BEYOND
MULDER AND SCULLY

BEYOND
MULDER AND SCULLY
THE MYSTERIOUS CHARACTERS OF "THE X-FILES"

ANDY MANGELS

A CITADEL PRESS BOOK
Published by Carol Publishing Group

A Citadel Press Book
Published by Carol Publishing Group
Citadel Press is a registered trademark of Carol Communications, Inc.

Editorial, sales and distribution, rights and permissions inquiries should be addressed to
Carol Publishing Group, 120 Enterprise Avenue, Secaucus, N.J. 07094

In Canada: Canadian Manda Group, One Atlantic Avenue, Suite 105, Toronto, Ontario
M6K 3E7

Carol Publishing Group books may be purchased in bulk at special discounts for sales
promotion, fund-raising, or educational purposes. Special editions can be created to
specifications. For details, contact: Special Sales Department, Carol Publishing Group,
120 Enterprise Avenue, Secaucus, N.J. 07094.

Manufactured in the United States of America
10 9 8 7 6 5 4 3 2 1

Library of Congress Cataloging-in-Publication Data
Mangels, Andy.
    Beyond Mulder and Scully : the mysterious characters of the X–
files / Andy Mangels.
        p.   cm.
    "A Citadel Press Book."
    Includes bibliographical references and index.
    ISBN 0–8065–1933–9
    1. X–files (Television program)   I. Title.
PN1992.77.X22M36   1997
791.45'72—dc21   97–47084
                                                                               CIP

For each of us in life, there are those who push us along,
give us the incentive to succeed,
or hold our hands in solidarity.

The career of a freelance writer is not a stable one.
For every writer who turns in reams of copy to their red-penned editors,
there are those out there who are struggling to turn the blank page
into a picture composed of words.

To these people I dedicate this book, my second:

Steven Watson,
my English teacher at Bigfork High School,
who pushed me hard because he knew I had the muse on my shoulder.

Ginny Traeger,
who welcomed me into her family's home when I was in college,
and helped me type my early assignments for print.

David Kaye,
who was my mentor when I came out, and who introduced me
to the world of Macintosh.

Finally,

my mother, Joanne Mangels,
who always nurtured the talents in me
and
my father,
who taught me to work hard and not skip the details.

Without the aid of these people,
I would have a lot more blank pages in my life.

CONTENTS

PREFACE

Okay, let's get the embarrassment out of the way first.

> "Fox's nighttime schedule is disappointing for action fans. Friday nights will find . . . *X-Files*, a male and female FBI team which investigates paranormal occurrences. Call it *Ghostbusters* meets *Unsolved Mysteries*."—"Andy Mangels's Hollywood Heroes," *Wizard* no. 25, September 1993

Yes, those were indeed my immortal words from the popular genre news column I've been producing for various magazines during the last decade. Now lest anyone jump to too many conclusions, there's nothing inherently wrong with my description other than that action fans would be disappointed. And given the initial reaction to *The X-Files*, mine was one of the most benign descriptions. *Entertainment Weekly*, which has since cozied up to the series and featured numerous wet-kiss articles, originally said, "This one's a goner."

When the series first premiered, I didn't much care for it. I've never been a big UFO buff—growing up at the time when books on the *Chariots of the Gods* were everywhere will do that to you—and the first two episodes were aimed straight at the heart of UFO lovers. I gave the series a try again with "Genderbender," but found it really weird, not entertaining.

It wasn't until midway through the third season, around the time of "Piper Maru," that I gave the series another chance. And I got hooked. Borrowing tapes of all of the previous episodes from a friend, I watched them at the rate of one or two a night, catching up to current time in about a month. By then, I was conversant with conspiracy theories, "Mulderisms," and the hundreds of *X-Files* web sites. I even knew to watch for Scully's ever-ready "Mulder, it's me" line before I became aware that people had actually catalogued them!

While stars David Duchovny and Gillian Anderson are certainly appealing, my attention was diverted more to the mysterious characters. We knew Mulder and Scully's basic past, but what was Skinner's story? Who were Deep Throat and Mr. X behind their quasi-mystic warnings and shadowy cameos?

And what was Cigarette-Smoking Man really up to? I resolved to find out more about the characters and about the actors who played them.

Beyond that, I noticed early on that the casting in the series was impeccable. Flawless. Superlative. There was never a moment that I wasn't pulled in to the roles the supporting actors were playing, even when I recognized them. And I recognized a lot of them. A decade of writing about science fiction, comic books, and horror projects in Hollywood makes one conversant with a lot of actors and actresses.

As the third season ended, I had begun buying all of *The X-Files* books, both authorized and unauthorized. But the most disappointing thing about them was the fact that not only did they barely even *mention* the guest stars (some didn't mention them *at all*), but that they didn't interview any of them. After all, it isn't Duchovny and Anderson who must swim through sewage in a rubber Flukeman outfit, or wear prosthetic limbs, or fight off rapes by invisible ghosts, or deal with gender-switching lovers and lightning bolt–throwing friends.

Mulder and Scully react to the events—and to the people—around them. They investigate and question and eventually do become involved, but not before we've seen that the guest characters exist on their own, free from the FBI's most unwanted couple. If it weren't for the guest stars, and the characters they make memorable, would the episodes be half as interesting?

As I bought *X-Files* book after *X-Files* book, each examining either series minutia or "real" paranormal case studies, I became increasingly frustrated. Eventually, I decided to write my own book, and *Agents X: The Unauthorized Guide to the Actors of The X-Files* was born. Originally, it was to have covered mainly the careers of "the big five": Mitch Pileggi, William B. Davis, Jerry Hardin, Steven Williams, and Nicholas Lea. Once the book landed at Carol Publishing, and went through a title change, we mutually decided to broaden the focus and spotlight dozens of the talented stars and guest stars who had walked through the doors of Ten Thirteen Productions.

The importance of these lesser known actors is undeniable. About costars Brad Dourif and Carrie Snodgress, David Duchovny said, in *Entertainment Weekly*, "My character comes across better in reaction to them. Thank God for the guest stars." In *Starlog Yearbook*, Gillian Anderson said, "We've been very fortunate to get some of the great guest stars we've gotten. It's always a wonderful boost for us to have those episodes where we have a great guest, because we get to be really challenged. A good guest star keeps you fresh, keeps you on your toes."

Vincent Schiavelli explains it a little better: "Naturally the guest cast in *The X-Files* creates the conflict of the story. If it were just Mulder and Scully, there wouldn't be any story. For example, something like *Star Trek*, in its various arrangements, can exist just on its own cast because the danger, the encroaching danger, can be something unseen. It can be something unknown or an interpersonal conflict. But obviously in this situation with two regulars . . . there's not terribly much conflict that can be generated. So of course it has to rely on the bringing in of outside characters."

Dan Butler agrees. "What's great about the show is [Mulder and Scully] are sort of set—in a way, the straight men of the series. They're not gonna vary that much, so it gives this vast leeway for really colorful guest shots."

Many of these colorful actors come from Vancouver, British Columbia, where the series is shot. Although Fox and Chris Carter initially cast many actors from Los Angeles and flew them up, they eventually came to realize the wealth of talent among the locals. "It's important that Canadian actors are getting this kind of recognition," said William B. Davis. "It's been a fight for the Canadian actor in the American film industry to be fully recognized." In her interview for this book, Megan Leitch said, "All the actors in the city wanted to work on that show, because it's a real *actors* show. That was the *hot* series to be on."

"Everyone who I've seen working on *The X-Files* is generally really good at doing what they do," said actor Christopher Allport. "They have to be because the scripts are very specific, and they demand a performance. They don't ask you to just stand there and talk. They don't cast a simple type. One of the reasons that the show is doing as well as it is, I think [is that] they're very, very good actors all the way down the line."

Many of those actors have appeared numerous times on the series, though not always in the same roles. In *X-Files Confidential*, coproducer Paul Rabwin addressed the frequent recasting of local actors. "The truth is, when you have the limited pool of actors in Vancouver, you tend to use the same ones periodically. On very small parts we have used an actor more than once in a season."

Casting director Rick Millikan said in *Entertainment Weekly*, "I look for people you won't recognize because I think it adds to the show's believability. Because even though everything on *The X-Files* is out there, you have to leave the viewers going 'Wow, you know, maybe that could happen.' When I bring actors in, I explain that it's a very laid-back [yet] intense-energy show. You want someone who's got a dark side, but it's not everything to them."

This book contains thirty-one actor interviews and over one hundred career profiles. I have attempted to make this the most complete guide yet to the actors of the series, though much material had to be cut due to space limitations.

As you read the book, you'll note many quotes attributed to other sources. Unlike almost all of the other unauthorized *X-Files* books on the market, I felt it was important to credit those who had done other interviews or profiles, especially if I was quoting their work. Having been swiped myself, as an author, I am keenly on the side of giving credit where credit's due.

So, dive into the world of mutants and abductees, of psychopaths and bureaucrats . . . and, ultimately, the world of talented actors and actresses.

And to paraphrase a popular saying, "Keep watching the credits."

How to Read the Episode Guides

Each episode in seasons One–Four opens with the airing number (e.g., X15 is the fifteenth episode), and the title (e.g., "Lazarus"), and the season (e.g., Season One).

The tables include a "Case Number," which is season/dot/airdate order/ number, followed by a parenthetical production number (as listed in the closing credits). Thus, 1.15/#15 (#1X14) is season one, episode fifteen, number fifteen, and production number 1X14.

This is followed by a "First Sighting" (original airdate), director and writer credits, and a guest cast list. That list is divided in two to three sections, separated by a space; first is front credits at the beginning of the show, second is end credits, and third is uncredited actors. In most cases, actor names are exactly as on-screen, though in some cases, middle names or initials have been added. In the case of character names, we have listed the most complete version of the name available, which is sometimes more complete or different than the on-screen credit.

Finally, each episode features a "Field Report" (episode synopsis) and "Witness Notes" (background material on actors or actor trivia), and many have "Witness Profiles" (spotlighting a specific actor or actress) and "Witness Interviews" (interviewing a specific actor or actress).

ACKNOWLEDGMENTS

A book of this nature does not come easily, nor without the aid of dozens of people. First and foremost, I would like to thank Peggy Schultz of the University of Southern California Cinema–Television Library. She went above and beyond the call of duty in helping research the most obscure credits. Fellow writer Scott Brick helped research contact numbers for over 150 actors and actresses. David Galvan provided me with three seasons of *The X-Files* a year before I started this book, when I finally started watching the series.

Transcription work is rarely a pleasure, but a group of friends helped transcribe the thirty-one interviews in this book. Thanks to Mary Ridge, Kehvan Zydhek, Jane "Lady Vader" Walpole, and Patrick Jones for their patience and transcription help. Patrick also gets a thank-you for his editing help, as does Thom Butts. Michael A. Martin, my *Star Trek* comic cowriter, loaned his laptop so I could work when I was out of town, and Ron Morrill helped double-check all the show credits.

Brandy "Xena-Woman" Swan loaned me a wealth of *X-Files* magazines that I don't have; Paula Mackey was a wonderful help with Mitch Pileggi material and photos; Delmo Walters ran down a bunch of photos in New York; Mark Evanier gave me advice and links to the animation industry; Frank Garcia and Paula Vitaris shared gossip, articles, and sessions of mutual frustration release; they all receive my gratitude and thanks.

One would think that a book like this would be a publicist's dream, but many publicists and agents were rather difficult to get help from. There are many who cooperated who shall remain nameless, but they should know they have my thanks, and their clients got my best attention. Special thanks go to Gregory Taylor at Disney Television for *Black Jack Savage* material, and to Ben Harrell at Mozark Productions for *Filthy Rich* material. Also, Greg "Pops" Bayless of the Asylum Street Spankers band provided a lot of help with Pileggi stage credits, as did Wanda V. Pierce and Alice Wilson; Robert A. Burns found me the out-of-print *Mongrel*. Thanks to them as well.

Grace and Cindy at Planet X and Debbie and Phil at Excalibur Comics deserve credit for breaking my bank with *X-Files* magazines and merchandise.

John at the Hollywood Book & Movie Poster Company and Pete at Larry Edmund's Books helped track down photos, and the crew at Portland's Movie Madness found some bizarre and obscure videos that I needed.

I'd also like to pass along thanks to Mike Lewis at Carol Publishing Group, who accepted the book, and Jack David at ECW Press, who *didn't*, but who gave me quite a bit of excellent publishing advice. And gratitude goes to Carrie Cantor, my editor, who waded through more *X-Files* trivia than she ever thought she could . . . and did so with good humor.

This book would not be nearly what it is without the help and cooperation of lots of actors. Thirty-one of them did interviews with me, and many, many more sent along information and photos so that the book could be more complete. I wish all of those who helped me much success in their careers. Special thanks go to Jerry Hardin and William B. Davis, who gave very generously of their time.

Finally, gratitude goes to my partner, Don Hood, who'll be glad not to have me pulling sixteen-hour days at the computer, next to piles of books, magazines, and photocopies, as I did for five months. He still has to listen to me saying "He was on *X-Files*" or "She was on *X-Files*" with almost every television show we watch these days, but he's gotten used to it by now.

BEYOND
MULDER AND SCULLY

THE MITCH PILEGGI FILE

Name: Mitch Craig Pileggi
Born: April 5, 1952; Portland, Oregon
Height: 6′ 2″
Weight: 200 lbs.
Hair: Brown
Eyes: Brown

Mitch Pileggi speaks at *The X-Files* convention in Austin, Texas on 19 November 1995.

Male sex symbol" is a tough sobriquet for anyone to accept, but *The X-Files* has more than a few men who fall into that category . . . at least if on-line polls are to be believed. One of the most popular male celebrities on the internet is Mitch Pileggi, the "surly pectoral god" and "brawny" actor who portrays FBI assistant director Walter S. Skinner. Perhaps it's the air of authority he generates on-screen: the glowering eyes behind the rounded glasses, the clenched lips, the bald head, the powerful frame barely hidden by his suits . . . Pileggi's Skinner is the gruff-but-lovable father figure, and fans have responded positively, bringing his role from occasional recurring character to full-fledged regular supporting actor.

Mitch Pileggi was born in Portland, Oregon, and although his family lived in the United States for several years, when Mitch was seven, the moving began. His father, Vito Pileggi (the family name is pronounced "Puh-ledgy" with emphasis on the second syllable) was an operations manager for a Department of Defense contractor. The family included mother Maxine, and six children, including brother Nick, and a sister (Mitch was the fifth child). The Pileggis lived in California and later San Antonio, Texas. When Mitch was ten years old, Vito got a new contract, and the family moved to Ankara, Turkey.

In an American high school in Ankara, Mitch got his first taste of acting, taking part in productions of *West Side Story, My Fair Lady*, and *Bury the Dead*, among others. He graduated high school in 1970, but decided not to pursue acting. Instead, Pileggi attended Fullerton College in California for a year, as well as the University of Maryland in Munich, Germany, and the University of Texas at Austin (where he received his business administration degree during the 1975–76 term). When he left college, he followed his father into his field, working as a desk-bound defense contractor monitored by the air force in various countries such as Turkey, Saudi Arabia, and Iran.

Mitch returned to the U.S. full time in his late twenties, fleeing a turbu-

1

lent Iran and settling back in Austin. He brought with him his wife, Debbie Andrews, a former "Army brat" whom he had married in 1978 after meeting in California. It was while in Austin that Mitch began acting in earnest, becoming a regular in the community theater groups of the area. He worked behind the scenes at the Zachary Scott Theatre Center, a non-profit organization. "At one time I did the books in the morning, I was the janitor in the afternoon, and I helped build sets in the afternoon also, and then I would do theater at night," Mitch said in the *Austin Chronicle*. "I really liked it there, and I came back a couple of years ago and did a play there. I have a lot of ties to Zach Scott. I· spent a lot of time cleaning up toilets in that theater."

From 1980 to 1983, Pileggi was a regular on theatrical stages, appearing in musicals from *Chicago*, where he sang solos and performed soft-shoe dance routines, to *Jesus Christ Superstar*, in which he played the role of Pontius Pilate. One of Mitch's most startling stage performances was in *Bent*, a play by Martin Sherman about a pair of gay lovers who are caught up in the tragedies of Nazi Germany in 1934. Pileggi played Max, a sexually promiscuous and unlikable sort, who barely escapes the Nazis with his lover. But the two are caught on their way to Amsterdam, and Max is forced by the Nazis to beat his lover to death, then is sent to a concentration camp for the following two years. Pileggi and his fellow actors' performances often brought the entire audience to tears.

Years later, in the summer of 1992, Pileggi would return to Austin after having some success in Hollywood. He took the lead in Terrence McNally's play *Frankie and Johnnie in the Clair de Lune*, playing the role of ex-con short-order cook Johnnie, a part played by Al Pacino in the 1991 movie adaption. Unlike Pacino, Pileggi spent the first ten minutes of both acts on stage . . . totally nude! Alice Wilson, who directed *Frankie and Johnnie* was initially concerned about the older female patrons of the arts, but later realized "I needn't have worried, because some of those older patrons came back and asked for specific seats where they could get a better view!"

Pileggi made his first break into Hollywood in 1982, when he was cast in *Mongrel*, a low-budget horror film set in Austin. Director-writer Robert A. Burns was intent on making a claustrophobic film about a boarding house seemingly besieged by a killer dog. Pileggi was cast in one of the film's two largest roles, Woodrow "Woody" Burkowski, the sadistic and grimy on-site manager of the boarding house. Though *Mongrel* was planned for theatrical release, it eventually ended up direct-to-video, although it is not in current release.

In 1983, spurred on by a role on the popular TV series *Dallas* and good feedback from an audition for the film *The Raggedy Man* (though he wasn't cast), Pileggi decided to move to California to pursue acting full-time. His wife, Debbie, decided to stay in Austin, and the marriage ended in divorce, an *amicable* one according to friends of the couple.

The road to success was tough over the next several years, and Pileggi found it difficult to find an agent. He kept busy working for his brother's company, installing window blinds. Yet when acting work started coming in, Pileggi was finding himself typecast. Due to his imposing size and lack of hair, Mitch was often cast as a thug or villain, on series such as *The A-Team* and

Downtown, the telefilms *Dalton: Code of Vengeance II* and *Three on a Match*, and features such as *Death Wish IV, Three O'Clock High*, and *Return of the Living Dead II*.

In 1989, Pileggi scored one minor psychopathic role, in the *Deliverance* wanna-be *Brothers in Arms*, and one major psychopathic role in Wes Craven's horror film *Shocker*. Craven had previously hit big with the character of Freddy Krueger, and he was attempting to reinvent the formula with a new character named Horace Pinker, a murderous TV repairman who gained the ability to jump in and out of people's bodies. Pileggi got the role of Pinker when he scared the film's producer, Marianne Maddalena, during the audition.

Unfortunately for Craven and Pileggi, *Shocker* was not the first in a new horror franchise; it did acceptably at the box office (and was a *huge* hit in South America), but did not do well enough to rate a sequel. Craven did use Pileggi again in *Night Terrors*, a telefilm pilot for a proposed TV horror anthology, and Mitch made an unbilled cameo in Craven's 1995 film *A Vampire in Brooklyn*.

The worst part of the *Shocker* fallout for Pileggi was that it further type-cast him in the psycho/tough-guy role. Although he played a few semi-benign characters in the years to come, he was once again cast as an about-to-be-electrocuted killer in the black comedy *Guilty As Charged*, played villainous roles in the series *Pointman, Models, Inc.,* and *Dallas* (he was back for three episodes) and the telefilms *Ravenhawk* and *Knight Rider 2000*. Pileggi even managed to give an overpoweringly threatening edge to his Internal Affairs investigator in *Basic Instinct*, where he was one of the few cast members who didn't look up Sharon Stone's skirt.

When not working in front of the camera, Mitch is often working out at the gym, keeping up the physique that sends female fans (and not a few male ones) swooning whenever *The X-Files* has a gratuitous shirtless scene. He's also a fan of rollerblading and plays softball and volleyball in Vancouver with cast and crew members from local series such as *Highlander*. He also rides horses and loves to read. Pileggi keeps two homes: one in Vancouver, and another in Valencia, California.

In December 1996, Pileggi wed Arlene Rempel, the Vancouver-based actress who plays star Gillian Anderson's stand-in on *The X-Files*. The two were wed during the show's Christmas break, in Hawaii. David Duchovny was Pileggi's best man.

Although his work on *The X-Files* and the promotional appearances he makes on the series' behalf have kept Pileggi fairly busy, this spring and summer, Pileggi was in Utah shooting scenes for a Fox television movie. The film, *Marabunta*, stars Pileggi as the recently widowed Sheriff Croy, who is raising his teenage son in the Alaskan wilderness. When vacationing entomologist Dr. Jim Conrad (Eric Lutes of *Caroline in the City*) discovers not only volcanic activity but also a swarm of hungry killer ants, panic comes to a peaceful and unsuspecting town. Together with Sheriff Croy and schoolteacher Laura Sills (Julia Campbell of *Men Behaving Badly*), Conrad begins a battle against the deadly army of ants that advances towards civilization.

It's a good thing that *Marabunta* has taken up much of his summer, because Pileggi's role in *The X-Files* movie, *Blackwood*, is reportedly almost nonexistent, with the actor only called for three days of filming. That's not the best reward for a character who has become one of the most popular supporting cast members of a hit series, but Pileggi *does* have a contract for several more years on *The X-Files*, and the movie appearance means that he'll survive the fifth season . . . good news indeed for the fans of the "surly pectoral god"!

Walter Sergei Skinner

The FBI couldn't ask for a sterner assistant director than Walter S. Skinner, the direct supervisor of agents Mulder and Scully. An ex-marine, Skinner seems often to be at odds with Mulder, though, in truth, he seems to see uncomfortable similarities between himself and the junior agent. Skinner is often stern with Agent Scully, though it's obvious he has a soft spot in his heart for the female agent.

On the other side of the desk, Skinner must constantly deal with the threatening presence of the Cigarette-Smoking Man—commonly known as CSM—the mysterious conspiracy-cloaked figure who once forced Skinner to shut down the X-Files section. Although Skinner has been controlled in the past by CSM, that control has slipped further as Skinner has seen direct threats to his own life from the overall conspiracy. In fact, in recent times, though Skinner and CSM have an agreement, both of them seem dangerously close to ending that agreement. . . in the most permanent fashion possible.

With his round-rimmed glasses and over-starched shirts, to say nothing of his stoically heroic actions, the character of Walter Skinner is a change for actor Mitch Pileggi. "In other characters I've done, I was pigeonholed and played a lot of psychos," he said in *Freetime*. "I think this is opening up new doors for me; it's showing people that I can play different types of characters other than I've played in the past."

Indeed, that typecasting may have been part of what kept Pileggi out of *The X-Files* in the beginning. The actor had auditioned twice for the series before he came in to audition for "Tooms." The role of Skinner was created by Glen Morgan and James Wong when Charles Cioffi was unable to film scenes as Section Chief Scott Blevins. "At the time I was shaving my head, and Chris Carter didn't think the look was right for the characters I was reading, which were both FBI agents," said Pileggi in the *Austin Chronicle*. "So I grew my hair back—all five of them—and the third time I went in with a kind of surly attitude because I hadn't been hired the first two times," he adds in the British *X-Files* comic. "Fortunately, that was the attitude they were looking for for Skinner."

Originally, the part was to have been a single episode guest star role, but as luck would have it, the producers decided to bring Skinner back. "They asked me to come back and have the recurring character the second season, especially during Gillian's pregnancy," Pileggi says in the *Austin Chronicle*. "Then at the end of the second season, they asked me if I wanted to sign a contract for six years, and I said, '*Absolutely*. Where do I sign?' "

Although he had inspiration for his character from his own dealings with the military while working for the Department of Defense, Pileggi based Skinner's character on someone a lot closer to home—his late father, who had passed away shortly after *The X-Files* began its run. "He had many people working for him with a lot of responsibility," Pileggi explained in *Entertainment Weekly*. "He was very stern in his dealings with employees, but he had a compassionate side, and the producers have finally let me start exploring that aspect of Skinner." Pileggi did not immediately realize how closely he was emulating his father until his family members brought it to his attention. "I didn't realize I was doing this until my family, my mom and my brothers and sister pointed it out . . . the way I move, the characteristics of the character are very similar to the way Dad was in the office," Pileggi said in an interview for the web site Office of the Assistant Director. "It wasn't something I was doing intentionally, I was just kind of doing it subconsciously"

And what about those looks? Bald or not, glasses or not, Pileggi gets squealing fans—female and male—wherever he goes. "He's the kind of guy who has command of a room just by getting up from his chair," said Chris Carter in *TV Guide*. "He looks like a real person, not a TV actor. And he's obviously got a very powerful sex appeal." Pileggi responded with "I never know how to respond to that sex symbol thing. I do notice whenever I'm referred to in the press as a sex symbol, it's always qualified by the word *unlikely*."

"Mitch came off as different, because he looked like a guy who had come up through the ranks," said James Wong in *Cinefantastique*. "He had a more virile look than the usual bureaucrat." Pileggi describes his look a little differently, noting that "I describe him as being perpetually constipated."

Indeed, the producers have gone out of their way as the seasons have progressed to give the fans what they want; not only more of *Skinner*, but *more of Skinner!* The fourth-season episode "Zero-Sum" even had a lengthy sequence that can only be described as "Skinner does *Striptease*." For a more revealing look at the character of Skinner, you need only keep reading.

X21 Tooms

Assistant Director Walter Skinner is introduced, and he's not pleased with Scully's work. He demands more frequent reports and more conventional investigation, chewing her out in front of Cigarette-Smoking Man. Later, he orders Mulder to stay away from Eugene Tooms or all of his friends in the Capitol won't be able to save him— or the X-Files—from the consequences. Finally, when the agents have gone, he coerces the first line of dialogue spoken by Cigarette-Smoking Man.

"He's got pressures from both sides," Pileggi said at a 1995 *X-Files* convention in Reno. "He's definitely got the Cigarette-Smoking Man. He's got superiors in the FBI who are stepping on his neck. The Cigarette-Smoking Man is . . . I think it's kinda like he's got something on Skinner. He's holding something over his head, and that's why he puts up with so much garbage from him. I think for the most part, he's definitely doing what he can, when he can, however he can, to support Mulder and Scully . . . You know, Mulder can be a pretty loose cannon, and he obviously never listens to much of what Skinner

5

has to say to him. (Laughs.) So, it's a tough situation. He's really kinda caught between a rock and a hard place, and he's trying to figure out how to handle it the best he can."

X25 Little Green Men   X26 The Host

Having already shut down the X-Files, Skinner and Cigarette-Smoking Man discover Mulder has left his assignment in "Little Green Men." Unfortunately, they don't know where he's gone, and neither does Scully . . . yet. Later, Skinner chews out Mulder and angrily kicks CSM out of his office.

In "The Host," Skinner sends Mulder to investigate a bizarre sewer death, an assignment that Mulder considers a punishment until the investigation yields a man-size human-like flukeworm. Skinner later admits that the case should have been an X-File, noting to Mulder that "We all take orders from someone."

"There was one episode where Mr. X tells them they have a friend in the FBI," said Pileggi in *Cinefantastique*, in relation to "The Host." "I guess he was implying that it was him, but in my eyes it's Skinner who's really the one who's the friend."

X28 Sleepless   X30 Ascension   X32 One Breath

In "Sleepless," Skinner gets very little airtime, mainly responding to Mulder's requests.

Skinner has three main scenes in "Ascension." First, he pulls Mulder off the case when Scully disappears. Later, he shows up at Skyline Mountain Summit to somberly confront the fact that Mulder may be responsible for the death of Duane Barry. Finally, when Mulder brings him slim evidence that Krycek is a coconspirator of Cigarette-Smoking Man, Skinner does his best to let Mulder know he believes. Knowing he can do nothing more powerful, Skinner reopens the X-Files. "That's what they really fear," he says.

When Mulder threatens to resign in "One Breath," Skinner relates a story to him about an experience he had when he was an eighteen-year-old marine in Vietnam. Three months into his tour of duty he killed a ten-year-old boy and lost his faith. Later, wounded and near death, he had an out-of-body experience. "I am afraid to look beyond that experience, Agent Mulder. You . . . you are not. Your resignation is unacceptable."

Pileggi often cites "One Breath" as his personal favorite episode, largely for the heart-baring scene between Mulder and Skinner. "I called Glen (Morgan) and Jim (Wong) up at Fox and thanked them for writing it because I thought it was a lovely scene," he said in *Cinefantastique*. "It really was a chance for Skinner to open up and show a side of himself to Mulder that hadn't been revealed yet, and really let him know that he was on his side."

X40 Colony   X41 End Game   X46 F. Emasculata

Angry that an FBI agent has been found dead in "Colony," Skinner terminates a case, and later informs Mulder of a family emergency. Then in "End Game," Skinner takes a more active part in the proceedings when Mulder needs help trading Samantha for a captive Scully. The encounter with the alien bounty hunter doesn't go as planned, and later, Skinner gets involved in a brutal brawl with the mysterious Mr. X to gain the whereabouts of Mulder.

In "F. Emasculata," Skinner must decide whether or not to let Mulder go public with word about a contagious disease. When Mulder demands to know where he stands, Skinner responds "I stand right on the line you keep crossing . . . I'm saying this as a friend: Watch your back. This is only the beginning."

Pileggi thinks that Skinner knows a lot more about Mr. X in "End Game" than most people realize. "I don't think he wanted to reveal himself to Mr. X and let him know that he knew who he was," Pileggi said in an interview for the Office of the Assistant Director Web page. "A lot of people weren't aware that Skinner had any idea about Mr. X, but I think Skinner knows about a lot of stuff that people don't know about. . . . And a lot of it he doesn't like."

Although he seems to be on Mulder's side, Skinner is a man walking a fence. "In [F. Emasculata] there's a shot where I'm standing [with] Mulder on one side and the Cigarette-Smoking Man on the other side," said Pileggi in the *Sci Fi* fall preview issue. "That's exactly where Skinner's at—he's caught right in the middle."

X49 Anasazi   X50 The Blessing Way   X51 Paper Clip

In this three-part episode, Skinner becomes heavily involved in the proceedings. In "Anasazi," he confronts Mulder about receiving secret files and brawls with the agent, then threatens Scully's job. In "The Blessing Way," after Scully is forced to resign from the FBI, Skinner steals the important DAT tape and brings it to her at Mulder's house, although Scully thinks Skinner is there to kill her. Finally, in "Paper Clip," Skinner agrees to turn the DAT tape back over to Cigarette-Smoking Man in exchange for Mulder and Scully's safety. He's double-crossed though, and severely beaten by CSM's agents. Skinner, however, has the last laugh when he brings out an oral historian who has memorized the DAT tape's contents. CSM is now apparently locked in a stalemate with Skinner.

The closing scene of "The Blessing Way" and opening scene of "Paper Clip" were tense and shocking, as Scully and Skinner leveled their guns at each other, until Mulder arrived and broke up the stalemate, forcing Skinner to lower his weapon. The confrontation brought up some major tensions in Skinner's relationship with Scully. "You don't know what his feelings are about Scully. Especially with the end where they have the standoff with the guns," Pileggi says in the *Austin Chronicle*. "That was actually a crushing blow for Skinner, for her to have reacted like that, because he really likes her a lot."

Skinner's feelings for Scully have been interpreted by some fans as being romantic, but Pileggi doesn't see them that way, as he further explains: "There are a lot of fans who want some type of romantic thing to happen between Skinner and Scully, which I think is ridiculous. His feeling for her—and even with Mulder—is, even though he's not that much older, more paternal."

The relationship between Skinner and Cigarette-Smoking Man, however, is far from caring. "The more and more the relationship with the CSM, the more contentious it became between the two of them, the happier I've been," Pileggi revealed in *XPose*. "When it culminated with the 'This is where you pucker up and kiss my ass' line, that was like 'Yes! Somebody needs to slap that man's face!' "

X59 Nisei   X63 Grotesque   X64 Piper Maru   X65 Apocrypha

In "Nisei," Skinner is annoyed at Mulder, who he thinks is withholding an important briefcase, while in "Grotesque," the assistant director is concerned about Mulder's mental health as he investigates a disturbing series of murders.

Later, in "Piper Maru," Skinner is gunned down by CSM's operatives in a restaurant after he reopens the investigation into Melissa Scully's death. In "Apocrypha," Skinner is rushed to the hospital, and Scully foils a final attempt on his life by his shooter (and the shooter of her sister), "Hispanic Man," Luis Cardinal.

Regarding his shooting and beating by Krycek and CSM's goons, his shooting by Hispanic Man, and the upcoming macing by his secretary and the fight with Mr. X, Pileggi had this to say in *Texas Monthly*, "I guess both Mulder and Scully have taken their fair share of beatings, now its my turn. I'm just waiting for the episode when Scully comes walking in to my office and starts smacking me around! She is the only one who hasn't."

X66 Pusher   X70 Avatar

Barely recovered from his wounds, Skinner is maced and badly beaten by secretary Holly, who's under the mind-controlling influence of "Pusher." But it's in "Avatar" that Skinner really gets the screen time. His wife, Sharon, is divorcing him after seventeen years of marriage, so he gets drunk and has sex with a woman he picks up in a bar. The trouble is, she's dead in bed the next morning, and Skinner is the prime suspect. Then it appears Skinner forced his wife to crash her car, and the assistant director keeps complaining about a frightening old woman in his dreams. It all ties in together with a plot by Cigarette Smoking Man to ruin Skinner and discredit the X-Files. But can the truth be found out in time to save the tight-lipped Skinner?

"Avatar" reveals Walter Skinner's middle name, "Sergei," which is the name of an old schoolmate of Chris Carter's.

" 'Avatar' began as a germ of an idea that David Duchovny came up with," Howard Gordon said in *Cinescape*. "It came from David saying 'Mitch is a great guy and Skinner is a great character —we don't use him enough.' We felt it was a good time in the season to deal with Skinner a little more, rather than have him just be a curmudgeonly foil for Mulder and Scully."

This was also the first time Pileggi had played a sex scene on the series (and one of the first in his acting career). Pileggi was also able to work again with Jennifer Hetrick, who played his wife, Sharon Skinner. The two had worked together on a 1991 telefilm called *Absolute Strangers*, in which Hetrick had been in a car accident and was in a coma (which is exactly what happened to her character in *this* episode). Mitch played a doctor at her bedside, but his scene was cut before the final print. "Maybe I looked a little too malevolent to be a physician" he said in *Shivers*. Still, he was quite enthused to work with the actress again. "When they were giving me the list of people for Sharon Skinner, they got to Jennifer's name and I said, 'That's her.' I've had a crush on Jennifer for years and years. She did a Campbell's soup commercial some years ago, and I told her I remembered her from that!"

X72 Wetwired   X73 Talitha Cumi   X74 Herrenvolk

Agent Scully goes ballistic in "Wetwired," causing Skinner to put out a warrant for her arrest. Then in the two-part "Talitha Cumi" and "Herrenvolk," Skinner tells Mulder his mother is in the hospital, warns Mulder that he can't help him find CSM, then helps Scully investigate the mystery that is Jeremiah Smith.

"Herrenvolk" is the first episode to feature an "also starring" designation for Mitch Pileggi.

X76 Teliko   X78 The Field Where I Died   X81 Tunguska
X82 Terma

Skinner barely appears in "Teliko," mainly showing up at the opening to introduce Scully to a man from the Center for Disease Control. He takes a much more active role in "The Field Where I Died," coordinating a task force of FBI and ATF agents in their raid and investigation of a cult.

In "Tunguska," Mulder brings a captive Krycek to Skinner's new apartment for safe-keeping. Skinner is happy to have him, and after gut-punching him, handcuffs him to an outside balcony railing to freeze overnight. Unfortunately, Krycek tosses a Russian courier off the balcony, leaving Skinner some explaining to do. Later, in

"Terma," Skinner presses Scully for information about the contents of a mysterious Russian pouch.

The scene where Skinner beat up Krycek was payback for the beating Skinner suffered at the hands of Krycek and his compatriots in "Paper Clip." The scene was a fun one to film for actors Pileggi, David Duchovny, and Nicholas Lea since in reality the trio are actually very good friends.

Note the first of the gratuitous Pileggi shirtless scenes in this episode when Mulder rousts Skinner to deliver Krycek to him. Also note that Skinner has moved to a new apartment, implying that a reconciliation with Sharon Skinner (hinted at in "Avatar") did not happen. Still, Skinner is on-again, off-again with the wedding ring. It's on for "The Field Where I Died," off for "Tunguska," and on again for "Paper Hearts."

X83 Paper Hearts   X84 El Mundo Gira   X87 Memento Mori
X89 Unrequited

Pileggi gets some great "Skinner constipation scenes" in "Paper Hearts." First he threatens to take Mulder off a case for hitting a prisoner, then relents as long as Scully keeps an eye on Mulder. When she fails to do so, and Mulder's bungling lets the killer loose with a gun, Skinner is not a happy man. In "El Mundo Gira," Skinner doesn't have much to do other than listen to reports, though there was a humorous dissolve from a graffiti painting of a bald alien/Chupacabra into the bald Skinner.

However, "Memento Mori" will go down as one of the two most important episodes for Skinner. When Mulder attempts to contact CSM to bargain for Scully's life, Skinner won't help him, talking him out of his plan. But when Mulder is gone, Skinner strikes a Faustian bargain with CSM on his own. CSM promises that Scully won't die, and that he'll extract what he wants from Skinner later. The deal will come back to haunt him.

"Unrequited" should have been a moving Skinner episode, as it deals with the rededication of the Vietnam Memorial. Although Skinner goes all out to find a killer who has ties to a paramilitary group called The Right Hand, his Vietnam background is barely mentioned at all. He does later save the life of General Benjamin Bloch.

X91 Max   X93 Small Potatoes   X94 Zero-Sum

In "Max," Skinner shows up at a bar moments after Agent Pendrell has been shot, ostensibly to place Louis Frish under military arrest. However, in light of the deal with CSM, it's possible he was en route to save Scully from CSM's assassin and showed up too late. Later, Skinner greets Mulder when he embarks from his plane, expecting to see the assassin, Scott Garrett. Mulder tells Skinner that Garrett "caught a connecting flight."

Skinner only has a brief scene in "Small Potatoes," but it's a hilarious one. Looking incredulously at a report on a case, Skinner questions the man who he thinks is Mulder but who is really the shape-changing Eddie Van Blundht.

The second biggest Skinner episode of the season came late in the year, but given that the entire "Zero-Sum" episode concentrated on Skinner, fans couldn't complain. CSM finally calls his marker due, and Skinner breaks dozens of laws. He intercepts e-mailed crime scene pictures sent to Mulder, cleans up the crime scene, incinerates the victim's body, steals the victim's blood samples, impersonates Mulder to a questioning detective, and confronts Marita Covarrubias! Later, Skinner is framed by CSM for the murder of the detective. Skinner is so angry at CSM that he shoots at him three times, point blank, as a warning. "If anything happens to her I will expose you," he growls, knowing that CSM has not cured Scully yet.

In "Zero-Sum," the producers treated fans to the most flagrantly gratuitous revealing flesh-fest yet. Pileggi, standing above the camera, legs spread and wearing white jockey underwear, slowly stripped off a shirt while the camera admired his body. Take *that*, Screaming Pileggians!

Although it answered the "boxers or briefs" question, "Zero-Sum" brings up other interesting questions. Why does Skinner care for Scully so deeply that he'll sell his soul and break the law for her? Is he in love with her? Does he feel somehow guilty for her disease or her abduction?

A season ago, Pileggi knew where Skinner's limits were, as related in a *Scarlet Street* interview. "He's definitely on Mulder and Scully's side. It's just a matter of him being stuck with the people he works for and his position. The only way that he can really get out of the situation is to leave and he ain't gonna do that. He's got a career. I think he came up from where Mulder is; I think he was in the same type of field work and he's elevated himself to where he is now. He's not going to just throw it away."

But as season four ended, Mulder felt he could no longer trust the assistant director, Scully was still dying of cancer, and Skinner, it appears, *has* thrown his career away. With several upcoming fifth season episodes spotlighting secondary cast members, it's clear that for Assistant Director Walter S. Skinner and actor Mitch Pileggi, there is much more to be revealed.

ACTOR CREDITS

MITCH PILEGGI

AMERICAN TELEVISION

Adam 12 (Syndicated)   Pileggi was in one episode. No information available.

The A-Team (NBC)   #64—"The Road to Hope," aired October 29, 1985 (fourth season). Role: Paul Winkle.

Alien Nation (ABC)   #7—"Night of the Screams," aired October 30, 1989 (first season). Role: Jean Paul Sartre, an evil Newcomer who is being hunted by a vengeful vigilante.

The Antagonists (CBS)   #3—"Full Disclosure," aired April 4, 1991 (first season). Role: Detective Haley.

China Beach (ABC)   #32—"With a Little Help From My Friends," aired March 7, 1989 (third season). Role: An E.O.D. Sergeant.

Dallas (CBS)   #143—"Barbecue Four," aired December 16, 1983 (seventh season). Role: ?; In the following three episodes, Pileggi recurs as Morrisey, who tangles with J. R. Ewing in a mental institution: #333—"Three-Three-Three (Part 1)," aired May 4, 1990 (twelfth season); #335—"April In Paris," aired November 2, 1990 (thirteenth season premiere); #336—"Charade," aired November 9, 1990 (thirteenth season).

Doctor, Doctor (CBS)   #29—"Ice Follies," aired November 15, 1990 (third season). Role: hockey coach.

Downtown (CBS)   #8—"Stan the Man," aired November 29, 1986 (first season). Role: Nick.

Falcon Crest (CBS)   #149—"Nowhere to Run," aired March 13, 1987 (sixth season). Role: ?; #211—"God of the Grape," aired November 10, 1989 (ninth season). Role: Eddie.

Get a Life (FOX)   #31—"Chris' Brain," aired January 19, 1992 (second season). Role: Nax.

Guns of Paradise (CBS)   #48—"The Valley of Death," aired February 8, 1991 (third season). Role: Rafe.

Hooperman (ABC)   #8—"Baby Talk," aired November 25, 1987 (first season). Role: Large Biker.

Hunter (NBC)   #135—"The Incident," aired October 24, 1990 (seventh season). Role: Danko.

Masters of Fantasy (Sci-Fi Channel)   "The *X-Files* Creators," aired June 7, 1996. Pileggi hosts this half-hour look at the creative team behind *The X-Files*.

Models, Inc. (FOX)   #29—"Sometimes a Great Commotion," aired March 6, 1995 (second season series finale). Role: Hitman hired to kill one of the main cast members at a wedding.

More Secrets of *The X-Files* (FOX)   aired May 10, 1996. Pileggi narrates this series recap.

O'Hara (ABC)   "Hot Rocks," aired December 5, 1987 (first season). Role: Webster.

Pointman (Syndicated)   #6—"My Momma's Back," aired March 2, 1995 (first season). Role: Dirkson, an ex-Navy SEAL who is an enforcer for the villain.

Roc (FOX)   title unknown, aired September 13, 1992 (second season). Role: Cop #1.

TELEVISION MOVIES

The Sky's No Limit (CBS),   aired February 7, 1984. Role: Jerry Morrow.

Dalton: Code of Vengeance II (NBC),   aired May 11, 1986. Role: Verbeck. This second pilot telefilm led to a series.

Three on a Match (NBC)   aired August 2, 1987 (pilot telefilm). Role: Bull Tully, a prison escapee.

Night Visions (NBC),   aired November 30, 1990 (pilot telefilm). Role: Keller.

Absolute Strangers (CBS),   aired April 14, 1991. Role: Doctor at the bedside of Jennifer Hetrick but his scene was cut from the telefilm. Pileggi would later team with Hetrick in *The X-Files* episode "Avatar."

Knight Rider 2000 (NBC),   aired May 19, 1991. Role: Thomas J. Watts, a recently released prisoner who is involved with murder, gun-smuggling, and other villainous deeds.

Trouble Shooters: Trapped Beneath the Earth (NBC),   aired October 3, 1993. Role: Thompson.

Pointman (Syndicated), aired December 3, 1994 (series pilot). Role: Benny.

Raven Hawk (HBO), aired July 20, 1996. Role: Carl Rikker, a villain who forces a little girl to kill her mother and father.

Marabunta (FOX), Planned for Fall 1997, on the Fox Tuesday Night Movie. Role: the widowed Sheriff Croy who is raising his teenage son in Alaska.

FEATURE FILMS

Mongrel. Released 1982 (1983 direct-to-video). Role: Woodrow "Woody" Burkowski, a demented boarding house manager who likes to play sick practical jokes on the boarders. This is Pileggi's professional premiere.

On the Line. Released December 1984. Also known as "Rio Abajo." Role: Stephens.

Death Wish 4: The Crackdown. Released November 1987. Role: the Cannery Lab Foreman, in a brief sequence fifty-four minutes into the film.

Three O'Clock High. Released October 1987. Role: Duke Herman, the sadistic, golf cart-driving school security guard.

Return of the Living Dead Part II. Released January 1988. Role: Sarge, a cigar-chomping Army sergeant sent in to contain the zombie menace.

Brothers in Arms. Released March 1989. Role: Caleb, a demented mounatin man who kills mountain climbers and attempts to rape the heroine.

Shocker. Released October 1989. Role: Horace Pinker, a killer who comes back from the dead and can jump into people's bodies, as well as into their television sets.

Guilty as Charged. Released April 1991 (direct-to-video?). Role: Robert Dominique, an unrepentant killer being jailed beneath a meat factory.

Basic Instinct. Released March 1992. Role: an Internal Affairs investigator who twice questions the lead detective, played by Michael Douglas.

It's Pat: The Movie. Released August 1994. Role: Concert Guard #2, who appears briefly backstage at a Ween concert sixty-eight minutes into the film.

Dangerous Touch. Released 1994. Role: Vince, a well-dressed hood who carries a straight razor.

Vampire in Brooklyn. Released October 1995. Role: Tony, an orange-suit wearing tough mobster who appears at the beginning of the film. This was an uncredited appearance.

THEATER

My Fair Lady. High school production.

West Side Story. High school production. Role: Tony.

Bury the Dead. High school production.

110 in the Shade (1980). Zach Scott Theatre, Dallas, Texas. Role: Noah Curry.

The Lark (1980). Zach Scott Theatre, Dallas, Texas. Role: La Tremorille.

Buried Child (1980). Zach Scott Theatre, Dallas, Texas. Role: Tilden.

Jesus Christ Superstar (1980). Zilker/Park Hillside Theater, Dallas, Texas. Role: Pontius Pilate.

Lone Star (1981). Zach Scott Theatre, Dallas, Texas. Role: Ray Caulder.

Chicago: The Musical (1981). Zach Scott Theatre and Genesius Productions, Dallas. Role: Amos Hart. Pileggi also had a solo and soft shoe routine.

Bent (1981). Center Stage at 6th Street, Dallas, Texas. Role: Max.

Rashomon (1982). Zach Scott Theatre, Dallas, Texas. Role: Tajomaru.

The Price (1982). Zach Scott Theatre, Dallas, Texas. Role: Victor Franz.

Frankie and Johnnie in the Clair de Lune (1992). Zach Scott Theatre, Dallas, Texas. Role:, Frankie.

OTHER CREDITS

The X-Files: Ruins (Harper Audio).   Running time: three hours on two cassette tapes. Pileggi is the narrator-performer in this audio adaptation of Kevin J. Anderson's novel.

Shocker "No More Mr. Nice Guy" the Music (SBK/Alive Records).   Run time: 40:45. Soundtrack available on CD and tape. Pileggi performs a rap duet with Alice Cooper (!) over the top of "Shockdance," by The Dudes Of Wrath. It is Track #6, and runs 4:31.

The X-Files: The Truth and the Light (Warner Brothers).   Running time: 48:36. Soundtrack available on CD and tape. Composer Mark Snow's themes from various episodes of *The X-Files* are woven together, with interspersed dialogue from several of the series actors. Mitch Pileggi has several dialogue snippets.

American Express. Running time: thirty seconds. Role: a man who's building a house in this commercial for the American Express Corporate Card.

SEASON ONE

X1 Pilot: The X-Files

Case Number: 1.01/ #1 (#1X79)
First Sighting: September 10, 1993
Directed by: Robert Mandel
Written by: Chris Carter

GUEST CAST	CHARACTER
Charles Cioffi	Division Chief Scott Blevins
Cliff DeYoung	Dr. Jay Nemman
Sarah Koskoff	Theresa Nemman
Leon Russom	Detective Miles
Zachary Ansley	Billy Miles
Stephen E. Miller	Coronor John Truitt
Malcolm Stewart	Dr. Glass
Alexandra Berlin	Orderly
Jim Jansen	Dr. Heitz Werber
Ken Camroux	Third Man
Doug Abrams	Patrolman
William B. Davis	Cigarette-Smoking Man
Katya Gardener	Peggy O'Dell
Ric Reid	Assistant Coroner
Lesley Ewen	FBI Receptionist
J. B. Bivens	Truck Driver

FIELD REPORT

Bellefleur, Oregon. A series of youth murders in Oregon draws the interest of Fox Mulder, a maverick FBI agent whose caseload includes the "X-Files." These are cases involving paranormal or extraterrestrial activity or other unexplained phenomena, and the higher-ups at the FBI seem intent on sabotaging Mulder's work. They assign Mulder a partner, agent Dana Scully, whose medical background and skeptical air may help her debunk—or discredit—Fox's theories. Though he doesn't initially trust Scully, Mulder wants to open her mind to "extreme possibilities."

In Oregon, the agents find young victims who Mulder thinks have been abducted. Indeed, when a grave is exhumed, the remains inside the coffin seem inhuman, and a metallic implant is embedded in the creature's nasal passage. The deaths are traced to Billy Miles, the supposedly comatose son of the local sheriff who Mulder thinks is under alien control. In the woods, Billy is freed from their control in a swirl of leaves and light, leaving the two FBI agents with more questions than answers. Scully reports her findings to the FBI panel that assigned her to work with Mulder and gives them the only remaining evidence: a metallic implant. The Cigarette-Smoking Man locks the implant away in a Pentagon storeroom with five others like it.

WITNESS NOTES

Dr. Heitz Werber, the therapist who hypnotizes Billy Miles at the end of the episode, is the same man who has worked with Fox Mulder for years, using deep-regression hypnosis to help him recover the memories of his sister's abduction.

Charles Cioffi would return in his role as Division Chief Scott Blevins in the fourth episode, "Conduit," but would not appear again until the final episode of the fourth season. Also, while the character is referred to in the credits and merchandising as "Section Chief," the nameplate on his door reads "Division Chief."

Actor **Cliff DeYoung** (Dr. Jay Nemman) is also well known as singer Cliff DeYoung. His band, Clear Light, recorded for Elektra Records in the 1970s. DeYoung later performed on Broadway, where he appeared in the hit production of *Hair*, as well as *Sticks and Bones*. Among DeYoung's many genre credits are roles in *The Craft* (1996), *F/X* (1986), *Dr. Giggles* (1992), *The Hunger* (1983), and a turn as Brad Majors in *Shock Treatment* (1981), the *Rocky Horror Picture Show* sequel. DeYoung's genre TV credits include Stephen King's *The Tommyknockers* (1993), the pilot for *Robocop: The Series* in 1994, and guest roles on *The Twilight Zone*, *Lois & Clark: The New Adventures of Superman*, *Time Trax*, and *Star Trek: Deep Space Nine*.

Sarah Koskoff (Theresa Nemman) appeared to be able to make her nose bleed on cue, but that was really special effects makeup by Toby Lindala. A thin tube was run through the girl's hair, down her forehead, and beside her nose. Shooting the actress in profile helped complete the illusion that the blood was actually coming from her nostrils. Koskoff recently appeared in Chris Carter's *Millennium* episode "Covenant."

Leon Russom (Detective Miles) appeared in the 1995 Fox telefilm, *Alien Nation: Body & Soul*, and guest-starred on the short-lived *Space Rangers*, and in the final episode of the CBS science fiction series, *Hard Time on Planet Earth*. He has recently had roles on *The Pretender* episode "Bazooka Jarod," as well as in *JAG*. He appeared as Mayor Krebs in the 1996 superhero film, *The Phantom*.

X2   Deep Throat

Case Number:	1.02 / #2 (#1X01)
First Sighting:	September 17, 1993
Directed by:	Daniel Sackheim
Written by:	Chris Carter

GUEST CAST	CHARACTER
Jerry Hardin	Deep Throat
Michael Bryan French	Paul Mossinger ("Redbird")
Seth Green	Emil
Gabrielle Rose	Anita Budahas
Monica Parker	Ladonna
Sheila Moore	Verla McLennon
Lalainia Lindbjerg	Zoe
Andrew Johnston	Lt. Col. Robert Budahas
Jon Cuthbert	Commanding Officer
Vince Metcalfe	Colonel Kissell
Michael Puttonen	Motel Manager
Brian Furlong	Lead Officer
Doc Harris	Mr. McLennen

FIELD REPORT

Ellens Air Force Base, Idaho. A pilot has disappeared from an air force base in southern Idaho, the sixth airman to go missing since 1963. Mulder is determined to investigate, despite the warning of a mysterious man in a restroom to drop this case. Mulder and Scully travel to Idaho, where they meet with the pilot's wife, who tells them of her husband's strange behavior prior to his disappearance. When the husband suddenly shows up, he's acting stranger still, and Mulder suspects his mind has been tampered with.

Mulder's theory is that the base is one of the places wreckage from the Roswell UFO was taken and that the military is experimenting with alien technology. Despite a painful warning from government thugs dressed in dark suits, Mulder sneaks onto the base at night and witnesses what appear to be UFOs. Before he can get off base, he is captured by base security and taken away. The next morning, Scully is alarmed to find herself under surveillance, but she gains the upper hand and forces the spy to take her to Mulder. His memory has been wiped clean, and he doesn't remember events of the last evening. Back in Washington, D.C., the mysterious man tells Mulder what he already suspects: *"They've* been here for a long, long time."

WITNESS NOTES

Although the official *X-Files* Web site and other sources list **Charles Cioffi** appearing as Division Chief Scott Blevins in this episode, he did not appear in it.

Michael Bryan French (Paul Mossinger) guest-starred as Jack Kerouac in the "Rebel Without a Clue" episode of *Quantum Leap*, and recently appeared in the action film *The Glimmer Man* (1996).

Gabrielle Rose (Anita Budahas) appeared in the genre hit *Timecop* (1994), as well as in three films written and directed by Canadian surrealist filmmaker Atom Egoyan: *Family Viewing* (1987), *Speaking Parts* (1989), and *The Adjuster* (1991).

Vince Metcalfe (Colonel Kissell) appeared in the 1995 telefilm of *The Omen*, filmed in British Columbia. Guest-starring in it were fellow *X-Files* actors Tom McBeath and Bill Dow.

Seth Green (Emil) acted in two low-budget horror films: *Arcade* (1993) and *Ticks* (1993). A rumor published in *Cult Times* says that Seth

Green and Lalainia Lindbjerg (Zoe) may have indulged in some method acting to play the scene where they're stoned in the diner scene. However, the veracity of said rumor is questionable; the magazine identifies Verla McLennen—a *character* played by Sheila Moore—as the *actress* who played Zoe.

X3 Squeeze

Case Number:	1.03/ #3 (#1X02)
First Sighting:	September 24, 1993
Directed by:	Harry Longstreet
Written by:	Glen Morgan & James Wong

GUEST CAST	CHARACTER
Doug Hutchison	Eugene Victor Tooms
Donal Logue	Agent Tom Colton
Henry Beckman	Detective Frank Briggs
Kevin McNulty	Fuller
Terence Kelly	George Usher
Colleen Winton	Lie Detector Technician
James Bell	Detective Johnson
Gary Hetherington	Kennedy
Rob Morton	Kramer
Paul Joyce	Mr. Werner

FIELD REPORT

Baltimore, Maryland. A series of bizarre murders in Baltimore arouse Scully's curiosity; people are being killed in rooms with no visible means of entry or exit. Even stranger is that, the victims' livers have been ripped out, seemingly by bare hands. Mulder joins in the investigation, much to fellow FBI agent Tom Colton's annoyance. When strange elongated fingerprints are found, Mulder matches them up against prints in murders past; every thirty years since 1903, six murders of the same type are committed.

At one of the past murder scenes, Mulder catches Eugene Victor Tooms slithering through a small air duct, but Tooms's alibi checks out and he passes a lie detector test. Despite that, Mulder and Scully find other evidence that Tooms may be the killer. Mulder surmises that he's a genetic mutant who can stretch his limbs and muscles to squeeze through small spaces, and that every thirty years he comes out of hibernation to eat six livers. The agents find his nest of newspaper

and bile but fail to catch Tooms. They won't have long to wait though; Scully is the sixth victim on Tooms's list!

WITNESS NOTES

Writers Glen Morgan and James Wong took their inspiration for this episode from the mysterious case of Jack the Ripper, a murderer in 1880s London's Whitechapel district whose final crime was committed in a room with seemingly no exit. Morgan also was inspired by the story of Richard Ramirez, the "Night Stalker," a Los Angeles–based serial killer who squeezed his way through windows and air ducts to get to his victims.

Donal Logue (Agent Tom Colton), a recent newcomer to film and television, has had roles in *And the Band Played On* (1993), *Little Women* (1994), *Jerry Maguire* (1996), *Diabolique* (1996), and *Dear God* (1997). This year, he starred in and produced an independent film called *Men With Guns*. Logue is perhaps most famous for his "Jimmy the cab driver" promos for MTV, and he recently appeared on the series *Public Morals*.

Terence Kelly (George Usher) has appeared in many TV series and telefilms, including the miniseries *Titanic* (1996), and Stephen King's *It* (1990), which also starred William B. Davis and Melinda McGraw.

Colleen Winton appeared in Chris Carter's *Millennium* episode "Covenant" as the murdered Mrs. Garry.

WITNESS PROFILE

DOUG HUTCHISON

Born: May, Dove, Delaware

One of *The X-Files'* most popular villains gained life through the measured acting of Doug Hutchison, an actor whose background and personality hardly prepared him to play a cannibalistic mutant. Born on an air force base in Delaware, Doug grew up in Detroit, Michigan, and Minneapolis, Minnesota. He got his first taste of acting at age nine with the role of Max Schmidt, the head elf in *The Day Santa Lost His Beard*. The young boy had originally wanted to be a priest, no doubt influenced in part by his parochial school teachers.

Instead, Doug pursued acting, first in Minneapolis and Chicago, then at the School of Drama at Juilliard in New York City. Leaving Juilliard after five months, Doug later studied with Richard Pinter and Sanford Meisner in New York. Hutchison also toyed with a music career, playing guitar and singing in the bands The Yuh-Uh-Uh-Uhs and Hot Bricks. The Yuh-Uh-Uh-Uhs recorded a tape of alternative music, *Vampire Chickens*, and filmed a video. Their music was eventually heard on the syndicated radio comedy/novelty show *"Dr. Demento."* Doug still writes and plays music.

Doug's film debut was *Fresh Horses* (1988), for which he gained glowing reviews. He was later cast in minor roles in *The Chocolate War* (1988), and *The Lawnmower Man* (1992). He continued to work on stage, winning a Dramalogue award for his portrayal of Jimmy Witteck in *The Other 5%*, and he began to make the rounds as a television guest star. He appeared in *Robin's Hoods, China Beach, Murder, She Wrote, The Young Riders, Diagnosis Murder, Love and War*, and had a recurring role in *Party of Five*.

Hutchison's agent called him at home one day to audition for a new Fox series about a pair of FBI agents, but when Doug picked up the script notes, there was practically no dialogue. All Eugene Tooms said was "yes, yes, no, no, yes, no, yes, no" as he was being interrogated. When Doug arrived for the audition, he found out that the character was a serial killer who ate livers. Fighting off a splitting headache, Hutchison walked into the audition room.

Writers Morgan and Wong recalled that they felt Hutchison looked much too young for the role. After director Harry Longstreet gave him an instruction to pretend to be stalking his victims, a bewildered Hutchison sat still for a moment, quietly repeating the directions. Then, he snarled at the director with "You want me to stalk you, you mother (expletive)?" The outburst scared Longstreet, but won over the writers. "He kind of turned a few shades of white," Hutchison recalled in a *Trekker* interview. "He looked at the producers, and they looked at him and they were kind of smiling. It was a very odd moment." Believing he'd lost the role, Hutchison went home, only to get a call from his agent telling him he'd gotten the part.

Hutchison's Eugene Tooms was an eerie character who gave you the chills just by looking at you with his yellow eyes (courtesy of a special pair of contact lenses). "I was really inspired by Anthony Hopkins's performance in *Silence of the Lambs*," Doug said in a *Starlog* yearbook interview. "I thought he had a grasp on stillness in that film which was incredibly powerful, because he had an inner life going on inside."

Hutchison's stunt double was a Seattle contortionist named Pepper whose main contribution to the episode was squeezing into the chimney on top of his victim-to-be's house. Pepper's flexible feat so amazed producer Goodwin that he let the scene stand with no added visual effects. When Hutchison rockets out of a heating vent, the scene was shot normally, then in front of a blue screen. This allowed visual effects artists to stretch Hutchison's body slightly, giving it a surreal and slightly inhuman shape.

After the first episode, Hutchison, a vegetarian, sent Chris Carter a frozen calf's liver to thank him for the role of Tooms. In *Trekker*, Doug said "It was fun after the episodes came out . . . to reveal that the liver-eating serial-killer-mutant was actually a vegetarian!"

In an interview in the British *The X-Files* magazine, Hutchison revealed that he wanted to do a sequel to "Squeeze" so badly that he wrote a sequel script, called "Dark He Was and Golden-Eyed," and sent it to Chris Carter. In return, the actor received a phone call from Fox's lawyers, telling him that legally, they could not allow anyone to read the script. In Hutchison's script Tooms "was in an experiment to find out how he could remain so young and immortal; he was infused with a drug that backfired." After Tooms escaped the asylum, he began "eating livers like M&Ms—he's on a rampage." Tooms's origin was also given, connecting him to a liver-eating Central American Indian god.

Despite the Fox lawyers, as fans know, Tooms's character *was* popular enough to warrant a sequel late in the first season ("Tooms," 1.21), written once again by Morgan and Wong. During that episode's final scene, where Mulder confronts Tooms in his nest underneath an escalator, Hutchison fought to play the scene naked. The producers had planned to have

Tooms in his animal control uniform, but, as Doug recalled in *Starlog* yearbook, "I just thought that was the silliest thing in the world, that I would be in a fetal position in my nest in my dog uniform. I wanted to be slimed, you know, from head to toe. I had pictured myself nude, like a caterpillar in a cocoon." After much discussion, the producers relented, and a very naked Hutchison was slathered with cold yellow sticky goop. "You sense that I come bursting out of there without a stitch of clothing on. It's something you catch on a subliminal level."

Hutchison has attended several of the *X-Files* conventions, always rallying the fans and calling for a third appearance of Tooms. Three years after Tooms's "death," his campaign seems unlikely to succeed. Meanwhile, when *X-Files* producers Glen Morgan and James Wong left the series to produce *Space: Above and Beyond*, they brought Hutchison on board as a recurring guest star. He played the role of Elroy-L, a human-looking android silicate who had allied himself with the alien Chigs, fighting against humanity. In this role, Hutchison's contact lenses had crosshairs painted on them.

More recently, Hutchison's credits have included the role of villainous redneck Pete Willard in the movie adaption of John Grisham's *A Time to Kill* (1996) as well as a small part in *Con Air* (1997). Hutchinson also appears in one of 1997's summer action movies, *Batman & Robin*, as the Golem, the head of a gang that inhabits the lair Poison Ivy wants as her own. Hutchison had previously worked with Joel Schumacher, on *A Time to Kill*, and was used to the flamboyant director's style. In *Batman & Robin*, Hutchison's face is covered with Day-Glo green and red makeup that glows eerily under black light. He might be completely unrecognizable except that, once again, he wears theatrical contact lenses, this time an iridescent blue.

In the fall of 1997, Hutchison was the "Polaroid Man" in the second season premiere of *Millennium*.

X4 Conduit

Case Number:	1.04/ #4 (#1X03)
First Sighting:	October 1, 1993
Directed by:	Daniel Sackheim
Written by:	Alex Gansa & Howard Gordon

GUEST CAST	CHARACTER
Carrie Snodgress	Darlene Morris
Michael Cavanaugh	Sioux City Sheriff
Don Gibb	Kip, Pennsylvania Pub Bartender
Joel Palmer	Kevin Morris
Charles Cioffi	Division Chief Scott Blevins
Shelley Owens	Tessa Sears
Don Thompson	Holtzman
Akiko Morison	Agent Leza Atsumi
Taunya Dee	Ruby Morris
Anthony Harrison	Fourth Man
Glen Roald	ME Worker
Mauricio Mercado	Coroner

FIELD REPORT

Sioux City, Iowa. Near Lake Okobogee, a teenage girl appears to have been abducted by aliens, while her little brother, Kevin, is left behind. Mulder wants to investigate, especially since the area is a hot spot for UFO activity. In Sioux City, Mulder and Scully find that the mother of the abducted girl had reported a UFO sighting back in 1967. Stranger still, Kevin is writing down binary code on page after page of paper. After Mulder sends the code to Washington for analysis, government agents descend on the family, claiming that Kevin's code was a classified defense transmission!

Later, the agents notice the last set of binary-code-filled papers Kevin had been working on spread out on the floor; the arrangement is a mural-sized picture of Ruby, his missing sister. Soon after, Mulder and Scully find Ruby dazed and walking in the woods. Medical tests show she was subjected to prolonged periods of weightlessness, but Ruby's mother won't allow her to talk to the agents. In the end, Mulder is distraught over the similarities between this case and that of his abducted sister, Samantha.

WITNESS NOTES

"Danny" is first mentioned in this episode. He is a friend of Mulder's who works at the Cryptology Section of the Bureau and helps him with data requests, fingerprint searches, and more. Danny has never been seen, though he has been mentioned in "The Erlenmeyer Flask," "Red Museum," "Avatar," and "Wetwired." Confusion over Danny's surname reigns in X-Phile ranks and the *X-Files* guidebooks: *The Truth Is Out There* lists Danny's surname as "Valodella," while the British book *X-Treme Possibilities* lists "Bernstein," *X-Files Confidential* lists two separate people as "Bernstein" and "Valadeo," and *The X-Files Declassified* lists both "Bernstow" and "Valodeo." No one connected to the series has cleared up the confusion.

This episode makes a big error by making repeated references to Michael Cavanaugh's character as the Sioux City sheriff, and his department as the sheriff's department. In Iowa (and most states), city cops are police, while county cops are sheriffs and deputies. Since it's the police department for Sioux City, it should properly be called the Sioux City Police department.

Carrie Snodgress (Darlene Morris) studied drama at Chicago's Goodman Theater School before embarking on a film and television career. In 1970, she won a Golden Globe Award and an Oscar nomination for her role as Tina Balser in *Diary of a Mad Housewife* (which also starred the Emmy Award–winning *X-Files* guest Peter Boyle). She retired from acting to become the companion of rock star Neil Young, with whom she had a son, Zeke. She remained out of the business for eight years until she was cast in Brian De Palma's telekinetic thriller *The Fury* (1978). She has since appeared in the acclaimed 1981 Broadway play *A Coupla White Chicks Sitting Around Talking*, and dozens of forgettable films, including *Trick or Treats* (1982), *The Attic* (1980), *L.A. Bad* (1985), and *Woman With a Past* (1994). Recently, she was the voice of Aunt Heloise on the *Phantom 2040* cartoon series.

Michael Cavanaugh (Sioux City Sheriff) had his first major stage role in the all-nude musical *Oh, Calcutta!* He began acting in films and television in the mid-seventies, appearing in such movies as *The Enforcer* (1976), *Gray Lady Down* (1978), and *Any Which Way You Can* (1980), as well as a lot of episodic television. Cavanaugh is no stranger to characters

named "Fox" who chase extraterrestrials. In 1986, he co-starred in the ABC series *Starman*, playing the role of Federal Security Agent George Fox, who relentlessly pursued Paul Forrester (Robert Hays), an alien inhabiting the dead body of a photographer.

Other genre credits of Cavanaugh's include appearances in Steven Spielberg's *Amazing Stories*, *Star Trek: The Next Generation*, *Lois & Clark: The New Adventures of Superman*, and in the computer game *Wing Commander IV: The Price of Freedom* (1995). He also appeared on the short-lived prime-time remake of *Dark Shadows* as Sheriff Patterson.

X5 The Jersey Devil

Case Number:	1.05/ #5 (#1X04)
First Sighting:	October 8, 1993
Directed by:	Joe Napolitano
Written by:	Chris Carter

GUEST CAST	CHARACTER
Claire Stansfield	The Creature
Wayne Tippit	Detective Thompson
Gregory Sierra	Dr. Diamond
Michael MacRae	Ranger Peter Boulle (Brouillet)
Jill Teed	Coroner Glenna
Tamsin Kelsey	Ellen
Andrew Airlie	Rob
Bill Dow	Paul (Dad, 1947 victim)
Hrothgar Mathews	Jack
Jayme Knox	Mom
Scott Swanson	First Officer
Sean O'Byrne	Second Officer
David Lewis	Young Officer
D. Neil Mark	SWAT Team Officer

FIELD REPORT

Atlantic City, New Jersey. Something inhuman is stalking the homeless in Atlantic City, killing them and gnawing on them. Mulder investigates alone, thinking it's the work of the fabled Bigfoot-like "Jersey Devil" but Scully doesn't want anything to do with the wild theory. Mulder catches sight of an animalistic female beast, but he is arrested by local authorities who are intent on keeping tourist trade unaware of the city's seedy side.

Mulder finds clues that the beast-woman may have been the mate of a feral man found dead in the woods. Later, he finds the woman and is menaced by her before Scully finally arrives and rescues him. After the police shoot the creature in the woods, a human bone is found in her digestive system. The case would seem to be closed, except for the bestial child of the creature, who waits in the woods.

WITNESS NOTES

Although the official spelling of the Ranger's name is "Peter Boulle," closed captioning lists it as "Peter Brouillet."

Actress **Claire Stansfield** (The Creature) stands 6'1" tall and what you saw of her on screen was almost all of her. She was naked for most of the episode, with hair tied over her breasts and a small G-string hiding those parts of her that could not be displayed on a Fox television series. David Duchovny previously worked with Stansfield on *Twin Peaks* and suggested her for the role to producers. Viewers who want to see more of Stansfield can check out "The Bounty Hunter" episode of Zalman King's *Red Shoe Diaries*. (The Showtime softcore anthology series is also the regular home of host-narrator David Duchovny.) Stansfield has also appeared in another Vancouver-filmed television series, the short-lived *Raven*, with Lee Majors, as well as a cyborg in *The Flash*, and *Frasier*. Feature film credits include *Gladiator Cop* and *Drop Zone*, both in 1994. Stansfield studied animal behavior at the zoo to prepare for the role. "I didn't want to come off as a she-woman of the jungle, running around half-naked like a female Tarzan," she said in a *TV Zone* interview. "They did a really good job . . . of not making me look like some model babe in a G-string."

One of **Gregory Sierra's** (Dr. Diamond) earliest film roles was as a gorilla sergeant in *Beneath the Planet of the Apes* (1970). He later appeared in the government-clones-sent-to-kill film *The Clones* (1973). On television, Sierra played twelfth precinct Detective Sgt. Chano Amenguale on the first season of *Barney Miller,* and later appeared as vice-squad Lt. Lou Rodriguez on the early episodes of *Miami Vice.* He starred on three seasons of *Sanford and Son,* one season of *Soap,* and was a regular on the short-lived *Zorro and Son.* Sierra's most prominent genre credit was on the 1988 NBC series *Something Is Out There*, spun off from a popular miniseries. Sierra played Lt. Victor Maldonado, the boss of L.A. cop Jack Breslin, who had gotten involved with a beautiful alien woman from outer space.

Wayne Tippit (Detective Thompson) guest-starred on the *Quantum Leap* episode "The Americanization of Machiko" and appeared semi-regularly on *Melrose Place* during the 1993–94 season.

Michael MacRae (Ranger Peter Boulle) guest-starred on the short-lived Ernest Borgnine Science Fiction series *Future Cop* and in the equally forgettable *Automan*, starring Desi Arnaz, Jr. Recently, McRae appeared on the "Worlds Apart" episode of *The Outer Limits*.

Tamsin Kelsey (Ellen) appeared in an *Outer Limits* episode called "Corner of the Eye." She also had roles in Stephen King's *Needful Things* (1993) and the recent "creature in the lake" kids film, *Magic in the Water* (1995).

X6 Shadows

Case Number:	1.06/ #6 (#1X05)
First Sighting:	October 23, 1993
Directed by:	Michael Katleman
Written by:	Glen Morgan & James Wong

GUEST CAST	CHARACTER
Barry Primus	Robert Dorlund
Lisa Waltz	Lauren Kyte
Lorena Gale	Ellen Bledsoe
Veena Sood	CIA agent Ms. Saunders
Deryl Hayes	CIA agent Webster
Kelli Fox	Pathologist
Tom Pickett	Cop
Tom Heaton	Groundskeeper
Jamie Woods-Morris	Ms. Lange
Nora McLellan	Jane Morris
Anna Ferguson	Ms. Winn

FIELD REPORT

Philadelphia, Pennsylvania. Lauren Kyte is having a bad week. First her boss commits suicide, then she's mugged. Too bad for her attackers that she has an invisible protector. When Mulder and Scully are called in to investigate, they find that the muggers' throats have been crushed—from the inside! When the agents talk to Lauren, they're menaced by their own car.

Lauren soon comes to realize that she's being haunted by the ghost of her boss, who had treated her as a surrogate daughter while he was alive. He leaves clues that he was murdered, and Lauren confronts his business partner, Dorlund. Mulder and Scully soon find they're not alone either; CIA agents are investigating Dorlund for sales of military parts to Mideast extremist groups.

WITNESS NOTES

Tom Braidwood's name is being stencilled over the parking-spot name of Howard Graves in one scene. Braidwood is an *X-Files* assistant director who later gained infamy as Frohike, one of the Lone Gunmen.

Barry Primus's (Robert Dorlund) film debut was in *The Brotherhood* (1968), but he really got his acting chops on a later role as Hermann Goering in *The Red Baron* (1971). As a star, he has an extensive list of B-movie credits, including *Avalanche* (1978), *Cannibal Women in the Avocado Jungle of Death* (1989), *Night Games* (1980), *Talking Walls* (a.k.a.: *Motel Vacancy*) (1985), *SpaceCamp* (1986), and *Denial: The Dark Side of Passion* (1991). And talk about your sidelines—the star Primus has shared the screen with the most is diva/actress Bette Midler! Primus had roles with the "Divine Miss M" in *The Rose* (1979), *Down and Out in Beverly Hills* (1986), and *Big Business* (1988). He also wrote and directed the Robert De Niro/Martin Landau film *Mistress* (1992) and was producer of the low-budget futuristic cyborg cop film *T-Force* (1994).

Lisa Waltz (Lauren Kyte) made her film debut in *Reckless* (1984). She played Amanda Gilbert, the wife of an abusive sheriff, in *Pet Semetary 2* (1992), and also appeared in the telefilms *Lifepod* (1993) and *Roswell: The UFO Cover-Up* (1994), which starred a number of other X-Files actors. Waltz has appeared on numerous television series, ranging from *thirtysomething* and *My So-Called Life* to *Northern Exposure* and *ER*. Waltz's latest role was as Kim Sayers's sister on NBC's *Dark Skies*. Lisa is a private pilot, and professes to be an expert at miniature golf.

X7   Ghost in the Machine

Case Number:	1.07/ #7 (#1X06)
First Sighting:	October 29, 1993
Directed by:	Jerrold Freedman
Written by:	Alex Gansa & Howard Gordon

GUEST CAST	CHARACTER
Jerry Hardin	Deep Throat
Rob LaBelle	Brad Wilczek
Wayne Duvall	Agent Jerry Lamana
Blu Mankuma	Claude Peterson
Tom Butler	CEO Benjamin Drake
Gillian Barber	Agent Nancy "The Iron Maiden" Spiller (Jane in credits)
Marc Baur	Man in Suit
Bill Finck	Sandwich Man
Theodore Thomas	Clyde

FIELD REPORT

Crystal City, Virginia. At the Eurisko World Headquarters, the chief executive officer is electrocuted in the high-tech office building, leaving him unable to pull the plug on the Central Operating System (COS). Mulder and Scully are brought into the investigation by Mulder's ex-partner, Jerry Lamana, who later unethically presents Mulder's profile of the killer as his own.

Blame for the death falls on Brad Wilczek, the genius creator of the COS, whose attempt to create artificial intelligence may have resulted in a computer with a sense of self preservation. The computer is indeed alive, kills Agent Lamana, and later imperils the lives of Mulder and Scully. Though they manage to shut COS down with a computer virus, the agents lose Wilczek, who is taken away by government agencies bent on using his knowledge for their own purposes.

WITNESS NOTES

Gillian Barber's character is named "Nancy Spiller" in the episode and in merchandising, but is listed as "Jane Spiller" in the credits.

Rob LaBelle (Brad Wilczek) played Terry in *Wes Craven's New Nightmare* (1994). He also has appeared in the psycho-thriller movie *The Temp* (1993) and in Todd Haynes's dark, edgy film triptych *Poison* (1991). He had a role in the female-cyborg-run-amok telefilm, *Running Delilah* (1994) and guest-starred on *Lois & Clark: The New Adventures of Superman*. La-Belle was unrecognizable as a Talaxian prisoner in the *Star Trek: Voyager* episode, "Faces," but he made a return appearance in a later episode, "False Profits." LaBelle spoke about his *X-Files* role in a *TV Zone* interview: "There was a brilliance and a great energy suggested in Wilczek. I found his thirst for knowledge more fascinating than anything else."

Blu Mankuma's (Claude Peterson) features include the adaption of Dean R. Koontz's *Watchers* (1988), as well as *Stakeout* (1987), *The Stepfather* (1987, with future *X-Files* and *Millennium* star Terry O'Quinn), and *The Russia House* (1990). In the third season of the syndicated vampire series *Forever Knight*, Mankuma played Captain Joe Reese, and he was the third-billed Sgt. Stan Parks on the syndicated *Robocop: The Series*. As a voice actor, you will hear him in the animated series *Beast Wars: Transformers* as Tigatron, and on *Reboot* as Gigabyte.

Wayne Duvall appeared in "Ghost in the Machine."

WITNESS INTERVIEW
WAYNE DUVALL

Born: May 29, 1958, Silver Spring, Maryland

When he was five years old, Wayne Duvall used to watch TV for a specific reason: to see his cousin Robert Duvall appear on shows like *The FBI*, *Combat*, and *The Mod Squad*. "He's the whole reason I got into acting," Wayne says. "I used to watch him and I knew that's what I wanted to do, too." As an adult, Wayne trained for seven years in the New York acting arena doing stage plays. He eventually headed west to try for a career in film and television, but it was slow going.

His film debut was in *Final Approach* (1991), followed by *Armed for Action* (1992). He later appeared in *Falling Down* (1993) with fellow *X-Files* guest star Raymond J. Barry and his famous cousin, as well as in *Disclosure* (1994). Wayne landed television work as well, including roles on *Valley of the Dolls*, *Picket Fences*, *Matlock*, *L.A. Law*, and *McGyver*.

In mid-1993, Duvall auditioned for the part of Jerry Lamana on a spooky new Fox series. Duvall's character was an FBI agent who used to work with Mulder in the Violent Crimes sec-

tion. Mulder agrees to help the desperate agent on his investigation into the death at Eurisko, but is later shocked to find Lamana has stolen his notes profiling the killer and passes them off as his own at an FBI meeting. Lamana wants up the ladder so badly that he doesn't see the unethical nature of his actions. Duvall remembers that he wasn't offered much background for his character other than what was in the script. "(Chris Carter) really didn't go into that history, especially since he thought, 'Look, we're going to kill him off in a half hour. We don't really need to know that much about him.'"

The first day of filming was the hardest on Duvall. He had to fly to Vancouver and jump right into filming. "I literally landed and I had to be at work and do the scene in the boardroom where I stole his report. It was midnight by the time we got to the scene and I was just exhausted and punchy. I was having trouble with my lines before filming, so I asked the prop guy if he would write down my speech on the big yellow pad that I had to look at when I did my report. So when you see me glancing down at my report, it's just my speech."

A later scene found the FBI agents at the home of computer genius Brad Wilczek. "He's in this real rich, fancy house, and he takes Gillian and David in and shows them a television screen to show them how artificial intelligence works. There's one point where there's this blank screen and if you freeze frame it you will see the reflection of the entire [camera] crew."

As is the fate of most ex-partners for Mulder and Scully, Duvall had a death scene as well, when the elevator in the Eurisko building plunges thirty floors with the unlucky agent inside. The elevator was actually on a sound stage. "They had this mock elevator up on some hydraulics to make it jolt. The rest of it was just camera work, with me writhing around on the floor." Lamana's death isn't witnessed, but is signified when the elevator security camera goes black.

Duvall is recognized often for his role on the show. "I just finished doing a movie last fall and I started getting all these calls like at the end of December, saying, 'Man, I saw you.' I thought they were talking about this movie I just did, called *My Fellow Americans*. It turns out is was just my *X-Files* rerun. Everyone watches that show, it's amazing."

What does the actor think of the premise for the series? "I am a believer in UFOs and I do believe that we have been visited before. The whole Roswell incident is interesting to me. It fascinates me. But, you know, I am not one of these people that is really obsessed with it or anything. We're silly to think we're the only life forms in the universe. But, yeah, I am fascinated with ghosts and all the paranormal stuff. Unfortunately, my episode was pretty much just about artificial intelligence gone awry."

Meanwhile, Duvall has kept himself very busy, appearing on *Jag, Murder One, ER,* and the *Wild Palms* miniseries, as well as in *Apollo 13* (1995), *The Fan* (1996), and the upcoming independent film *Skeletons* (1997). Duvall also has a large role in Paramount's action-adventure thriller *The Flood,* in which he plays opposite Morgan Freeman and Christian Slater.

X8 Ice

Case Number: 1.08/ #8 (#1X07)
First Sighting: November 5, 1993
Directed by: David Nutter
Written by: Glen Morgan & James Wong

GUEST CAST	CHARACTER
Xander Berkeley	Dr. Hodge
Felicity Huffman	Dr. Nancy Da Silva
Steve Hynter	Dr. Denny Murphy
Jeff Kober	Bear
Ken Kerzinger	John Richter
Sonny Surowiec	Campbell

FIELD REPORT

Icy Cape, Alaska. A team of scientists drilling Arctic core samples are slaughtered, seemingly by each other if the videotape is to be believed. "We are not who we are," says one scientist before turning a shotgun on a fellow scientist. Mulder and Scully fly north to investigate, along with a professor of geology, a toxicologist, a physician, and a pilot. The pilot, Bear, is bitten by a dog that was living with the scientists, and it's soon clear that the bite transferred a parasite into his body.

The parasite is a worm that quickly takes over the hypothalamus gland in the brain, causing extreme agression to anything that hosts it. As a storm traps the survivors in the cabin, the threat of infection with the parasite drives them to the brink of paranoia. Is Mulder infected, and will Scully be able to find a cure for the parasite before everyone is killed?

WITNESS NOTES

Though there are many similarities between this episode and the two movie versions of *The Thing* (1951 and 1982)—as well as the novella on which it was based, *Who Goes There?* by John W. Campbell, Jr.—writer Glen Morgan has stated that the episode was based on an article in *Science News*. Interestingly enough, the production designer who built the Arctic complex, Grame Murray, had also worked on John Carpenter's above-mentioned remake of *The Thing.*

The border collie featured in this episode is either the father or mother (sources vary) of Blue, David Duchovny's ever-present dog companion.

Felicity Huffman (Dr. Nancy Da Silva) has a short list of credits since her debut in 1988's *Things Change,* but that list does include a role on the TV miniseries *Stephen King's Golden Years* as Terry Spann, the icy head of security at the secret government research facility, Falco Plains. On that series she played most of her scenes with future *X-Files* performers R. D. Call and Ed Lauter.

Steve Hytner (Dr. Denny Murphy) was a regular in the cast of *Disney Presents: The 100 Lives of Black Jack Savage*, a short-run Stephen J. Cannell show that starred future *X-Files* regular Steven Williams, and was co-produced by Glen Morgan and James Wong. He also appeared in the cult horror film *The Prophecy* (1996) and in the flop pulp action film *The Shadow* (1994).

Montana-born actor **Jeff Kober** (Bear) played Dodger on *China Beach* and Guy Stafford on *Falcon Crest*. He also had roles in the film version of *Alien Nation* (1988), was a satanic killer in *The First Power* (1989), and was killed in both *Candyman* (1992) and *Terminator 2: Judgment Day* (1991). He played a guest role as an alien visitor on an episode of *V*, and had a starring role in the comic book–inspired flop *Tank Girl* (1994) as Booga, the half-man, half-kangaroo "Ripper" lover of the title character. Unable to stay away from those prosthetics for long, Kober returned to the makeup chair to play Daedalus, the Nosferatu clan leader, in last year's Fox vampire series *Kindred: The Embraced*. A talented artist, Kober also painted all the artwork that was seen in the background on that show.

Ken Kirzinger, whose grisly fate as John Richter is sealed in the opening sequence, is the stunt coordinator for *The X-Files*.

Since his film debut in *Mommie Dearest* (1981), **Xander Berkeley** (Dr. Hodge) has appeared in a number of genre films, including *Attack of the 50 Foot Woman* (1993), *Candyman* (1992), *Deadly Dreams* (1988), *Terminator 2: Judgment Day* (1991), *Apollo 13* (1995), and the flop Pamela Anderson comic book–based film, *Barb Wire* (1996). His most *X-Files*-like project so far? That would have to be the made-for-TV film *Roswell: The UFO Cover-up*, a 1994 project starring Kyle McLachlan and Martin Sheen.

Makeup man Toby Lindala created a latex neck for Berkeley to use in one scene. The prop came complete with blood and a wriggling worm. "They had to film a shot of me slicing the neck with a scalpel, and you could see this worm squirming around," Berkeley said in *TV Zone*. "Unfortunately, everyone got grossed out by the whole thing when they looked at the dailies, so they decided not to put it in the episode."

X9 Space

Case Number:	1.09/ #9 (#1X08)
First Sighting:	November 12, 1993
Directed by:	William Graham
Written by:	Chris Carter

GUEST CAST	CHARACTER
Ed Lauter	Lt. Col. Marcus Aurelius Belt
Susanna Thompson	Michelle Generoo
Tom McBeath	Scientist
Terry David Mulligan	Mission Controller
French Tickner	Preacher
Norma Wick	TV Reporter
Alf Humphreys	Second Controller
David Cameron	Young Scientist
Tyronne L'Hirondelle	Data Bank Scientist
Paul Des Roches	Paramedic

FIELD REPORT

Houston, Texas. Astronaut Marcus Aurelius Belt has been having flashbacks lately; during his spacewalk, he was attacked by a phantom form. When he sees Viking Orbiter pictures of Mars—and what appears to be a face in the craters—the nightmares return. Belt is now supervisor of NASA's space shuttle program, but the latest lift-off seems to have been sabotaged. Mission Control communications commander Michelle Generoo asks Mulder and Scully to come down to the Cape and investigate the sabotage, especially because her fiancé will be serving on the next shuttle mission.

Mulder has a case of hero worship for Lieutenant Colonel Belt, and it clouds his judgment as the mission proceeds. The shuttle launches fine, but once in space it is attacked by the ghostly form that has been living inside Belt. Even as the astronauts panic because of an oxygen leak that could cause the shuttle to burn up on reentry, Lt. Col. Belt wrestles with the alien presence inside his body and mind.

WITNESS NOTES

Susanna Thompson (Michelle Generoo) has appeared in *Alien Nation: Dark Horizon* (1994) as well as twice on *Star Trek: The Next Genera-*

tion and once on *Star Trek: Deep Space Nine*. In the latter appearance, an episode called "Rejoined," Thompson drew both controversy and raves for her role as Trill scientist Lenara Kahn, a woman who shared a lingering on-screen lesbian kiss with series regular Terry Farrell (Lieutenant Dax). In an interview with *TV Zone*, Thompson recalled that "preparing for the role of Michelle Generoo, I really tried to get into that military/scientific sort of mind set and all the responsibility that goes along with being the head of NASA communications." The role was difficult to fully prepare for though, given a host of last-minute changes to the script. "I think some of this might have had to do with what they were and were not allowed to show in terms of NASA."

Terry David Mulligan (Mission Controller) starred in the "Weeds" episode of Chris Carter's *Millennium*.

Ed Lauter appeared in "Space."

WITNESS INTERVIEW

ED LAUTER

Born: October 30, 1940, Long Beach, New York

At the time he was cast, Ed Lauter was the biggest name actor to appear on *The X-Files*. With almost a hundred film and television credits to his name, Lauter's steely gaze and bald head were instantly recognizable among the ranks of character actors.

The son of a Broadway actress of the twenties, Lauter always had an interest in acting. He graduated from C. W. Post College with an acting degree in hand, but then entered the army, where he served in a special forces unit. After spending some time in the theater scene—and the stand-up comedy scene in Greenwich Village—he finally appeared in a show that became a hit, Broadway's multiple-award-winning *The Great White Hope*.

That show brought Lauter to the attention of Hollywood casting directors, and he migrated west in the early seventies, making his film debut in the western *Dirty Little Billy* (1972), followed quickly by Joseph Wambaugh's *The New Centurions* (1972). In the years that followed, he racked up an impressive list of credits, including a critically acclaimed role as the sadistic Captain Knauer in *The Longest Yard* (1974) and a role in Alfred Hitchcock's final film, *Family Plot* (1976). Lauter was immediately a favorite of Hitchcock's. "After we finished the film I was at a function where they were honoring him and he called me over to the table and introduced me to his wife, and said very sweetly 'Ed, I want you to be in my next film, *The Short Night*.' It would have been Sean Connery and Liv Ullmann, and I had the third lead." Unfortunately, Hitchcock died before he was able to complete the film.

Although action and suspense films became his stock in trade, Lauter did appear in a number of genre films, including a remake of *King Kong* (1976), *Magic* (1978), the telefilm *The Clone Master* (1978), Stephen King's *Cujo* (1983, with *X-Files* star William B. Davis), *The Rocketeer* (1991), and *Digital Man* (1995). Lauter played Sheriff Cain on the trucker drama-comedy *BJ and the Bear*, but is best remembered on series television for his role as General Louis Crewes on Stephen King's *Golden Years* miniseries.

The *X-Files* casting director contacted Lauter specifically for the role of ex-astronaut Lt. Col. Marcus Aurelius Belt. "I enjoyed playing the character and I'm very proud of it," Lauter says, while on location for a telefilm in Vancouver. "I had to react to these creatures possessing me and coming out of me. I had a very dramatic scene in my office where I come unglued, and they have to come and carry me off and take me away. It held an audience's interest and gave me a chance to do something that I hadn't really done with that much force. It was kind of like letting everything hang out, screaming and carrying on."

What does Lauter think about the themes and conspiracies the show espouses? "On the cover-ups, it's definitely something to think about. They are coming up with so much evidence—the conclusion that there is life out there other than ours is becoming more and more obvious. That there is some credibility with that—it's a morass of ideas and theories and nobody, I think, has the *real* answer. Who knows what's out there? It's for us to discover." Still, Lauter's own feelings are closer to the skeptical Scully's than to Mulder's. "I believe very much in science, and I appreciate facts. Show me facts. Prove it to me."

In the last few years, Lauter has been featured in such films as *Born on the Fourth of July* (1989), *True Romance* (1993), *Leaving Las Vegas* (1995), HBO's *The Tuskegee Airmen* (1995), and *Mulholland Falls* (1996). Last year, he also starred in *Ravenhawk*, a movie that featured Mitch Pileggi.

What's next up for Ed? He's already filmed a Family Channel telefilm called *Marriage Is Forever*, and a movie about gambling called *Top of the World*, with Dennis Hopper and Peter Weller. This summer he may be taking part in a little film project called *Blackwood*, the first *X-Files* movie. "Chris [Carter] says 'You know, I want to look for something for you because I really want to work with you again.' We're talking about my appearing in that. If not that, he'd like me to be in *Millennium*."

Fans should also try to track down the April 1997 issue of *Vanity Fair*, which contains a photo spread on the *leading* character actors in Hollywood by Annie Lebowitz. "Lee Marvin was a character actor, but he played leads. Dustin Hoffman is a character actor, but he plays leads. Gene Hackman is a character actor who plays leads. Joe Pesci is a character actor who plays leads. I love [being] a character actor and would love to get a shot at playing leads a couple of times. [Annie] put me right in there with some very wonderful people. I was very proud. It had people like Rob Steiger, Linda

Hunt, Kathy Bates, J. T. Walsh, Emmet Walsh . . . all the wonderful people that *work*. I am proud to be in the same orbit with these guys. I think Hitch [Hitchcock] is probably smiling down [from] up there."

X10 Fallen Angel

Case Number:	1.10/ #10 (#1X09)
First Sighting:	November 19, 1993
Directed by:	Larry Shaw
Written by:	Howard Gordon & Alex Gansa

GUEST CAST	CHARACTER
Frederick Coffin	Section Chief Joseph McGrath
Marshall Bell	Commander Calvin Henderson
Scott Bellis	Max Fenig
Jerry Hardin	Deep Throat
Brent Stait	Corp. Taylor
Alvin Sanders	Deputy Sheriff J. Wright
Sheila Paterson	Gina Watkins
Tony Pantages	Lt. Fraser
Freda Perry	Mrs. Wright
Michael Rogers	Lt. Griffin
William McDonald	Dr. Oppenheim
Jane MacDougall	Laura Dalton
Kimberly Unger	Cheif Karen Koretz

FIELD REPORT

Townsend, Wisconsin. After an alien spacecraft crashes, the government evacuates the area, declaring that there has been a toxic chemical spill. Deep Throat tells Mulder about the crash, but when Mulder surreptitiously photographs the site, he is captured. Imprisoned by military agents, Mulder meets Max Fenig, a young member of the National Investigative Committee of Aerial Phenomena (NICAP). Scully comes to get Mulder, warning him that his actions may cause the X-Files unit to be shut down.

By the time Mulder returns to Wisconsin, all hell has broken loose. An invisible alien pilot from the crashed UFO has horribly burned several pursuing soldiers, another alien ship has appeared on Army radar, and Max Fenig is having seizures, which Mulder discovers are related to having been abducted by aliens. As Mulder pursues the invisible pilot and Max

Fenig into a warehouse, he is shocked to witness Max being abducted by the second UFO. Later, back in Washington, Mulder defiantly questions a government committee regarding the truth about the incident. In the background, Deep Throat is busy saving Mulder's butt.

WITNESS NOTES

Burly actor **Frederick Coffin** (Section Chief Joseph McGrath) has had roles in the feature films *Shoot to Kill* (1988), *Hard to Kill* (1990), *If Looks Could Kill* (1991), and *Wayne's World* (1992). On television, he guest-starred on Steven Spielberg's *Amazing Stories* and the revival of *The Twilight Zone*. In the "Night of the Visitors" episode of *Something Is Out There*, Coffin played an author who had just published a book about his abduction by aliens.

Marshall Bell (Commander Calvin Henderson) appeared as a regular in NBC's short-lived hip-hop musical series of 1990, *Hull High*. Bell has done two films with Arnold Schwarzenegger: *Twins* (1988) and *Total Recall* (1990). He also appeared in the low-budget suspense film *The Vagrant* (1992), *A Nightmare on Elm Street 2: Freddy's Revenge* (1985), and Robert A. Heinlein's *The Puppet Masters* (1994). He recently played the vigilante executioner title role in Chris Carter's *Millennium* episode "The Judge."

Vancouver actor **Scott Bellis** is a familiar sight on the planks of local stages, especially with the Shakespearean theater group Bard on the Beach. He's been nominated for five Jessie Awards (local theater awards) in both leading and supporting roles. In 1994, he appeared in three movies: *Intersection, Little Women*, and the time-travel movie *Timecop*. He has also had guest roles on *MacGyver, Neon Rider, Black Stallion,* and *Street Justice*, the 1995 telefilm, *The Man Who Wouldn't Die*, as well as *Johnny's Girl, Courting Justice,* and *Shame*. Recently, he appeared in UPN's science fiction pilot film, *THEM*.

The X-Files's Vancouver casting director Lynne Carrow was very proud of finding Bellis for the role of Max Fenig. In a *Cinefantastique* article, she noted "Scott Bellis was just fabulous. I really fought to get Scott cast. They kept saying 'No, the role of Max will have to come out of L.A.' And I kept saying 'No, you've got to see this guy. . . . Of course he ended up being one of the most popular characters." Indeed, the *X-Files* producers thought Bellis did such a great job with the role that they brought Max Fenig back on the series for a two-parter towards the end of season four: "Tempus Fugit" and "Max." "Fenig was an interesting character," said producer/writer Howard Gordon in the British *The X-Files* magazine. "[He was] a neurotic, paranoid conspiracy theorist who's almost a precursor to the Lone Gunmen."

X11   Eve

Case Number:	1.11/ #11 (#1X10)
First Sighting:	December 10, 1993
Directed by:	Fred Gerber
Written by:	Kenneth Biller & Chris Brancato

GUEST CAST	CHARACTER
Harriet Harris	Dr. Sally Kendrick, Eve 7 / also Eves 6 and 8
Erika Krievens	Cindy Reardon / Eve 9
Sabrina Krievens	Teena Simmons / Eve 10
Jerry Hardin	Deep Throat
George Touliatos	Dr. Katz
Tasha Simms	Ellen Reardon
Janet Hodgkinson	Waitress
David Kirby	Ted Watkins
Tina Gilbertson	Donna Watkins
Christine Upright-Letain	Ms. Wells
Gordon Tipple	Detective
Garry Davey	Hunter
Joe Maffei	Guard #1
Maria Herrera	Guard #2
Robert Lewis	Officer

FIELD REPORT

Greenwich, Connecticut, and San Francisco, California. In Greenwich, Teena, a catatonic young girl waits in the front yard, while her father sits in the backyard, drained of blood. In the hospital she tells agents Mulder and Scully of red lightning and men from the sky. Mulder notes the connection to cattle mutilations, and the two agents are shocked to find that an identical murder took place in San Francisco at the exact same time. Even more bizarre, the agents find that the girl in California, Cindy, looks identical to Teena.

When Teena is kidnapped, Scully traces information about the girls to Dr. Sally Kendrick, who was performing unauthorized genetic experiments at about the time the girls were born. Meanwhile, Mulder is given information from Deep Throat about a government genetic cloning experiment that was conducted in the 1950s. The female clones were named Eve, and Mulder soon learns that one of the grown Eves is actually Dr. Kendrick, and that she has kidnapped Teena and Cindy to raise them. But not all is as it seems with the oddly calm little girls, and sometimes murder can hide in the smallest of hearts.

WITNESS NOTES

Teena and Cindy are the names of Glen Morgan's and James Wong's wives.

Erika and Sabrina Krievens (Cindy Reardon and Teena Simmons) are young twin actresses from Vancouver, British Columbia. Child labor laws prevented the producers from using Los Angeles–based twins in the role.

George Touliatos (Dr. Katz) has been active in Hollywood since the late seventies. Some of his genre film credits include *Prom Night* (1980), the wretched futuristic car movie *Firebird 2015 A.D.* (1981), *The Swordsman* (1993), *Red Scorpion 2* (1994), and *Gladiator Cop* (1994). He also appeared in the B-movie *Robbers of the Sacred Mountain* (1983), whose claim to fame was that it is supposedly the first made-for-cable movie. On TV, he has been seen on episodes of *The Twilight Zone, Ray Bradbury Theater, Forever Knight*, and the "Blood Brothers" episode of *Outer Limits*.

Robert Lewis appeared most recently in the "522666" episode of Chris Carter's *Millennium*, which had an eerie similarity to the Oklahoma City bombings.

WITNESS PROFILE
HARRIET SANSOM HARRIS

Texas-born Harriet Sansom Harris has been acting since she was a young girl. Her talent paid off when she was accepted into the prestigious Juilliard School in New York. After grad-

uation, Harris spent three years with The Acting Company, a repertory theater group. She went on to other regional theater work before landing roles in both off-Broadway and Broadway productions, acting in such prestigious plays as *Macbeth* (as Lady Macduff) and *Hamlet* (as Ophelia) at the New York Shakespeare Festival, and in *The Crucible* and *Man and Superman* at the Roundabout Theater.

Her film debut was in the vampire comedy *Transylvania Twist* (1990). She later appeared as the lead characters' blind daughter, Francie Williams, in *Stephen King's Golden Years*, the miniseries that also starred a number of future *X-Files* actors.

Harris starred in the original cast of *Jeffrey*, an off-Broadway play about a gay man afraid to have sex. She played all the female roles (including a brief appearance as Mother Theresa), winning her both accolades and the friendship of writer Paul Rudnick. He later wrote a role for her in *Addams Family Values* (1993), which caught the attention of the producers of *Frasier*. Beginning in 1993, Harris played the role of Frasier's chain-smoking agent, Bebe Glazer.

The talented actress continued to guest-star on various television shows, including Fox's *The Crew, Doctor, Doctor, Murphy Brown, Sisters, Chicago Hope*, and *Ellen*. She also played the regular role of Vivian Buchanan on CBS's *The Five Mrs. Buchanans*. Some of her film roles have included *Quiz Show* (1994) and the visually stunning new version of *Romeo and Juliet* (1996).

Harris was a favorite of the *X-Files* producers for her work in "Eve," and when Glen Morgan and James Wong left the series to create *Space: Above and Beyond*, they cast her in the episode "Eyes." Chris Carter also recently used Harris again, as Maureen Murphy, in the *Millennium* episode "Loin Like a Hunting Flame."

X12 Fire

Case Number: 1.12 / #12 (#1X11)
First Sighting: December 17, 1993
Directed by: Larry Shaw
Written by: Chris Carter

GUEST CAST	CHARACTER
Amanda Pays	Inspector Phoebe Green
Mark Sheppard	Bob the Caretaker/Cecil L'Ively
Dan Lett	Sir Malcolm Marsden
Laurie Paton	Lady Marsden
Duncan Fraser	Beatty
Phil Hayes	Driver #1
Keegan Macintosh	Michael
Lynda Boyd	Miss Kotchik, Female Bar Patron
Christopher Gray	Jimmie
Alan Robertson	Gray-Haired Man

FIELD REPORT

Cape Cod, Massachussetts. Someone is killing members of the British Parliament, lighting them on fire in unexplainable ways. Scotland Yard Inspector Pheobe Green arrives in Washington, D.C., to ask the help of Mulder, her former lover from Oxford, in keeping Sir Malcolm Marsden safe while he visits Cape Cod. Mulder admits to Scully that he is deathly afraid of fire and that he suspects Green is playing head games with him.

The arsonist behind the murders is an unassuming man named Cecil L'Ively, a man with pyrokinetic powers (the ability to start fires with his mind). L'Ively is indeed stalking Marsden, and when Mulder and Green go undercover to find him, the results are explosive. Mulder's life is saved by firemen, and later Scully figures out who the arsonist is. It all ends in flames at Marsden's vacation home, where Mulder must overcome his fear of fire and work with Scully and Green to stop L'Ively.

WITNESS NOTES

Mark Sheppard (Cecil L'Ively) may seem a familiar face on the screen, but he just *seems* familiar. Born in London, the son of *Max Headroom* actor W. Morgan Sheppard, Mark became a professional musician at age fifteen, eventually playing with performers like Robyn Hitchcock, The Television Personalities, and the aptly-named Irish group Light a Big Fire. He's won awards for his stage work in Los Angeles, but has been featured in only two films: *In the Name of the Father* (1993) and *Lover's Knot* (1996). Sheppard also appeared in the "Spider in the Tower" episode of *M.A.N.T.I.S.*, a series which featured many future *X-Files* actors and was created by the co-creator of

Dark Skies, Bryce Zabel. That particular *M.A.N.T.I.S.* episode was directed by future *X-Files* director Kim Manners. Coming up, look for Sheppard as a regular cast member of Rysher's new syndicated action series, *Soldier of Fortune, Inc.*, airing in the fall of 1997.

Dan Lett (Sir Malcolm Marsden) also doesn't have many screen credits and what he has are mainly Canadian productions. He's appeared in guest roles on the television series *E.N.G.*, *Due South*, and *Wind at My Back*. His film credits include *Paris, France* (1993) and *Sugartime* (1996). And if the character Malcolm Marsden's name looks familiar, you've been watching the credits. It's the name of the first-season *X-Files* hairstylist.

Amanda Pays starred in "Fire."

WITNESS PROFILE
AMANDA PAYS

Born: June 6, 1959, London, England

Amanda Pays studied drama in her years of education at the Marist Convent in England. When she finished her schooling in London, she embarked on a successful career in modelling and commercials, traveling the world on shoots.

At the age of twenty-two, she was one of England's top models, but what she really wanted to do was act. She began training at

London's Academy of Live and Recorded Artists, and soon made her debut, starring with George Segal, on HBO's *The Cold Room* (1984). Other film roles followed, including appearances in *Oxford Blues* (1984), *The Kindred* (1987), and the undersea monster movie, *Leviathan* (1989).

Science fiction fans will know Pays most from two series she appeared on as a regular: *Max Headroom* and the critically acclaimed one-season CBS series, *The Flash*. On *Max Headroom*, she played the leading role of Theora Jones, the assistant to reporter Edison Carter/Max Headroom, a computer-generated video star of the future (played by Matt Frewer). One of her other *Headroom* costars, W. Morgan Sheppard, is the father of her *X-Files* costar, Mark Sheppard.

Several years later, Pays was cast as Christina "Tina" McGee on *The Flash*, a gorgeously stylish super-hero series based on the comic book character. McGee was a scientist at S.T.A.R. labs, and was the only person in the world who knew that police scientist Barry Allen was really the fastest man on Earth.

In this episode of the *X-Files*, a number of personal interplay scenes that deepened the relationship between Green and Mulder were shot but cut in the editing process. Chris Carter wanted to show that Mulder had a history with women. "I just thought it was an interesting choice to use Amanda Pays and to make a villainess out of her," he said in *Cinefantastique*. "Everybody on the internet loves to hate Phoebe."

X13 Beyond the Sea

Case Number: 1.13/ #13 (#1X12)
First Sighting: January 7, 1994
Directed by: David Nutter
Written by: Glen Morgan & James Wong

GUEST CAST	CHARACTER
Brad Dourif	Luther Lee Boggs
Don S. Davis	Captain William Scully
Sheila Larken	Margaret Scully
Lawrence King	Lucas Jackson Henry
Fred Henderson	Agent Thomas
Don MacKay	Warden Joseph Cash
Lisa Vultaggio	Liz Hawley
Chad Willett	Jim Summers
Kathrynn Chisholm	Nurse
Randy Lee	Paramedic
Len Rose	ER Doctor

FIELD REPORT

Raleigh, North Carolina. After leaving her parents' home for Christmas dinner, Scully is startled from sleep to see her father sitting in a chair in her bedroom mouthing silent words. Moments later, she is even more startled to receive a call from her mother, telling her that her father has just died. Scully looks, but the spectre of her father is gone.

Scully is soon caught up in the case of death-row inmate Luther Lee Boggs, who is sentenced to be executed within days. Boggs claims to have become psychic, and he offers Scully a chance to talk with her father beyond the grave if she'll arrange a stay of execution. Reversing roles, Mulder is the skeptic, especially when Boggs trips up on a test. But Boggs's information does help lead Scully to rescue a kidnapped pair of college students, and she must make a choice to help Boggs or to see him go to his execution without ever knowing if he did indeed have a message from her dead father.

WITNESS NOTES

Missouri-born actor **Don S. Davis**, who appeared here for the first time as Captain William Scully, also appeared in David Lynch's eerie cult series *Twin Peaks* as Major Garland Briggs. Davis really was a military man; he was a captain in the U.S. Army, and had been stationed in Korea during the Vietnam war. His work as a theater teacher at the University of British Columbia led to extra work on *MacGyver*, where he was the stunt double for Dana Elcar, who played series regular Peter Thornton. Davis guested on other shows, such as *J.J. Starbuck* and *21 Jump Street*, and eventually began to receive starring roles. He was in *Watchers* (1988), *Midnight Matinee* (1989) with William B. Davis, *The Omen IV: The Awakening* (1991), Stephen King's *Needful Things* (1993), and recently appeared in the movie *The Fan* (1996). Although he died in this episode of *X-Files*, Davis would reprise his role as Captain Scully in the second season episode,

"One Breath." The silent words Davis was uttering as a ghost were actually St. Matthew 6: 9-13, the Lord's Prayer.

Vancouver native **Chad Willett** (Jim Summers) was a four-year regular on the Canadian series *Madison*, and has appeared on one episode of *Outer Limits*. Most recently, he played the regular role of astronaut Peter Engel on the syndicated series *The Cape*.

The names of the two killers in this episode, Luther Lee Boggs and Lucas Jackson Henry, were taken from real life serial killer Henry Lee Lucas, whose later accomplice in crime was Ottis Toole. Lucas claims to have murdered hundreds of men and women from his first kill in 1951 until his capture in 1983. A rash of recantings and changed testimonies has led police to question exactly how many victims Lucas (and Toole) killed, but the estimated number is well over one hundred. Henry Lee Lucas is currently awaiting his execution on death row at a Huntsville, Texas, prison.

WITNESS PROFILE
BRADFORD C. DOURIF
Born: March 18, 1950, Huntington, West Virginia

With Luther Lee Boggs, Brad Dourif adds yet another psycho to his credit list. Indeed, the actor's resume is full of wild-eyed unbalanced characters, almost to the exclusion of any other type. Dourif has made a strong foothold as a character actor, and his rare forays into television are almost always genre-related.

Dourif made his film debut in the 1975 film *One Flew Over the Cuckoo's Nest*, playing the innocent, stammering Billy Bibbitt and received an Academy Award nomination, a Golden Globe Award for Best Supporting Actor, and a British Oscar for Best Supporting Actor for the role. Several other future *X-Files* guest-stars also appeared in the critically acclaimed film, including Vincent Schiavelli ("Humbug"), Michael Berryman ("Revelations"), and Sydney Lassick ("Elegy").

Dourif's first leading role was as an obsessed preacher in director John Huston's *Wise Blood* (1979), but the film failed at the box office. Dourif has worked steadily since then, mostly in B movies and genre films. His most famous role was as serial killer Charles Lee Ray (do all serial killers have the middle name of "Lee"?)

before his soul was trapped in the body of a "Good Guys" doll, at which point he became Chucky, the killer doll in the trio of *Child's Play* movies (1988, 1990, 1991), the last of which starred future *X-Files* guest Perrey Reeves.

Some of Dourif's other genre credits include *Spontaneous Combustion* (1989), *Critters 4* (1991), *Graveyard Shift* (1990), *The Eyes of Laura Mars* (1978), *The Exorcist III* (1990), *Grim Prairie Tales* (1989), Dario Argento's *Trauma* (1992), and *Color of Night* (1994). Dourif was awarded the "Fangoria Chainsaw Award for Best Supporting Actor" for his role in *Body Parts* (1991). As if those weren't enough to certify his membership in the Weirdo Actors Guild, Dourif worked with cult director David Lynch twice, with roles in *Blue Velvet* (1986) and *Dune* (1984). This year, Dourif has a role in the upcoming fourth *Alien* film, *Alien: Resurrection*.

On television, Dourif worked with Oliver Stone and Bruce Wagner on the *Wild Palms* miniseries, and appeared in the 1995 Disney remake of *Escape to Witch Mountain*. His earliest television work was the telefilm *Sergeant Matlovich vs. the U.S. Air Force* (1978), which told the story of a gay veteran's fight to stay in the military. Series television roles for Dourif have included a recurring role in *Star Trek: Voyager* and guest shots on *Babylon 5* and *Tales From the Crypt*. He most recently played the role of wacko Millennium-group wannabe Dennis Hoffman in "Force Majeure," an episode of Chris Carter's *Millennium* series.

Dourif was cast in this *X-Files* episode at the request of writers Morgan and Wong, but it required some wrangling by Chris Carter. Because Dourif was more expensive than the *X-Files* guest-star budget allowed, Carter had to get permission to cast him. Carter called Fox president Peter Roth at home, on Thanksgiving, to get Roth to sign off on the extra fees. In *X-Files Confidential*, Morgan says "We fought pretty hard for Brad Dourif, and Chris came through for us. *Cuckoo's Nest* is a movie that means a lot, and to have Brad Dourif saying our lines just meant the world to me."

Director David Nutter was happy to be working with the actor as well, as he revealed in *Cinefantastique*. "Brad Dourif came in and my job there was to create a setting where he could be what he really wanted to be . . . basically I let him have the stage."

X14 GenderBender

Case Number:	1.14/ #14 (#1X13)
First Sighting:	January 21, 1994
Directed by:	Rob Bowman
Written by:	Larry Barber & Paul Barber

GUEST CAST	CHARACTER
Brent Hinkley	Brother Andrew
Michele Goodger	Sister Abigail
Peter Stebbings	Marty/Brother Martin [Male]
Kate Twa	Marty [Female]
Nicholas Lea	Michael
Mitchell Kosterman	Detective Horton
Paul Batten	Brother Wilton
Doug Abrahams	FBI Agent #2
Aundrea MacDonald	Pretty Woman
John R. Taylor	Husband
Grai Carrington	Tall Man
Tony Morelli	Cop
Lesley Ewen	FBI Agent #1
David Thomson	Brother Oakley

FIELD REPORT

Steveston, Massachussetts. Thinking he's about to get lucky, a man picks up a woman in a dance bar. In the hotel room, they have sex, but the man chokes to death after they've finished. As his female partner leaves, her body changes into that of a man. Mulder and Scully are dispatched to investigate, as this is the fifth post-coital death in the area in six weeks. Each corpse contains high amounts of pheremones, a stimulant which heightens sexual attraction.

Oddly enough, the agents' investigation lead them to the community of the Kindred, a reclusive (apparently religious) sect that prefers to have little contact with the outside world. When Mulder and Scully press their investigation on the Kindred, they find more strangeness than they thought possible—through rituals the Kindred can change their sex. It seems that the killer is a rogue member of the group. Scully is almost seduced and Mulder is almost trapped in an organic underground catacombs before they both escape. But now that their secret is out, what will become of the Kindred?

WITNESS NOTES

The chant sung by the Kindred was written by *X-Files* co-executive producer Paul Rabwin. It was sung by Rabwin and six other singers.

Brent Hinkley (Brother Andrew) has been featured in several films whose titles could be reflective of this episode of *The X-Files* including *Zapped Again!* (1990) and *Martians Go Home* (1990). Other genre films he has appeared in include *Jacob's Ladder* (1990), *The Silence of the Lambs* (1991), *Mom and Dad Save the World* (1992), *Carnosaur* (1993), and Tim Burton's *Ed Wood* (1994).

Michele Goodger (Sister Abigail) appeared in *The Accused* (1988), *Shoot to Kill* (1988), *Who's Harry Crumb?* (1989), *The Hitman* (1991), and *Little Women* (1994). She had a regular role as Belle Ramsey on the television series *The Adventures of the Black Stallion*.

When **Mitchell Kosterman** (Detective Horton) reappeared in "Sleepless," he was *Lieutenant* Horton of the NYPD. It's unclear whether the character is supposed to be the same person or not.

X15 Lazarus

Case Number:	1.15/ #15 (#1X14)
First Sighting:	February 4, 1994
Directed by:	David Nutter
Written by:	Alex Gansa & Howard Gordon

GUEST CAST	CHARACTER
Christopher Allport	Agent Jack Willis
Cec Verrell	Lula Phillips
Jackson Davies	Agent Bruskin
Jason Schombing	Warren James Dupre
Callum Keith Rennie	Tommy Phillips
Jay Brazeau	Professor Varnes
Lisa Bunting	Doctor #1
Peter Kelamis	O'Dell
Brenda Crichlow	TV Reporter
Mark Saunders	Doctor #2
Alexander Boynton	Clean-Cut Man
Russell Hamilton	Officer Daniels

FIELD REPORT

Baltimore, Maryland. Scully is on a stakeout with violent crimes agent Jack Willis, her ex-partner and ex-boyfriend. They're soon involved in a bloody bank robbery, and both Willis and the robber, Warren Dupre, are shot. At the hospital, both die at the same time, but Willis is eventually revived. Later, he leaves the hospital, but only after cutting the wedding ring off the finger of Dupre's corpse. Stranger still, the tattoo that Dupre had is now appearing on Willis' forearm!

Mulder is the first one to voice a theory, that Willis has been taken over by Dupre's spirit, but Scully refuses to believe him. Willis kills Dupre's brother-in-law, who he thought betrayed him, and lures Scully into a trap. Willis tries to convince Dupre's wife/accomplice that he is really Dupre, but she betrays him again (as she did at the bank robbery). Even as he dies a second time, Willis/Dupre tries to reconcile with Scully, and takes the scheming Lula Phillips to the other side as he/they go.

Christopher Allport appeared in "Lazarus."

WITNESS NOTES

Cec Verrell (Lula Phillips) has had a number of bizarre genre roles, beginning with her role as a hooker in *Runaway* (1984), the Tom Selleck/Gene Simmons futuristic suspense film. She later appeared with wrestling star "Rowdy" Roddy Piper in *Hell Comes to Frogtown* (1987), the Western werewolf movie *Mad at the Moon* (1992), and in the pilot telefilm *Nick Knight*. Verrell was also a cast member of the Navy-sanctioned CBS series *Supercarrier*.

Jackson Davies (Agent Bruskin) also starred in *Runaway* with Verrell, as well as over a dozen films and telefilms shot in British Columbia. He played another FBI agent, named Lusk, in *Stakeout* (1987), and costarred with *X-Files* actor William B. Davis in the pilot telefilm *Diagnosis of Murder* (1992). Davies was also a recurring character in *MacGyver*.

Jason Schmobing, a.k.a. Jason Scott Schombing (Warren James Dupre), played Officer Ronnie Lopez on *The Commish*.

WITNESS INTERVIEW
CHRISTOPHER ALLPORT

Born: June 17, 1947, Boston, Massachusetts

California-based actor Christopher Allport has "done it all from the top to the bottom," with a heavy emphasis on telefilms. He debuted on the soap opera *Another World*. Allport later ap-

peared as a regular on a season of *Dynasty*, as well as on episodic television including *Diagnosis Murder, Doogie Howser, M.D., Matlock, Murder, She Wrote,* and *Beverly Hills 90210*. His genre credits include a *Quantum Leap* episode "Last Dance Before an Execution," as well as a *Twilight Zone* episode called "Examination Day." More recently, he has guested on *The Sentinel,* the "Live Hard, Die Young, and Leave a Good-Looking Corpse" episode of *Kindred: The Embraced,* and *The Pretender*.

Some of Allport's movie credits include William Friedkin's *To Live and Die in L.A.,* the 1983 Emmy award–winning *Special Bulletin* (1983), the forgotten slasher film *Savage Weekend* (1980) with later *X-Files* guest William Sanderson, and the horror film *Dead and Buried* (1981). He later appeared in Tobe Hooper's remake of *Invaders From Mars* (1986) and *Jack Frost* (1996), a film about a killer snowman.

Because Allport's show was in the first season, he admits that "there was no real cachet to doing *The X-Files*. It was just another show at that point." He knew Chris Carter from the producer's days as a writer for *Surfer* magazine. "We used to play paddle tennis every Sunday." The role of agent Jack Willis found Allport sharing many of his scenes with Gillian Anderson. He was, after all, playing the role of Scully's ex-partner and ex-boyfriend. "It was clear as we were shooting it that she had done a lot of work around that relationship [and] who this guy had been to her. When we said goodbye at the end of the show, we were both crying. We both had invested a lot into it. That was very early for her on that show, too. She wasn't quite sure who her character was yet, and she was still defining it."

The "presence" of another actor helped Allport. "David Nutter showed me a previous episode that he had directed that had Brad Dourif on it. And he kept talking about how great Brad Dourif was. They showed the episode during lunch hour, and it just got my competitive juices really going—he kept talking about Brad Dourif this and Brad Dourif that. I made it a priority early on to make them forget who Brad Dourif ever was." Did he succeed? "I think, yes, certainly. I don't think I erased Brad Dourif's name, but I think they certainly remembered my episode."

As the episode opens, agents Willis and Scully are involved in a shootout at a bank, and Willis is hit by a blast from a pump-action shotgun. Was that difficult? "Oh, come on! I was doing a show with Bob Forrester a couple of weeks ago in Dallas. We just sat there for about an hour trading, guessing how many times we've died, and how many different ways we've died over the years in our careers. You just *do* it. Basically, it's just a dance. It's a physical thing that you do. You've gotta go with the gunshot the way you're blown and move, and there's [blood] squibs all over you—there's nothing you have to act, particularly.

"Dying is another story. When I was doing that show, I swear to God we were working so hard, that when it came time to be doing that stuff, that whole last scene, I literally saw parts of my life flash in front of me. My *own* life. Flashing in front of my eyes. And I wasn't willing any of this. I began to just see—as if I was drowning—I began to see my life flash in front of my eyes. It was me working on the character! And everything else that was going on. Once you've been acting for a long time, there's a kind of automatic thing that goes on, an unconscious process. You just trust that it's going to do its work."

Speaking of work, *The X-Files* is notorious in Hollywood as a difficult shoot. "I've never worked so hard on an episodic show before. David Nutter was the director of that episode,

and he is a very good director, and he will not let a shot go by if it's not right." And while Allport was busy, he says star David Duchovny was even busier. "They were reshooting a previous episode that hadn't quite finished yet, and that's what he would do on his lunch break—he'd go off and shoot some more, shoot something else. The intensity of the set was tremendous and very good, very focused."

After Jack Willis died, the soul of his killer, Warren Dupre, entered his body. Allport now not only had to play one character, but two! Dupre was left-handed. Was that an issue for Allport? "I'm a lefty—no problem! I didn't have to do much right-handed stuff because Jack Willis is right-handed, and because I'm the guy inside of him, I'm left-handed." Still, switching back and forth between personalities was tricky. "I kept having to turn to David [Nutter] and saying, 'Are you getting who this is right now?' 'Cause sometimes it was the bad guy, sometimes it was the agent, and sometimes it was a mixture of both. And they threw so much at me! The diabetes, the critical wound in the stomach, all this stuff coming at me. [Laughs.] Just tell me, how do you act 'diabetes'? You can't! You can act the insulin—the coma, the shock and all of that, but . . . a character with diabetes? What am I supposed to do? You can't act that."

Allport didn't have a problem cutting off his (Dupre's) own finger in the morgue scene. "This is why David is such a good director. He did it all with the montage. They only show me picking up the surgical scissors, looking down, and then you hear this *snap*, but you never saw the cut." However, a location shoot was unnerving for Allport. "We shot the hospital scenes in a location up there that was an asylum for the criminally insane. It was very spooky there. If you wandered off the set, just down to another floor, you felt like you were in a very haunted and sad place. You could almost feel the horror of the place."

Allport found working on *The X-Files* a good experience. "I really got on film what I wanted. Certainly in the end, when I was crying, and when I killed her [Lula Phillips]. You really believe the love that the character had for the woman who betrayed him. That's what I wanted to show more than anything else. He was a horrible psychopath but he truly loved this person."

Allport has recently had more discussions with Chris Carter. "We've talked a lot about a *Millennium*. I almost went up this season to play Lance's [Henriksen] brother but it didn't work out. When I saw Chris up in Vancouver this past trip, we definitely talked about doing one next season."

Years after his episode of *X-Files* was filmed, Allport has become a fan of the series (his favorites are "Humbug," "D.P.O.," and "Musings of a Cigarette Smoking Man"), but what excites him the most? "I have my own *X-Files* trading card!" And that's something he could *never* have gotten from his work on *Dynasty*.

X16   Young at Heart

Case Number:	1.16/ #16 (#1X15)
First Sighting:	February 11, 1994
Directed by:	Michael Lange
Written by:	Scott Kaufer & Chris Carter

GUEST CAST	CHARACTER
Dick Anthony Williams	Agent Reggie Purdue
Alan Boyce	Young John Irvin Barnett
Christine Estabrook	Agent Henderson
Graham Jarvis	NIH Doctor
Jerry Hardin	Deep Throat
Robin Mossley	Dr. Joe Ridley
Merrilyn Gann	Prosecutor
Gordon Tipple	Joe Crandall
William B. Davis	Cigarette-Smoking Man (as CIA Agent)
Courtney Arciaga	Young Progeria Victim
David Petersen	Older John Irvin Barnett
Robin Douglas	Computer Specialist

FIELD REPORT

Washington, D.C. A note left behind at a jewelry store robbery makes a reference to Fox Mulder, but all the clues point to John Barnett, a criminal Mulder put behind bars, and who died in prison four years ago! Fox begins investigating with his ex-partner, Reggie Purdue, but Agent Purdue is killed by a man who claims to be John Barnett. Mulder reluctantly brings Scully in on the case.

What they find is scientific testing gone awry. Dr. Ridley, the man who pronounced

Barnett dead, had his medical license revoked for unsanctioned experimentation involving reversing the aging process. Ridley tells Scully that Barnett was the last of his experiments, and that he can regenerate his limbs and his life, much in the same way a salamander can. Barnett is negotiating with secret government operatives to sell them Ridley's research, and the government is willing to lose Scully to Barnett's revenge if that's the price they need to pay.

WITNESS NOTES

The black-and-white film footage of the doctor and his young patients with progeria was an emotional time for the crew. Coproducer Paul Rabwin had contacted the Progeria Society, and Courtney Arciaga, a little girl who suffered from the aging disease, was flown up to Vancouver to film the footage.

Dick Anthony Williams (Agent Reggie Purdue) has been a character actor in Hollywood since the mid-seventies, debuting in *Dog Day Afternoon* (1975). His credits include the thriller *The Deep* (1977) and *Edward Scissorhands* (1990), the telefilm of Aldous Huxley's *Brave New World* (1980), and the miniseries adaption of James A. Michener's *Space* (1985). Williams co-starred with David Duchovny in *The Rapture* (1991), as Henry.

Alan Boyce (Young John Irvin Barnett) has acted in numerous independent film projects, including *Totally F***ed Up* (1993) and *Skin and Bone* (1996).

Christine Estabrook's (Agent Henderson) debut role was in the acclaimed film *The Bell Jar* (1979). Her other credits include the telefilm *The Lost Honor of Kathryn Beck* (1984) with Steven Williams and the films *The Usual Suspects* (1995) and the forgettable psychic comedy *Second Sight* (1989). Recently, she played the role of frosty flight attendant supervisor Lenora Zwick on the Fox sitcom *The Crew*.

Graham Jarvis (NIH Doctor) has been working in Hollywood since 1969, when he appeared as the music teacher in the counterculture film *Alice's Restaurant* (1969). He continued to be involved in music-related projects throughout his career, including the film *R.P.M.* (1970), and a regular role as Bob

Dyrenforth on two syndicated seasons of *Fame*. His only genre credits are roles in the bizarre suburban cannibal comedy *Parents* (1989), and one of the few roles in Stephen King's *Misery* (1990), as well as parts on *Star Trek: The Next Generation* ("Unification Part I"), *Tales From the Crypt*, and *The Twilight Zone*.

X17 E.B.E.

Case Number:	1.17/ #17 (#1X16)
First Sighting:	February 18, 1994
Directed by:	William Graham
Written by:	Glen Morgan & James Wong

GUEST CAST	CHARACTER
Jerry Hardin	Deep Throat
Allan Lysell	Chief Rivers
Peter LaCroix	Ranheim (a.k.a. Frank Druse; Druce in closed-captioning)
Bruce Harwood	Byers
Dean Haglund	Langly
Tom Braidwood	Frohike

FIELD REPORT

Mattawa, Washington. The "conspiracy" kicks into gear after an Iraqi pilot shoots down a UFO and it crashes near a U.S. base on the Iraq/Turkey border. Later, Mulder tries to question a trucker who said he saw a UFO, but the local sheriff won't allow it. Mulder becomes convinced that the trucker's cargo is actually an E.B.E. (Extraterrestrial Biological Entity) salvaged from the Iraqi UFO, and he decides to get help from an unlikely source.

Mulder and Scully visit the offices of the government watchdog group, conspiracy theorists The Lone Gunmen. Afterward, Mulder is given a lead from Deep Throat that turns out to be misinformation. Mulder and Scully manage to track the trucker to Washington state, where they use phony credentials to enter a secret government installation. There, Mulder confronts Deep Throat about the existence of extraterrestrial life (and death). The experience leaves Mulder wondering whether he can trust his informant or not.

WITNESS NOTES

Both of the fake IDs that Mulder and Scully use bear the names of *X-Files* assistant directors: Mulder's is Tom Braidwood and Scully's is Val Stefoff. Does this mean that the same "fictional" Tom Braidwood whose name was being stencilled onto a parking space at HTG Industrial Technologies (in "Shadows") is now working for the government in their Northwest Facility?

Allan Lysell (Chief Rivers) has appeared in a number of *MacGyver* episodes and in the horror film *The Fly II* (1989).

X18 Miracle Man

Case Number:	1.18/ #18 (#1X17)
First Sighting:	March 18, 1994
Directed by:	Michael Lange
Written by:	Howard Gordon & Chris Carter

GUEST CAST	CHARACTER
R. D. Call	Sheriff Maurice Daniels
Scott Bairstow	Samuel Hartley
George Gerdes	Reverend Calvin Hartley
Dennis Lipscomb	Leonard Vance
Walter Marsh	Judge
Campbell Lane	Margaret Hohman's father
Chilton Crane	Margaret Hohman
Howard Storey	Fire Chief
Iris Quinn Bernard	Lillian Daniels
Lisa Ann Beley	Nurse Beatrice Salinger
Alex Doduk	Young Samuel
Roger Haskett	Deputy Tyson

FIELD REPORT

Kenwood, Tennessee. Mulder and Scully investigate the Miracle Ministry, a traveling religious revival with headliner Samuel Hartley. Ten years ago, Samuel miraculously brought Leonard Vance, a severely burned man, back to life. Recently though, Samuel's healing touch has had a disturbing turn; two of the people he healed died shortly thereafter. Samuel is arrested by the local sheriff, who has a personal vendetta against the boy. He purposely puts two men into the same jail cell as Samuel, and the two men beat the healer to death.

With Samuel dead, Mulder and Scully must discover the true cause of the healing deaths.

They trace clues to Leonard Vance, who has been traveling with the ministry. Vance has his own reasons for wanting Samuel dead, but the ghostly vision that appears to him drives him over the edge. A puzzled Mulder and Scully also find that Samuel's body has disappeared, with a nurse claiming he revived from the dead and walked out on his own!

WITNESS NOTES

Actor Don S. Davis, who plays the recurring role of Captain William Scully, was the dialect coach for this episode, working with the actors to get their Southern accents right.

R. D. Call (Sheriff Maurice Daniels) is a regular on *EZ Streets* as Michael 'Fivers' Dugan and was an evil Enforcer in the water-logged *Waterworld* (1995). He is best remembered by genre fans for his chillingly ruthless portrayal of Jude Andrews, the government killer from the CIA-like organization known as The Shop in *Stephen King's Golden Years* miniseries. That role pitted him against—and had him murder—several future *X-Files* guest actors.

Dennis Lipscomb (Leonard Vance) has had a career full of cop roles, including multiple guest shots on *Hill Street Blues*, which led to creator Steven Bochco hiring him as a regular in the short-lived police musical series, *Cop Rock*. Lipscomb was also a regular on *Wiseguy* as Sid Royce and on *In the Heat of the Night* as Mayor Findlay. In a role with odd ties to his *X-Files* character, Lipscomb played a character involved in the seemingly miraculous resurrection of dead prison inmates on the "Resurrection" episode of *Lois & Clark: The New Adventures of Superman*.

Roger Haskett (Deputy Tyson) was an ER doctor in the "Maranatha" episode of Chris Carter's *Millennium*.

WITNESS PROFILE

SCOTT BAIRSTOW

Born: April 23, Steinbach, Manitoba, Canada

Scott Bairstow is best known as the scruffy disillusioned gunslinger Newt Call on the syndicated television series *Lonesome Dove* and its follow-up, *Lonesome Dove: The Outlaw Years*.

In 1993 his role as Jesse in the telefilm *There Was a Little Boy* garnered him critical acclaim, with the *Los Angeles Times* calling him "a dynamic young actor." His work caught the attention of Disney executives who needed a young male lead for their feature film *White Fang 2: Myth of the White Wolf* (1994). Those who watched *Lonesome Dove*, based on Larry McMurtry's Pulitzer Prize–winning novel and the Emmy award–winning miniseries, were probably surprised at Bairstow's turn on *The X-Files*. As Newt Call, Bairstow was unshaven, scruffy, and thirtyish; as the reluctant religious healer Samuel Hartley, he was haunted but young.

Bairstow had experience with supervising producers/writers Howard Gordon and Alex Gansa prior to his work on this episode of *The X-Files*. He had shot an ABC pilot for them called *Country Estates* (that same pilot got *them* their jobs on *The X-Files!*). "I called him to specifically read for this part," said Howard Gordon in *Cinefantastique*. "He was doing *White Fang 2*, and he had a three-picture deal at Disney, and his agent wasn't letting him do television. So I called Scott directly and implored him to do it. He read the script and he loved it."

With the cancellation of *Lonesome Dove* after two seasons (1994–1996), Bairstow has completed work in three 1997 films: *Wild America, Black Circle Boys*, and the telefilm *Killing Mr. Griffin*.

X19 Shapes

Case Number:	1.19/ #19 (#1X18)
First Sighting:	April 1, 1994
Directed by:	David Nutter
Written by:	Marilyn Osborn

GUEST CAST	CHARACTER
Ty Miller	Lyle Parker
Michael Horse	Sheriff Charles Tskany
Donnelly Rhodes	Jim Parker
Jimmy Herman	Ish
Renae Morriseau	Gwen Goodensnake
Dwight McFee	David Gates (Lawyer)
Paul McLean	Dr. Josephs

FIELD REPORT

Browning, Montana. A father and son are attacked by a creature, but when shot, it turns out to be a Native American man named Joe Goodensnake. Mulder and Scully arrive, and Mulder links the case to J. Edgar Hoover's very first X-File, in the same region. He theorizes that some Native American men have the power to turn into wolves. That's bad news for Lyle Parker, who was wounded by the beast in the earlier battle.

When his own father is ripped to shreds and Lyle is found naked and dazed nearby, the plot thickens. Mulder visits a tribal elder, Ish, who tells him the legend of the manitou, a creature that resurfaces every eight years. When Mulder tries to warn Scully, he discovers that she's already left the hospital with Lyle. Mulder and the sheriff race to the Parker home to save Scully from the creature Lyle has become in the night.

WITNESS NOTES

Glen Morgan and James Wong did an uncredited rewrite on Osborn's script.

Ty Miller (Lyle Parker) was a regular on the Western series *The Young Riders* and on *Hotel*, based on Arthur Hailey's novel. He also appeared in the recurring role of Prospero in the low-budget Full Moon science fiction movies *Trancers 4: Jack of Swords* (1994) and *Trancers 5: Sudden Death*. And who directed these two Science Fiction B movies? None other than David Nutter, the director of this *X-Files* episode.

Michael Horse (Sheriff Charles Tskany) appeared regularly on *Twin Peaks*, as Deputy Tommy "Hawk" Hill. He worked with David Duchovny on some episodes, in which Duchovny played transvestite FBI agent Dennis/Denise Bryson. In *Wrapped in Plastic*, Horse relates a story from filming this *X-Files* episode. He had a photo of himself with Duchovny in drag and showed it to the makeup artist. "'You know, I used to date David's sister,' David didn't say anything." Horse made his film debut as Tonto in the much-maligned 1981 film *The Legend of the Lone Ranger*. He later appeared in *Passenger 57* (1992), the telefilm *Lakota Woman: Siege at Wounded Knee* (1994), two episodes of Steven Spielberg's

Amazing Stories, and as a regular on the 1992 syndicated series revival of *The Untouchables*, as well as the Canadian series *North of 60*. He was one of the narrators in the 1995 documentary series *500 Nations*, which detailed the history of the Native American tribes. You may also be familiar with Horse from his cartoon voice roles; he's on *Gargoyles* (as Sergeant Peter Maza), *The Tick*, and *Duckman*.

A native Canadian, **Donnelly Rhodes** (Jim Parker) was a contract player for Universal in the sixties. He was a common guest star on *Mission: Impossible* as well as on *The Wild, Wild West*, and he even tucked an episode of *Tarzan* into his resumé in 1966. Rhodes had a three-year role on the soap opera *The Young and the Restless* as Phillip Chancellor, Sr. In 1984, he moved up to Vancouver, British Columbia, to take the role of veterinarian Dr. Grant 'Doc' Roberts in the popular Canadian series *Danger Bay* (1984), which was seen in the U.S. on the Disney Channel. The versatile Rhodes also had a role in the telefilm *Dalton: Code of Vengeance II* (1986), which co-starred Mitch Pileggi. Rhodes's genre roles have included individual episodes of *The Starlost*, *The New Adventures of Wonder Woman* ("A Date With Doomsday"), *Sliders* ("Greatfellas"), and *Outer Limits* ("Worlds Apart"). Rhodes also appeared as Pete Dumont in "Broken World," an episode of Chris Carter's *Millennium*.

Jimmy Herman (Ish) has been in five films since his debut in *Dances With Wolves* (1990), including *Blind Justice* (1994) as a shaman, *Medicine River* (1994), and the telefilms *Geronimo* (1993), *Warrior Spirit* (1994), and *Crazy Horse* (1996).

X20   Darkness Falls

Case Number: 1.20/ #20 (#1X19)
First Sighting: April 15, 1994
Directed by: Joe Napolitano
Written by: Chris Carter

GUEST CAST   CHARACTER
Jason Beghe   Ranger Larry Moore
Tom O'Rourke   Steve Humphreys
Titus Welliver   Doug Spinney

David Hay	Clean-Suited Man
Barry Greene	Bob Perkins
Ken Tremblett	Dyer

FIELD REPORT

Olympic National Forest, Washington. Thirty loggers have vanished in the woods, victims to a glowing green horde of mites. But that's not what the local forest ranger and the logging company security man believe; they blame the men's disappearance on eco-terrorists. Mulder and Scully arrive to investigate, and quickly meet one of those eco-terrorists, Doug Spinney. Spinney says that the deaths came from a force that was trapped within the trees that the loggers cut down, and Mulder theorizes that the mites could be ancient insect eggs mutated by radiation from the nearby volcano.

Quick escape from the remote cabin they're sharing is impossible, and the agents are forced to spend the night hoping their generator won't fail as light tends to keep the insects away. Security man Humphreys is cocooned by the mites when he ventures into the night. Spinney, Ranger Moore, Mulder, and Scully attempt to escape in a car, but eco-terrorist spikes in the road stop their progress. And as the car's power dies down, the mites descend toward the agents, trapping them in their vehicle.

WITNESS NOTES

Tom O'Rourke (Steve Humphreys) is best known for his role as company boss A. J. Trask in the short-lived NBC sitcom *Working Girl*, which was a spin-off from the film that starred Melanie Griffith, Harrison Ford, and Sigourney Weaver. The series also starred a newcomer to Hollywood, Sandra Bullock.

Why is it that **Titus Welliver** (Doug Spinney) always has the role of the troublemaker? In his film debut, *Navy SEALS* (1990), he played an annoying redneck at a bar. In the 1990 telefilm *The Lost Capone*, he played gangster Ralph Capone. He followed that one up by playing Al Capone in the film *Mobsters* (1991), before switching sides to play a mace-happy bad cop in *The Doors* (1991). He also was in an early episode of the horror series *Tales From the Crypt*, entitled "Forever Ambergris." Most recently, Welliver was the ulti-

mate bad guy, a ruthless mobster vampire on Fox's *Kindred: The Embraced*; he played Cameron, a member of the Brujah clan. The leader of that clan was fellow *X-Files* actor Brian Thompson.

Jason Beghe appeared as Ranger Larry Moore in "Darkness Falls."

WITNESS PROFILE

JASON BEGHE

Born: March 12, 1960, New York City, New York

Actor Jason Beghe has been a friend of David Duchovny's since they were teens. The two met in Manhattan's prestigious Collegiate Preparatory School, where Duchovny had gotten in on a scholarship, at age thirteen. Beghe and Duchovny hung out with Billy Wirth, who would later become an actor as well. After Duchovny graduated Princeton and left his post-graduate studies at Yale, Beghe encouraged Duchovny to pursue acting as well, convincing him to attend classes at The Actors Studio and helping to get him to audition for commercials. Beghe had himself decided to be an actor when he was twenty-five, and began taking acting lessons from Wynn Handman. When they weren't working on stage or auditioning for roles on screen, Beghe and Duchovny worked together as bartenders.

Years later, Duchovny would repay Beghe for his encouragement by getting him cast in this *X-Files* episode.

Beghe's first film role was in *Compromising Positions* (1985). He followed that up with a role in the critically acclaimed telefilm about the murder of a gay military cadet, *Dress Gray* (1986). Other film roles include *Thelma & Louise* (1991), the telefilm *Treasure Island: The Adventure Begins* (1994), and the cable telefilm werewolf-cop thriller, *Full Eclipse*. Beghe's biggest starring role was in the horror film *Monkey Shines* (1988), in which he played Allan Mann, a quadriplegic man who trains a monkey to help him. Jason can be seen soon in the 1997 Demi Moore film, *G. I. Jane*.

In *The Duchovny Files*, Beghe is quoted on his feelings about acting: "As an actor, you not only give the audience something that you've put a lot of time into but also share a part of yourself with them. If it's a good role you also discover something about yourself in the process. I don't know what could be more exciting."

Beghe told *TV Zone* that "Larry Moore was just a vehicle for me to go up and hang out with Duke (Duchovny). Unfortunately, the conditions for filming couldn't have been worse. It was raining, snowing, and freezing up there . . . but all we did was laugh the entire time."

X21 Tooms

Case Number:	1.21/ #21 (#1X20)
First Sighting:	April 22, 1994
Directed by:	David Nutter
Written by:	Glen Morgan & James Wong

GUEST CAST	CHARACTER
Doug Hutchison	Eugene Victor Tooms
Paul Ben Victor	Dr. Aaron Monte
Mitch Pileggi	Assistant Director Walter S. Skinner
Henry Beckman	Detective Frank Briggs
Timothy Webber	Detective Talbot
Jan D'Arcy	Judge Kann
Jerry Wasserman	Dr. Plith
Frank C. Turner	Dr. Collins
Gillian Carfra	Christine Ranford
Pat Bermel	Frank Ranford
Mikal Dughi	Dr. Pamela Karetzky
Glynis Davies	Nelson (Tooms's attorney)
Steve Adams	Myers (state's attorney)
Catherine Lough	Dr. Richmond
William B. Davis	Cigarette-Smoking Man
Andre Daniels	Arlan Green

FIELD REPORT

Baltimore, Maryland. Eugene Victor Tooms is up for parole, and at his commitment hearing Mulder appears as more insane than Tooms. The killer is freed, and he goes to live with the Greens at their halfway house. Tooms resumes his job with animal regulation, but Mulder is keeping a close eye on him, in a manner edging dangerously close to harassment.

Meanwhile, Scully meets the new assistant director, Walter S. Skinner, who demands better reports and more conclusive evidence from her and agent Mulder. Cigarette-Smoking Man watches silently nearby. Mulder and Scully continue investigating Tooms's past, finding evidence that dates back to the 1933 murders. While Mulder sleeps, Tooms slithers into his house and frames Mulder, saying the agent attacked and badly beat him. Mulder is ordered to stay away from Tooms, but he and Scully find that Tooms's final murder has been committed. The agents must track Tooms to his nest, underneath the escalator of a shopping mall, before the mutant enters hibernation.

WITNESS NOTES

Jan D'Arcy (Judge Kann) is yet another veteran of *Twin Peaks*, on which she played Sylvia Horne.

Frank C. Turner (Dr. Collins) was a regular character on *Lonesome Dove: The Outlaw Years*, (Unbob, the simple-minded townsman). His genre credits include two episodes of *Ray Bradbury Theater*, an episode of *Outer Limits* ("If These Walls Could Talk"), and an episode of *Poltergeist: The Legacy*. With his gaunt scarecrowish looks he's been a fixture in horror movies such as *Watchers* (1988), *The Fly II* (1989), Stephen King's *It* (1990), and Stephen King's *Needful Things* (1993).

Paul Ben-Victor (Dr. Aaron Monte) appeared with fellow *X-Files* star Brad Dourif in the horror film *Body Parts* (1991). He's also appeared in a variety of B movies, including *Assault of the Killer Bimbos* (1987) and *Red Scorpion 2* (1994), as well as a few hit films, including *Tombstone* (1993). His professional name is spelled with—and without—a hyphen.

Henry Beckman starred in "Squeeze" and "Tooms."

HENRY BECKMAN

Born: November 26, 1921, Halifax, Nova Scotia

Perhaps no one in this book has quite as many acting credits as Henry Beckman, whose resumé contains nine Broadway plays, over one thousand television appearances, and hundreds of feature films. As a Canadian actor, he's proud to have won two Genie awards (the Canadian equivalent to the Oscar), though he notes that they make "great bookends." In 1977, he was awarded the Queen Elizabeth Silver Jubilee Medal for his contributions to Canadian culture.

Beckman enlisted in the Canadian Army on September 1, 1939, attaining the rank of acting sergeant before exiting the military after five and a half years and enrolling at the Academy of Dramatic Arts in New York. Beckman hit Hollywood in the post–World War II years, originally playing bit parts before becoming a well-known character actor. Name an actor or actress, and odds are that Beckman has appeared in a movie or television show with them, from Sean Connery to the Monkees.

Regular roles for Beckman have included Colonel Douglas Harrigan on *McHale's Navy* and George Anderson on *Peyton Place*, as well as parts in *I'm Dickens—He's Fenster* and *The Lieutenant*. Utilizing his knowledge of Hollywood, Beckman wrote the book "How to 'Sell' Your Film Project" (Pinnacle Books, 1979), a reference book that has become a standard at film schools and colleges. He's now working on finishing his second book, "Hollywood With Its Pants Down," a humorous remembrance of stars he's worked with or met.

Among Beckman's genre TV credits are guest shots on *My Favorite Martian, Tarzan, Rod Serling's Night Gallery, The Starlost, The Immortal, Ray Bradbury Theater, The Six Million Dollar Man, Poltergeist: The Legacy,* and both the original *Twilight Zone* and the eighties revival series. He also appeared in the "Mr. R.I.N.G." episode of *Kolchak: The Night Stalker*. Chris Carter has long admitted that the Kolchak series was his main inspiration for *The X-Files*.

Beckman got the *X-Files* job through his Vancouver agent. "I went up and did it and apparently they liked it so well that they called me back for another episode," Beckman says, before adding "which didn't make *me* mad at all. I thought it was a pretty good role. I outfoxed all the machines and found the damn corpse myself!"

Having worked on so many series and shows, did the veteran actor know the series was going to be a big hit? "Oh yeah, I kind of felt it in my bones. We had a party at my house and the producer of *Peyton Place* said to me, 'What do you think?' I said, 'I think it's going to be a tremendous hit.' I knew this *X-Files* was going to be okay, because people are into that sci-fi stuff. It's a lot bigger than I thought it was going to be, that's for darn sure! And then you have *Millennium* splintering off from that." Beckman still watches the show "when I'm at home. My family enjoys it. My wife likes it."

Besides his second book, Beckman is trying to produce a film with his son. *The Head, Guts and Soundbone Dance*, based on a play, has an ecological message. "I'm now rapidly becoming an environmental wacko," he says, only half-jokingly. "The average citizen doesn't understand what's happening to our oceans. They're being decimated right, left, and center." In the meantime, he's still in front of the cameras, where's he's been for almost fifty years; he recently shot a series of thirty-five Canadian commercials for Ford.

X22 Born Again

Case Number:	1.22/ #22 (#1X21)
First Sighting:	April 29, 1994
Directed by:	Jerrold Freedman
Written by:	Howard Gordon & Alex Gansa

GUEST CAST	CHARACTER
Brian Markinson	Tony Fiore
Mimi Lieber	Anita Fiore
Maggie Wheeler	Detective Sharon Lazard
Dey Young	Judy Bishop
Andrea Libman	Michelle Bishop
P. Lynn Johnson	Dr. Sheila Braun
Leslie Carlson	Dr. Spitz
Richard Sali	Felder
Dwight Koss	Detective Rudy Barbala
Peter Lapres	Harry Linhart

FIELD REPORT

Buffalo, New York. After a little girl found outside a police station is questioned, the detective who was questioning her launches himself out the window to his death. Another cop brings in Mulder and Scully on a referral, and they discover that the little girl is strange indeed. Based on their own questioning of the girl, Mulder surmises that she might be the reincarnation of Charles Morris, a policeman who was killed nine years ago, at about the time of her conception!

Little Michelle does indeed seem to have psychokinetic powers, and she mutilates her dolls in the same manner as the dead policemen: the right eye gouged out and the left arm missing. After another cop is killed with Michelle nearby, the truth begins to come out; three crooked cops were responsible for Morris's death, and two of them are now dead. Mulder and Scully find the final cop, Tony Fiore, being menaced by Michelle, but can they stop the spirit of Morris from killing his final victim?

WITNESS NOTES

"Tony Fiore" appears to be a popular name for crooked cops in Vancouver-based genre shows. It was also the name of a villainous detective in the *Forever Knight* episode "Dead Issue," broadcast on October 6, 1992. That Tony Fiore was played by actor Marc Strange.

Brian Markinson (Tony Fiore) has appeared in both *Star Trek: Voyager* and *Star Trek: The Next Generation*, as well as in Fox's telefilm *Alien Nation: Millennium* (1996), UPN's *The Sentinel*, and the film *Wolf* (1994). Recently, he appeared in the blockbuster hits *Apollo 13* (1995) and *Volcano* (1997). Markinson told *TV Zone* about the hijinks of this episode's finale. A fireplace poker was supposed to fly up and hit Brian in the head. "The poker itself was hard rubber, not steel. The prop guy squatted down out of frame . . . he was supposed to throw this poker and have it sort of glance off the back of my head." After several practice runs to get the stunt right, the cameras rolled. "To everyone's surprise, especially mine, the poker hit me straight on the temple. I saw stars. I have a feeling that's the take they used, too. I just went down and kind of crashed. It took a little while to get my wits about me."

Maggie Wheeler (Detective Sharon Lazard) a.k.a. Maggie Jakobsen, had her first regular gig as a sketch player on Lorne Michaels's short-lived 1984 NBC series *The New Show*. Jakobsen became a regular on *These Friends of Mine* (but was unceremoniously dumped when the show became *Ellen*), and has a recurring role on *Friends*. At one time, she dated David Duchovny, whom she starred with in the movie *New Year's Day* (1989), the film in which Duchovny did his much-ballyhooed nude scene. Wheeler recently told *Entertainment Weekly*: "We were boyfriend and girlfriend for quite a few years before that, so I'd already seen him naked."

Dey Young (Judy Bishop) was a regular on the short-lived ABC rescue series *Extreme*. She also appeared on "The Masterpiece Society" episode of *Star Trek: The Next Generation*.

Young **Andrea Libman** (Michelle Bishop) appeared in *Little Women* and *Andre* (both 1994), and in *The Odyssey*. She is the voice of Andraia on the computer-animated *Reboot* series.

Mimi Lieber starred in "Born Again."

WITNESS INTERVIEW
MIMI LIEBER

Born: March,1 Cleveland, Ohio

Raised in in Los Angeles, Mimi Lieber saw Hollywood around her constantly, so as an adult she moved to New York. "I lived the life of the late seventies downtown theater scene New York actor. You know, the black-leotard thing. I did real weird experimental theater. And then I ended up getting all these huge rock-and-roll movies as a dancer, which brought me back to L.A., and that eventually led into the nice career I've got now." Lieber was one of the principal dancers in *Grease* and *Sgt. Pepper's Lonely Hearts Club Band* before she started doing guest star shots on television and films.

So what are some of the TV credits? "Somehow I cornered the market on the 'Concerned-Undereducated-Cop's-Wife,'" Mimi laughs. "You know, it's a neighborhood. I've played every Connie, Theresa, and Maria on television. With a dialect of the five boroughs of Manhattan." Those roles includes guest shots on *Civil Wars*, *The Commish*, *Night Court*, *Beverly Hills 90210*, *Melrose Place*, *L.A. Law*, *Diagnosis Murder*, the failed coroner drama *Leaving L.A.*, multiple episodes of *Wiseguy*, and two episodes of *Seaquest DSV*. Mimi recurred on

Dreamworks' *High Incident* as a "loud, ballsy attorney," while at the same time recurring as Meshack Taylor's Cuban love-interest on *Dave's World.*" And then, of course, there is *Friends*, on which she was one of Matt Le Blanc's six Tribiani sisters.

Lieber's film credits include Ron Howard's directorial debut *Night Shift* (1982), *Protocol* (1984), the serial-killer-enters-into-a-computer flop *Ghost in the Machine* (1993), the pyrokinetic romantic comedy *Wilder Napalm* (1993) written by future *X-Files* script writer Vince Gilligan, and *Corrina, Corrina* (1994) with Steven Williams. In the future, she'll appear in Warren Beatty's next film, currently under the working title *Bulworth.*

Among the special skills listed on Lieber's resumé are motorcycle riding, skiing, and "killer scream." She was only able to exercise her screaming ability for a short time while working on *The X-Files*, however and only then after the episode had wrapped filming.

Mimi loved shooting *The X-Files*, but found it harder to deal with than some other series. What was difficult about the shoot? "Well, I'm sure most actors on that show would say there are elements that you have to sort of deal with as if they're 'normal.' This eight-year-old girl is my dead husband! 'Action!' You find out from your current husband, who is bound and gagged on the floor, that this child in my living room—in the middle of the night—is the *soul* of my ex-husband, and, by the way, I killed him! In maybe a thirty-second close-up of me, (I have to) receive that information, process it, and ask the child not to kill my current husband. An intense close-up on me and I have to register that I understand it and yet, I don't want this man to die!"

Working with young Andrea Libman, who played the possessed Michelle Bishop, added another oddity to the job. "Her performance was *incredibly* creepy," shudders Lieber. "And then, I'd walk past her trailer and she'd be sort-of doing hopscotch with her little sister or brother and her mom. And I remember it was like 'Oh my God! She's just a normal kid!' But I had just spent hours and hours with a child, who looks like a child, and has the silent self-possession of a very sad adult. That was wild! She was very sweet, she had a tiny little high voice . . . but the performance was so creepy that it was hard to accept that she was just a cute little kid when she *was* being one!"

Lieber remembers one other thing about the show (here's where the killer scream comes in). At the episode's end, Tony Fiore locks his wife, Anita (Lieber), in the upstairs bedroom, and it's obvious that there's trouble. "And then (the girl) comes in and starts to put him through hell! The director didn't want me making any noise, even though glass is breaking, and things made of iron are flinging into walls downstairs. Now I am *not* an argumentative guest star, but I did speak up on behalf of what I felt was the reality of the situation. 'How can I (be quiet)? I'd be terrified, for my own safety, if nothing else.' I felt Anita should be screaming and trying the door."

The director, however, wouldn't listen to Lieber. "He wanted me to be docile and obedient in a situation where human primal instinct would make you fight. Of course, in post-production, they realized that was the case, and I went in and had to loop all of that [screaming]. I went in to the looping stage and watched the entire scene of him being thrown about in the living room, and every time there was a loud crash, I had to figure out another, 'What's going on? Help me! I'm trapped!' Without that, it would have been bizarre!"

Overall, Lieber found the *X-Files* experience a positive one, and she is often recognized for her role there, as well as for her role on *Friends*. But *The X-Files* holds something stronger in her heart. "It was challenging as an actor, without any of the common obstacles to just doing good work. In a one-hour episodic show, sometimes things are very, very rushed. This was a show where we had to accomplish difficult emotional changes, and there was a script and an organization that supported that sort of strong work."

X23 Roland

Case Number: 1.23/ #23 (#1X22)
First Sighting: May 6, 1994
Directed by: David Nutter
Written by: Chris Ruppenthal

GUEST CAST	CHARACTER
Zeljko Ivanek	Roland Fuller/Dr. Arthur Grable
Micole Mercurio	Mrs. Stodie
Kerry Sandomirsky	Tracy
Garry Davey	Dr. Keats
James Sloyan	Dr. Frank Nollette
Matthew Walker	Dr. Ron Surnow
Dave Hurtubise	Dr. Larry Barrington
Sue Mathew	Agent Lisa Dole

FIELD REPORT

Colson, Washington. At a laboratory where an experimental jet engine is being developed, strange things are happening. A scientist, Dr. Surnow, is killed when he is sucked into the engine, and it appears that autistic janitor Roland Fuller is responsible. The first death on the project was its originator, Arthur Grable, who was killed in a car accident but whose head was kept in a cryogenic chamber. Mulder and Scully arrive to investigate, but find themselves running in circles.

Dr. Keats is next to be killed, when Roland dunks his head in liquid nitrogen and drops the corpse, shattering the head into hundreds of frozen fragments. Mulder and Scully find out that Roland is actually the twin brother of Arthur Grable, and Mulder surmises that Grable's cryogenically-preserved brain might be sending murderous thoughts to his autistic brother. The final surviving doctor, Frank Nolette, raises the temprature in Grable's chamber, then confronts Roland at the project site. Roland gets the better of him and locks Nolette in the wind tunnel of the jet engine. Will the doctor be torn apart at mach 15, or will Mulder and Scully arrive in time to save him?

WITNESS NOTES

Micole Mercurio (Mrs. Stodie) starred in the telefilm *Roe vs. Wade* (1989) with Jerry Hardin.

Kerry Sandomirsky (Tracy) made her feature film debut in *Midnight Matinee* (1988), a Canadian horror film that also starred William B. Davis and many other *X-Files* actors. She was a semi-regular on *Wiseguy*.

Garry Davey (Dr. Keats) recently had the role of Ranger Chet in "Paper Dove," the first season finale of Chris Carter's *Millennium*.

James Sloyan (Dr. Frank Nollette) has done

quite a bit of genre work, including the musical fantasy film *Xanadu* (1980), the 1987 telefilm *Bigfoot*, two episodes of *Buck Rogers in the Twenty-fifth Century*, *Misfits of Science*, *New Adventures of Wonder Woman*, *Quantum Leap*, *Strange Luck*, *Star Trek: The Next Generation* ("The Defector" and "Firstborn"), *Star Trek: Deep Space Nine* ("The Alternate"), and *Star Trek: Voyager* ("Jetrel").

Zeljko Ivanek played Roland Fuller in "Roland."

WITNESS PROFILE
ZELJKO IVANEK

Born: August 15, 1957, Ljubijana, Yugoslavia

Yugoslavian actor Zeljko Ivanek studied at Yale University and the London Academy of Music and Dramatic Art. He has recieved two Tony award nomination for his roles in Broadway plays. One of his first feature films found him as the lead character in *The Sender* (1982), which dealt with psychic transmissions of nightmares. He also appeared in such films as *Mass Appeal* (1984), *Courage Under Fire* (1996), *The Associate* (1996) with Jerry Hardin, and *Donnie Brasco* (1997). He has a recurring role as State's Attorney Ed Danvers on *Homicide: Life on the Streets*, and he recently had a startling turn as a paranoid militia man who takes doctors hostage in a convenience store in

an episode of *Chicago Hope*. Look for him coming up in the pilot for *Enemy*, a potential Fox series based on a Dark Horse Comics series.

For this episode of *The X-Files*, Ivanek apparently nailed the part of Roland Fuller on his first reading. The actor was the first to audition for the role, and while the producers tested the other ten actors who were there to read for the part, Ivanek was clearly the favorite. "It was short notice, and I didn't have time to do much research," Ivanek said in *Entertainment Weekly*, referring to Roland's autistic savant character. "But it came to me very easily. Once you feel it in your bones, it plays itself."

Chris Carter was clearly pleased with Ivanek's work. This year, he cast him in the "Walkabout" episode of *Millenium*. There, the intense actor played the role of the odd Dr. Daniel Miller, who may or may not be helping Frank Black get rid of his psychic abilities.

And if you're wondering how to pronounce his name (everyone does), it's ZHEL-ko Ee-VAH-nek.

X24 The Erlenmeyer Flask

Case Number:	1.24/ #24 (#1X23)
First Sighting:	May 13, 1994
Directed by:	R. W. Goodwin
Written by:	Chris Carter

GUEST CAST	CHARACTER
Lindsey Lee Ginter	Crew-Cut Man
Anne DeSalvo	Dr. Anne Carpenter
Simon Webb	Dr. William Secare
Jerry Hardin	Deep Throat
Jim Leard	Captain Roy Lacerio
Ken Kramer	Dr. Terrance Allen Berube
Phillip MacKenzie	Medic
William B. Davis	Cigarette-Smoking Man
Jaylene Hamilton	WDT *Newscan* Reporter
Mike Mitchell	First Uniformed Cop
John Payne	Fort Marlene Guard

FIELD REPORT

Georgetown, Maryland. A fugitive from the police, Dr. William Secare, leaves a trail of green blood as he escapes, and Deep Throat informs Mulder that he'll want to follow this up. Mulder and Scully trace the fugitive's car to Dr.

Berube, who claims no knowledge of the incident. Berube is later killed by a mysterious government man with a crew-cut. Mulder is contacted by Secare, and clues lead him to a warehouse where five full-grown, *living* humans are floating in tanks.

Meanwhile, Scully has analyzed a flask of liquid from Secare's lab that is labelled "Purity Control." She is shocked to find that it is a plant enzyme used in gene therapy, and that it contains neucleotides that are found nowhere in nature. Deep Throat later tells Mulder that the five humans were terminally ill patients who were given alien-human hybrid DNA in an experiment and that Secare is now the only survivor. When Mulder attempts to save Secare, he is taken captive by the crew-cut man. Deep Throat and Scully must work together to steal an alien fetus—the extraction donor for Purity Control—to trade for Mulder's life. But though Mulder is released, Deep Throat is shot and killed, and Scully loses the fetus. In the aftermath, the X-Files are closed down by the FBI.

Lindsey Lee Ginter starred in "The Erlenmeyer Flask" and "Red Museum."

WITNESS NOTES

Anne DeSalvo (Dr. Anne Carpenter) has had recurring roles on both *Taxi* and *Wiseguy* (as Gina Grosset), as well as roles in *Arthur* (1981), *D.C. Cab* (1983), *Burglar* (1987), and *Radioland Murders* (1994). She also directed her first feature film in 1997, *Women Without Implants*.

Simon Webb (Dr. William Secare) also played a doctor in two of his previous roles: the telefilm *Miles From Nowhere* (1992), and *Happy Gilmore* (1996).

WITNESS INTERVIEW

LINDSEY LEE GINTER

Born: December 13, 1950, Alameda, California

Can you imagine the man who killed Deep Throat working in a pizza parlor? That's what Lindsey Ginter did at one time. The imposing actor began acting in high school. He was later accepted into the American Conservatory Theater in San Francisco, but a broken foot scuttled his plans. The actor-to-be became a stockbroker instead, eventually moving to New York,

where he worked as a building supervisor, and later at Vinnie's Pizza.

Ginter got back into acting in the late seventies, mainly working in repertory theaters but eventually starring in the Broadway play *Fifth of July*, directed by John Landis. In 1990, Ginter got himself an agent, changed his look, "and started playing bad guys. That worked for me. That's when I started working steadily doing episodic television. [I also did] a lot of authority figures—military or policemen. You wouldn't really qualify them as bad guys, but they are fairly authoritative and tough. [On screen] I've been killed and knifed and stabbed and shot . . . all those things," he laughs. "I've died a thousand deaths."

Some of Ginter's movie roles have included Sergio Leone's *Once Upon a Time in America* (1984), *Beverly Hills Cop III* (1994) with future *X-Files* guest Timothy Carhart, and four semi-genre telefilms for Mahagony Pictures: *Mercenary*, *The Outsider*, *Mars*, and *True Blue*. He recently filmed a Universal science fiction film, *Time Master*, and this fall, Ginter will begin filming *Simple Simon*, with Bruce Willis and Alec Baldwin. Ginter's recent appearance on *NYPD Blue* as a rapist who cuts up his landlord into multiple pieces earned quite a bit of attention, especially when Dennis Franz's character, Andy Sipowitz, practically battered Ginter's character to death.

As for science fiction roles, Ginter appeared as a sheriff in Fox's 1995 miniseries remake of *The Invaders*, which guest-starred *X-Files* semi-regular Roy Thinnes. He was in the two-part "The Camp Counselor" episode of UPN's *Deadly Games*. He played a criminal trapped in a cave with Hercules in the "A Rock and a Hard Place" episode of the syndicated hit, *Hercules: The Legendary Adventures*. Ginter later starred as a Superman-hating general in an episode of *Lois & Clark: The New Adventures of Superman*, and also showed up in the season finale of *Dark Skies*.

Before he got his role as Crew-Cut Man, Ginter had auditioned for several other roles on *The X-Files*. "I think I had auditioned for them two or three times . . . and they didn't cast me. I was down doing *Walker: Texas Ranger* and they called up my agent and offered me the role that I did. Apparently I'd impressed them sufficiently enough with the earlier auditions that I didn't have to reaudition, so they gave me the part of Crew-Cut Man."

For series that use handguns and other firearms, special training for the actors is usual. However, Ginter didn't need any extra training. "I've shot everything from AK-47's to grenade launchers to 'street sweepers,' which is like a shot gun . . . single action, 50 caliber sniper rifles, MP5s [a German semi-automatic], Glocks . . . I mean I can go on and on. I've shot everything. You have to pay the proper respect to the tool, and make sure that you're shooting off center. You don't actually directly aim the thing at somebody. The way it looks [on film], you can't really tell. You want the actor that you're pointing the gun at to feel comfortable."

When Crew-Cut Man was brought back in the second season episode "Red Museum," the character was killed off at a slaughterhouse. "I had the script. I knew I was gonna be whacked at the end of the episode. That was kind of a bummer. [Laughs.] One always hopes that you could have a running role. I don't know how they would do that with me . . . [maybe] continually coming back and killing off all their informants [and doing their] 'wetwork.'"

Ginter found the experience of working in the slaughterhouse strange. "I've never been in a slaughterhouse. The sight of rows and rows— and racks—of beef, hearts, and lungs stuck on these meat hooks as far as you can see . . . it's a pretty strange sight." Did that turn the actor off to meat? "No, not at all. It made me hungry, actually!"

THE JERRY HARDIN FILE

Name: Jerry Wayne Hardin
Born: November 20, 1929, Dallas, Texas
Height: 6' 1"
Weight: 175 lbs.
Hair: Brown, with grey
Eyes: Blue

Jerry Hardin

Few characters on *The X-Files* have had more effect on the continuation of Agent Mulder's ongoing search for the truth than Deep Throat. The first in a short line of secretive informants, the fatherly Deep Throat gave information freely to the questioning Mulder, offering him leads and clues in his eternal search for the Truth, and giving him the knowledge that someone in the world besides him knew that "they" were already here. As viewers would later learn, Deep Throat had ties to Mulder's past; thus it is, in retrospect, no surprise that Deep Throat gave his life for the cause of Agent Mulder. Even his dying words, "Trust No One," have had a profound effect on agents Mulder and Scully in their work on the X-Files.

Deep Throat was played by veteran actor Jerry Hardin, who has been appearing on stage and screen since the 1950s. Born in Dallas, Texas, and raised on ranches in Mesquite and Beaumont, small towns outside the city of Dallas, Hardin was an only child who grew up riding horses and attending rodeos. Eventually his father remarried and he got a half-brother and two half-sisters, but most of his youth was solitary.

"I don't know that I always wanted to be an actor," Hardin said from his home in Los Angeles. "I was pretty much involved in the kinds of things that would lead you into the field. That is to say that in church or in school, I was always involved in plays or in public presentations of one kind or another, so essentially, I was drawn to that. I also was never afraid of making a fool of myself in public, which I suppose is a good start."

"In high school I belonged to all of the speech and drama organizations . . . though in my part of the world anyone who was seriously considering being a performer was very strange indeed," he laughs. "But I won a scholarship to go to college [Southwestern University in Georgetown, Texas] and that sort of gave me some encouragement. At college I was hired as the student technical assistant to the theater department and became an integral part of the theater department. I helped build a couple of theaters there and ended up teaching scenery building to senior students. We did a broad range of things. We had four major productions and five minor productions a year, and I was in all of them." Hardin earned his Bachelor of Fine Arts degree at Southwestern.

In his senior year of college, he won a prestigious Fullbright scholarship to study in Europe. "That pretty much sealed it." Hardin used the scholarship to attend the Royal Academy of Dramatic Art in London from 1951 to 1953. Hardin saved half of his scholarship for the first year so that he could stay on for a second, then won a second grant.

Hardin returned to the United States in 1953 and joined the Barter Theatre in Arlington, Virginia, which toured in the winter time and allowed him to play stock in the summer. Hardin eventually became an assistant producer and a director there. Repertory theater was a new experience for Hardin, though he spent about eleven or twelve years in regional repertory companies. "For my money, it was a poor way to make a living but it was a good way to be an actor because I was onstage virtually every night for eleven years, rehearsing in the day time and playing at night." The typical repertory schedule—nine months winter contract and three months summer contract—played hell with Hardin's personal life, but he still married and had children, all in the midst of moving from one theater to another.

Hardin's wife, Dianne Hill, is currently an acting teacher in Los Angeles and manages a studio called Young Actors Space. Kellie Martin (*Christie, Life Goes On*), Chad Allen (*Dr. Quinn, Medicine Woman, My Two Dads*), and Nicholle Tom (*The Nanny*) are a few of her more successful clients. Hardin and Hill have two children, both of whom are involved in show business. Son Shawn Hardin is vice president and executive director of New Media at NBC and is involved in the internet network that Microsoft and NBC have created. Daughter Melora Hardin has been a guest star on dozens of series, played the lead role in the *Dirty Dancing* television series and other short-lived series, and appeared in such films as *The Rocketeer* and *Soul Man*.

Hardin made his first inroads into film and television while still in the theater on the west coast. His first movie role was in the cult hit *Thunder Road* (1958), which he filmed in North Carolina with Robert Mitchum. "I got my SAG [Screen Actors Guild] card then. I was a young actor at the Barter Theatre in Virginia, and Bob Mitchum came looking for actors to work in this film he was going to shoot down in North Carolina. He hired me and I went down and had several weeks work." Later, when the movie came out, a friend told Hardin to go to a New York movie theater. "There is a scene where I am sprawled across the hood of a car talking to Bob Mitchum. They had done a cardboard cutout of me leaning across the hood of that car, and here was this six-foot cardboard cutout sitting in front of this theater. I thought, 'Damn! I've arrived! I've made it.' "

Hardin was only in one other film during that period, which he has forgotten the name of. He also appeared in some of television's last live theater shows in New York. "I actually did some of the last *live* long-form. We did *What Makes Sammy Run?* live, if you can believe it. I remember doing that in Brooklyn and everybody running like a bat out of hell from one set to another, with cables and cameras and people dressing while they are running . . . It was the very tail end of the live television performances. I remember that with great fondness . . . how crazed it was."

With a taste of Hollywood, Hardin moved to the Los Angeles area in 1972 or 1973, anticipating an easy move into a specific genre of Hollywood. As he explains, "I was brought up riding horses and dealing with animals, cattle, and what have you, on the ranch. I thought what they need in Hollywood is an actor who can act *and* ride a horse, and do it well. But when I arrived in Hollywood the western was a dead issue," he laughs. Hardin was able to make some breaks though, thanks to friends in the theater. "In some ways it was easier than it would have been had I come here absolutely cold turkey, because I had introductions to various agents. It was a slow beginning but eventually it built into something."

One western that was running at the time was *Gunsmoke*, but Hardin was working as an assistant producer and director at L.A.'s Barter Theatre. "I was doing a show every night, doing eight shows a week, when I was offered a small role on *Gunsmoke*. I could not take it because you have to be pretty far up the ladder before any movie company will guarantee that you will be off the set in time to go to a show." Hardin later did get a role on *Gunsmoke*, however, as well as other western roles in various miniseries. He thinks that his first TV role was probably an episode of *Ironside*.

Hardin eventually found extensive work as a character actor, appearing regularly in series of the seventies and eighties, often playing authority figures such as cops and judges. He particularly enjoyed working with James Garner on *The Rockford Files*, appearing in three episodes in the course of that series. Hardin also did a lot of work "looping other people's work. They would hire someone in Timbuktu that they didn't like very much and they would hire me to come in and do the vocal acting for this person's work."

In 1982, Hardin got his first regular series role, on a surprise hit sitcom called *Filthy Rich*. "It went to the top of the ratings!" The series (created by Linda Bloodworth) followed the adventures of the unscrupulous and snobby Becks, whose patriarch died, leaving a video-taped will behind. One of the stipulations of his will was that his illegitimate son, "Wild" Bill Westchester (Jerry Hardin), and his family would live in the family mansion, Toad Hall. The resulting storylines were a send-up of *Dallas* and *Dynasty*, with a little bit of *The Beverly Hillbillies* thrown in. Hardin's co-stars on the series were Forrest Tucker, Delta Burke, and Dixie Carter, among others.

Filthy Rich premiered again in the fall, but CBS kept moving it on the schedule. "It failed as a result of poor planning; they jumped in too quickly and didn't have enough lead time to do the work that everybody was capable of doing. Most of the people involved had theater backgrounds and were used to working in an ensemble situation and could have created a really good company."

Over the years, Hardin has had some involvement with science fiction. He did various voices in the original 1981 *Star Wars* radio dramas for National Public Radio. "I had never done a radio show before and it was a new experience for me. I enjoyed being involved and it was a new skill." He also appeared in series such as *Starman, Time Trax*, and *Star Trek: Voyager*, but his most famous role other than Deep Throat was that of Samuel "Mark Twain" Clemens in two episodes of *Star Trek: The Next Generation*.

Hardin had "always thought of Twain as an interesting character. So when the opportunity came to play him [in *Star Trek*], I went out with some determination to get it if I possibly could, and I did. While we were doing the first episode the line producer took me aside and said [I] should do Twain. Then Les Landau, who was directing the episode, eventually said the same thing to me, so that got my attention . . . I went back and read some of Twain's works, which I hadn't done since I was a child. I was fascinated by him. He was enormously contemporary, and he was funny. I felt a kinship to him because he had been a cowboy and a silver miner. So when I went back for the second episode, I said 'Well, you guys talked me into it. I'm going to do a show with Mark Twain's material.' Les Landau said 'Good. I'll direct it. When do we start?' "

What developed out of that was a one-man show, *Mark Twain: On Man and His World*. Clocking in at an hour and forty-five minutes, the show is quotes and monologues by Twain, arranged and connected by Hardin. "I do the full wardrobe and makeup and the whole deal, and to the best of my ability duplicate what Twain did in his later years in his platform performances all over the world . . . come on and talk about things that interested him. There is nobody on the stage but me. If I screw up, I'm in a lot of trouble."

Hardin's take on Twain is different than that of Hal Holbrook, another actor famed for his portrayal of Twain. "I am much more attracted to the fact that Mark Twain was a cowboy and a silver miner and a riverboat pilot and a printer. He became a journalist and a writer by accident, and his fascination with the stories of miners and characters about town is something that I identify with in a big way. The character that I see in Twain is very much attached to those kinds of roots and I think Hal has chosen to do much more the man who was the friend and raconteur with royalty and with the famous. We have a different take on the man."

Hardin most recently went to Europe to appear at a science fiction convention in Manchester, England, and to perform the *Mark Twain* show in Galway, Ireland. The *X-Files* connection helps draw in an audience overseas who may not be familiar with Twain, or with Hardin himself. "*X-Files* is very popular and it's a way of people recognizing who I am. Ordinarily they recognize my face (but) they don't know my name." Playing up *The X-Files* in press materials is "a way of identifying who is playing Mark Twain, and we found that it works very well."

Hardin is in negotiation to put on the *Twain* show onstage in Los Angeles, though no plans have been firmed up yet. Still, he is happy to be back in the theater. "The theater is my first love. If I could have made as good a living I probably would have stayed in the theater. I enjoy that the most. That's the drug of being an actor. When the curtain goes up it's your show. In film, it's everybody else's show. They can do everything to you in film, the camera can be somewhere else, you can be in shadow, they can even put somebody else's voice in there, they can change your timing. When the curtain goes up onstage it's your show. They may fire you when the show is over, but as long as the curtain is up, it's you and the audience and there is something quite exciting and fulfilling about that."

THE X-FILES

One of Hardin's film appearances was as a lawyer in the malevolent law firm in the film *The Firm*. Reportedly, Chris Carter had seen Hardin in the film and chose him for the role of Deep Throat. "That's a story that I read somewhere," Hardin says, adding that "Chris never told me that. I went in to read for him just like I would for anybody else, and he hired me. Whether he had any real background on me at that point in time I don't know."

The series was just getting started, so Hardin had no clear indication that his would be a recurring character. "As far as I was concerned it was a one-shot deal. I was just a guest star on the show. But it continued to happen, and it happened all the way through that first season!"

"The whole experience of playing Deep Throat was always a rather odd one," he says, "because it was generally a day or two of intense shooting, be on the set early in the morning and work till late at night, and then I was through. And I *only* worked with David. I never met Gillian until the episode in which they shot me. So I had been in seven episodes and David was the only one I knew. I really didn't know anybody else on it."

Hardin chuckles, bringing up the first meeting of Deep Throat and Mulder, in a restroom. "That whole experience was odd I suppose. Any time you start out a relationship with other actors in the john or in the toilet, you know it is an odd place to go." Still, Hardin is appreciative of his guest role. "David is a hard worker, he's focused, it was always pleasant to work with him. I did become aware later in the process that he was beginning to be enormously fatigued. He was telling me the whole experience of doing twenty-some-odd episodes in which you're hardly ever off camera is a killer. Everybody wants to do that kind of work because it's nice to have a regular check coming in, but the reality of it is that it takes its toll in terms of energy and focus and desire."

Hardin notes that the role was never completely conceptualized by himself, or the writers. "It was always a question of solving the immediate problems. Often times when you do a series, the director or writer will sit down and there is a kind of bible discussion about who this character is, what their background is, where they are going, how they are going to be treated by the writers. That was never true of Deep Throat. I never knew where it was going, or *if* it was going. Each episode was out of the blue; they would call my agent and say 'Is Jerry available?' And even sometimes when I wasn't available they would work around it so that I could be available. They would adjust to other jobs . . . for that I was enormously grateful.

"I just did that job and there was never a discussion about where the part was going. The only discussion that I ever heard was generally in the makeup trailer. David would speculate on what the real relationship was—who was Deep Throat? He thought Deep Throat ought to be his long lost father. I think another theory was that Deep Throat actually was an alien. But these were things we discussed in the makeup trailer before the day began just for the fun of it."

So what were Hardin's internal theories and motivations about the character? "I was always looking for ways to justify what I saw as essentially a writer's device. Deep Throat, in my opinion, was created initially as a way to move the plot forward in a rapid way. If you look back at the things that Deep Throat was given to do, in a two-minute or three-minute scene he had to dump an enormous amount of information into Mulder's head from which the rest of the episode would proceed. So it was an expositional tool. I saw my job as an effort to make that interesting and seemingly flow naturally from the needs of the character. Sometimes that was easy and sometimes that was a pain in the ass. The language used was always oblique, it was never direct. That's an unusual kind of writing, in television certainly, and was an interesting challenge from the actor's viewpoint."

When was Deep Throat a pain in the ass? "Because everybody [on the show] knew there were long speeches [for Deep Throat], there would be great pressure to do them at an enormous pace. My sense of it under those circumstances is that if you say it at a tremendous pace, the information doesn't necessarily communicate because it goes by so fast. Sometimes that was hard to do; you being the actor were placed in a position of trying to find a way to justify what was needed to move the story on at that point, but still have it come from a visceral place."

The name "Deep Throat" is most commonly associated either with the infamous porn movie or with the secret government informant that was involved in the Watergate scandals with *Washington Post* reporter Bob Woodward. Hardin didn't study up on that real-life character "because I didn't really think of him as being that guy or even *like* that guy. What eventually turned out to be given [as] facts about Deep Throat were much different than I imagine whoever Deep Throat was for [Woodward]." Hardin's Deep Throat "is a man who was a Green Beret, who worked for the CIA, and who obviously, at the point in time that the audience is introduced to him, is in a position of extraordinary access to information. Somehow or other you have to find some excuses for that. How does he have that kind of information and under what circumstances and how can he exercise it without being caught?"

Hardin continues, explaining the motivations he came up with for Deep Throat. He notes that people in government are sometimes "in positions where they feel like there are certain kinds of things that ought to be known, that really should be in the public domain, but for whatever influences exist at the time you can't just put it out there. You can't dump it because it has either political impact or it has emotional impact that has a down side associated with it. If you make the assumption that there are *indeed* aliens, and that this man knows about them, I think it is easy to make the leap of faith that he feels like everybody needs to be prepared for this and needs to have the information there. If he announces it then he ceases to have access to that information because the government will shut it off. Or whoever or whatever his source is becomes *no longer* a source. In order to protect his own sources and his own involvement, he needs an avenue . . . and I think Mulder is that avenue. That was my idea of why it was done the way that it was done. Whether or not that is what Chris [Carter] thought I don't know, because we never discussed it."

Despite the fact that he's come back to the series several times since his shocking death at the end of the first season, Hardin has not been asked to appear in *The X-Files* movie. Still, the actor appears at science fiction conventions all over the world, and is amazed by the response he gets from fans. "The whole *X-Files* phenomenon has been an interesting phenomenon for me. When you come right down to it I probably don't have more than four or five minutes of screen time [and yet] the fans still remember Deep Throat and they are still attached to him. They keep asking me over and over again if Deep Throat is going to come back." Hardin has found the fans in other countries more intense than his American fans. "I was in Australia and England and it's a much more intense following than *Star Trek* has had in some ways."

So with *The X-Files* tapping in to a streak of paranoia and mysteries, distrust of the government, and alien conspiracies, what does Hardin believe to be the Truth? "In a general sense I think all governments have secrets and I think that it is imperative that they do. It is the nature of functioning as a controlling body; it is also the nature of the human animal. Everybody has some things that are private to the ongoing process of living. Governments *have* secrets: I think sometimes they are *good* secrets and sometimes they are *bad* secrets."

But are they the kind of secrets that Deep Throat would be hiding? "As to the question of aliens, I don't have any belief in that, and I have serious doubts about other humanoid life forms other than our own. There may be other kinds of life, but it is probably amoebaelike. I am, in that sense, not a dyed-in-the-wool science fiction fan. It's a wonderful challenge as an actor to imagine those things and to function in that world, but I personally don't believe it and I don't give credence to all of the unidentified flying object crazes that hit everything from Roswell to the latest Arizona light in the sky."

X2 Deep Throat   X7 Ghost in the Machine   X10 Fallen Angel

An unidentified man approaches Mulder in a restroom in the episode "Deep Throat" and warns him off from a case he is investigating. Later, the man, Deep Throat, meets Mulder on a running track. Promising to feed information to Mulder when it's in his best interests to do so, Deep Throat answers Mulder's question "They're here, aren't they?" with an ominous "Mr. Mulder, they've been here for a long, long time."

Mulder questions Deep Throat in "Ghost in the Machine" about why the Department of Defense is running an investigation into his case, and is told that the computer genius is close to developing an adaptive learning computer. Later, after the genius has disappeared, Deep Throat tells Mulder that "They can do anything they want."

Mulder investigates a supposed alien crash site thanks to Deep Throat's tip in "Fallen Angel." Deep Throat later apparently saves Mulder's career when an FBI Office of Professional Responsibility Committee orders him fired. Section Chief McGrath confronts Deep Throat for countermanding the Committee's decision, and Deep

Throat warns him to keep his friends close, "but keep your enemies closer."

The scene that closes "Fallen Angel" implies that Deep Throat is someone high up in the FBI; high enough to directly and unquestionably countermand Mulder's dismissal. However, from here on, Deep Throat's actions are more careful, perhaps implying that he knows he may have overstepped his bounds.

X11 Eve   X16 Young at Heart   X17 E.B.E.

In "Eve," Deep Throat feeds Mulder information about the Litchfield eugenics experiments of the 1950s, which have resulted in the clone-like Eves. He also arranges to allow Mulder and Scully to see the incarcerated Eve 6 at an insane asylum.

Deep Throat tells Mulder about the government's interest in Dr. Barnett's experimentation of reversal of aging in "Young at Heart."

For the first time that he is aware of, Fox is misled by Deep Throat when the informant gives Mulder a faked photograph of a UFO in "E.B.E." Later, at a power plant, Mulder is captured by soldiers and is surprised to see Deep Throat there. Deep Throat lets Mulder see a chamber that used to house a live E.B.E. (Extraterrestrial Biological Entity) and tells him that he is one of the three people alive to have killed an alien. When he was with the CIA in Vietnam, he shot an alien that survived after the Marines shot its UFO down over Hanoi.

Deep Throat contacts Mulder via clicks on his phone in "Eve," but in "E.B.E.," Mulder shines a blue light out his window and awaits a phone call from Deep Throat. In that same episode, Mulder tells Scully about his informant and states that he'd never lie to Mulder only to have Deep Throat lie to him in the next scene! It's implied that Deep Throat is still with the CIA, though he has gone rogue by leaking secrets to Mulder to atone for the past in which he killed the alien.

In regards to the eugenics experimentation, Hardin said in *Starlog* that " 'Eve' was a rather scary one, and one which may or may not have been science fiction. I was particularly interested in the revelation of the experiment in which the government was involved." And about "Fallen Angel," he said, "That was the first episode in which it seems possible that Deep Throat is not on Mulder's side; that he might be misleading Mulder rather than directing him in an honest fashion."

X24 The Erlenmeyer Flask

Deep Throat shows his true colors in "The Erlenmeyer Flask." First, he tells Mulder to watch a newscast about a manhunt, later telling the agent that he's "never been closer." After Mulder tracks down the site of "purity control" experiments, Deep Throat confirms that the government has been experimenting with creating alien-human hybrids. Scully has her first meeting with the mysterious informant, who warns her that she'll need something to trade with the bad guys in exchange for a captured Mulder's life. But when it comes time to make the trade, Deep Throat insists on making it. He is shot and killed by the Crew-Cut Man, and as he dies, he tells Scully to "Trust No One."

In this episode, when Scully calls the informant "Deep Throat," it is the first time that he is ever referred to by that name on the series.

Hardin found the demise of Deep Throat as surprising as anyone. However, he could take solace in one thing: "When the script was sent to me, there was a little note on it from [Chris] Carter saying 'No one ever really dies in *The X-Files.*' I didn't have any feeling about being cut out of the series or any of those kinds of things, I just simply didn't know what was the upshot of all that was. I was interested in that particular [episode] because it was the longest period of time that I had worked on the show. Also it was the most complete kind of character development. There were little snippets of things before, but this had a strong through-line and therefore was more interesting to play."

After an exhausting night shoot for Deep Throat's death scene—during which the crew was fighting to finish before dawn—a wet and cold Hardin accompanied Chris Carter away from the set. "We went back down to the makeup trailer and the honey wagons, and they had a little champagne and a balloon or two to bid me farewell. That was nice; a breakfast of champagne after a night of shooting. Kind of an odd way to go."

X50 The Blessing Way   X73 Talitha Cumi   X80 Musings of a Cigarette-Smoking Man

As Fox Mulder hovers between life and death in "The Blessing Way," he sees visions of his father and Deep Throat, who convince him to keep pursuing the truth.

Deep Throat also makes a brief reappearance in "Talitha Cumi," when the shape-changing Jeremiah Smith briefly morphs into Deep Throat to unnerve Cigarette-Smoking Man.

It's Christmas Eve 1991 in "Musings of a Cigarette-Smoking Man," and Deep Throat calls CSM when an alien has been captured. Viewing it in a medical chamber, CSM asks "How many historic events have only the two of us witnessed together, Ronald? How often did we make or change history? And our names can never grace any pages of record. No monument will ever bear our image. And yet once again, the course of human history will be set by two unknown men standing in the shadows." Then, after losing a coin toss, Deep Throat enters the chamber and shoots the alien.

Even after his character's death on the series, Hardin was called back to appear again as Deep Throat, as Chris Carter had hinted. "My whole relationship to that show has always been momentary because there has never been a chat about where it goes from here. Actually the funny part of it was that I always thought 'Well, it's over,' but then the last time I worked was the morphing scene Chris directed. When it was over, he said 'Well thank you, it's been fun to work with you again. Now we have found a way to bring Deep Throat back!' "

Although Deep Throat is given a name, "Ronald," in "Musings of a Cigarette Smoking Man," the basic veracity of the story is called into question as canon due to the fact that the entire episode is Frohike's version of what he *thinks* he's uncovered about Cigarette-Smoking Man's past.

Other Deep Throat Appearances

Several X-Files episodes have made reference to the secretive past of Deep Throat. Among them are:

X51. In the old photo that Mulder and the Lone Gunmen examine in "Paper Clip," besides Bill Mulder and Victor Klemper, a young Cigarette-Smoking Man, a young Deep Throat, and a young Well-Manicured Man are obvious; the other three men's identities are not clear.

X65. Young Deep Throat makes his first appearance in "Apocrypha," in a scene in which he, young Bill Mulder, and young Cigarette-Smoking Man visit the bedside of a Navy man who's dying from radiation burns gained in a salvage operation in 1953. The Navy man thought he was salvaging a downed plane carrying a bomb, but it was really a UFO.

ACTOR CREDITS ───────────────────

JERRY HARDIN

AMERICAN TELEVISION

Alfred Hitchcock Presents (NBC) #5—"Final Escape," aired October 27, 1985 (first season). Role: Warden.

Ally McBeal (Fox) #4—"The Affair," aired September 29, 1997 (first season). Role: A priest presiding at a very awkward funeral.

Amazing Grace (NBC), Hardin appeared in one episode. No information available.

Baretta (ABC)— "The Appointment," aired March 9, 1978 (third season). Role: unknown.

Dallas (CBS) #67—"The Making of a President," aired January 30, 1981 (fourth season). Role: unknown. #245—"Ten Percent Solution," aired March 13, 1987 (tenth season). Role: Judge Loeb.

Dark Justice (CBS) Hardin appeared in one episode. No information available.

Dr. Quinn, Medicine Woman (CBS) Hardin plays the recurring role of Dr. Cassidy, a critical and rude Denver doctor who is often at odds with Dr. Quinn. #18—"The Race," aired September 25, 1993 (second season premiere). #81—"Dead or Alive, Part I," aired February 3, 1996 (fourth season) #82—"Dead or Alive , Part II," aired February 10, 1996 (fourth season). #96—"Malpractice," aired October 5, 1996 (fifth season).

Evening Shade (CBS) Jerry Hardin played the recurring role of Billy. #40—"Going to the Chapel, Part II," aired February 24, 1992 (second season). #41—"Going to the Chapel, Part III," aired March 2, 1992 (second season).

Family (ABC) Hardin appeared in one episode. No information available.

Family Classics (CBS) Broadcast live from a theater in New York. Role: unknown. "The Three Musketeers, Parts I & II," aired December 2, 1960 and December 7, 1960.

Family Ties (NBC) "Fool For Love," aired January 23, 1986 (fourth season). Role: Mr. Bidney.

Father Murphy (NBC) "The First Miracle, Part I," aired April 4, 1982 (second season). Role: Ray Walker.

The Feather and Father Gang (ABC) #1—"Feather and Father" (a.k.a. "Two Star Killer"), aired December 6, 1976 (first season series premiere). Role: unknown.

Filthy Rich (CBS) Hardin played series regular Wild Bill Westchester, a working-class man whose family must share a mega-million inheritance and mansion with the snooty rich Beck family. The series premiered August 9, 1982, and ran through June 15, 1983, with fifteen episodes total.

Golden Girls (NBC) #20—"Adult Education," aired February 22, 1986 (first season). Role: Professor Cooper, an evening course teacher who makes a pass at his student, Blanche.

Gunsmoke—(CBS) "The Foundling," aired February 11, 1974 (nineteenth season). Role: Bob Ranger.

Harry-O (ABC) #13—"Accounts Balanced," aired November 21, 1974 (first season). Role: Doorman. #40—"Forbidden City," aired February 26, 1976 (second season). Role: George Dillard.

Highway to Heaven (NBC) #4—"Song of the Wild West," aired October 17, 1984 (first season). Role: unknown.

I'll Fly Away (NBC) #5—"All God's Children," aired October 21, 1991 (first season). Role: unknown.

The Incredible Hulk (CBS) #79—"Sanctuary," aired November 6, 1981 (fifth season). Role: Sheriff.

Ironside (NBC) Hardin appeared in one episode. No information available. This was his first role in Hollywood, and appears to be uncredited.

Jag (CBS) #30—"Full Engagement," aired February 21, 1997 (second season). Role: Mechanic.

Knot's Landing (CBS) #12—"Bottom of the Bottle, Part I," aired March 20, 1980 (first season). Role: Bartender. #316—"The Torrents of Winter," aired January 9, 1992 (thirteenth season). Role: Billy Reed.

L.A. Law (NBC) Hardin played District Attorney Malcolm Gold, a recurring role. #1—"L.A. Law," aired September 15, 1986 (first season premiere). #11—"El Sid," aired December 11, 1986 (first season) #56—"Leave it to Geezer," aired March 30, 1989 (third season). #83—"The Last Gasp," aired May 17, 1990 (fourth season). #101—"As God Is My Codefendant," aired April 4, 1991 (fifth season). #121—"From Here to Paternity," aired March 26, 1992 (sixth season).

Little House on the Prairie (NBC) Hardin appeared in one episode. No information available.

Lois & Clark: The New Adventures of Superman (ABC) #8—"The Green Green Glow of Home," aired November 14, 1993 (first season). Role: Wayne Irig, the man who first finds Kryptonite.

Mad About You (NBC) #13—"Togetherness," aired January 13, 1993 (first season). Role: Al, Jamie's grumpy client.

Matlock (NBC) #101—"The Broker," aired December 4, 1990 (fifth season). Role: Avery

"A. C." Campbell, a man accused of murdering his partner, then appears to commit suicide.

Melrose Place (FOX)   Hardin played the recurring role of Dennis Carter, the vengeful baby-snatching father of the late Reed Carter in the third season episodes. #66—"In-Laws and Outlaws," aired September 26, 1994. #67—"Grand Delusions," aired October 3, 1994. #73—"And Justice for None," aired November 14, 1994. #80—"They Shoot Mothers, Don't They?," aired January 16, 1995.

Miami Vice (NBC)   #30—"Bushido," aired November 22,1985 (second season). Role: unknown.

Midnight Caller (NBC)   Hardin plays the recurring role of Travis Quarry. #59—"City of Lost Souls, Part I," aired May 7, 1991 (third season) #60—"City of Lost Souls, Parts II and III," aired May 10, 1991 (third season, two-hour series finale).

Murder, She Wrote (CBS)   #210—"Northern Explosion," aired January 2, 1994 (tenth season). Role: Hamish McPherson. #221—"A Nest of Vipers," aired September 25, 1994 (eleventh season premiere). Role: Norman Gilford. Hardin appeared in two more episodes, but no information on these appearances is available.

Murphy Brown (CBS)   #189—"All in the Family," aired January 8, 1996 (eighth season). Role: Colonel Sherwood, the father of Corky Sherwood.

Mystery Science Theatre 3000 (Comedy Central)—"Mitchell," aired 1988 (fifth season). Role: a police desk sergeant. This episode contained the edited version of the 1975 feature film, *Mitchell* (see film section for further information).

Orleans (CBS)   Role: recurring character of Gillenwater, a crazy lawyer vying for the attention of Gloria. Hardin appeared in four or five episodes, but credits can only be found for the following two. #1—"Pilot," aired January 8, 1997 (first season, two-hour series premiere). #4—"Hijack," aired January 29, 1997 (first season).

Paradise (CBS)   #34—"The Gates of Paradise," aired January 6, 1990 (second season). Role: Uncle Peter.

Picket Fences (CBS)   #5—"Frank the Potato Man," aired October 23, 1992 (first season). Role: Dave Piper, a dairy farmer who owns a cow whose udder explodes and a five-legged goat.

Quantum Leap (NBC)   #69—"Roberto! January 27, 1982," aired March 11, 1992 (fourth season). Role: Saxton.

Remington Steele (NBC)   #51—"A Pocketful of Steele," aired November 20, 1984 (third season). Role: Lowell McKenzie, a bank vice president. (Steven Williams also appeared in this episode.)

The Rockford Files (NBC)   #50—"Coulter City Wildcat," aired November 12, 1976 (third season). Role: Walter Link. #75—"The Mayor's Committee From Deer Lick Falls," aired November 25, 1977 (fourth season). Role: Knute Jacobs. #118—"Deadlock in Parma," aired January 10, 1980 (sixth season, series finale). Role: the corrupt Mayor Sindell.

Sara (CBS)   Hardin played the recurring role of Frank Dixon. #1—"Title Unknown," aired February 13, 1976 (first season premiere) #2—"Title Unknown," aired February 20, 1976 (first season).

Starman (ABC)   #22—"The Test," aired May 2, 1987 (first season finale). Role: Gus.

Star Trek: The Next Generation (Syndicated)   #16—"When the Bough Breaks," aired February 13, 1988 (first season). Role: Radue, leader of the sterile child-stealers of Aldea. #125—"Time's Arrow, Part I," aired June 20, 1992 (fifth season finale). Role: Samuel "Mark Twain" Clemens. #126—"Time's Arrow, Part II," aired September 26, 1992 (sixth season premiere). Role: Samuel "Mark Twain" Clemens.

Star Trek: Voyager (UPN)   #8—"Emanations," aired March 13, 1995 (first season). Role: Dr. Neria, a thanatologist (a doctor who specializes in the study of death).

Sunday Showcase (NBC)   Broadcast live from a theater in New York. Role: unknown.

"What Makes Sammy Run? Parts I & II," aired September 27, 1959, and October 4, 1959.

Time Trax (Syndicated)   #3—"To Kill a Billionaire," aired February 1, 1993 (first season). Role: Presiding Appellate Judge Benedict Choate, a fugitive from the future.

The Twilight Zone (Series Two) (CBS)   #20—"Profile in Silver," aired March 7, 1986 (first season). Role: Lyndon B. Johnson.

Who's the Boss (ABC)   Jerry Hardin played the recurring role of Dr. Graham in three or four episodes in a row. It is assumed that the first two are "Savor the Veal, Parts I and II", aired August 22–23, 1992, but that is unconfirmed. #196—"Savor the Veal, Part III," aired August 24, 1992 (ninth season).

WKRP in Cincinatti (CBS)   #13—"Fish Story," aired sometime between December 1978 and February 1979 (first season). Role: Officer Plyler.

Young Maverick (CBS)   #8—"Half Past Noon," aired January 30, 1980 (first season finale). Role: Purnell Sims.

TELEVISION MOVIES

From Earth to the Moon (HBO),   aired Late 1997. Role: unknown.

The Second Civil War (HBO),   aired March 15, 1997. Role: Colonel McNally.

Pandora's Clock (NBC),   aired November 10–11, 1996. Role: Priest aboard a doomed flight.

Soul of the Game (HBO),   aired April 20, 1996. Role: Baseball commissioner Happy Chandler.

Secrets of the Bermuda Triangle (ABC),   aired April 4, 1996. (pilot telefilm). Role: Slick.

A Streetcar Named Desire (CBS),   aired October 29, 1995. Role: Doctor who takes Blanche DuBois away. (Note that the credits misspell his name as "Harden.")

Where Are My Children? (network unknown),   aired 1994. Role: T.K. Macready.

Murder of Innocence (CBS),   aired November 30, 1993. Role: Mort Webber.

Plymouth (ABC),   aired May 26, 1991. (pilot telefilm). Role: Lowell, one of the townspeople in an Oregon community that relocates to a mining base on the moon.

Hi Honey—I'm Dead (FOX),   aired April 22, 1991. Role: Cal.

Once More, With Feeling (network unknown),   aired late eighties/early nineties. Role: unknown.

Quiet Friendly Little Town (network unknown),   aired late eighties/early nineties. Role: unknown.

Uncommon Knowledge (network unknown),   aired late eighties/early nineties. Role: unknown.

Please Stand By (network unknown),   aired late eighties/early nineties. Role: unknown.

Hometown Boy Makes Good (HBO),   aired 1989. Role: Desmond City Mayor Bob Chestnutt, who is having an affair with the lead character's mother.

Roe vs. Wade (NBC),   aired May 15, 1989. Role: Honorable Judge Goldberg at the U.S. District Court in Dallas, Texas.

Roots: The Gift (ABC),   aired December 11, 1988. Role: Dr. Reynolds.

The Town Bully (ABC),   aired April 24, 1988. Role: Mayor Artie Lyons.

Bluegrass (CBS),   aired February 28–29, 1988. Role: Brock Walters (in part two of the miniseries).

LBJ: The Early Years (NBC),   aired February 1, 1987. Role: unknown.

Do You Remember Love (CBS),   aired May 21, 1985. Role: Dave McDonough.

Attack on Fear (CBS).   Also known as *The Light on Synanon*. Aired October 10, 1984. Role: Sheriff Bergus.

Wilderness Women (network unknown),   aired mid-eighties. Role: unknown.

Celebrity (NBC),   aired February 12–14, 1984. Role: Jonah Job.

Mysterious Two (NBC), aired May 31, 1982. Role: unknown. This telefilm has eerie connections to the recent Heaven's Gate catastrophe. The story concerns two aliens visiting Earth in an effort to enlist converts to travel the universe with them.

Thou Shalt Not Kill (NBC), aired April 12, 1982. Role: unknown.

World War III (NBC), aired January 31, to February 1, 1982. Role: General Philip Olafson.

In Love With an Older Woman (CBS), aired 1982. Role: unknown.

The Children Nobody Wanted (CBS), aired December 5, 1981. Role: Dr.Watson.

Angel Dusted (NBC), aired February 16, 1981. Role: unknown.

Gideon's Trumpet (CBS), aired April 30, 1980. Role: Sheriff Mel Cobb.

Friendly Fire (ABC), aired April 22, 1979. Role: unknown.

The Chisolms (CBS), aired March 29, 1979, to April 19, 1979. Role: pioneer Jonah Comyns in parts two and three of this four-part miniseries.

Roots II (ABC), aired February 1979. Role: unknown.

Kate Bliss and the Ticker Tape Kid (ABC), aired May 26, 1978. Role: Bud Dozier, a party guest.

Alambrista! (PBS), aired October 16, 1977. Role: Man in a café.

Washington Behind Closed Doors (ABC), aired September 6–11, 1977. Role: unknown.

The 3,000 Mile Chase (NBC), aired June 16, 1977. Role: Manager.

The Gardener's Son (PBS), aired January 6, 1977. Role: Patrick McEvoy, the father of a poor, troubled boy in the 1870s (played by Brad Dourif).

Oregon Trail (NBC), aired January 10, 1976. Role: Macklin.

Guilty or Innocent: The Sam Sheppard Murder Case (NBC), aired November 17, 1975. Role: Chief Ed Kern.

Hurricane (ABC), aired September 10, 1974. Role: Neill.

Miracle on 34th Street. Hardin appeared in one of the three versions cited below, but no confirmation can be found as to which one. CBS—aired December 14, 1955. NBC—aired November 27, 1959. CBS—aired December 14, 1973.

Delaney (network unknown), no information available.

FEATURE FILMS

The Ghosts of Mississippi. Released December 20, 1996. Role: unknown.

The Associate. Released October 1996. Role: Harley Mason.

The Firm. Released June 1993. Role: Royce McKnight, a managing partner in a sinister law firm. This role reportedly inspired Chris Carter to cast Hardin as Deep Throat.

Pacific Heights. Released September 1990. Role: Bennett Fidlow.

The Hot Spot. Released September 1990. Role: George Harshaw.

Blaze. Released December 1989. Role: Thibodeaux.

War Party. Released 1989. Role: Sheriff.

The Milagro Beanfield War. Released March 1988. Role: Emerson Capps.

Little Nikita. Released March 1988. Role: Chief Jim Brewer, assigned to the San Diego office of the FBI, who sends an agent out on a covert assignment on his own. Perhaps this is where Deep Throat got his start?

Valentino Returns. Released 1987. Role: Ray Horner, a holy-roller preacher in a carnival tent.

Wanted: Dead or Alive. Released January 1987. Role: John Lipton.

Big Trouble in Little China. Released June 1986. Role: Pinstripe lawyer in the film's opening who has proof of the paranormal demonstrated to him by a Chinese man.

Let's Get Harry. Released 1986. Role: Dean Reilly, a government worker who leaks information to a rescue squad en route to Colombia.

Warning Sign. Released August 1985. Original title was *Biohazard.* Role: Vic Flint.

The Falcon and the Snowman. Released 1984. Role: Tony Owens.

Mass Appeal. Released November 1984. Role: Mr. Dolson.

Heartbreakers. Released September 1984. Role: Warren Williams.

Cujo. Released August 1983. Role: Masen.

Honkytonk Man. Released December 1982 . Role: Sheriff Snuffy, a Southern sheriff with a hilarious accent and an Errol Flynn moustache.

Tempest. Released August 1982. Role: Harry Gondorf.

Missing. Released January 1982. Role: Colonel Sean Patrick.

Heartland. Released 1981. Role: Cattle Buyer.

Reds. Released November 1981. Role: Harry

Honky Tonk Freeway. Released August 1981. Role: Florida's governor.

1941. Released December 1979. Role: Map man.

Head Over Heels. Released October 1979. Also released as *Chilly Scenes of Winter.* Role: Bill Patterson, the boss of the lead character.

Wolf Lake. Released 1978. Also released as *The Honor Guard.* Role: Wilbur.

Mitchell. Released 1975. Role: Police Desk Sergeant. This film was later done as a *Mystery Science Theater 3000* episode (see TV section).

Our Time. Released March 1974. Also known as *Death of Her Innocence.* Role: unknown.

Sleeper. Released December 1973. Role: Doctor who opens Woody Allen's pod.

Born of Water. Released circa 1973. Role: Pastor James Clayton Hewlitt in this independent religious film.

Run Mickey Run. No information available.

Thunder Road. Released April 1958. Role: Niles Penland, a kid who drove a whiskey delivery car. Hardin's first on-camera acting job.

THEATER

Mark Twain: On Man and His World. Hardin plays Samuel "Mark Twain" Clemens in this one-man show, which has been performed in several theaters and countries, as follows: Paramount Center for the Arts, Bristol, Tennessee (March 1994); Barter Theatre, Kingsport (March 1994); Eastman Employee Center, Kingsport (March 1994); Virginia; Starfest Safari, South Florida (April 1996); Chaplaincy Centre, Edinburgh (August 1996); Australia; Galway, Ireland (August 1997).

Moon for the Misbegotten. Front Street Theatre, Memphis, Tennessee. Role: Hogan.

Who's Afraid of Virginia Woolf? Front Street Theatre, Memphis, Tennessee. Role: George.

Imaginary Invalid. Front Street Theatre, Memphis, Tennessee. Role: Argon.

Romeo and Juliet. Arena Stage, Washington, D.C. Role: Mercutio.

The Physicists. Pennsylvania State University. Role: Beutler.

Blood Wedding. Pennsylvania State University. Role: Leonardo.

Right You Are, If You Think You Are. The Alley Theatre, Houston, Texas. Role: Penza.

The Tenth Man. The Alley Theatre, Houston, Texas. Role: Zitorsky.

The Price. Stage West, Springfield, Massachusetts. Role: Walter.

The Lovers. Stage West, Springfield, Massachusetts. Role: Andy.

Thousand Clowns. Stage West, Springfield, Massachusetts. Role: Murray.

After the Fall. Manitoba Theatre. Role: Quentin.

Mandragolo. Manitoba Theatre. Role: The Priest.

OTHER CREDITS

The X-Files: The Truth and the Light (Warner Brothers). Running time: 48:36. Soundtrack available on CD and tape. Composer Mark Snow's themes from various episodes of

The X-Files are woven together, with interspersed dialogue from several of the series actors. Hardin has several dialogue snippets.

Star Wars: Radio Drama (National Public Radio). Aired 1981. This thirteen-part radio drama expanded on the blockbuster *Star Wars* film, with many scenes not included in the original film. Hardin performed many voices for the series. The series is available on CD and tape from Highbridge Audio.

SEASON TWO

X25 Little Green Men

Case Number: 2.01/ #25 (#2X01)
First Sighting: September 16, 1994
Directed by: David Nutter
Written by: Glen Morgan & James Wong

GUEST CAST	CHARACTER
Mitch Pileggi	Assistant Director Walter S. Skinner
Mike Gomez	Jorge Concepcion
Raymond J. Barry	Senator Richard Matheson
William B. Davis	Cigarette-Smoking Man
Les Carlson	Dr. Troisky
Marcus Turner	Young Fox Mulder (Age 12)
Vennessa Morley	Young Samantha Mulder (Age 8)
Fulvio Cecere	Aide to Senator Matheson
Deryl Hayes	Agent Morris
Dwight McFee	Blue Beret Commander
Lisa Ann Beley	FBI Cadet/Student
Gary Hetherington	Lewin/Mulder's Apartment Stakeout Man
Bob Wilde	Rand

FIELD REPORT

Arecibo, Puerto Rico. Mulder is dispatched to a site in Puerto Rico by his ally, Senator Matheson. His purpose is to make contact before a Blue Beret UFO retrieval team can destroy all evidence. Scully hacks his files and goes to look for Mulder, who has found a Mexican man that seems to have seen aliens. Running into the jungle, the man is frightened to death, and Mulder returns to the Arecibo station, where he himself is visited by aliens.

Scully finds Mulder unconscious at the station, and the two of them barely manage to escape with the papers and reel-to-reel recordings which Mulder says will be proof of the visitation. Back at FBI headquarters, Mulder gets royally chewed out by A.D. Skinner, while a smirking Cigarette-Smoking Man watches. The only tape reel Mulder managed to escape with is empty; his proof has vanished.

WITNESS NOTES

Senator Richard Matheson is named for famed science fiction and horror author Richard Matheson. Some of his most famous works are the vampire novel *I Am Legend* and *The Shrinking Man*, filmed as *The Incredible Shrinking Man* from Matheson's adaptation. In Hollywood, Matheson was highly sought after; he wrote fourteen episodes of *The Twilight Zone*, several scripts for *Star Trek* and *Rod Serling's Night Gallery* as well as a number of Roger Corman horror films of the 1960s. Matheson also scripted both *Kolchak* pilot films, *The Night Stalker* (1972) and *The Night Strangler* (1973), and more recently, the enduring time-travel love story, *Somewhere in Time* (1980), based on his novel.

The producers originally wanted Darrin McGavin to play the role of Senator Matheson, giving a nod to the man who had played the lead in *Kolchak, The Night Stalker*, Chris Carter's inspiration for *The X-Files*. However, McGavin wasn't available. In *X-Files Confidential* writer James Wong notes "I'm not sure what happened. Our casting director called before we started second season and spoke to McGavin's agent and said, 'We want him for the first show; lock him up, and we're willing to pay the price.' By the time it came down to getting him, suddenly the agent said. 'He doesn't know about the show' or 'He's not available.' "

In the flashback sequences (set on November 27, 1973), young Fox Mulder wants to watch *The Magician* on television shortly before Samantha's abduction. *The Magician* was a one-season NBC series which starred Bill

Bixby as Anthony Blake, an illusionist and escape artist who used his talents to help people in danger and fight crime. The November 27th episode was "Lady in a Trap," and in it, Blake uses his powers to help locate a rare book which has been stolen from a museum.

Mike Gomez (Jorge Concepcion) had previously appeared in "La Bizca," a *21 Jump Street* episode directed by David Nutter. His other *X-Files* connection was his appearance in *The Milagro Beanfield War* (1988), which starred Jerry Hardin. Other credits for Gomez include two episodes of *Star Trek: The Next Generation*: "The Last Outpost" and "Rascals."

Les Carlson (Dr. Troisky) appeared in two David Cronenberg films, *The Dead Zone* (1983) with future *X-Files* star William B. Davis, and the violence-on-video creep-out *Videodrome* (1983).

Marcus Turner, making his first appearance in this episode as the young Fox Mulder, may have *also* been making his screen debut with this role. No credits prior to 1994 can be found for the young actor, though after this he appeared in the telefilms *Falling From the Sky: Flight 174* (1995) and *Prisoner of Zenda, Inc.* (1996). He also had a role in the film *Ronnie & Julie* (1996).

Raymond J. Barry appeared in "Little Green Men" and "Nisei."

WITNESS INTERVIEW
RAYMOND J. BARRY
Born: March 14, 1939, Hempstead, New York

Coming from a theatrical background, Raymond J. Barry first showed up on the Hollywood scene in the mid-seventies, appearing in a variety of movies before landing his only regular television role on the short-lived 1987 CBS series *The Oldest Rookie*. There, as Lieutenant Marco Zaga, he was in charge of Detective Gordon Lane, who was played by future *X-Files* guest-star Marshall Bell. Some of Barry's roles in later years have included playing Tom Cruise's father in *Born on the Fourth of July* (1989), and the father of the murdered boy in the critically acclaimed *Dead Man Walking* (1995). Late in 1997, Barry will appear in *Flubber*, starring Robin Williams, a Disney remake of *The Absent-Minded Professor* (1961). In addition to his ongoing film and stage work, Barry's newest enterprise is his first book, *Mother/Son and Other Plays*, an anthology of five of his plays published by Chicago Plays.

Hardcore *X-Files* fans will be most interested to know that Barry co-starred in a 1992 movie called *The Turning*, which happened to feature a very young Gillian Anderson in her first professional role. "She had maybe two or three scenes, and she was just beginning her career," says Barry. "I think she was very good in that film." When told that the film was *finally* being released to capitalize on Anderson's fame, Barry was amused. "That's probably true, because the film stinks. It's just badly directed, and the editing . . . it was written in such a way that all the locations are in the same room for the first fifty percent of the film. The eye gets absolutely no variation, whatsoever. And it just doesn't work. It finally comes a little bit to life in the second half, but it's not a very good film."

On *The X-Files*, Barry was cast as Senator Matheson, a man who is not only on the Intelligence Committee, but who is also the only confidant who watches out for Agent Mulder in Congress. How did Barry get cast in that role? "They called my agent and asked me if I wanted to do it, and at the time I could use the money, so I did it. [Laughs] I try to stay away from television. I find the medium to be, I don't know, a step below film, and I try to stay clear of it if I can. If I'm broke I'll do it. At the time I was broke." [Laughs]

The following season, the producers wanted Barry back for "Nisei." "I got another call about a year later, to do the same character, and there was a negotiation snare. They have a very set fee they pay to people to be invited guests, and it's low. I wanted twice what they offered and they bandied back and forth. It didn't matter to me one way or the other if I was going to do it by that time because I wasn't broke. So, finally they came up with the money but it was only after probably a week of telephone tag between my agent and the producers. I didn't know what all the fuss was all about. We're not talking about much bread and obviously they're making a fortune.

"At one juncture I received a message, 'Would you do it for the usual fee just as a favor to me?' I didn't know these guys. If a producer walked in front of my face I'd never recognize him or know his name. And they actually had the audacity to ask me to do them a *favor*. God, I hate to tell you how many years I spent making like ten cents an hour, and these guys are asking me to do them a favor and work for scale. [Laughs] While they are making *millions*. God knows how much money these producers make on a series as successful as that. But I guess if they break policy for one actor they feel like they've compromised themselves, or something. I don't know what goes on in people's minds with regard to that, but it's all about money.

"Actually, you know, the real truth of the matter is, I love saying no. I've spent so many years going through what I've just described to you—the struggle of being an actor—that it gives me great pleasure to say, 'No, thanks. Thanks, but no thanks.'"

Despite the negotiation hassles, Barry didn't have any problems once he arrived on set. "I didn't have a negative time [on *The X-Files*]. My agents were dealing with all that. When I finally showed up and did it . . . it was pleasurable. I prepared, I knew my words. Everybody is very cool in terms of just 'let's get this thing done.' I'll tell you something. What complaint could anyone have? You walk out there, they've got all the food on the table, you got your chair with your name on it. How could

you possibly complain? God forbid I would have to do an honest day's work. You know what I mean?"

X26 The Host

Case Number:	2.02/ #26 (#2X02)
First Sighting:	September 23, 1994
Directed by:	Daniel Sackheim
Written by:	Chris Carter

GUEST CAST	CHARACTER
Mitch Pileggi	Assistant Director Walter S. Skinner
Darin Morgan	Flukeman
Matthew Bennett	First Workman (Craig)
Freddy Andreiuci	Detective Norman
Don MacKay	Charlie
Marc Bauer	Agent Brisentine
Gabrielle Rose	Dr. Zenzols
Ron Sauve	Foreman (Ray)
Dmitri Boudrine	Russian Engineer
Raoul Ganee	Dmitri
William MacDonald	Federal Marshal

UNCREDITED
| Steven Williams | Mr. X/Telephone Caller |

FIELD REPORT

Newark, New Jersey. A Russian freighter has brought something to New Jersey with it. It lives in the sewage, is incredibly strong, and likes to lunch on humans. Mulder investigates a half-eaten sailor who washes up on the shore, but considers the assignment busy work. However, when Mulder consults with Scully, she finds a large fluke wriggling around in the sailor's liver. A sewer worker is later attacked, and after he's questioned by Mulder, he coughs up another fluke.

At a sewage processing plant, the workers backflush the system, trapping a human-like white creature with a sucker-like mouth. Mulder and Scully work together to examine the creature, much to A.D. Skinner's annoyance, but when the government tries to take the creature in for incarceration, it escapes into a Porta-Potty outside a campground. Mulder and Scully must find the "Flukeman" before it can escape into the sewers, where it has already begun to hermaphroditically breed.

Matthew Bennett (First Workman, Craig) has appeared in a number of telefilms, including *A Killer Among Friends* (1992), *Just One of the Girls* (1993), and *When Secrets Kill* (1997).

Freddy Andreiuci (Detective Norman) played Bill in *Witchcraft V: Dance With the Devil* (1992) and had a role in *Power of Attorney* (1995).

Dmitri Boudrine (Russian Engineer) played another Russian, Andrei Petrovich Melnikov, in the Chernobyl-themed "Maranatha" episode of Chris Carter's *Millennium*.

WITNESS PROFILE

DARIN MORGAN

As a child, Darin Morgan never wanted to put on rubber suits and swim through sewers, nor did he imagine himself an Emmy award–winning writer. He liked going to the movies with his father, but yearned to play professional baseball. When his older brother, Glen, began acting in high school, Darin got involved in the theater as well. Eventually, both brothers were enrolled in the same film course at Loyola Marymount University. There, Morgan learned an appreciation of silent films and comedy actors like Buster Keaton and Charlie Chaplin and learned that physical comedy and slapstick did not always mean pratfalls.

Morgan began writing scripts and teleplays, but his career seemed destined to go nowhere. Brother Glen, now working with James Wong on Vancouver-based TV series such as *The Commish* and *21 Jump Street*, helped his brother get acting jobs in those shows: he played Sal on the "Charlie Don't Surf" episode of *The Commish* and homeless street kid Skid on the "Blinded by the Thousand Points of Light" episode of *21 Jump Street*.

When Glen Morgan and James Wong became writers and co-executive producers of *The X-Files*, Glen tried to get his brother interested. He eventually convinced Darin to climb into the rubber suit of the Flukeman, but the job was demanding. A full-body cast of Darin was made, with the actor crouching on a bicycle seat to maintain the correct shape. The finished Flukeman suit took six hours to put on, and Morgan couldn't remove it until filming was finished for the day. During one day of shooting, Morgan was in the suit for twenty hours.

The urethane rubber suit also soaked up water, making it extremely heavy to wear when wet. The grotesque pull-on mask did not have any holes for the nose, meaning Morgan had to breathe through his mouth only. Eating was next to impossible, as he could not eat and breathe at the same time. And because this episode was filmed in July at Canada's Iona Island Sewage Treatment Plant, the suit was very hot *and* very smelly. If Chris Carter brings back Flukeman (as the episode's denouement suggested), Morgan has said he won't be the one in the suit.

David Duchovny never saw Darin Morgan out of his Flukeman suit. Months later, when Morgan was flying to Vancouver to work on "Humbug," the writer/actor sat next to Duchovny on the plane. Half an hour into the flight, he asked Duchovny for an autograph signed "To my nemesis, Fox Mulder." When a perplexed Duchovny asked for an explanation, Morgan revealed that he had been Flukeman.

Glen Morgan had prevailed upon Darin to try writing a script for *The X-Files'* second season, and Morgan created the opening teaser for "Jose Chung's 'From Outer Space.'" Darin also helped his brother out of a story pinch by suggesting the psycho postal worker in "Blood," and aided him in storyboarding the episode. Darin was invited to join the writing staff by producer Howard Gordon and given a nine-week contract. Darin's scripts included the second-season episode "Humbug" and the third-season episodes "Clyde Bruckman's Final Repose," "War of the Coprophages," and "Jose Chung's 'From Outer Space,'" (although he had some uncredited rewrites on "Quagmire," including the death scene for QueeQueg, the dog he had introduced in "Clyde Bruckman's Final Repose"). Darin's scripts were infamous for their bizarre humor and black comedy and for the way that they kept the characters of Mulder and Scully completely in character, even in the midst of absurd circumstances. Darin won a 1996 Emmy award for "Outstanding Writing for a Drama Series" for "Clyde Bruckman's Final Repose."

And then Darin retired. "I'm just tired of writing this show," he said in *Sci Fi Universe*.

"It's only my fourth episode, I know, but there's a quick burnout factor in episodic TV. There is a certain deadline pressure. And dealing with the censors and the network is just hard."

Morgan was pulled back to *The X-Files* to act in one fourth season episode, "Small Potatoes." There, he played the hapless Eddie Van Blundht, a man with a tail who could change his physical appearance to look like anyone. Though the episode was written by Vince Gilligan, it had all the elements of a "Darin Morgan script."

X27 Blood

Case Number:	2.03/ #27 (#2X03)
First Sighting:	September 30, 1994
Directed by:	David Nutter
Original Story:	Darin Morgan
Teleplay by:	Glen Morgan & James Wong

GUEST CAST	CHARACTER
William Sanderson	Ed Funsch
John Cygan	Sheriff Spencer
Kimberly Ashlyn Gere	Mrs. McRoberts
George Touliatos	County Supervisor Larry Winter
Bruce Harwood	Byers
Dean Haglund	Langly
Tom Braidwood	Frohike
Gerry Rosseau	Mechanic
Andre Daniels	Harry McNally
William MacKenzie	Bus Driver
Diana Stevan	Mrs. Adams
David Fredericks	Security Guard
Kathleen Duborg	Mother
John Harris	Taber
B. J. Harrison	Clerk

FIELD REPORT

Franklin, Pennsylvania. Postal worker Ed Funsch gets laid off and you know there's going to be trouble. Especially when he's been seeing phrases like "KILL 'EM ALL" on electronic readouts. Mulder is in town investigating a rise in homicide for the Behavioral Science unit of the FBI; seven people have killed twenty-two others in the last six months. Mulder notes that the only link in the crimes is the destruction of electronic readouts. When the agents question a woman about another murder, she goes psy-cho and tries to stab Mulder before being shot by the sheriff.

In her autopsy, Scully notes an incredibly high adrenalin level and traces of a chemical which could be causing hallucinations. After he winesses workers shoveling insects onto yards in the area, a bewildered Mulder captures a Eurasian cluster fly and takes it to the Lone Gunmen. They are able to identify the hallucinogenic chemical as an experimental insecticide which causes fear responses. Soon, Mulder and Scully discover that strange crop-dusting tests are being conducted on the citizens of Franklin. But even as they race against time to test the town's populace for exposure to the chemical, Edward Funsch is packing up his rifle and heading to the clock tower of the Franklin Community College.

WITNESS NOTES

The clock-tower shootings by Funsch are based on the real Texas Tower massacre. On August 4, 1966, just before noon, Charles J. Whitman climbed up into the tower at the University of Texas. His marine-issue duffle bag contained two rifles, a pistol, a revolver, over seven hundred rounds of ammunition, a sawed-off shotgun, numerous knives, and food . . . including Spam. Whitman began spraying the crowd below with his high-powered rifle and other guns. He killed thirteen people and wounded thirty-four others before Austin police were able to shoot him. When an autopsy was later performed on Whitman, a huge tumor was found pressing into the part of his brain that controls aggression.

In this *X-Files* episode, the nurse buzzing the doorbell is actually buzzing the word "KILL" in morse code.

Bob Newhart connection #1: Ex–Air Force man **John Cygan** (Sheriff Spencer) played the role of cynical comic book creator Harlan Stone in the ABC sitcom *Bob*, which starred Bob Newhart. However, he is best remembered for his regular role as Paulie Pentangeli on *The Commish*, a series that also featured future *X-Files* stars Melinda McGraw and Nicholas Lea.

Kimberly Ashlyn Gere (Mrs. McRoberts) is a woman of many names. As Ashlyn Gere, she has appeared in approximately seventy-five hardcore porn movies, has modeled for *Penthouse* magazine, and is the winner of several industry porn awards, including "Best Actress" for the alien gender-switching sex film, *Chameleons*. As Kim McKamy, she has appeared in many horror and exploitation movies such as *Lunch Meat* (1987), *Evil Laugh* (1986), *Creepozoids* (1987), *Angel III: The Final Chapter* (1988), and *Fatal Instinct* (1991). In the spring of 1994, Gere had been visiting a friend at a strip club when Glen Morgan recognized her and asked for a card. Since he couldn't produce his own business card, Gere suspected a casting couch–type ploy, but reluctantly gave him her number. Days later, Gere got a call from Morgan, and she returned the call to an office on the Fox lot. "I couldn't believe it," Gere said in an interview in *Femmes Fatales*. "I couldn't give the time of day to a producer of *The X-Files!*"

With her character in this *X-Files* episode, Gere recalls that "Glen and Jim bring a lot of very slight innuendos into all of their characters . . . For me to play a character whose fear was the fear of being raped was their way of being a little catty." In *X-Files Confidential*, Glen Morgan reveals that "[Gere] was trying to go legitimate, and we were trying to be punks and ruffle feathers." Although producer Robert Goodwin questioned Gere's casting, Morgan stood behind it, comparing the stunt to G. Gordon Liddy's appearances on *Miami Vice*. "It's a weird, cool thing to do, and she's a better actress than Gordon was." Later, as Kimberly Patton, Gere was cast with a recurring role as Feliciti OH on *Space: Above and Beyond*, the Fox series created by Glen Morgan and James Wong.

WITNESS INTERVIEW
WILLIAM SANDERSON

Born: January 10, 1948, Memphis, Tennessee

Bob Newhart connection #2 : Like many actors in this book, you'd recognize William Sanderson if you saw him. His slight Tennessee drawl, weather-beaten brow, and expressive eyes would pull you in, but you may not be able to immediately place him. That is, until he would say "Hi, I'm Larry, this is my brother Daryl, and this is my other brother Daryl." "A lot of people saw the *Newhart* show," Sanderson ad-

William Sanderson went postal in "Blood."

mits with a mirthful sigh. "*Newhart's* never going to go away."

Sanderson is also easily recognizable from his work as the childlike android inventor J. F. Sebastian in *Blade Runner*. Then there's the recent noirish pseudo-Western, *The Last Man Standing*, with Bruce Willis and Christopher Walken. Indeed, perusing Sanderson's long resumé reveals he's appeared in over forty movies—big hits such as *Coal Miner's Daughter* (1980), *The Onion Field* (1979), *The Rocketeer* (1991), and John Grisham's *The Client* (1994), and not so popular movies including such horror fare as *Nightmares* (1983), *Man's Best Friend* (1993), *Mirror, Mirror* (1990), *Skeeter* (1993), and *Hologram Man* (1995). Television credits include both *Lonesome Dove* miniseries and the recent *Andersonville* miniseries, as well as Stephen King's *Sometimes They Come Back*. Episodic work has ranged from *Married . . . With Children* to *Mann and Machine*, with stops along the way for *The Pretender* and *Babylon 5*.

Sanderson grew up in Memphis, the son of a landscape designer and an elementary school teacher. He did a two-year stint as an army medic, and then decided to pursue a law degree. He decided not to take the bar exam, opting instead to launch himself into the world of acting, his lifelong dream. He worked in local theaters and honed his skills as a bartender, eventually moving to New York. Soon after beginning acting training, Sanderson appeared in a number of Off-Broadway productions, including *The Taming of the Shrew, To Kill a Mockingbird*, and *Marat/Sade*. A few movies followed. Then came *Newhart* and *Blade Runner* (both in 1982), and Sanderson's career took off.

Sanderson was cast in *The X-Files* at the request of director David Nutter, who has since used the actor in an episode of *ER* as well. "I really like David Nutter," Sanderson says. "I suspect that it was *Blade Runner* that caused him to hire me. I didn't have to audition for him. He showed the producer some tapes." Once Sanderson arrived on set, he didn't discuss his character, the pissed-off postal worker Ed Funsch, with anyone else. "Funsch was kind of a normal guy, originally, and he was just an innocent worker who got fired from his job. I loved what they did with the ending. I liked that he didn't have long hair and earrings and he just sort of *became* obsessive."

In the episode's most explosive scene, Funsch was in a clock tower shooting at bystanders below. The scene is full of kinetic wild energy, and Sanderson clearly relished the job. "I got to release some feeling, some anger, shoot up the place. Drink, cry . . . I just had fun." But was it cathartic fun? "I'm scared of that word. I may have thought that when I was younger, but it's just fun. It's like playing cops and robbers when you're little. I wouldn't want to do that exclusively. I like to play dads and all kinds. But, to be honest, I like these [roles] because you can really get paid for becoming enraged."

Much of what made it into the actual episode came from the "pre-slate preparation," before Sanderson was actually supposed to "play" the scene. As Sanderson got into character and rehearsed, Nutter captured the actions, resulting in an edgy multiple-angle MTV editing style that disoriented the viewers and allowed them to feel Funsch's madness.

Sanderson's enthusiasm extends to almost everything he's done. That includes recent voice work for cartoon shows. On *Batman: The Animated Series*, he was Karl Rossum in "His Silicon Soul" and other episodes. "They called my commercial agent, and said they wanted a guy like in *Blade Runner*. And my agent said,

'Well I represent him!' I was just sure I'd get over there and get fired. [Rossum] was a scientist, similar to a character I'm playing on *Jumanji* [the animated series]. They're often eccentric. I've done a lot of [eccentric scientists]." He admits that he really enjoys doing animation voices. "I like them because you don't have to dress up, and they don't care what you look like."

Upcoming, look for Sanderson in a small independent film, *Eating Las Vegas,* and the TNT miniseries *The George Wallace Story*, as well as another cult project for TNT . . . the prequel movie of *Babylon 5*! So, with a thriving career, is Sanderson happy? "I just thank God every day that I make a living at something I love!" The unfortunate Ed Funsch never shared that sentiment.

X28 Sleepless

Case Number:	2.04/ #28 (#2X04)
First Sighting:	October 7, 1994
Directed by:	Rob Bowman
Written by:	Howard Gordon

GUEST CAST	CHARACTER
Mitch Pileggi	Assistant Director Walter S. Skinner
Nicholas Lea	Agent Alex Krycek
Jonathan Gries	Salvatore Matola
Steven Williams	Mr. X
Tony Todd	Corporal Augustus D. "Preacher" Cole
Don Thompson	Henry Willig
David Adams	Dr. Francis Girardi
Michael Puttonen	Dr. Pilsson
Anna Hagan	Dr. Charyn
William B. Davis	Cigarette-Smoking Man
Mitch Kosterman	Detective Lieutenant Horton
Paul Bittante	Team Leader
Claude DeMartino	Dr. Grissom

FIELD REPORT

New York, New York. Mulder receives a mysterious tape telling him about a man who is found internally burned to death with no sign of fire in the room. Just the case to investigate with eager-beaver new partner Alex Krycek, who is freshly assigned to Mulder in tow. The man, Grissom, ran a sleep disorder clinic, and he's connected to a marine special forces unit that was in Vietnam. All members of that unit have died except for one man, the haunting Augustus Cole, known as "Preacher" to his unit mates. And Cole is missing.

Mulder finally meets his mysterious government informant, Mr. X, who tells him that Cole's unit was used in sleep deprivation experiments aimed at creating a super soldier who had no need for sleep. The result has left Cole awake for the last twenty-four years, and Mulder surmises that Cole has developed a psychic power which allows him to make dreams seem real enough to kill. Mulder has a tough time finding Cole, but when he does Krycek kills the soldier, claiming he saw a gun in his hand. Later, Krycek reports to his real boss, Cigarette-Smoking Man.

WITNESS NOTES

The actors who played the Vietnamese killers in one soldier's hallucinations could not speak English. Director Rob Bowman had a difficult time getting them not to look at the camera and crew.

Jonathan Gries (Salvatore Matola) has been steadily working since the mid-seventies, and has appeared in a wide variety of genre projects. His early role in the telefilm *Helter Skelter* saw him featured with future *X-Files* star Steve Railsback, and he worked with Jerry Hardin on the religious film *Born of Water*. He appeared in three horror films, *TerrorVision* (1986), *The Monster Squad* (1987), and *Fright Night II* (1988). He was a series regular on Fox's *Martin* for two seasons, and most recently has been a regular on NBC's *The Pretender*, on which he plays The Center's computer hacker, Broots.

WITNESS PROFILE

TONY TODD

Born: December 4, Washington, D.C.

Tony Todd was raised by his Aunt Clara in Hartford, Connecticut. A two-year scholarship to the University of Connecticut led to a scholarship offer from the Eugene O'Neill National Theater Institute. While there, he became involved with many of the local repertory companies, and even began teaching playwriting to local high school students.

Tony Todd starred in "Sleepless."

Later, while performing in *Johnny Got His Gun* at New York's Westbank Theater, Todd was greeted backstage by movie director Oliver Stone, who offered the actor the role of Sergeant Warren in *Platoon* (1986). He followed that up with a role in the independent film *Sleepwalk* (1986), which featured Chinese fairy tales that came to life, and co-starring roles in *Bird* (1988) and *Lean on Me* (1989) followed.

Standing an imposing six-foot-five, Todd has had quite a variety of horror film roles, starting with an appearance in *Voodoo Dawn* (1989), followed by a starring role in George Romero's remake of *Night of the Living Dead* (1990) and a guest appearance on the TV series *Werewolf*. In 1992, he garnered the title role in Clive Barker's *Candyman* film, based on the author's short story, "The Forbidden." That film was popular enough to warrant a sequel, *Candyman: Farewell to the Flesh* (1995), in which Todd's tragic character of Daniel Robitaille—the man who became Candyman—was explored further.

Todd also had a role as Grange, the top henchman of the villainous Top Dollar, in *The Crow* (1994), and on television, he starred in three *Black Fox* telefilms in 1994 and 1995, and the critically acclaimed CBS miniseries *True Women* (1997). More recently, he has had starring roles in *Sabotage* (1996) and *The Rock* (1996).

On television, Todd is a favorite of the *Star Trek* producers, although he didn't get the first role he had tried out for: Geordi LaForge. Todd has appeared as K'urn, the Klingon brother of Worf on three episodes of *Star Trek: The Next Generation* and *Star Trek: Deep Space Nine*, but his most memorable role was when he played the adult Jake Sisko on a flash-forward episode of *Deep Space Nine* called "The Visitor." Todd also had a recurring role on *Homicide: Life on the Street,* and has guest-starred as the character of Gladius on *Hercules: The Legendary Journeys* and as the doomed Cecrops in "The Lost Mariner" episode of *Xena: Warrior Princess.*

In a *Starburst* interview, Todd admitted that he identified with his character in this episode of *The X-Files.* "Actors don't get a lot of sleep, but then I do my best thinking, not drinking, at night." The actor was pursued for the role by the casting directors, and since it was one of the shows on Todd's list of series he was interested in, the role was arranged quickly. His scenes were filmed over three days, after which he caught the red-eye flight to New Orleans to report to the set of *Candyman: Farewell to the Flesh* the next morning.

Of his role as Cole, Todd told *TV Zone* "I don't necessarily see Cole as a villain. He is someone whose brain has been tinkered with and from what I could see, he just wants to be put out of his misery. In that final confrontation he's actually holding a Bible. He uses his psychic abilities to make Krycek think it's a gun and that's why he shoots him. Augustus wants to go to sleep, so that adds a touch of poetry to the part."

More recently, Todd has been featured in the film *Wishmaster* (1997), a horror film directed by Robert Kurtzman and also starring horror veterans Robert "Freddy Krueger" Englund and Kane "Jason Vorhees" Hodder. Todd has also completed starring roles in the acclaimed independent festival film *Driven* (1996), and *Stir* (1997). Further in the future, a third *Candyman* film is under discussion, and Todd has the title role in the BBC/UPN miniseries, *Shaka Zulu: The Citadel* (1997–98). Sounds like Tony Todd's acting slate will keep him sleepless for quite a while to come.

X29   Duane Barry

Case Number:	2.05/ #29 (#2X05)
First Sighting:	October 14, 1994
Directed by:	Chris Carter
Written by:	Chris Carter

GUEST CAST	CHARACTER
Steve Railsback	Duane Barry
Nicholas Lea	Agent Alex Krycek
C.C.H. Pounder	Agent Lucy Kazdin
Stephen E. Miller	Tactical Commander
Frank C. Turner	Dr. Hakkie
Fred Henderson	Agent Rich
Barbara Pollard	Gwen
Sarah Strange	Kimberly
Robert Lewis	Officer
Michael Dobson	Marksman #2
Tosca Baggoo	Supermarket Clerk
Tim Dixon	Bob Morris
Prince Maryland	Agent Janus
John Sampson	Marksman #1

FIELD REPORT

Marion, Virginia. An alien abductee, afraid the aliens are coming back for him, takes four people hostage in an office building in Richmond. Mulder and Krycek are brought in by negotiator Agent Lucy Kazdin, who figures that Mulder will be able to talk enough "UFO-talk" to get Duane Barry to release his hostages. Mulder is stunned to find out that Barry is an ex-FBI agent, and when the chance arrives, Mulder swaps himself for a wounded hostage. Barry wants to talk to Mulder as badly as Mulder wants to hear the abductee's experiences.

Scully's research on Barry shows he's dangerously delusional, and shortly thereafter Barry is shot and captured. When he is examined, doctors find implants within his skull and abdomen that couldn't have come from any human source. Scully takes one of the implants and exposes it to a supermarket scanner, only to have the machine go crazy. That night, as a bright light comes for him, Barry escapes and kidnaps Scully from her apartment.

WITNESS NOTES

The aliens in this episode were all played by nine- and ten-year-old girls.

Sarah Strange (Kimberly) was Maura in "Force Majeure," an episode of Chris Carter's

Millennium. Co-starring with her in that episode was this episode's co-star C.C.H. Pounder.

WITNESS PROFILE

C.C.H. POUNDER

(Carol Christine Hilaria Pounder)

Born: December 25, 1952, Georgetown, British Guyana, South Africa

Perhaps the best-known African-American character actress in the business, C.C.H. Pounder came from very humble beginnings. Born in Guyana, Pounder was raised on a sugar cane estate. In Africa, she saw her first live theater: a Kabuki rendition of *The Tea House of the August Moon*, which mesmerized her. Pounder later studied theater in Sussex, U.K. and New York, and eventually worked both on off-Broadway and Broadway, where she caught the eye of Bob Fosse. He cast her in his film *All That Jazz* (1979), and a career in Hollywood soon beckoned. Although she appeared in the critically acclaimed film *Prizzi's Honor* (1985), Pounder really shot to fame with her role as Brenda in *Bagdad Cafe* (1988). Roles in almost thirty films followed, including *Postcards From the Edge* (1990), *Sliver* (1993), and the recent film, *Face/Off* (1997).

Pounder has had dozens of roles in genre films and series, including the feature films *Robocop 3* (1993) and *Tales From the Crypt: Demon Knight* (1995), the telefilms *Psycho IV: The Beginning, Lifepod,* and Fox's *White Dwarf*. Recently, Pounder was in the vocal cast of Disney's direct-to-video sequel, *Aladdin and the King of Thieves* (1996), and she is most commonly seen as Dr. Angela Hicks on NBC's *ER*, a recurring role that has helped raise her profile even higher.

C.C.H. Pounder was nominated for an Emmy Award as Outstanding Guest Actress in a Drama Series for her role as Agent Lucy Kazdin in this episode of *The X-Files*, though she did not win. Still, she remains a favorite of Chris Carter, who has cast her as a recurring character in *Millennium*, where she plays Millennium group member Cheryl Andrews. Her appearances so far have included "The Judge," "Weeds," and "Force Majeure." This fall, look for Pounder to play a lead role in NBC's miniseries *The House of Frankenstein*.

X30 Ascension

Case Number:	2.06/ #30 (#2X06)
First Sighting:	October 21, 1994
Directed by:	Michael Lange
Written by:	Paul Brown

GUEST CAST	CHARACTER
Steve Railsback	Duane Barry
Mitch Pileggi	Assistant Director Walter S. Skinner
Nicholas Lea	Agent Alex Krycek
Sheila Larken	Margaret Scully
Steven Williams	Mr. X
Meredith Bain Woodward	Dr. Ruth Slaughter
William B. Davis	Cigarette-Smoking Man
Michael David Simms	FBI Agent
Peter LaCroix	Dwight
Steve Makaj	Patrolman
Peter Lapres	Video Technician
Bobby L. Stewart	Deputy

FIELD REPORT

Skyland Mountain, Virginia. Mulder finds out that Scully has been kidnapped and that Duane Barry is taking her to the Blue Ridge Parkway's Skyland Mountain tram. Skinner orders Mulder to stay off the case, but Fox goes after Barry anyhow. Krycek tells Cigarette-Smoking Man where Mulder's going and follows. As Mulder rides toward the mountaintop in a tram, Krycek kills the tram operator down below and stops the tram, leaving Fox hanging perilously high above the mountainside.

When he finally makes his way to the mountaintop, Mulder finds an exhultant Barry. The man explains to Mulder that he traded Scully to the aliens to stop them from taking him. Barry tells Mulder that the military is in on the abduction, and later, under the care of Krycek, Barry chokes and dies. Mulder tells Skinner he thinks Barry was poisoned and tries to get help from Matheson, but Mr. X warns him off. Shortly thereafter, Mulder finds that Krycek is a traitor, and the young agent disappears. Skinner, siding with Mulder and acknowledging that there is some sort of conspiracy, reopens the X-Files.

That is indeed Gillian Anderson's pregnant belly you see in Mulder's imagined alien experimentation. Several weeks after filming this episode, on September 25, 1994, Anderson gave birth to her daughter, Piper.

The song playing on Mulder's radio in this episode is "Red Right Hand," by Nick Cave and the Bad Seeds. It would later be used in the first X-Files soundtrack, *Songs in the Key of X*.

Michael David Simms makes the first appearance in his recurring role as an FBI agent in this episode. He also played Special Agent Tom Babich in the "Lamentation" episode of Chris Carter's *Millennium*. Could they be the same guy?

Steve Railsback appeared in "Duane Barry" and "Ascension."

WITNESS PROFILE
STEVE RAILSBACK

Born: November 16, 1948, Dallas, Texas

Although he had appeared in two prior films— the ghost story *The Visitors* (1972) and *Cockfighter* (1974)—Steve Railsback rose to prominence playing Charlie Manson in the telefilm miniseries *Helter Skelter* (1976). He then played the role of Private Prewitt in the miniseries *From Here to Eternity*, following

that up by starring in the title role of the critically acclaimed *The Stunt Man* (1980). Railsback cowrote the POW telefilm *The Forgotten* (1989) with Keith Carradine and James Keach; he also directed *The Spy Within* (1994), starring Theresa Russell and Scott Glenn.

Somewhere, Railsback's career seemed to take a left turn. Although he continued to work almost constantly, most of the projects he was cast in were either low-budget or forgettable. Many of them were also science fiction or horror films, including *Escape 2000* (1981), *Trick or Treats* (1982) with fellow *X-Files* guest Carrie Snodgress, *Deadly Games* (1982), *Lifeforce* (1985), *Blue Monkey* (1987), the Sharon Stone flick *Scissors* (1991), *Alligator II: The Mutation* (1991), *Sunstroke* (1992), and *Nukie* (1993). Recently, he had a role in the abysmal comic book–based film *Barb Wire* (1996).

Chris Carter pursued Railsback for the role of Duane Barry in the *X-Files* two-parter, which had been constructed largely to deal with Gillian Anderson's pregnancy. In the book *The X-Files Declassified*, Chris Carter is quoted as saying that "He is the person I wanted, the only person I ever thought of for the role. He really became the part, and I think also that the levels of your actors rise to that."

In an interview with *Cinescape*, Railsback said "I like [Duane Barry]. I always believed he was telling the truth and he had just had it up to here with not being believed." The actor had never seen the series, but had appreciated the script and the sample episodes Fox sent him for review. "The script is what excited me. It was written as [well] as any screenplay I'd ever read."

Although "Ascension" was directed by Michael Lange, the first part, "Duane Barry," was both written and directed by Chris Carter, who was making his directorial debut. "Chris is very actor savvy for someone who's not an actor," said Railsback. "He really knows how to talk to actors . . . he just let me create, which is a great feeling."

At a 1995 speech at the University of Southern California Graduate Screenwriting Program, Chris Carter explained one element of Railsback's alien abduction sequence. "If you remember the episode where the drill drilled into the guy's teeth, you actually saw the effect of the drill. The special effects guy actually put a pipe into the actor's mouth—Steve Railsback's mouth—and shot water out of his mouth so that when you added a special effects laser, it made it look like it was truly drilling his teeth, which made it all that much more painful."

Railsback currently stars in Fox's new science fiction series *The Visitor*.

X31 3

Case Number: 2.07/ #31 (#2X07)
First Sighting: November 4, 1994
Directed By: David Nutter
Written By: Glen Morgan & James Wong
Original Script: Chris Ruppenthal
Writers: Chris Ruppenthal, Glen Morgan, & James Wong

GUEST CAST | CHARACTER
Justina Vail | The Unholy Spirit
Perrey Reeves | Kristen Kilar
Frank Military | John / The Son

Tom McBeath | Detective Gwynn
Malcolm Stewart | Commander Carver
Frank Ferrucci | Detective Nettles
Ken Kramer | Dr. Browning
Roger Allford | Garrett Lorre
Richard Yee | David Yung
Brad Lorre | Fireman
Gustavo Moreno | The Father
John Tierney | Dr. Jacobs
David Livingstone | Guard

UNCREDITED
Guyle Frazier | Officer

FIELD REPORT

Los Angeles, California. Mulder follows a series of vampiric killings to Los Angeles, telling the police there that similar killings have taken place in Memphis and Portland. One man is dead, and Mulder tells them that there will be two more before the killer—or killers—move on. Mulder tracks down newly hired employees at local blood banks and arrives with the police at the Hollywood Blood Bank, finding the new night watchman, "John," slurping blood hungrily.

After John tells them that he's "The Son," and that "The Father" and "The Unholy Spirit" are still loose, he's burned to death by sunlight. Clues lead Mulder to the gothic nightspot,

Club Tepes. There he meets and is seduced by a beautiful young woman named Kristen, who all but confesses to the murders. Later, the police search Kristen's home, but find no sign of her, only blood-filled bread in the oven. Mulder waits for Kristen to return, and discovers that she's on the run from the vampiric trio. Mulder and Kristen have sex, and then face down the trio of vampires.

WITNESS NOTES

This is the *only* episode which has not featured Gillian Anderson in any manner.

Justina Vail (The Unholy Spirit) worked with director David Nutter on four episodes of the syndicated series *The Adventures of Superboy*: "The Road to Hell, Parts I and II," and "Threesome, Parts I and II." In that latter two-parter, she played Dr. Odessa Vexman, a villainess who teamed up with longtime Superboy enemies Metallo and Lex Luthor.

Frank Military (John / The Son) also appeared on an episode of *The Adventures of Superboy*, though not one directed by Nutter. He was the eponymous shrinking hero-wannabe "Microboy." **Tom McBeath** (Detective Gwynn) appeared in the religious-themed "Kingdom Come" episode of Chris Carter's *Millennium*.

Tom McBeath (Detective Gwynn) appeared in the religious-themed "Kingdom Come" episode of Chris Carter's *Millennium*.

WITNESS PROFILE

PERREY REEVES

Although she would not make her feature film debut until *Child's Play 3* (1992), Perrey Reeves had a successful start to her career on the small screen. She appeared in the sci-fi telefilm *Plymouth* with future *X-Files* star Jerry Hardin and had a recurring role on ABC's *Homefront*. Reeves has had numerous guest roles on television, including appearances in the "Poison" episode of *21 Jump Street*, the "Dead Man Sliding" episode of *Sliders*, and the "Child's Play" episode of *The Flash*.

Reeves first met David Duchovny in May 1993. She and her mother came into Fred Segal's in Santa Monica, the same clothing store that Duchovny was shopping in. She wanted lingerie, he wanted a suit (with money from his *Kalifornia* paycheck), but he couldn't decide between a gray or a blue suit. Her advice was to buy both.

Reeves and Duchovny dated for the next few years, during which time she was cast in the *X-Files* role. She played Kristen, a woman who may or may not have believed herself to be a vampire, but who definitely had a bewitching effect on Fox Mulder. Not coincidentally, Duchovny's first love scene of the series was played with the actress.

Reeves lived in Los Angeles, and her and David's work schedules only allowed the two of them to see each other on the weekends. They sublet a house together on Point Grey in Vancouver, and spent as much time as possible with each other. Both were vegetarians, and both practiced yoga; Perrey left Duchovny notes on the refrigerator containing advice from Deepak Chopra.

In *X-Files Confidential*, cowriter James Wong blames the negative fan reaction to "3" on Reeves. "I think that because the two of them have a sexual relationship off-screen, there was a kind of tension missing that you have with two people who *haven't* messed around. The whole thing is that she should have been so alluring and there would be a chemistry between them, and there wasn't at all. That's why I think it wasn't successful."

Duchovny and Reeves ended their relationship in late 1995 or early 1996. According to the book *The Duchovny Files*, the managers for both actors issued press releases about the breakup.

X32 One Breath

Case Number:	2.08/ #32 (#2X08)
First Sighting:	11 November 1994
Directed By:	R. W. Goodwin
Written By:	Glen Morgan & James Wong

GUEST CAST	CHARACTER
Sheila Larken	Margaret Scully
Melinda McGraw	Melissa Scully
Mitch Pileggi	Assistant Director Walter S. Skinner
Steven Williams	Mr. X

William B. Davis	Cigarette-Smoking Man
Don S. Davis	Captain William Scully
Jay Brazeau	Dr. Daly
Nicola Cavendish	Nurse G. Owens
Lorena Gale	Nurse Williams
Bruce Harwood	Byers
Dean Haglund	Langly
Tom Braidwood	Frohike
Ryan Michael	Overcoat Man
Tegan Moss	Young Dana Scully

FIELD REPORT

Georgetown, Maryland. Margaret Scully is buying a headstone for Dana Scully's grave when news reaches her and Mulder: Scully has been found, and she's alive! Scully is comatose and Mulder can't find any information about where she was or how she got to the hospital. The Lone Gunmen do their best to find out what the mysterious substance in Scully's blood is, even as her New Age sister tries more mystical ways to save her life.

Deep in her subconscious mind, Scully sees herself in a boat on a lake, tethered to the shore by a frail rope. After a man steals Scully's blood sample, Mulder gives chase, but the man is executed by Mr. X, who tells Mulder to back off. Later, Mulder is left a clue to Cigarette-Smoking Man's address; he breaks into the apartment and confronts the conspirator at gunpoint. CSM is smug and unruffled, and Mulder resigns from the FBI. Mr. X offers him the promise that answers will come from men searching his apartment that night, but a torn Mulder spends the time with Scully, who finally awakens from her coma, with no memory of what happened during her abduction.

WITNESS NOTES

Nurse Owens is named after the grandmother of writer-producer Glen Morgan.

Nicola Cavendish (Nurse G. Owens), is a Vancouver-based actress with a very long list of theatrical credits, including the Broadway play *Blithe Spirit*. Born in England, she was raised in the Okanagan village of Kaleden and attended the University of British Columbia, where she graduated with a bachelor's degree in theater. She has done numerous voices for *Sesame Street* and was a regular on two Canadian television series, *Zig Zag* and *Red Serge Wives*. She had a role in *American Boyfriends* with future *X-Files* star Nicholas Lea, and in Stephen King's *It*, which also featured William B. Davis and Melinda McGraw. She's also been in an episode of the popular swords-and-Immortals series *Highlander*.

WITNESS PROFILE
MELINDA McGRAW
Born: October, 25, Nicosia, Cyprus, Greece

Like series star Mitch Pileggi, actress Melinda McGraw spent her early childhood outside the United States. McGraw's father was a diplomat for the Agency of International Development under the Kennedy administration and was living in Cyprus when Melinda was born. She lived in Beirut and Pakistan until her family relocated to the U.S. when she was four. Melinda grew up in Dover and Cambridge, Massachusetts, and eventually became involved with the Boston Children's Theater.

Melinda attended Bennington College for two years, then was accepted to London's Royal Academy of Dramatic Arts, later appearing in several West End productions and British regional theater plays. Although she had a smattering of guest roles on television, McGraw returned to the U.S. in 1989, when she appeared on *Quantum Leap* ("A Little Miracle") and garnered a recurring role on *The Human Factor* as Rebecca Travis. Her first regular gig was on the Vancouver, B.C.–based cop drama *The Commish*, on which she played an ambitious and bright ex-FBI agent, Cyd Madison, who became Eastbridge's new chief of detectives (as of the second-season premiere).

It was while working on *The Commish* that McGraw met Nicholas Lea, who had a recurring guest role on the series as Officer Enrico "Ricky" Caruso. The two soon became romantically involved. Strangely, neither of them returned for the series' fourth season, although by then, Lea had begun his role as Krycek on *The X-Files*. Glen Morgan and James Wong had written a number of episodes of *The Commish* and wrote the part of Melissa Scully with McGraw in mind. It was originally intended that Melissa Scully would become a love interest for Fox Mulder, but plans changed and the script dictated that her character be killed instead.

Since her character's untimely death on *The X-Files* (see episodes 3.01 and 3.02), McGraw has been busy guest-starring on shows such as *Cybill*, *The Larry Sanders Show*, and Dan Akroyd's new sitcom, *Soul Man*. She has also returned to the stage in the Los Angeles area, as both an actor and producer.

X33   Firewalker

Case Number:	2.09/ #33 (#2X09)
First Sighting:	October 18, 1994
Directed by:	David Nutter
Written by:	Howard Gordon

GUEST CAST	CHARACTER
Bradley Whitford	Dr. Daniel Trepkos
Leland Orser	Jason Ludwig
Shawnee Smith	Jesse O'Neil
Tuck Milligan	Dr. Adam Pierce
Hiro Kanagawa	Peter Tanaka
David Kaye	TV Reporter Eric Parker
David Lewis	Vosberg
Torren Rolfsen	Technician

FIELD REPORT

Mt. Avalon, Washington. A volcanic research team finds something very odd on the video feed of a robotic camera: a moving shadow in the depths of the volcano where nothing living could possibly survive. Mulder and Scully arrive to investigate, finding the project office in disrepair and the remaining crew members fearful for their lives. It appears that a visionary volcanologist, Daniel Trepkos, may have gone mad, and his notes reveal that he has found a subterranean organism that might be a silicon-based lifeform.

Mulder descends into the volcano to stop Trepkos while Scully stays behind to analyze growths found in one dead scientist's throat. The agents soon discover that spores are growing in each member of the research team, and that they are highly contagious if they burst near other humans. Now, Mulder has to stop the murderous Trepkos, and Scully is menaced by Jesse, whose growth is about to burst and infect her with the spores!

The special effects scene in which the volcanic spores burst from the characters' necks in this episode was very complex. "The bladders in the neck were a design that Adam Behr and I put together," says makeup man Toby Lindala in *Shivers*. "[It was] a condom with concentric circles of plastic and wire glued around it so they could fold in on themselves and get as flat as the wire was wide. When they were inflated, they would extend out to make it look as though this parasite was actually pushing itself out from the inside. We made a cast of Hiro [Kanagawa], who had this thing come out of his neck." An effects man then sat just out of the shot with a pollen blower, and when the camera had come in for the close-up, "we see the pollen blow past this fake neck that we had set up . . . we just broke the foam latex skin, which was pre-scored, and jammed it through."

Bradley Whitford (Dr. Daniel Trepkos) is a Juilliard-trained actor who has worked almost exclusively in film, including roles in *Revenge of the Nerds II: Nerds In Paradise* (1987), *Young Guns II* (1990), *Scent of a Woman* (1992), *Robocop 3* (1993), and the presidential farce *My Fellow Americans* (1996). He had the lead role of San Francisco private eye Dave Brodsky in the short-lived NBC detective spoof *Black Tie Affair*.

Leland Orser (Jason Ludwig) has been featured in a number of recent hit genre films. He was the crazed victim in the massage parlor in *Seven* (1995), a technician in *Independence Day* (1996), and a character named "Test Tube" in John Carpenter's flop sci-fi film *Escape From L.A.* (1996). Late this year, look for him in the role of Purvis in *Alien: Resurrection*.

Shawnee Smith is a self-proclaimed military brat whose acting career began at the age of eight on stage and in commercials, leading to a small role in the film version of *Annie* (1982). Her role in *Crime of Innocence* (1985) won her the Youth in Film Award for Best Actress, and at fifteen, she became the youngest theater actress ever to win the Drama-Logue Award for her role in *To Gillian on Her Thirty-seventh Birthday*. As a teenager, Smith appeared in the telefilm *Bluegrass* (1988) with Jerry Hardin, the remake of *The Blob* (1988), and *Who's Harry Crumb?* (1989). More recently, she has appeared in the miniseries Stephen King's *The Stand*, where she played the lover of Randall Flagg, the Dark Man (she got the part after the original actress, Diane Lane, unexpectedly got pregnant). Smith recently appeared in her second horror miniseries, Stephen King's *The Shining*, in which she played a waitress.

Tuck Milligan (Dr. Adam Pierce) first appeared in the miniseries *North and South* (1985) and later in the telefilm *Apollo 11*. Feature film credits include *The Russia House* (1990), the new adaptation of John Steinbeck's *Of Mice and Men* (1992), and *Heaven's Prisoners* (1996).

X34   Red Museum

Case Number:	2.10/ #34 (#2X10)
First Sighting:	December 9, 1994
Directed by:	Win Phelps
Written by:	Chris Carter

GUEST CAST	CHARACTER
Paul Sand	Gird Thomas
Steve Eastin	Sheriff Mazeroski
Mark Rolston	Richard Odin a.k.a. Dr. Doug Herman
Lindsey Lee Ginter	Crew-Cut Man
Gillian Barber	Beth Kane
Bob Frazer	Gary Kane
Robert Clothier	Old Man
Elisabeth Rosen	Katie
Crystal Verge	Woman Reading Words
Cameron Labine	Rick Mazeroski
Tony Sampson	Brad
Gerry Naim	1st Man
Brian McGugan	1st Officer

FIELD REPORT

Delta Glen, Wisconsin. A teenage boy is found wandering a road, nearly naked, and with the words "He Is One" written in red marker on his back. Mulder and Scully arrive to investigate, but the local sheriff blames the problems on a local vegetarian cult, the Church of the Red Museum. Delta Glen is a beef farming community, and the Red Museum members' beliefs don't sit well with the locals. After a girl is found dazed and nearly naked, the leader of the Red Museum is taken into custody.

Meanwhile, Mulder and Scully are taken to a farm where bizarre experimentation on cattle is taking place. The cows are being given a genetically engineered growth hormone, and a local farmer believes it to be the cause of the nasty behavior townspeople have been exhibiting. The agents soon find evidence that a local doctor, who had treated all of the carved-up teens since their births, may have been conducting experiments on them. The youths have all been injected with Purity Control, the alien DNA that Scully analyzed in "The Erlenmeyer Flask."

WITNESS NOTES

This episode's surprise denouement—the death of Crew-Cut Man—was controversial. Producer Glen Morgan was surprised at the cavalier way in which Chris Carter did away with Crew-Cut Man. In the British *X-Files* magazine, he says "I wanted it to be that this guy died [and] they never knew who he was. No name, no serial number, no record. My feeling—and Chris knows this—is that [Crew-Cut Man] should have been better developed. He's [even] shot offscreen! Geez, this is the guy who killed Deep Throat, and it's just kind of tossed away."

Paul Sand (Gird Thomas) is a Tony award–winning Broadway actor. In 1974, he starred in his own CBS TV series, *Paul Sand in Friends and Lovers*, in which he played an incurably romantic bass violinist who played with the Boston Symphony Orchestra. Later, Sand became a regular on *St. Elsewhere* as Dr. Michael Ridley. Credits he'd probably like to forget include a role in the Village People "biopic" *Can't Stop the Music* (1980), and the lead in the *Wonder Woman* episode "Disco Devil," in which he played a villainous disco dancer with the power to steal secrets from the minds of musically hypnotized government officials.

Steve Eastin (Sheriff Mazeroski) has been seen in a number of genre projects. On TV, he has appeared in *Starman, The Six Million Dollar Man*, and the 1978 telefilm *The Clone Master* (one of his earliest roles). Film credits include *A Nightmare on Elm Street 2: Freddy's Revenge* (1985), the alien body-jumping movie *The Hidden* (1987), *Sliver* (1993), the low-budget Full Moon film *Robot Wars* (1993), and the recent *Con Air* (1997).

Mark Rolston (Richard Odin) took a while to settle on a career. As a child, he was a ballet dancer. As a teen, he was a basketball player. As an adult, he tackled acting in a big way, touring the United States in a prestigious production of *Richard III*. Rolston's film credits include two successful genre films: *Aliens* (1986) and Stephen King's *The Shawshank Redemption* (1994). His credits also include some less successful genre films: *Scanner Cop* (1994) and Roger Corman's *Humanoids From the Deep* (1996). Rolston discussed his character in an interview with *TV Zone*. "Richard Odin is removed, self-obsessed, and above all, eccentric. I play a lot of bad guys, so the fact that there was a nice twist at the end when, in fact, we aren't the bad guys, was interesting." In one scene in the episode, Odin is communicating with his followers via the computer, and director Win Phelps wanted Roslton to experiment with his body language as he typed. "I'm sure there are quite a few unprinted takes where I must have looked like Mozart banging away on those keys."

Brian McGugan (1st Officer) is both an actor and a playwright. He has appeared in *The Outer Limits, The Commish, MacGyver, Bordertown*, and the telefilm *The Death of the Incredible Hulk*. He produced a twelve-part video series, *Reel Pro Files*, which documented Vancouver's entertainment industry.

SPECIAL CONSPIRACY NOTES

This episode was planned as a cross-over with *Picket Fences*, a quirky award-winning drama on CBS. Both series were productions of Twentieth-Century Fox Television, and Chris Carter was a big fan of David Kelly's series. *Picket Fences'* plots were sometimes as bizarre as *The X-Files'* plots, with serial killers and serial bathers sharing screen time with spontaneously combusting mayors, abducted circus elephants, and dishwasher suicides. At the time, *Picket Fences* aired Fridays at 10 P.M. on CBS, immediately following *The X-Files* on Fox, and a two-part cross-over would be easy.

Carter and *Fences* creator David E. Kelley met at a parking lot at the Twentieth-Century Fox studios, where they hatched the cross-over idea. "I wrote a script and showed it to David. And he liked it and decided to continue the story," said Carter in an *Entertainment Weekly* interview. After serious work on the project was finished, including scheduling David Duchovny to appear on *Picket Fences*, CBS scuttled the cross-over, forcing the shows to re-think their strategies. CBS's reason for killing the idea is that they didn't want people to watch the Fox network at 9:00 P.M. instead of watching CBS.

The rethought *Picket Fences* episode does still have some direct references to *The X-Files*. "Away in the Manger" aired one week after "Red Museum" on December 16th, 1994. In this story, Rome, Wisconsin's sheriff, Jimmy Brock (Tom Skerritt) and his deputies find a dead cow in a truck, its stomach cut open. Medical Examiner Carter Pike (Kelly Connell) suspects strange genetic experiments involving cows and injections of alien DNA, based on reports he's heard from nearby Delta Glen about recent FBI activities.

An exasperated Agent Morrell from the FBI is called, but when he claims nothing is happening in Delta Glen, Pike presses the issue. "Well then, what was the FBI doing in Delta Glen? What about the teenage rapists and the plane crash and the people in red frocks who won't eat meat?" After Pike accuses him of a cover-up, Agent Morrell says "That's an unsolved case, and it doesn't involve you."

It is discovered that cows are being used as replacement wombs for women who want to give birth but may not be able to carry the child to term. Rome's mayor-to-be, Rachel Harris (Emmy winner Leigh Taylor-Young), is stuck at the heart of the controversy when it's revealed that her own child is being birthed by a cow! Sounds like an *X-Files* episode after all.

X35 Excelsis Dei

Case Number: 2.11/ #35 (#2X11)
First Sighting: December 16, 1994
Directed by: Stephen Surjik
Written by: Paul Brown

GUEST CAST | CHARACTER
Teryl Rothery | Nurse Michelle Charters
Sab Shimono | Gung Bituen
Frances Bay | Dorothy
Erick Christmas | Stan Phillips
David Fresco | Hal Arden

Sheila Moore | Mrs. Dawson
Jerry Wasserman | Dr. John Grago
Tasha Simms | Laura Kelly
Jon Cuthbert | Tiernan
Paul Jarrett | Upshaw
Ernie Prentice | Leo Kreutzer

FIELD REPORT

Worcester, Massachusetts. A nurse at the Excelsius Dei nursing home is raped by an invisible attacker. Mulder and Scully arrive to investigate the claim of Nurse Charter, who has filed a suit against the government because she must return to work where her accused attacker—seventy-four-year-old Hal Arden—has continually sexually harassed her. At the home, a doctor has been using an experimental drug to help treat Alzheimer's patients, but the results may not be what he hopes for. Especially with Stan Phillips.

An older man is choked by an invisible hand and an orderly is pushed out the window and killed. An older woman, Dorothy, tells Scully she can commune with spirits that exist in the home. Mulder discovers that out that an Asian orderly, Gung, has been giving some of the patients medicinal mushroom tablets. The tablets, also used by mystical shamans, have possibly unleashed an opening to the spirit world. Mulder and Nurse Charters are imperiled in a bathroom by the spirits, but when Stan goes into a seizure, the ghosts disappear.

WITNESS NOTES

Sab Shimono (Gung Bituen) played an elder in *Waterworld* (1995), and was a regular in both the movie and the TV series of *Gung Ho*, as Mr. Saito. He also played the role of Lord Norinaga in *Teenage Mutant Ninja Turtles III* (1993).

Frances Bay (Dorothy) is another veteran of David Lynch's weird *Twin Peaks*, where she played Mrs. Tremond. In feature films, she has been in the horror films *The Attic* (1979) starring fellow *X-Files* guest star Carrie Snodgress, *Nomads* (1986), *The Pit and the Pendulum* (1990), *Arachnophobia* (1990), *Critters* (1991), *The Paperboy* (1994), and John Carpenter's *In the Mouth of Madness* (1995).

Erick Christmas (Stan Phillips) has played two well-known clerics. He was a priest in the cult film *Harold and Maude* and had a reoccurring role on *Cheers* as Sam Malone's parish priest. He was also a time-warp scientist in *The Philadelphia Experiment*, which inspired the later second-season *X-Files* episode "Død Kalm." Roles the actor would like to live down? He was Senator Polk in *Attack of the Killer Tomatoes* (1980) and Mr. Carter in the *Porky's* trilogy (1982–85). So *that's* where he learned the sexually harassing behavior he used as Stan Phillips!

David Fresco (Hal Arden) has a career that stretches back to the film *Queen of the Burlesque* (1946), and that includes guest shots on the original *Mission: Impossible* and *Twilight Zone* series, as well as appearances on the femme fatale detective series *Honey West* and *Rod Serling's Night Gallery*.

Sheila Moore (Mrs. Dawson) had a role as the mother of a molested girl in "The Well Worn Lock" episode of Chris Carter's *Millennium*.

Teryl Rothery was in "Excelsis Dei."

WITNESS INTERVIEW

TERYL ROTHERY

Born: November 9, Vancouver, British Columbia

As a little girl, Tery Rothery used to use her Pez dispenser as a communicator, pretending she was the girl with whom Captain Kirk would fall in love and—finally—settle down with.

Years later, Rothery has never appeared on an episode of *Star Trek*, but she's got quite a few science fiction series to her credit, including guest shots on *M.A.N.T.I.S.*, two episodes of *The Outer Limits*, *Two*, and *Profit*. She's also just landed the recurring role of Doctor Frasier on the new *Stargate SG-1* series from Showtime. She's been featured in the Loch Ness monster-style movie *Magic in the Water* (1995) and the kangaroo ninja movie *Warriors of Virtue* (1997). And, of course, she was the nurse caretaker at this episode's Excelsius Dei nursing home, where she played probably the wettest on-land scene in *X-Files* history!

Rothery had actually auditioned for *The X-Files* several times before landing this role. She had tried for the role of Lula Phillips in "Lazarus," the role of mentally challenged Tracy in "Roland," and later for the part of the vampiric Kristen in "3." But then came Nurse Michelle Charters. "They knew my work. It was just a matter of finding the right role. And this was the one that seemed to work."

In the episode itself, Nurse Charters is such a bitch that it's hard to identify with her. But the writers originally planned to stack the cards even further. As revealed in the book *The Truth Is Out There*, the Nurse Charters character was originally written as a lesbian. That element of the character was deleted, says Chris Carter in that book, because "it just felt gratuitous at that point." Given that *The X-Files* has never had a *positive* gay character on the series, the producers apparently realized that having its first gay character negatively portrayed might cast *The X-Files* in a poor light. Then again, that apparent sensitivity didn't stop them from featuring a stereotypical gay serial killer in the over-hyped pilot of Chris Carter's *Millennium*.

"In the original script, Charters was also going to be gay," confirms Rothery. "In the section where they come in and they're interviewing me in my home, I talked about how a man smells a certain way and what happened. [Then] my lover then comes in and she's behind me. In the audition [they wanted] a lot of disdain for men as well. So it put her on that different type of edge, the way they were going. And then they changed the direction and said 'No, we're not going to have that at all.' "

In the opening scene, Charters is raped by

invisible ghosts. Rothery admits that the scene "was challenging for me because I couldn't play off of anybody. There was nobody there, so I had to create my own stuff. It was me throwing myself and flipping myself on the bed and trying different things. That process was fun. It was fun to really conjure up—as an actress—to have to play off my own stuff and my own imagination. And I had a great time doing it."

Explaining further, Rothery says "You're in this room and your imagination is so powerful. You're alone and it's quiet and they start it with 'somebody slam the door.' The sound of a slamming door always gets the adrenaline going for me. They had crew down below the bed, and they actually had a vibrator on the bed. They had wire that you can't see, and some guy down [below], pulling the bed. The vibration of the bed and the movement—I blocked out all the other things and I was so in the moment. That was frightening!"

The scene was reminiscent of the ghostly rape scene in *The Entity*, a 1983 horror film. But unlike the more graphic R-rated ghostly rape in that film, Rothery notes that in "Excelsis Dei," "they didn't have the clothes ripping. What they had was the Velcro wrist bands that are on the hospital beds. I moved my arms as if he—or they—were throwing my arms back, and the bands snapped closed on my wrists." To get that effect, the scene was shot in reverse. Rothery began with her hands in the wrist bands and then someone behind the scenes ripped off the bands using fishing line. Another part of the scene would have had Rothery levitate. "I was going to get fitted with this body cast thing, to help levitate me. But time wouldn't permit it, so we weren't able to do that."

In a later scene, David Duchovny and Rothery were floating in a specially built tank containing 3,300 gallons of water. Duchovny's sense of humor kept the actress's spirits up during filming. "There was a scene where we're submerged in this tank in the bathroom and it's late, and we got punchy. They had heated the water for us, to about 90 degrees, so it was quite warm. I remember the two of us having to hang in this [tank], because we couldn't come out. I don't know how many hours we did

hanging in this tub. David would crack lines . . . let's just say bathroom humor."

Not all was fun and games on the set though. The episode was filmed at the Riverview Mental Institution in Coquitlam, British Columbia, just outside Vancouver. "There are rumors, of course, that it's haunted," admits Rothery. "You hear various stories from the crew. I've shot other things there and the energy in the building is just frightening. If you go right up to the top in the attic, you see the cages and it's just . . ." She stops for a moment, admitting that the memory has given her goosebumps. "I remember this one incident where a producer went to use the restroom, and it's like, eerily quiet, and it's just scary. He opened the restroom door and this whole flood of water came out! There was no leakage, there was no seepage of water under the door!" Another haunting story from the Institution happened to both a set/costume person and another member of the crew that Teryl knew, in which a bloody woman approached them and asked for a cigarette, then disappeared.

For Rothery, it's incidents like these that give some credence to the paranormal. What does she think about UFOs and other paranormal activites? "I believe when people say they've seen things, [that] they've seen a UFO. Absolutely. I don't know if I have my own philosophy or my firm belief. I'm just very open to the possibilities."

And who knows? When contact *is* established with aliens, Pez dispensers may just be the key to communication.

X36 Aubrey

Case Number:	2.12/ #36 (#2x12)
First Sighting:	January 6,1995
Directed by:	Rob Bowman
Written by:	Sara B. Charno

GUEST CAST	CHARACTER
Terry O'Quinn	Lieutenant Brian Tillman
Deborah Strang	Detective B. J. Morrow
Morgan Woodward	Harry Cokely
Joy Coghill	Mrs. Thibedeaux
Roby Driscoll	Detective Joe Darnell
Peter Fleming	Officer #1

| Sarah Jane Redmond | Young Mom |
| Emanuel Hajek | Young Cokely |

UNCREDITED
| Stephen Saban | Police Photographer |

FIELD REPORT

Aubrey, Missouri. After telling her boss that she's carrying his child, Detective Morrow inexplicably finds herself out in a field, digging up the remains of legendary FBI agent Sam Cheney, who disappeared in 1942. Cheney had been investigating a string of serial murders wherein women were raped and murdered, with the word "sister" carved into their chests. Scully reopens Cheney's case, even as Lieutenant Tillman tells her another murder has turned up with the same m.o.

The suspect thought to have been the murderer was recently released from prison, but at seventy-seven, and with an alibi, he couldn't have done the latest murder. Morrow wakes from a nightmare to find "sister" carved into her chest and a sack of human remains buried under the floorboards of her family house. As Scully and Mulder investigate further, they find that Morrow may have more than one skeleton in her family closet.

WITNESS NOTES

This is the only episode so far with no repeat guest actors.

In *X-Files Confidential*, Chris Carter says "**Deborah Strang**, who played B. J., was topnotch, and we put her in for an Emmy nomination. Morgan Woodward was excellent as well." Director Rob Bowman adds "I just thought she did a great job of coloring the character and making her believable." Strang had previously appared in a short film, *Memorial*, which was written by Sara Charno, the writer of this *X-Files* episode.

Stephen Saban, who is an extra playing a police photographer at one of the grave sites (look for him in a leather jacket and a baseball cap), is a reporter for *Details* magazine. While working on a story on the series for the February 1995 issue, he was drafted as an extra. When he asked Deborah Strang if she was worried that X-Philes would scrutinize her every moment, her reponse was "Like the size of my butt?"

Morgan Woodward (Harry Cokely) appeared in two episodes of the original *Star Trek* series: "Dagger of the Mind" and "The Omega Glory." He was recently the very creepy man in the iron lung in the "Force Majeure" episode of Chris Carter's *Millennium*. His past in Hollywood includes a tremendous number of Western movies and television series since 1955, plus three appearances on *Logan's Run* and roles in episodes of *Planet of the Apes*, *Salvage One*, *Project UFO*, and *The Incredible Hulk*.

Joy Coghill (Mrs. Thibedeaux) appeared with future *X-Files* guest Steve Railsback in *Blue Monkey* (1987), with a number of other *X-Files* guests in the telefilm *Omen IV: The Awakening* (1991), and in David Cronenberg's early horror film *They Came From Within* (1975).

WITNESS PROFILE
TERRY O'QUINN

Born: July 15, 1952, Newbury, Michigan

As a child, Terry O'Quinn (some sources list "Quinn" as his real surname) wanted to be a performer, though he considered singing to be a more attractive career than acting. He began acting in college, then moved to regional theaters up and down the eastern seaboard. He performed on Broadway in *Curse of the Aching Heart* and in many off-Broadway productions as well.

O'Quinn's film debut was in *Mahler* (1974), a biopic about the composer Gustav Mahler. In the years since, he has been featured in over fifty feature films and telefilms, averaging five or six projects a year since the late eighties. He appeared in the telefilm *Roe vs. Wade* (1989) and the recent feature *Ghosts of Mississippi* (1996), both also starring Jerry Hardin.

O'Quinn's biggest role to date was as the chameleonlike marriage-minded killer in *The Stepfather* (1987), a chilling low-budget effort that spawned a less-effective sequel, *The Stepfather II* (1989), in which he also starred. Although his eyes and smile can be warm and inviting, O'Quinn's ability to give the chilling edge of lunacy by the slightest sidelong glance got him cast in a lot of horror films to follow. He was Sheriff Joe Haller in Stephen King's *Silver Bullet* (1985), Dr. Linden in *Pin* (1988), and a detective in *Amityville: A New Generation* (1993). Other genre credits include the silly *SpaceCamp* (1986), and the comic book–based *The Rocketeer* (1991), in which he played millionaire Howard Hughes.

O'Quinn spoke briefly about his *X-Files* appearance in *XPose*: "When I worked on that *X-Files* episode, the entire cast and crew seemed like a well-organized and well-oiled machine. They were concerned about the quality of the product and handled everything like complete professionals. So, I found the idea of working with a group like that very appealing."

Despite an admitted unease on television, O'Quinn has recently been a recurring character on three series: he was in several episodes of *Jag*, and was the sinister Reilly on five episodes of NBC's failed science fiction series, *Earth 2*. But it would take Chris Carter to utilize O'Quinn's appeal fully on the new-for-1996 Fox series, *Millennium*.

In *Millennium*, Carter cast O'Quinn as Peter Watts, a high-up member of the Millennium Group. The group bordered on the edge of law enforcement; it is clearly not a government group, but is respected by most law enforcement and government agencies. Peter Watts works closest with Frank Black (Lance Henricksen), a weather-beaten man with the power to visualize past acts of violence, thereby taking authorities a step closer to solving crimes.

The first season of *Millennium* ended in May, and O'Quinn appeared in thirteen of the twenty-two episodes: "Pilot," "Gehenna," "522666," "Blood Relatives," "The Wild and the Innocent," "Loin Like a Hunting Flame," "Force Majeure," "Sacrament," "Walkabout," "Lamentation," "Powers, Principalities, Thrones, and Dominions," "Broken World," and "Maranatha."

O'Quinn recently appeared in the 1997 film *Shadow Conspiracy*, a feature that also starred Charlie Sheen, Donald Sutherland, and sometime *X-Files* player Charles Cioffi. Coming this fall, O'Quinn returned for the second season of *Millennium*, where Peter Watts plays a larger role, and he will reprise the role in *The X-Files* movie, *Blackwood*, making it the first filmed *X-Files/Millennium* crossover.

X37 Irresistible

Case Number:	2.13/ #37 (#2x13)
First Sighting:	January 13, 1995
Directed by:	David Nutter
Written by:	Chris Carter

GUEST CAST	CHARACTER
Bruce Weitz	Agent Moe Bocks
Nick Chinlund	Donald Addie Pfaster
Deanna Milligan	Satin
Robert Thurston	Jackson Toews
Glynis Davies	Ellen
Christine Willes	Agent Karen F. Kossef
Tim Progish	Mr. Fiebling
Dwight McFee	Suspect
Denalda Williams	Marilyn
Maggie O'Hara	Young Woman
Kathleen Duborg	Prostitute
Mark Saunders	Agent Busch
Clara Hunter	Coed

FIELD REPORT

Minneapolis, Minnesota. A mortuary worker is caught taking a lock of hair from the corpse of a woman and is fired. Later, when a grave is desecrated, Mulder and Scully are brought in to investigate. Scully is particularly troubled, and Mulder classifies the perpetrator as an "escalating fetishist" whose interest in death and corpses may soon lead to murder. Mulder's right, as Donnie Pfaster kills a prostitute and takes pieces of her as keepsakes.

A botched stalking lands Pfaster in jail, but he's not the police suspect in the case. Pfaster sees Dana Scully while he's behind bars, and after he's released, he decides she will be his next victim. As Mulder tracks down clues that implicate Pfaster, the death fetishist runs Scully off the road and takes her captive. Her worst fears come true as a terrified Scully realizes she's about to be the victim of a serial killer.

WITNESS NOTES

The morphing images over Pfaster's body and face were inserted after filming, not only because morphing effects *need* to be inserted after filming, but also because Chris Carter realized that without the effects, nothing in the show was an X-File! The psychopathic death fetishist was as real as any other cop-show villain until the extra demonic morphing touches were added.

Nick Chinlund (Donnie Pfaster) made his screen debut in the low-budget horror film *The Ambulance* (1990) and later appeared in *Lethal Weapon 3* (1992) and *Eraser* (1996.) He starred in an episode of Zalman King's erotic anthology series *Red Shoe Diaries*, hosted by David Duchovny. "Nick came in and he had a kind of androgynous quality that worked," Chris Carter said in *X-Files Confidential*. "I thought he looked like Joe College, but he could scare the hell out of you." Check out that quality on display in summer 1997's *Con Air* and in the upcoming live action *Mr. Magoo* movie.

Bruce Weitz starred in "The Fighter" episode of *Highlander*.

WITNESS PROFILE

BRUCE WEITZ

Born: May 27, 1943, Norwalk, Connecticut

Born during World War II, young Bruce Weitz had the traditional boyhood dreams of the era. When he grew up, he wanted to be a fireman or a cowboy. But a dare from high school classmates found Weitz cast in the junior class play, and the actor was hooked. Weitz came to Los Angeles in the mid-seventies, where he became a staple guest star on the series of the time. His big break came in 1981 when school chum Steven Bochco told him he was writing a pilot for a new cop show and asked Weitz to play a

role. The show was *Hill Street Blues*, and Bochco wanted Weitz for the role of vice cop Johnny (J. D.) LaRue. Weitz liked the script, but argued for the part of scruffy detective Mick Belker. He auditioned for the network, and won the role.

And who could forget Weitz in the role of growling Belker, more apt to bite a criminal than to cuff him? Unable to express his feelings, Belker was most frustrated when his mother called, generally while he was booking a snickering suspect. Belker's frequent undercover assignments were almost always a comedic highlight of the sometimes somber series; he was a female nurse, he was a Hassidic Jew, he was a homeless man, he was a street-corner hooker . . . viewers never knew what to expect. The series was a critical hit and lasted six seasons. In 1984, Weitz won an Emmy Award for Outstanding Supporting Actor in a Drama Series for his role on *Blues*.

Post–*Hill Street Blues*, Weitz has been a staple of "true life" telefilms and has been a cast member of several series, including *Anything but Love*, on which he played Mike Urbanek during the third season, and the short-lived *Byrds of Paradise*, on which he was Dr. Murray Rubinstein. He recently voiced the villainous Lock-Up on an episode of *Batman: The Animated Series*, and recurs as the voice of Bruno Manheim on the WB network's *Superman* animated series.

Fans of *The X-Files* will want to search out one episode of *Highlander*. In "The Fighter," Weitz plays a scrappy Immortal who promotes boxers through the ages. Also starring in that episode is a pre-Krycek Nicholas Lea.

X38 Die Hand Die Verletzt

Case Number: 2.14/ #38 (#2x14)
First Sighting: January 27, 1995
Directed by: Kim Manners
Written by: James "Chargers" Wong & Glen "Bolts, Baby!" Morgan

GUEST CAST	CHARACTER
Dan Butler	Jim Ausbury
Susan Blommaert	Phyllis H. Paddock
Heather McComb	Shannon (Kate) Ausbury

Shaun Johnson
P. Lynn Johnson
Travis MacDonald
Michele Goodger
Larry Musser
Franky Czinege

Laura Harris
Doug Abrahams

Pete Calcagni
Deborah Brown
Dave Duran
Barbara Ausbury
Sheriff John Oakes
Jerry Thomas (a.k.a. Jerry Stevens)
Andrea
Paul Vitaris

FIELD REPORT

Milford Haven, New Hampshire. The local Parent-Teachers Committee of Crowley High School seems normal enough—until they end their meeting with a candle-lit chant to Satan! A boy is later killed in the woods, his body found with the eyes and heart cut out. Mulder and Scully arrive to investigate, and things begin to get even stranger. A rain of toads pelts the agents, water drains counter-clockwise, and a creepy substitute teacher named Mrs. Paddock is hiding the boy's heart and eyes in her desk drawer.

After a teen in Mrs. Paddock's class experiences flashbacks and slashes her wrist with a dissecting scalpel, Mulder manages to get one of the parents, Ausbury, to admit that they've been using their own children in satanic rituals. Now, it appears that the devil has come to Milford Haven! Ausbury is later eaten whole by a huge Burmese python, and the remaining members of the cult decide they must sacrifice Mulder and Scully to appease the devil. But Mrs. Paddock has other plans, and they don't involve the deaths of the FBI agents.

WITNESS NOTES

Franky Czinege's character is named "Jerry Thomas" in the credits, but is identified as "Jerry Stevens" in the dialogue. Shannon Ausbury is also called "Kate" in the episode.

"Paul Vitaris" is named after online X-Phile Paula Vitaris, a writer whose thoughtful and informative pieces on *The X-Files* have been printed in *Cinefantastique* and the British *The X-Files* magazine.

Crowley High School is named after Edward Alexander "Aleister" Crowley, a British occultist who was heavily involved in the field of modern witchcraft and Wicca, but who dabbled in Tantrism, Freemasonry, and other "magick" practices. According to many sources, Crowley was heavily addicted to drugs, but never harmed his disciples. His main teaching was based in the self-written "Law of Thelema," which stated "Do what thou wilt shall be the whole of the Law." Crowley died in 1947, having authored almost a hundred books, including "The Book of Thoth," which outlined his study of tarot, and the "Holy Books of Thelema," which contained the mystical system that Crowley taught to his followers.

Heather McComb (Shannon [Kate] Ausbury) made her professional debut as Zoe in *New York Stories* (1989). She was the spark-throwing teen superhero, Jubilee, in Fox's 1996 pilot telefilm *Generation X*, based on the Marvel comic series. Heather also appeared in "The Wild and the Innocent," an episode of Chris Carter's *Millennium*. Most recently, the young actress joined the cast of NBC's *Profiler* for the last half-dozen first-season episodes as Frances Malone, the rebellious daughter of Bailey, head of the Violent Crimes Task Force.

Creepy actress **Susan J. Blommaert** (Phyllis H. Paddock) also appeared in Stephen King's *Pet Sematary* (1989) and Tim Burton's *Edward Scissorhands* (1990). She has guest starred on *Tales From the Crypt* ("Four-Sided Triangle") and had a recurring role as Judge Steinman on *Law & Order*. In a weird coincidence, Blommaert also played a biology teacher in a commercial for Butterfinger candy bars! Nobody better lay a finger on her butterfinger!

WITNESS INTERVIEW
DAN BUTLER

Born: December 2, 1954, Huntington, Indiana

How did television's most macho (fictional) radio sportscaster end up as snake chow? Dan Butler is familiar to most readers as Bob "Bulldog" Briscoe on NBC's highly-rated sitcom, *Frasier*, but his career encompasses much more than that.

It all began in Fort Wayne, Indiana, where young Dan used to entertain the family at gatherings. He was cast in a local production of *The Music Man*, and was bitten by the acting bug. Butler went on to perform in many regional theaters before making his debut on Broadway in Harold Pinter's *The Hot House*. He was later in the Broadway show *Biloxi Blues* as well as several off-Broadway plays. He also wrote the book and lyrics for three musicals: *The Case of*

Dan Butler appeared in "Die Hand Die Verletzt."

the Dead Flamingo Dancer, A Tap of Fable Murder, and Mystery Musical. While performing in Terrence McNally's The Lisbon Traviata at Los Angeles's Mark Taper Forum, Butler was approached by the casting director for Frasier.

Butler had already done some television and film work before Frasier, including The Manhattan Project (1986) and the critically-acclaimed AIDS film Longtime Companion (1990). He also holds the distinction of being one of the two cast members to appear in both film versions of Thomas Harris's famous Hannibal Lecter novels: Manhunter (1986), adapted from the novel Red Dragon; and The Silence of the Lambs (1991), whose FBI cadet Clarice Starling character was one of the inspirations for the character of Dana Scully. Later films have included Captain Ron (1992), Rising Sun (1993), Dave (1993), and The Fan (1996).

The talented actor made a stir in Hollywood circles when he wrote and performed the autobiographical play The Only Thing Worse You Could Have Told Me in 1994. The play features fourteen vignettes about what being gay means to Butler, and is titled after the negative reaction Butler's father had when his son came out to him. The play, which has received much critical acclaim, has been scripted by Butler for a feature film version, which Frasier star Kelsey Grammer will produce.

Butler was cast in The X-Files shortly after The Only Thing Worse caused a stir in Los Angeles, but the subject never came up on the X-Files set. "At that point I had done it in L.A., but I hadn't done it in New York," said Butler. "Really, there hadn't been a lot of press about it, so it wasn't like [I was] walking in with a sandwich board on."

How did he get cast in the role? "It was right around Christmas and I had a couple weeks off from Frasier and this offer came through. I read the script and I had grown up terrified of snakes, so I thought this would be a good way to get over it. It was a great script. I was intrigued by the whole idea of disillusionment of faith. It just happened to have the twist that this was about faith being witchcraft, instead of Christianity, or another religion. And I also loved that you heard both sides of the abuse issue. You were never clear who was telling the truth. Whether it was my daughter or me . . . I'm glad they never gave an answer."

The scene where the snake devours Butler's character whole is the episode's highlight, and is, in fact, the genesis of the entire script, according to the writers. Butler laughs at the dread he had facing the scene. "The big joke was 'Oh, they're going to film that particular scene the last day, so just in case I'm constricted to death, they'll have it all in the can!' So, when the schedule came out, sure enough that was the last scene they were going to shoot!

"They had two snakes. One was a twenty-foot python, and the other was fourteen-foot python. Both, as I understood it, had been owned by an exotic dancer before. They also had the front part of another snake as an animatronic robot, for when it had to twist around me in one shot. At other points, when you see it almost strangling me to death, they wrapped the real snake around me a couple times. Then they had to tug it from behind, because if it doesn't recognize you as food, it won't constrict."

Well, that's amazing snake fact no. 1, but Butler found out more facts. "There's a big difference between [these snakes and] snakes that slither and are poisonous and will bite and kill me. You know, I shivered a bit when I saw the python the first time. But then they brought it out, and about five of us got over there and put it over our shoulders. They breathe very loudly, and they sniff you. It sounds [something] between a dog and a hiss. And it's like a thigh muscle. They're very beautiful . . . and cold. I had forgotten about them being cold-blooded."

The creepiest on-camera moments came for Butler when "they had handcuffed me to the railing, so my back was to the snake coming down the steps. All I heard was that 'whwhwh, whwhwh' [sound of the snake moving] as it's coming, and I had no idea where it was. There's nothing they can do except pinch its tail to get it to move forward. They can't guide it. You can't train a snake where to go."

Dan chuckles at the memory. "They had these steps so that you could see in between each step, so they had a camera from above, [another] from below, and [another] underneath the stairs. Well the first time they did this, I could hear the cameramen underneath the steps going 'Wait I can hear it, but I don't know where it is.' Then, all of a sudden, I heard them go 'Oh my God!' It had gone down a crack between the wall and the steps, instead of going right down the steps, and was hovering over their heads!"

The scene took quite a while to film, due to other logistical problems. "I felt sorry for the snake, because it would get halfway down the steps, and then its weight would catapult it the rest of the way down. It got scared and pulled back to strike. The snake wranglers had to stuff it into the burlap bag. They realized, 'That's enough for *this* snake. Let's bring the next one in.' It had had enough of being tossed around."

X39 Fresh Bones

Case Number:	2.15/ #39 (#2x15)
First Sighting:	February 3, 1995
Directed by:	Rob Bowman
Written by:	Howard Gordon

GUEST CAST	CHARACTER
Bruce Young	Pierre Bauvais
Daniel Benzali	Colonel Wharton
Jamil Walker Smith	Chester Bonaparte
Matt Hill	Private Harry Dunham
Callum Keith Rennie	Groundskeeper
Steven Williams	Mr. X

Kevin Conway	Private John "Jack" McAlpin
Katya Gardner	Robin McAlpin
Roger Cross	Private Kittel
Peter Kelamis	Lieutenant Foyle

UNCREDITED
Adrien Malebranche	Skinny Man accosting Scully

FIELD REPORT

Folkstone, North Carolina. Private McAlpin, a soldier at the Folkstone Immigration and Naturalization Service Processing Center dies after driving his car into a tree that has been carved with voodoo markings. Mulder and Scully investigate the suicide, which is the second in two weeks, and the soldier's wife tells them she thinks it was a voodoo curse. Base commander Colonel Wharton says that the Center's imprisoned Haitian refugees are angry at his men, and the soldiers are under enormous stress. One of the refugees, Pierre Bauvais, an alleged voodoo practitioner, tells the agents that the refugees only want to go home.

When McAlpin turns up as a walking zombie, Mulder and Scully find that the other dead soldier is missing as well. Wharton blames the curse on Bauvais, and has the man beaten to death. Mr. X tells Mulder that Wharton wants revenge on the Haitians for the death of his men on their last mission to Haiti. The truth about the matter is even stranger than the agents imagine; Wharton is actually the voodoo priest, and Bauvais isn't quite as dead as he seems!

WITNESS NOTES

The Rottweiler dog of the cemetery groundskeeper is named Wong, a reference to the now ex- *X-Files* writer/executive producer.

Matt Hill (Private Harry Dunham) has had small roles in several horror films, including *Watchers* (1988), the telefilm *The People Across the Lake* (1988), and the Canadian film *Midnight Matinee* (1988), with William B. Davis. In *Teenage Mutant Ninja Turtles III* (1993), Hill filled out the animatronic costume of Raphael. He was also the English voice of the character Ryo on the Japanese cartoon *Ronin Warriors*.

Callum Keith Rennie (Groundskeeper) is a relative newcomer to acting in front of the camera. He's had roles in the time-travel film *Timecop* (1994), and *Unforgettable* (1996).

Kevin Conway (Private John "Jack" McAlpin) seems to be a mystery man. He is *not* the same Kevin Conway who has had roles dating back to 1972's *Slaughterhouse Five*, and stretching up to 1993's lead role in *Gettysburg*. Due to the similarity of the names, finding credits for the Kevin Conway who appeared in this episode of *The X-Files* is difficult. May we suggest a middle initial, Kevin?

Daniel Benzali was a voodoo military man in "Fresh Bones."

WITNESS PROFILE

DANIEL BENZALI

Born: January 20, 1950, Rio de Janeiro, Brazil

Bald actor Daniel Benzali came to Hollywood in the mid-eighties following a successful stage career. His most famous stage credit was as General Juan Peron in Hal Prince's West End production of Tim Rice and Andrew Lloyd Webber's *Evita*. Much later, in the summer of 1993, Benzali would originate the stage role of butler Max von Mayerling, the one-time director and husband of Norma Desmond, in Andrew Lloyd Webber's musical version of *Sunset Boulevard*. Benzali can be heard on the World Premiere Cast recording of the show.

Benzali's early work in front of the camera was unremarkable, though he appeared in the 1985 James Bond movie, *A View to a Kill*, starring Roger Moore. He followed that up with the telefilms *The Return of Sherlock Holmes* (1987) and *Roe vs. Wade* (1989) with Jerry Hardin. Recently, he played the White House Chief of Security Nick Spikings in *Murder at 1600* (1997).

On television, Benzali played the doctor who performed heart surgery on Captain Picard in the *Star Trek: The Next Generation* episode "Samaritan Snare" and also appeared on *Star Cops* and *Law & Order*. He also had a recurring role on *L.A. Law*—and an *NYPD Blue* guest shot for producer Steven Bochco, who decided to cast Benzali in his newest project. The role of lawyer Ted Hoffman in the first season of ABC's *Murder One*, won Benzali great reviews and a higher Hollywood profile. In 1995, Benzali was nominated for the Golden Globe award as Best Actor for his role in *Murder One*; the same year, *X-Files* star David Duchovny was nominated for the award as well.

X40 Colony

Case Number:	2.16/ #40 (#2x16)
First Sighting:	February 10, 1995
Directed by:	Nick Marck
Story by:	David Duchovny & Chris Carter
Written by:	Chris Carter (teleplay)

GUEST CAST	CHARACTER
Peter Donat	William Mulder
Brian Thompson	The Pilot
Dana Gladstone	"Dr. Landon Prince" / "Dr. James Dickens" / Gregor clones
Megan Leitch	Samantha Mulder clone
Tom Butler	CIA Agent Ambrose Chapel
Mitch Pileggi	Assistant Director Walter S. Skinner
Tim Henry	Federal Marshal
Andrew Johnston	Agent Barrett Weiss
Rebecca Toolan	Mrs. Mulder
Ken Roberts	Motel Proprietor
Michael Rogers	1st Crewman
Oliver Becker	2nd Doctor
James Leard	Sergeant Al Dixon
Linden Banks	Reverend Calvin Sistrunk
Bonnie Hay	Field Doctor

Kim Restell	Newspaper Clerk
Richard Sargent	Captain
David L. Gordon	FBI Agent

UNCREDITED

| Capper McIntyre | First Jailer |
| Michael McDonald | Military Policeman |

FIELD REPORT

Germantown, Maryland. A "Russian" pilot who has crash-landed in the Arctic Circle is rescued, and later turns up in a Scranton, Pennsylvania, abortion clinic. There, he kills a doctor with a stiletto-spike blow to the neck, and green fluid oozes from the wound. Mulder is sent clippings of two other such deaths of abortion clinic doctors who all look exactly alike, all have no identifiable pasts, and whose bodies have never been found in their burnt-down clinics.

The Pilot tracks down another of the doctors and kills him, then murders an investigating FBI agent and takes his shape when Mulder and Scully arrive. Mulder soon discovers that the doctors are all Russian clones, but before he can investigate further, he's called back to his home. A woman claiming to be the grown Samantha Mulder has arrived, warning Fox that the cloned "Gregors" raised her and that an alien bounty hunter (The Pilot) is after her to kill her. Scully tries to protect the last four Gregor clones, but the morphing Pilot kills them all, then corners her in her hotel room disguised as Mulder.

WITNESS NOTES

Chris Carter once again tried to get *Kolchak* star Darren McGavin to take a role on the series—Bill Mulder—but the actor turned him down.

Dana Gladstone (Gregor clones) appeared in two episodes of Steven Spielberg's *Amazing Stories*, episodes, the latter of which, "Gershwin's Trunk," he played composer George Gershwin. He also played historical figure Erich Von Stroheim in the 1994 telefilm *Young Indiana Jones and the Hollywood Follies*.

Tom Butler (CIA Agent Ambrose Chapel) is a very active Vancouver actor who has also done some stuntwork on film. He has appeared in over thirty films and telefilms, and has had guest roles on most of the Vancouver-based television series, including *The Sentinel* (once), *The Commish* (twice), and *The Outer Limits* (three times). He appeared in one other project with paranormal overtones: *Scanners 2: The New Order* (1991). Of course, it could be argued that a role in *Ernest Rides Again* (1993) is akin to a paranormal circumstance. Butler also did stuntwork on *Bloodfist VII: Manhunt*, which featured Steven Williams.

Ken Roberts (Motel Proprietor) also appeared on Chris Carter's *Millennium*, in the episode titled "Sacrament."

Megan Leitch was the clone of Samantha Mulder in "Colony" and "End Game."

WITNESS INTERVIEW
MEGAN LEITCH

Born: November 9, Kamloops, British Columbia

It can be said that *The X-Files* would not exist if it wasn't for Samantha Mulder. After all, Fox Mulder has based his whole life on finding his sister. Was she abducted by aliens, the government, or someone else? In the two-part episode "Colony" and "End Game," the FBI agent began to find some of the answers to his questions. He was also reunited with his sister, fully grown into a beautiful young woman. And yet, even as he was convinced his quest was over, Samantha was revealed to be a clone, and then killed. Mulder's search for the Truth had to continue . . .

Embodying the character of the grown-up Samantha Mulder is Megan Leitch, a pretty Canadian actress who has been active in both the theater and the film/television industry boom north of the border. On stage, she has been nominated for the Sterling Award for Best Actress for her role as Juliet in the Citadel Theatre's production of *Romeo and Juliet*. She was also nominated for the prestigious Jessie Richardson award for Best Actress for her role in *Toronto, Mississippi* at the Touchstone Theatre.

Leitch has had an active life on the small screen as well, with guest roles on *The Black Stallion*, *Kids in the Hall*, *The Commish*, *Two*, and *The Sentinel*. She was in the miniseries of Stephen King's *It*, along with William B. Davis and Melinda McGraw, and played a whacked-out nun in *Omen IV: The Awakening* (1991). She's also had roles in feature films: H.P. Lovecraft-based *The Resurrected* (1991) and *Knight Moves* (1993), as well as the comedy rockumentary *Hard Core Logo* (1997).

So how did the talented actress manage to be cast in one of the most important roles on one of the hottest series on television? To start with, Leitch had an unusually fast audition process. While visiting her family in British Columbia for Christmas, she was called in to audition. "There was rumor that they had [the role] cast in L.A. or something, and there was a problem. I got called in with six other girls, and we read for the part." Megan was called back the following week for a second reading, then was told she had the part. Leitch was not a regular viewer of the series, which she felt was a blessing at the audition. "I think that would have put more pressure on me if I had known how big it was."

When they were filming the first episode, a magazine reporter was on set, covering the series. Because of the surprise revelations about Samantha, security was tight. "Chris [Carter] gave me this first script and he said 'You have more to do in the second one, but we are still rewriting.' Chris actually called me in to talk about the character. He was unsure at that point whether he wanted it released that I was actually a clone of the sister. We talked about what I could say or couldn't say to the interviewers, and then he sort of filled me in a bit more on the story."

Did Carter specifically state whether or not this is *really* a clone of Samantha Mulder? "No, he hasn't specified that. I don't know any more than you do. My idea was that he'd make Fox fairly stupid if they introduced somebody else who *isn't* me. But if they did want to bring Samantha down, then I'd have to be cloned from people who know who Samantha is. Right? But they may change that . . . I don't know."

In one scene in "End Game," Samantha and the Pilot topple off a bridge into the water far below. "We were shooting that very late—it was about four in the morning—and I think [the stuntwoman] did it in one take. It was quite a plunge, and it was very cold. We were all in wet suits when we were dealing with the water but it was freezing cold. But [the stuntwoman] hit her head. She thought she was fine when she got out of the water. She went home, and when she woke up the next morning, she was calling her boyfriend by the wrong name! She is a very good stuntwoman, but no matter what they do or how much they practice, it's dangerous." The stuntwoman, who had a bit of a concussion, recovered, and later worked with Leitch on another series.

Megan thinks that at least one of the Samantha clones could still be on the loose. "I've seen other episodes since—with the children working on the farm—and there could be any number of clones." Indeed, while there is only one Samantha seen in "Colony," five Samantha clones are seen in "End Game." How was the effect achieved? "They had me walk through the scene, and they just set up the camera angles and I played the scene with stand-ins. They had a girl who had her hair like mine, and who, from the back of the head, looked like me. They would shoot the angle from the woman in the lab coat with the person's back to me, and then they would switch the camera around and put me in that place and the woman in the lab coat turned around a bit and change the angle of the camera."

That's all easy enough to do, but what about the scenes with two or more Samanthas facing the camera? "Where it got down to a real shot where there's supposed to be two of us side-by-side, they have something called a split camera. It shoots one-half on one side and one-half on the other, and they put it together somehow with the technology that they have. There is a line on the screen and they were very specific about the marks for that—about what I could do and what I couldn't do when I was filming that scene."

Leitch only got to do one melt-down scene in the two-parter. In "End Game," when her body is pulled from the river, it dissolves into the clone-body green goo that viewers have come to expect. Makeup man Toby Lindala did a facial casting of Leitch to get her likeness. Then, "what they did is they built different wax heads with the green underneath," Megan remembers. "I actually have a Polaroid of my head in with all the green heads. When they would light them on fire, the wax melted and the green goo came out from underneath the face mold."

Will we be seeing the grown-up Samantha Mulder—or her clones—any time soon? "They put me on hold last year, in April," she admits. "This January they put me on hold again for a double episode. If an actor is put 'on hold,' that means that they put you on hold for the number of days that they would want to use you. If you get any other jobs, you have to let them know first, so that they can book you first. It means that they're thinking of using you for those days."

Unfortunately, neither of the holds resulted in an actual appearance for Leitch. Still, she's hopeful. "I think they're still figuring out how to handle it. Because they are writing the episodes in advance, that's when they're saying 'Shall we bring Samantha back in? Do we want to use the eight-year-old young Samantha, or the older Samantha? How is the story developing?' When I left, people said 'Well, you know the door is open for you to come back.' "

Given her enthusiasm for *The X-Files*, it's clear that Leitch is ready for that door to open any time. Indeed, as the manuscript for this book was being finished, the *X-Files* producers told Leitch that her character may come back early in season five!

X41 End Game

Case Number:	2.17/ #41 (#2x17)
First Sighting:	February 17, 1995
Directed by:	Rob Bowman
Written by:	Frank Spotnitz

GUEST CAST	CHARACTER
Steven Williams	Mr. X
Peter Donat	William Mulder
Brian Thompson	The Pilot
Megan Leitch	Samantha Mulder clone
Colin Cunningham	Lieutenant Terry Wilmer
Mitch Pileggi	Assistant Director Walter S. Skinner
Garry Davey	Captain
Andrew Johnston	Special Agent Barrett Weiss
Allan Lysell	Able Gardner
J. B. Bivens	Sharpshooter
Oliver Becker	2nd Doctor
Beatrice Zeilinger	Paramedic
Bonnie Hay	Field Doctor

FIELD REPORT

Deadhorse, Alaska. In the Beaufort Sea, near where the Russian pilot crashed, a radio signal is coming from two hundred meters below the ice. A U.S. submarine that investigates is trapped. Meanwhile, "Mulder" morphs into the Pilot and takes Scully hostage, intending to trade her for Samantha Mulder. Fox's sister tells him that the clones are alien colonists who came to Earth to experiment on alien/human hybrids. She also reveals that the only way to kill the alien bounty hunter is to pierce the base of his skull.

When a trade is to be made for Scully, the Pilot dives off a bridge while holding Samantha, evading an FBI sharpshooter that Skinner has provided. Mulder has been left information that leads him to a clinic, where clones of Samantha tell him that his real sister is still alive. The Pilot attacks Mulder and burns the clinic, and Mulder pulls out all the stops to find him. When Scully tries to contact the shadowy Mr. X, it's Skinner that greets—and beats—the informant; later, Scully finds that Mulder has gone to Alaska, chasing the Pilot. The Pilot tells him that his sister is alive before disappearing in a submarine beneath the ice. Mulder practically freezes to death before Scully helps revive him.

WITNESS NOTES

In the original script, writer Spotnitz had crafted a scene where Mulder picks up his sister on a bridge while heading to the clinic, only to have her morph into the bounty hunter right before his eyes. They wrestle for control of the car, crash it, and Mulder heads for the clinic (where the Samantha clones are) with the bounty hunter in hot pursuit. The scene was cut from the script and never filmed, as it would have added several days to the shooting schedule.

This is the first episode in which *every single* actor had already appeared or would later appear in another episode of the series.

Colin Cunningham (Lieutenant Terry Wilmer) appeared in the feature films *Hard Evidence* (1995) and *Robin of Locksley* (1996), as well as the telefilm *Captains Courageous* (1996).

J. B. Bivens (Sharpshooter) appeared as a deputy in the "Broken World" episode of Chris Carter's *Millennium*.

X42 Fearful Symmetry

Case Number:	2.18/ #42 (#2x18)
First Sighting:	February 24, 1995
Directed by:	James Whitmore, Jr.
Written by:	Steven DeJarnatt

GUEST CAST	CHARACTER
Jayne Atkinson	Willa Ambrose
Lance Guest	Kyle Lang
Jack Rader	Ed Meecham
Bruce Harwood	Byers
Tom Braidwood	Frohike
Jody St. Michael	Sophie the Gorilla
Charles Andre	Ray Floyd
Garvin Cross	Red Head Kid
Tom Glass	Trucker Wesley Brewer

UNCREDITED	
Bubbles	The Invisible Elephant

FIELD REPORT

Fairfield, Idaho. An invisible force trashes cars, breaks windows, and kills a road-crew workman. Down the road, an elephant appears, forty-three miles from the zoo it escaped from! Mulder and Scully investigate, and Mulder claims that the elephant must have been invisible. As the agents investigate at the zoo, they discover the Wild Again Organization (WAO) has been trying to shut the zoo down. Mulder also finds out from the Lone Gunmen that the area is a hotspot for UFO activity, and that no animal in the zoo had ever been pregnant.

After a WAO photographer is mauled by a tigress that has become invisible, Scully finds out that both the elephant and the tigress were pregnant. Mulder thinks that the animals are being abducted by aliens and impregnated, and questions Sophie, an intelligent gorilla kept by Willa Ambrose. Sophie communicates with Fox by sign language that she's afraid that the light in the sky will take a baby away from her. When the zoo is shut down, the WAO makes their attempt to free Sophie, but the attempt leaves one person dead and Mulder trapped in a room with the agitated gorilla.

WITNESS NOTES

Dean Haglund does not appear as Langly in this episode, making the Lone Gunmen a duo for a change.

The videotape of the elephant being abused at the zoo was actual footage used in animal rights propaganda films.

Jayne Atkinson (Willa Ambrose) appeared as a cast member in the one-season NBC miniseries family drama, *A Year in the Life*, and as the mother in the later NBC movie family drama *Parenthood*. She later played the role of Annie Greenwood in both *Free Willy* (1993) and *Free Willy 2: The Adventure Home* (1995), both of which featured big killer whale but no invisible elephants.

Lance Guest (Kyle Lang) was born in 1960, in California. Early in his career he landed the regular role of "Lance" (wonder where they got the name?) on the *Lou Grant* series. He later appeared as a regular cast member of *Knots Landing* and *Life Goes On*. He was a victim in *Halloween II* (1981) and *Jaws: The Revenge* (1987), but he redeemed himself as the heroic lead of *The Last Starfighter* (1984), one of the first movies to use extensive computer animation.

Jack Rader (Ed Meecham) has over thirty feature and telefilm credits to his name, but they seem to break down thematically. There are the prison movies, such as the telefilm *Alcatraz: The Whole Shocking Story* (1980) and *Penitentiary III* (1987); there are the disaster telefilms, such as *Flight 90: Disaster on the Potomac* (1984), *Big One: The Great Los Angeles Earthquake* (1989), and *Fire! Trapped on the 37th Floor* (1990); and there are the organism-that-kills-humans movies like *The Blob* remake (1988) and *Outbreak* (1995). The reader can decide which of the three categories *Amityville IV: The Evil Escapes* (1989) falls into.

Jody St. Michael (Sophie the Gorilla) is a renowned mime who is no stranger to monkey roles. She also played a gorilla in the film *Gorillas in the Mist* (1988). As in that movie, her suit here was constructed by famed special effects makeup man Rick Baker and his company, which won an Oscar for his work on the film.

X43 Død Kalm

Case Number:	2.19/ #43 (#2x19)
First Sighting:	March 10, 1995
Directed by:	Rob Bowman
Story by:	Howard Gordon
Teleplay by:	Howard Gordon & Alex Gansa

GUEST CAST	CHARACTER
John Savage	Henry Trondheim
David Cubitt	Captain Barclay
Vladimir Kulich	Olafsson
Stephen Dimopoulos	Ionesco
Claire Riley	Dr. Laskos
Robert Metcalfe	Nurse
Dmitry Chepovetsky	Lieutenant Richard Harper
Mar Anderson	Halverson
John McConnach	Sailor

FIELD REPORT

Tildeskan, Norway. The crew of a U.S. Navy destroyer abandons ship, but when they're found in their lifeboats eighteen hours later, the survivors have all aged to old men. Mulder theorizes that the ship sailed through a temporal wormhole, resulting in the premature aging of the crew. He and Scully head to Norway to investigate and are taken to the ship. They soon find that the ship, commissioned in 1991, looks twenty to thirty years old and that the bodies of

the dead crew members still aboard are mummified. Is time moving faster on the ship?

When the agents and their ferryman rest, they wake up thirty years older. Although they find a pirate who is seemingly unharmed by the aging disease, they discover themselves getting weaker and weaker. Scully theorizes they're being poisoned by free radicals attacking their DNA, and Mulder discovers the water has been tainted. When the last of the clean water is caught in a flooded sewage hold, Mulder and Scully seem destined to die of old age within hours.

WITNESS NOTES

The various actors who had to endure the makeup for the aging sequences were indeed losing time; the makeup sessions took three to four hours each!

David Cubitt (Captain Barclay) is a relative newcomer to the camera, making his earliest appearances in the telefilm *Silent Motive* and the feature film *Run* (both in 1991). Since that time, he has appeared in several movies, the "Dark Matters" episode of *The Outer Limits*, and *E.N.G.* Currently, he stars in the Canadian series *Traders* as Jack Larkin.

Vladimir Kulich (Olafsson) can be seen in the low-budget flicks *Necronomicon: Book of the Dead* (1996) and *Red Scorpion 2* (1994). Recently, he costarred in the miniseries *Pandora's Clock* with Jerry Hardin.

WITNESS PROFILE

JOHN SAVAGE

Born: August 25, 1950, Long Island, New York

John Savage, whose real name is reportedly John Youngs, began working in film in the early seventies, where he appeared in a number of forgettable films and telefilms before breaking out with *Eric* (1975), a "true story" telefilm in which he played Eric Lund, a young athlete who fights back after being diagnosed with leukemia. A few years later, a second pair of breakthrough roles arrived. The first role was in *The Deer Hunter* (1978), a powerful film about three steel workers who are sent to fight in Vietnam. The second was a lead role in *The Onion Field* (1979), a harrowing cop film based on a book by Joseph Wambaugh.

John Savage appeared in "Død Kalm."

Savage went on to play roles in the film version of the musical *Hair* (1979), *Salvador* (1986), and *The Godfather, Part III* (1990). In the nineties, his career has taken a downturn; though he still works regularly, it is in projects like Roger Corman low-budgeter *Carnosaur 2* (1995), as well as *Red Scorpion 2* (1994) and *White Squall* (1996). Savage will appear in three independent feature films in 1997: *Little Boy Blue*, *Club Vampire*, and *Amnesia*.

In *X-Files Confidential*, director Rob Bowman says that "John Savage proved to be a very interesting man to work with. He is very intelligent, but he's used to a feature schedule." In feature filming, actors generally only have a small amount of lines to learn for each day, whereas in television episodic filming, they must keep a much higher concentration of the script in their heads. "His being slightly uncomfortable helped in the playing of his character," adds Bowman.

X44 Humbug

Case Number:	2.20/ #44 (#2x20)
First Sighting:	March 31, 1995
Directed by:	Kim Manners
Written by:	Darin Morgan

GUEST CAST

GUEST CAST	CHARACTER
Jim Rose	Dr. Blockhead / Jeffrey Swaim
Wayne Grace	Sheriff James Hamilton
Michael Anderson	Mr. Nutt
The Enigma (Paul Lawrence)	The Conundrum
Vincent Schiavelli	Lanny
Alex Diakun	Curator
John Payne	Jerald Glazebrook, the Alligator Man
George Tipple	Hepcat Helm
Alvin Law	Reverend

UNCREDITED

Debis Simpson	Waiter
Blair Slater	Older Glazebrook
Devin Walker	Younger Glazebrook

FIELD REPORT

Gibsonton, Florida. The sideshow freak "alligator man" is killed in his swimming pool by an unseen creature, drawing Mulder and Scully to southern Florida, where circuses and sideshows spend their off-season time. At the funeral, Dr. Blockhead erupts from beneath the coffin, pounding a nail into his chest and making a spectacle of himself. The town is teeming with sideshow performers, leading the agents into a land where *they* are the bizarre oddities.

They check into a hotel run by a midget and meet Lanny, a drunk ex-sideshow man who has a small congenital twin growing out of his side. The murders of the sideshow "freaks" mount, and Mulder and Scully find themselves puzzled, especially by a man whose entire body is covered by a puzzle tattoo and who eats raw fish he catches in the river as well as buckets full of crickets. The real killer is Leonard, the parasitic twin that has found a way to leave Lanny's body and is trying to find a new host. But can the agents find a scurrying cannibalistic mutant twin in the midst of a funhouse?

WITNESS NOTES

The song playing at Hepcat Helm's studio in this episode is "Frenzy," by Screamin' Jay Hawkins. It would later be used in the first *X-Files* soundtrack, *Songs in the Key of X*.

Of the rumors (and blooper reel) that Anderson ate a cricket, the actress has denied the stories many times. However, she did put a cricket in her mouth. As she explained in *Entertainment Weekly*, "There was this [tattooed guy] sitting in front of me eating two hundred [live bugs] at a time, chomping on them, and I'm not gonna put one in my mouth?"

Two of the performers are real sideshow attractions. **Jim Rose** (Dr. Blockhead) founded the Seattle-based troupe The Jim Rose Circus Sideshow in 1990, and has toured with the group around the country. Their most famous session, other than *The X-Files*, was when they toured with the Lollapalooza Tour in 1992. Rose himself often reclines on a bed of nails, offers his neck up as a human dartboard, swallows razor blades and other sharp unconsumables, puts spoons up his nose, staples dollar bills to his forehead, catches bullets in his teeth, and ends the show by pressing his face into broken glass! For more on Jim Rose, see his book, *Freak Like Me*, or visit his official website at http://www.ambient.on.ca/jimrose/

Despite his skills on stage, Jim Rose had never been in front of the camera as an actor before and needed line readings from off-camera to complete his scenes. He later made his second acting appearance on an episode of the ABC children's horror series, *Bone Chillers*.

The Enigma (The Conundrum) has been with the Sideshow since the beginning, though he was originally known as Slug, the Sword Swallower. On stage, he used to swallow swords, but now he mainly eats slugs and bugs live. And yes, those really are his tattoos covering him from head to toe. His wife is a tattoo artist and contortionist known as Katzen; the original black lines for the tattoo were done in 1992 and Katzen and other tattoo artists have been filling the puzzle pieces in with blue over the years. According to Chris Carter in a 1995 speech at the University of Southern California, "That is not a real fish [The Enigma is eating]. He offered to do it, but with very many takes he would have gotten sick."

Wayne Grace (Sheriff James Hamilton) has a host of genre credits, none of which involve circus freaks. He was also a cop in *Friday the 13th: The Final Chapter* (1984), Stephen King's *The Running Man* (1987), and *Scanner Cop* (1994), although he switched departments to become a fire chief in "The Bribe," an episode of HBO's *Tales from the Crypt*. He also appeared in *Wizards of the Lost Kingdom II* (1985), *Slumber Party Massacre III* (1990), the "true-life" UFO abduction movie, *Fire in the Sky* (1993), and Clive Barker's *Lord of Illusions* (1995).

Michael J. Anderson (Mr. Nutt) is a little person who appeared in *Twin Peaks* as "The Man From Another Place."

John Payne (Jerald Glazebrook) is not really afflicted with icthyosis, the disease which creates alligator-like skin in humans and which is the affliction suffered by most real freak show Alligator Men. The makeup effects were by Toby Lindala, who in a *Shivers* interview said "John had that beautiful, sobering voice, and it was a great way of portraying the character." ·

Vincent Schiavelli appeared in "Humbug."

WITNESS INTERVIEW

VINCENT SCHIAVELLI

Born: November 11, 1948, Brooklyn, New York

With his soulful eyes, unruly hair, and his penchant for playing unusual or eccentric characters, Vincent Schiavelli is instantly recognizable. Patrick Swayze's phantom guide in *Ghost* (1990)? The organ grinder in *Batman Returns* (1992)? Both were Schiavelli, carving another uniquely strange notch in his acting belt. He also appeared in *One Flew Over the Cuckoo's Nest* (1975), *The Happy Hooker* (1975), *The Adventures of Buckaroo Banzai* (1984), H.P. Lovecraft-inspired *The Lurking Fear* (1994), Clive Barker's *Lord of Illusions* (1995), and

The People vs. Larry Flynt (1996). "I enjoy finding the humanity of these very strange people," Schiavelli says, laughing. "It would be interesting sometime if I got to play just an ordinary joe. But I have the feeling the audience would sit there saying, 'Yeah, and now he's going to *what*?'"

Schiavelli is a favorite of genre TV casting directors and has appeared in *Otherworld, Star Trek: The Next Generation, MacGyver, Highlander, M.A.N.T.I.S., Tales From the Crypt, Baywatch Nights,* and HBO's new series *Perversions of Science.* In animation, Vincent did a memorable vocal job as the voice of magician Zatara on *Batman: The Animated Series.*

Schiavelli was in Vancouver working on another show when a meeting was set up at the offices of 10-13. "I got a meeting with Chris Carter, and said, 'Listen, if I do this show it would really make my wife very, very, happy.'" Schiavelli is married to Carol Mukhalian, a concert harpist. "My wife's a big *X-Files* fan. So, a few weeks later they called with this part."

The actor is also a fan of the series itself. As a veteran of hundreds of projects, what does Schiavelli think it is about *The X-Files* that works? "First of all, I think the two main characters work tremendously well. Because they, as characters, are so relatively *ordinary* human beings, you don't question their veracity in terms of their searching. You don't question their veracity because, you know, she's a doctor, and he's an agent, and they always wear these dark, somber-looking clothes. [Laughs.] They're very straight arrows, and I think their ability to play that enhances the really far out notions that are explored in the different scripts."

In "Humbug," Schiavelli plays Lanny, a man who has a small parasitic twin growing out of his side. The twin, Leonard, is not only murderous, but exceptionally ugly as well, looking rather too close to the alien baby from the miniseries *V: The Final Battle.* Not surprisingly, both creatures were grotesque puppets. Leonard was difficult to work with, according to Vincent. "I'm never going to work with that guy again! What a prima donna he was!" Schiavelli laughs. "They did a torso cast. He was kinda strapped on. It wasn't glued on as I recall. There were several of them. There was

one that moved, there was one that was stationary . . . several of those little brothers, in various forms."

"Humbug's" other co-stars included Jim Rose and the Enigma, from the Jim Rose Circus Sideshow. Schiavelli never did see the entire act, but he saw more than viewers did. Rose's penchant for odd bits of masochism was entertaining on set, though a scene where he's pounding a nail into his nose made the crew wince. "What I thought was interesting about the way that they cut [the episode] was that they cut it to look like he wasn't pounding the nails up his nose, which he actually *was* doing. When you see it, it looks like it's fake. They did that on purpose, obviously, because it's just too grim to think about!"

Schiavelli enjoyed working with David Duchovny and Gillian Anderson, although he admits to being amazed when Anderson put the live cricket in her mouth. In another scene between Lanny and Scully, the two characters try to peek beneath each others' bathrobes— Scully to see the parasitic Leonard, Lanny to see Scully's cleavage. "Everyone had a hard time keeping a straight face. We were both kind of checking each other out. A couple times we both started laughing and couldn't stop."

Was Lanny the weirdest role Schiavelli has ever done? "Actually, he was a pretty ordinary guy, in a way. He was just a poor, schmucky guy, you know what I mean? This guy was just this poor circus freak who had this brother attached, who was getting out at night and chewing on people. You know, a cannibalistic twin?" The actor thinks for a moment, then adds "I think I've played weirder characters. Certainly the guy I just played for the new Bond movie is a lot weirder. He kills people for a living."

Schiavelli is talking about the upcoming eighteenth James Bond film, *Tomorrow Never Dies,* in which he plays a German killer for hire named Dr. Kaufman. Schiavelli is also working on a film project about a character actor who becomes incredibly famous that has caught Disney's interest. Proud of his Sicilian heritage, Schiavelli is also finishing up his second book, *Bruculinu, America,* remembrances of Sicilian neighborhoods in Brooklyn told in stories and recipes. The book will be published by the Chapters imprint of Houghton Mifflin in the spring of 1998. The versatile actor has already written one cookbook, *Papa Andrea's Sicilian Table* (Citadel Press) and has also contributed to various newspapers and magazines.

Despite the fate of Lanny's twin in "Humbug" (he's apparently eaten by The Conundrum), don't look for any recipes for parasitic-twin meatloaf. Schiavelli may play strange characters on the screen, but when it comes to cooking, he's much more down to earth.

X45   The Calusari

Case Number:	2.21/ #45 (#2x21)
First Sighting:	April 14, 1995
Directed by:	Michael Vejar
Written by:	Sara B. Charno

GUEST CAST	CHARACTER
Helene Clarkson	Maggie Holvey
Joel Palmer	Charlie and Michael Holvey
Lilyan Chauvin	Golda
Kay E. Kuter	Head Calusari Elder
Ric Reid	Steve Holvey
Christine Willes	Agent Karen F. Kosseff
Bill Dow	Dr. Charles Burk
Jacqueline Danieneau	Nurse Castor
Bill Croft	Calusari #2
Campbell Lane	Calusari #3
George Josef	Calusari #4
Oliver Wildsmith	Teddy Holvey
Jeremy Isaac Wildsmith	Teddy Holvey

FIELD REPORT

Arlington, Virginia. A toddler follows a floating balloon across a train track at a kiddie park, resulting in his death when the train hits him. Months later, Mulder reopens the case, finding some evidence in photo blow-ups that there may have been some form of poltergeist activity in connection with the death. Questioning the family, Mulder and Scully are surprised by the Romanian grandmother, who tells the boy's mother that she married the devil.

The old woman seems to both love and fear Charlie, the surviving child of the Holveys. She attempts to have him exorcised by Romanian holy men, known as "Calusari," but the experience ends with her being pecked to death by chickens that were once dead themselves! The real culprit is Michael, the stillborn twin brother of Charlie who is angry at his family and means to kill them from beyond the grave. Will Scully become the ghostly boy's next victim, or will the Calusari exorcise Michael in time?

WITNESS NOTES

The line Charlie says while standing above his dying grandmother is indeed in Romanian. He is saying "You are too late to stop us."

Helene Clarkson (Maggie Holvey) appeared in the telefilm *Woman on the Run: The Lawrencia Bembenek Story* (1993), and the feature films *Bury Me in Niagara* (1993) and *Blood & Donuts* (1995).

Joel Palmer (Charlie and Michael Holvey) makes his second appearance on *The X-Files* with this episode. Palmer first took to the stage at the age of three, as a shoeshine boy in a stage production of *Hello, Dolly!* His on-camera debut was shortly thereafter in a commercial for Mattel Toys. He had a starring role in *Far From Home: The Adventures of Yellow Dog* (1995) and guest roles on *Outer Limits* and *Poltergeist: The Legacy*, as well as *Sesame Street*.

Lilyan Chauvin (Golda) was a regular on the short-lived TV series *Cafe Americain* as Madame Dussolier. She also appeared in the genre films *Silent Night, Deadly Night* (1984), which engendered controversy with its Killer Santa theme, *Predator 2* (1990), *Universal Soldier* (1992), and *Pumpkinhead II: Blood Wings* (1994). She also has credits stretching back to Elvis Presley's *Tickle Me!* (1965) and the Tony Curtis/Janet Leigh film *Perfect Furlough* (1959).

Kay E. Kuter (Calusari Elder) is most famous for his role as farmer Newt Kiley on *Petticoat Junction* and its spin-off, *Green Acres*, but his career stretches back into the fifties, where he appeared in the original *Sabrina* (1954), *Guys and Dolls* (1955), and the awful science fiction film *The Mole People* (1956). Other genre credits include *The Last Starfighter* (1984), *Zombie High* (1987), and *Warlock* (1989).

Christine Willes appears again in her role as social worker Agent Karen F. Kosseff, a character based on the social worker wife of coexecutive producer Paul Rabwin. Willes is a very busy theatrical actress in Vancouver, with over twenty-six productions to her credit, including *A Streetcar Named Desire, Sex Tips for Modern Girls, More Sex Tips for Modern Girls, Steel Magnolias,* and the touring company of *Angry Housewives.* On television, she's had guest roles on *21 Jump Street, The Commish,* and *The Outer Limits.* She is also a voice and speech coach who has worked with many of the actors in this book.

X46 F. Emasculata

Case Number: 2.22/ #46 (#2x22)
First Sighting: April 28, 1995
Directed by: Rob Bowman
Written by: Chris Carter & Howard
                    Gordon

GUEST CAST	CHARACTER
Charles Martin Smith	Dr. Osborne
Dean Norris	U.S. Marshal Tapia
John Pyper-Ferguson	Paul
William B. Davis	Cigarette-Smoking Man
Angelo Vacco	Angelo Garza
Mitch Pileggi	Assistant Director Walter S. Skinner
Morris Panych	Dr. Simon Auerbach
Lynda Boyd	Elizabeth
John Tench	Steve
Alvin Sanders	Bus Driver
Kim Kondrashoff	Bobby Torrence
Chilton Crane	Bus Station Mother
Bill Rowat	Dr. Robert Torrence
Jude Zachary	Winston

FIELD REPORT

Cumberland Prison, Virginia/Costa Rica. In Costa Rica, a scientist examines a sore on a dead boar, only to have it explode in his face. He dies hours later, but the disease is willfully spread. A package with a sore-covered pig's leg is shipped to Cumberland Prison, where several inmates are infected. Among those infected are Paul and Steve, who escape from the prison shortly thereafter, unaware that they're now carrying a deadly contagion. Mulder and Scully arrive to investigate, but the federal marshals warn them to stay out of it. Scully stays at the now-quarantined prison in an attempt to find out more, while Mulder joins the hunt for the missing prisoners.

Mulder finds the men, but one of them escapes after infecting his girlfriend. Meanwhile, Dr. Osborne has become infected at the prison and he tells Scully of the cover-up that's happening due to Pinck Pharmaceuticals and their government contracts. Scully has a near miss at infection, while Mulder has a tense standoff with the dying Paul—and his young hostage— aboard a bus. And once it's all said and done, it appears that Cigarette-Smoking Man and his cronies have covered up the viral experiment.

WITNESS NOTES

Chris Carter wrote the part of gas station attendant Angelo Garza for his Los Angeles production assistant Angelo Vacco. Despite his messy death, Vacco would return in the third season finale for another death scene.

Charles Martin Smith (Dr. Osborne) was discovered by a talent agency while appearing in a school play. He was cast as Terry "Toad" Fields in George Lucas's *American Graffiti* (1983). He reprised that role in *More American Graffiti* (1979), and later appeared in the dreadful slasher film *The Campus Corpse* (1977), *Starman* (1984), and the award-winning *The Untouchables* (1987). Other credits on his diverse list include *Herbie Goes Bananas* (1980), the AIDS film *And the Band Played On* (1993), the telefilm *Roswell: The UFO Cover-Up* (1994), and two recent television miniseries: *Streets Of Laredo* (1995) and *The Beast* (1996). As a director, Smith has helmed the low-budget horror film *Trick or Treat* (1986), the cartoon-based live action film *Boris and Natasha* (1991), and *Fifty/Fifty* (1993). He also directed three episodes of Glen Morgan and James Wong's *Space: Above & Beyond* ("The Dark Side of the Sun," "Ray Butts," and "Pearly"), and more recently directed for the *Buffy the Vampire Slayer* TV series.

Dean Norris (U.S. Marshal Tapia) plays authority figures in most of his movie roles. He was a SWAT team leader in both *Gremlins 2: The New Batch* (1990) and *Terminator 2: Judgment Day* (1991) and a police detective in *Disorganized Crime* (1989), *Hard to Kill* (1990), and *Playmaker* (1994). His genre credits include *Total Recall* (1990), Stephen King's *The Lawnmower Man* (1992), the HBO werewolf-cop movie *Full Eclipse* (1993), *It Came From*

Outer Space II (1996), and a role in the "We Shall Overcome" episode of NBC's *Dark Skies*. He also appeared with Jerry Hardin in *The Firm* (1993).

John Pyper-Ferguson (Paul) is most recognizable for his role as the hapless thief Pete Hutter on Fox's late, lamented western *The Adventures of Brisco County, Jr.* He has also appeared in a variety of genre television projects, including *MacGyver, Star Trek: The Next Generation, Legend, Viper, The Watcher, The Outer Limits, Poltergeist: The Legacy*, and the pilot for *The Osiris Chronicles*. He was nominated for a 1997 Canadian Gemini Award for his guest role as Cullen on *Highlander* in the episode "Courage." Pyper-Ferguson has appeared in the feature films *Pin* (1988), *Stay Tuned* (1992), *The Unforgiven* (1992), and *Hard Core Logo* (1996). He recently guest starred as Jim Gilroy in "The Wild and the Innocent," an episode of Chris Carter's *Millennium*.

During the scenes where Paul holds the young boy hostage, makeup man Toby Lindala was hidden underneath the bus seats, operating an air-pump tube which made Pyper-Ferguson's "sore" makeup pulse and throb. Each boil was wired with two separate tubes so that different colors of pus could spew different distances.

Lynda Boyd (Elizabeth) was in an episode of Chris Carter's *Millennium* entitled "Blood Relatives," That episode also costarred fellow *X-Files* actress Nicole Parker.

X47 Soft Light

Case Number: 2.23/ #47 (#2x23)
First Sighting: May 5, 1995
Directed by: James Contner
Written by: Vince Gilligan

GUEST CAST   CHARACTER
Tony Shalhoub   Dr. Chester Ray Banton
Kate Twa   Detective Kelly Ryan
Kevin McNulty   Dr. Christopher Davey
Steven Williams   Mr. X

Nathaniel Deveaux   Detective Barron
Robert Rozen   Doctor
Donna Yamamoto   Night Nurse
Forbes Angus   Government Scientist

Guyle Frazier   First Officer (Barney)
Steve Bacic   Second Officer
Craig Brunanski   Security Guard

FIELD REPORT

Richmond, Virginia. In a hotel, an executive is swallowed up by the shadow of Dr. Chester Banton, who the unscrews a hallway lightbulb and runs away. One of Scully's students, Detective Kelly Ryan, asks for her help on the case, and Scully and Mulder arrive to check out the scene. This is the third crime scene at which someone has disappeared, leaving only an oily black blotch on the floor. Mulder suspects it was spontaneous human combustion, but notes that the light has been unscrewed. Later investigation reveals more unscrewed lights at the missing persons' homes, and a connection is found: all of the men recently arrived by train.

The agents track down and capture Chester in a train station, where the lighting is diffuse and soft. He's terrified the government wants to steal his scientific secrets and his "black hole" shadow. Indeed, after Mulder tells Mr. X about Chester, the mysterious informant tries to abduct the shadow-man. Chester returns to Polarity Magnetics, Inc., where the accident that caused his weird powers originally happened. There, he tries to get fellow scientist Dr. Christopher Davey to help him but it turns out the man is working for Mr. X! When Mulder and Scully arrive, a shadow burned into the wall implies Chester is dead, but is he really, or does Mr. X have control of him?

WITNESS NOTES

Tony Shalhoub (Dr. Chester Ray Banton) was a regular character on *Wings* as cabbie Antonio Scarpacci. He's also been in the films *Barton Fink* (1991), *Honeymoon in Vegas* (1992), and *Addams Family Values* (1993). In the summer 1997 film *Men in Black*, Shalhoub played the role of Jack Jeebs, an alien turned pawnbroker. When confronted by the alien-hunting Men in Black, Jeebs's head is shot off, only to grow a new one moments later.

"He's basically a good man," said Shalhoub of his *X-Files* character in a *TV Zone* interview. "Banton's not evil or a killer. It's his scientific inquisitiveness about this dark matter that gets the better of him. Suddenly he's in way over his head and he tries to figure out how he can reverse the process or, ultimately, do away with himself so that he doesn't harm any more people." Shalhoub also noted that the *X-Files* cast and crew often sang the song "Me and My Shadow" during filming.

Kate Twa (Detective Kelly Ryan) appeared in the films *Devotion* (1995) and *Big Bully* (1996).

Steve Bacic (Second Officer) played a lead role in the "Covenant" episode of Chris Carter's *Millennium*.

Kevin McNulty appeared in several episodes of *The X-Files* including "Soft Light."

WITNESS INTERVIEW

KEVIN McNULTY

Born: December 8, 1955, Penticton, British Columbia

Kevin McNulty has been in over forty telefilms, almost twenty feature films, and nearly every television series based in Vancouver: *Bordertown, Cobra, M.A.N.T.I.S., The Marshal, The Commish, 21 Jump Street, The Sentinel, Outer Limits, Viper, Two, Wiseguy, Highlander,* Showtime's *Stargate SG-1,* to name a few. In fact, finding a Vancouver project that *doesn't* have McNulty in it is tough, and *The X-Files* is no exception. With three episodes already under his belt—"Squeeze," "Soft Light," and

"Apocrypha"—it's only a matter of time before he'll be back on the 10-13 sound stages.

McNulty began doing theater in high school, and upon graduation, enrolled at Washington State University. After a year and a half, he returned to Vancouver and resumed his theatrical work. Somewhere around 1986, the television and film industry began flocking to British Columbia, and McNulty started working in a new medium. "The casting directors up here—the people that they worked from were the theater people, because that's the only people they knew. I was kind of lucky, because I was a medium-profile theater actor. I slid over to the film and TV rather easily."

When McNulty auditioned for *The X-Files*, the series had just barely been picked up by Fox, and only a thirteen-episode commitment had been made. Discussing his first *X-Files* episode, McNulty wants to clear up a logical leap that fans—and other *X-Files* books—have made. McNulty's character in "Squeeze," named "Fuller," is not the same person as his character in "Apocrypha," the similarly-named "Agent Brian Fuller." "No, no. The 'Squeeze' guy was head of Violent Crimes in the FBI, and he never came back. We never saw him again," says McNulty. "I think at the time [of 'Apocrypha'] they said, 'Well, don't worry about it. It was so long ago that nobody's gonna make a connection and we'll just leave the name as it is.' But the first guy was head of Violent Crimes, so he was *up there* in the FBI. Agent Fuller was just an agent. I suppose that's what happens, when a show takes off and people start to look at it in detail, right? These things pop up."

While he doesn't have much to say about "Squeeze," McNulty remembers that he got called back for auditions at the beginning of the second season, though he wasn't cast immediately. The role they wanted McNulty for was a new regular supporting character. "I think at the time, they wanted to establish this agent who bugged Mulder, who sat in the boardroom and just laughed at everything Mulder said. They thought that I was the right guy for it." However, since he was filming *Serving in Silence* in Vancouver and *Children of the Dust* in Calgary (concurrently!) he couldn't take the role.

After that scheduling snafu (the planned

new character was never used on *The X-Files*) McNulty stayed on the producer's minds. "By the end of the season, they needed this scientist. I don't even think I auditioned for 'Soft Light.' They just said, 'Here is the role. He'll be good for this role.'"

If you think that's the end of the story, you're wrong. Welcome to the *confusing* world of casting. In the third season, McNulty was cast as agent Brian Fuller in "Apocrypha," but the role was fairly small and the actor didn't expect anything else from it. Two days after opening in a theatrical play, *The X-Files* producers phoned the actor to reappear as agent Fuller in "Unrequited." He wasn't able to get out of his theatrical contract, so the offer went to fellow actor, Ryan Michael, who was working at Kevin's home as a finishing carpenter, and the role was changed to agent Cameron Hill.

Most of McNulty's scenes in his three episodes of *The X-Files* are rather straightforward: no aliens, no special effects, no stunts. Even his death scene in "Soft Light" is muted. "I end up being the bad guy in that one. I sell out to Mr. X, then he kills me. You hear the shot and my head just slumps into the camera. So I died at the end of that one."

You can almost hear McNulty grinning when he adds "and then I got resurrected as Agent Fuller." For one of Vancouver's busiest character actors, resurrection is an everyday occurrence.

X48 Our Town

Case Number:	2.24/ #48 (#2x24)
First Sighting:	May 12, 1995
Directed by:	Rob Bowman
Written by:	Frank Spotnitz

GUEST CAST	CHARACTER
Caroline Kava	Doris Kearns
John Milford	Walter "Chic" Chaco
Gary Grubbs	Sheriff Tom Arens
Timothy Webber	Jess Harold
John MacLaren	George Kearns
Robin Mossley	Dr. Vance Randolph
Gabrielle Miller	Paula Gray
Hrothgar Matthews	Mental Patient (Creighton Jones)
Robert Moloney	Worker
Carrie Cain Sparks	Maid

FIELD REPORT

Dudley, Arkansas. Meat is murder in this small town, as George Kearns finds out when a girl leads him to a woodland clearing where a circle of people—and a man in a tribal mask—behead him. Kearns was a meat inspector, and he had been planning to shut down a local processing plant, Chaco Chicken, which had gross health violations. When Mulder and Scully arrive in town, a woman at the plant begins to hallucinate and takes her manager hostage. After the police are forced to shoot the woman, Scully performs an autopsy, finding out in the process that the beautiful *young* woman was born in 1948!

Later, Mulder and the police drag the river and find nine headless skeletons whose bones appear to have been boiled. Mulder thinks there's cannibalism at work here, and visits Walter Chaco's house, where he finds a trophy cabinet full of severed heads. Mulder may be too late though, as Scully has been captured by Chaco and the tribal masked man, and they're preparing to decapitate her at a bonfire ceremony. Will Scully become part of the Chaco Chicken slogan: "Good People, Good Food?"

WITNESS NOTES

Caroline Kava (Doris Kearns) played NYPD Detective Jean Harp in three of Richard Crenna's "Janek" telefilms, including *Murder Times Seven* and *Murder in Black and White*. She also wrote, directed, and produced an award-winning short film, *Polio Water* (1995). Other credits include *Little Nikita* (1988) with Jerry Hardin, and *Born on the Fourth of July* (1989). In the *Quantum Leap* episode "The Leap Home," she played lead character Samuel Beckett's mother.

John Milford (Walter Chaco) was born in 1929, and has had a career in Hollywood since the mid-sixties, where he appeared in shows such as *Gunsmoke, The Untouchables, Men Into Space*, the original *Outer Limits, The Invaders, Voyage to the Bottom of the Sea*, and *Land of the Giants*. In the seventies, Milford guested on *Bigfoot and Wildboy, The Phoenix, Planet of the Apes, The Invisible Man, Gemini*

Man, *The Six Million Dollar Man, The Bionic Woman, Buck Rogers in the Twenty-fifth Century, Spider-Man,* and *Wonder Woman.* And in the highbrow department, he also had a regular role as LAPD Captain Dempsey in *Enos,* the one-season spin-off of *The Dukes Of Hazzard.*

Gary Grubbs (Sheriff Tom Arens) hit Hollywood in the late seventies, working steadily as a character actor. He played Deputy Hamilton to Jerry Hardin's Sheriff Cobb in the telefilm *Gideon's Trumpet* (1980) *and* Deputy Jim Bob to Jerry Hardin's Sheriff Snuffy in the the feature film *Honkytonk Man* (1982). Grubbs later appeared in *The Court Martial of Jackie Robinson,* with *X-Files* star Steven Williams, but as far as we can tell, he did not play a deputy there.

"I love Gary Grubbs, the guy who played the sheriff," said writer Frank Spotnitz in *Shivers.* "For weeks, me, Rob Bowman, Howard [Gordon], and some of the other people kept imitating him, because we thought he played that part perfectly."

Timothy Webber (Jess Harold) is a Toronto-based actor who has appeared in many Canadian films. Early work includes the horror film *Terror Train* (1980), *Midnight Matinee* with William B. Davis, the time travel movie *Millennium* (1989), and the controversial film *The Boys of St. Vincent* (1993), about sexual abuse of young boys by Catholic clergymen.

X49 Anasazi

Case Number:	2.25/ #49 (#2x25)
First Sighting:	May 19, 1995
Directed by:	R. W. Goodwin
Story:	David Duchovny & Chris Carter
Teleplay by:	Chris Carter

GUEST CAST	CHARACTER
Peter Donat	William Mulder
Floyd Red Crow Westerman	Albert Hosteen
Nicholas Lea	Alex Krycek
William B. Davis	Cigarette-Smoking Man
Mitch Pileggi	Assistant Director Walter S. Skinner
Michael David Simms	Senior FBI Agent
Renae Morriseau	Josephine Doane

Ken Camroux	Second Senior Agent
Dakota House	Eric Hosteen
Bernie Coulson	The Thinker (a.k.a. Kenneth J. Soona)
Bruce Harwood	Byers
Dean Haglund	Langly
Tom Braidwood	Frohike
Mitchell Davies	Stealth Man
Paul McLean	Agent Kautz

UNCREDITED

Aureleo Dinunzios	Antonio
Chris Carter	Third Senior Agent
R. W. Goodwin	Gardener
Byron Chief Moon	Father

FIELD REPORT

Farmington, New Mexico/Washington, D.C. The morning after an earthquake, Navajo teenager Eric Hosteen finds a strange humanoid skeleton and a large silver object buried just under the earth in a canyon. Meanwhile, a computer hacker has gained access to the "MJ" files, and shadowy government men from Germany, Japan, and Italy join Cigarette-Smoking Man. The Lone Gunmen arrive at Mulder's apartment to arrange a meeting between him and the hacker. Mulder meets the man, who gives him a digital audio tape (DAT) of the MJ files, which supposedly has all of the Department of Defense (DOD) UFO records from the 1940s forward.

As the conspiracy closes in around them, Mulder and Scully attempt to decipher the tape, only to discover it's written in Navajo code. Skinner confronts Mulder, then Scully, threatening them with expulsion from the FBI if they're hiding anything. Cigarette-Smoking Man meets with Bill Mulder, whose name is in the DOD files, while Mulder tries to arrange a meeting with Mr. X, and Scully finds a Navajo translator. Shortly thereafter, Krycek kills Bill Mulder, framing Mulder for the crime. Fox manages to track down Krycek, but Scully stops him from killing the rogue agent by shooting her own partner in the shoulder.

Fox and Scully go to New Mexico, where "code-talker" Albert Hosteen tells them of the Anasazi, a Native American tribe which may have been abducted by aliens. In the DOD files, Scully finds references to herself and Duane Barry, and she returns to Washington to see Skinner. Fox investigates the metal object in the canyon. He discovers it's a train boxcar filled with what appear to be dead aliens. Mulder is trapped inside when Cigarette-Smoking Man and his clean-up troops arrive and napalm the boxcar.

WITNESS NOTES

Chris Carter makes his first and only appearance in front of the cameras in the scene where Scully is interrogated. (He's sitting at the end of the table.) Director/producer R. W. Goodwin also appears in a brief cameo as a gardener.

Dakota House (Eric Hosteen) was a regular character on the Canadian television series, *North of 60*. He also appeared in the 1993 telefilm *The Diviners*.

Peter Donat played the role of Bill Mulder on several episodes of *The X-Files*.

WITNESS PROFILE

PETER DONAT

Born: January 20, 1928, Kentville, Nova Scotia

Canadian-born Peter Donat is the nephew of actor Robert Donat (not the son, as has been reported elsewhere). He attended the Yale School of Drama, and later appeared both on Broadway and on off-Broadway from 1952 to 1962, winning the Theater World Award for Best Featured Actor in 1957 for his role in *The First Gentleman*. From 1958–1964, Donat also appeared with the Stratford Shakespeare Festival in Canada.

Although he dabbled some in Hollywood, with a role in the 1958 film *Lost Lagoon*, among others, Donat stayed true to the theater. In 1968 he moved to San Francisco and began appearing with the American Conservatory Theater (ACT). During the last twenty years, Donat has appeared in well over fifty productions with ACT, and has directed and written plays as well, including *Sherlock Holmes and the Shakespeare Solution*.

Donat has had film roles in *The Godfather: Part II* (1974), *The Hindenburg* (1975), *The China Syndrome* (1979), *Tucker: The Man and His Dream* (1988), and *The Game* (1997). Telefilm work has included *Mazes and Monsters* (1982) and *Earth Star Voyager* (1988). More recently, Donat played the evil Dr. Mordecai Sahmbi on the syndicated science fiction series *Time Trax*. His genre guest roles include appearances on *Future Cop*, *The Invisible Man*, *Salvage One*, *Voyagers*, and the revived *Outer Limits* series, where he played an evil prep school principal.

Donat shared some of his thoughts on the *X-Files* experience in a letter: "My involvement with *The X-Files* was very sudden and has been very sporadic. It is very well and cleverly produced with a lot of filming know-how and commitment. The role of Fox's father is of great interest to me, of course, but we have had no discussions regarding his great and painful *secret*. I'm sure this will eventually be revealed even though, or perhaps *especially* now that he is dead.

"David Duchovny is very devoted to the series, obviously, and is just fine to work with. I have not yet met his partner-in-crime, Gillian Anderson, but look forward to that at a later date. The hours are long and very concentrated, often going well into the night and early mornings, so the demands on those in the continuing leading roles are immense, especially David, who bears up very well."

Given that Peter Donat has made two appearances on *The X-Files* after his death in this episode, I have no doubt that the actor will be back on the series in the future . . . perhaps to reveal that "great and painful secret!"

THE STEVEN WILLIAMS FILE

Steven Williams.

Name: Steven Williams
Born: January 7, Memphis, Tennessee
Height: 6' 2½"
Weight: 175
Hair: Black
Eyes: Black
Marks: Mustache or beard

His information came with a price, and working with him meant that Agent Mulder knew that he was being used. In a fight, he was as likely to head butt his opponent as to throw a punch, and he wasn't afraid to execute anyone who stood in his way. His loyalty seemed to the cause of truth at times, and to the cause of the conspiracy at other times, but it really lay wholly with the plans he made for himself and his own cause. He was, as they say, not your father's informant. No surprise then that the character played by veteran actor Steven Williams was known only by one letter . . . a letter that defined a generation and named a series . . . X.

Though the roots of Mr. X are steeped in mystery, the background of actor Steven Williams is not so hidden. Williams was born in Memphis, Tennessee, and lived in the nearby farming community of Millington on the farm of his maternal grandparents. His grandfather was a Baptist preacher, giving the young man a religious base in his upbringing. When he was nine, Steven and his mother moved to Chicago, Illinois. A smart kid, he skipped two grades in school. Williams later graduated from Wendell Phillips High School, and enrolled in the General Motors Institute, the local automaker's engineering school.

With the Vietnam war going on, Steven was drafted to serve in the U.S. Army. Luckily, he was not sent to Vietnam but was instead sent to Gilhausen, Germany, where he served in the Army's 2nd Armored Division for two years. It was there that Williams discovered a new passion: boxing. While in the Army, he would become the divisional champion of the United States Army Boxing Team, Middleweight Division.

After he received an honorable discharge, Williams returned to Chicago and began working as a postman. After delivering the mail in sub-zero temperatures for a while, he decided to head for a warmer job. "I actually wanted to be a singer," Williams said in *Cult Times*. "My hero was Johnny Mathis and I wanted to be just like him, but I never did anything about it. I found myself working in the apparel business selling women's clothing in an exclusive area in Chicago. A lot of my customers were employed at the various ad agencies around town, and they would come in and say, 'Boy, you look nice in a shirt and tie. You should try modeling.' Eventually I thought, 'What the heck. If they all think I can do it, then let's give it a shot.' "

Williams quit his job in 1972, and his modeling career did take off, with print ads and commercials using him in their campaigns. Steven began to make other connections as well, in the theater world. He and two friends founded Earth Productions, which toured schools, libraries, and youth centers, presenting adaptations of the classics for the children. "That was one of the best experiences of my professional life," he said in an interview for his official Web site.

Williams also began auditioning for the stage, and began to get roles in the bustling theater scene in Chicago. He worked steadily for the next several years, turning in dynamic performances in such plays as *Taming of the Shrew*, *Purlie*, *All Honorable Men*, and the experimental science fiction play, *Warp*. Over the years, Williams would perform in other cities, earning two nominations for the prestigious Joseph Jefferson Award for the musicals *Joplin* (in which he played all eight male roles, including jazz pianist Scott Joplin) and *Cinderella Brown*. Even today, with his film and television career keeping his slate full, Williams returns to the theater; in Los Angeles and New York he recently won critical acclaim for his role as a family patriarch in *The Letter*.

The Chicago theater work led to other auditions. Williams garnered small roles in such African-American films as the dramatic *Cooley High* (1975), the acclaimed *Mahogany* (1975), and *Monkey Hustle* (1976). In 1979, Williams was cast in a film that would give him much wider exposure: *The Blues Brothers*. Williams played one of a pair of state troopers who chased the title characters throughout the film, usually suffering indignities as a result. The role of a lawman was a switch for Williams, but set a pattern; much of his career would see him as an authority figure.

In 1980, with *Blues Brothers* in release, Williams went to Los Angeles for the first time for publicity on *Dummy*, a telefilm he had done with LeVar Burton and Paul Sorvino. He moved there permanently in 1982, where he began to get steady work as a television guest star and film actor. He appeared on popular shows such as *Dallas* and *L.A. Law*, and a number of action series created by Stephen J. Cannell. And in the dubious honors distinction, he was reportedly the *only* African-American actor of note to guest star in the good ol' boys Southern series *The Dukes of Hazzard*.

In two roles, Williams dealt with issues he still had from his younger days. "I costarred with Chuck Norris in *Missing in Action II*," Williams said in his Web site interview. "The film is a reminder to me that the war in Vietnam is not over. There are men still missing and a negative effect from support that was not given to the men that returned. And a lack of support for the men that are missing. When I was drafted into the Army, I found myself in Germany just as the war in Vietnam was escalating. Even now I wonder why I was passed over. Although I am happy that I didn't have to face what other young Americans faced on those jungles, with the terrible choice of kill or be killed, I still feel the guilt that I think that all of us who missed that war feel. At the time I questioned what I was being saved for."

In 1985, Williams landed his first regular TV role on the series *The Equalizer*, where he played the recurring character of Lt. Jefferson Burnett, an NYPD cop who sometimes worked with private detective Robert McCall, the title character. Williams appeared in six episodes of the first season, then left the series. He didn't have long to wait, though, before gaining another cop role that would make him famous.

Stephen Cannell premiered a new Fox series in April 1987. *21 Jump Street* dealt with social issues with a youthful—and at that time, unknown—cast of young actors including Johnny Depp, Peter DeLuise, Dustin Nguyen, and Holly Robinson. They played young officers who worked undercover at local high schools, dealing with drugs, gangs, prostitution, and other problems of city youth. The group was initially overseen by Captain Richard Jenko (played by Frederic Forest), though he left the series after the sixth episode. Williams was brought in with the seventh episode as Captain Adam Fuller, a by-the-book police officer who was respected and admired by his subordinates. Williams stayed on through the five seasons of *Jump Street*, during which time the series won praise from youth groups for its responsible storylines dealing with social issues.

After starring in ninety-seven episodes of the series, Williams took a new step in his career. He made his directorial debut, directing the final episode, "Second Chances," which aired in May 1991. Today, *21 Jump Street* is in syndication in over sixty countries. The series was also recently purchased by the FX cable network.

Williams didn't stay unemployed for long, jumping into a new series immediately after finishing *Jump Street*. Glen Morgan and James Wong, who were executive story editors and writers for *Jump Street*, were developing a new series with Cannell for Disney. Though actor Stoney Jackson played the title role in the pilot for *Disney Presents: The 100 Lives of Black Jack Savage*, Williams was cast in the role for the short-lived series that followed, which aired in the spring of 1991.

Savage played the roguish ghost of a seventeenth-century pirate, doomed to live for eternity inside a castle unless he used his supernatural powers to save a hundred lives. But if he ventured outside the castle, bat-like creatures known as "Snarks" could capture him and pull him down to Hell! When a high-profile Wall Street criminal, Barry Tarberry (Daniel Hugh Kelly) escaped to the Caribbean island of San Pietro, he just happened to hole up in Savage's castle. The two soon struck a bargain; working together, they would save as many lives as possible, commuting Savage's sentence and making up for Tarberry's misdeeds. The series only lasted seven episodes, but is remembered by fans as an enjoyable and quirky series that deserved a better life.

Williams returned to guest-star status after *Black Jack Savage*, working again in theater and film as well. His largest film role was in *Jason Goes to Hell*, the ninth and final *Friday the 13th* film. He played the role of Creighton Duke, a craggy bounty hunter who seemed to be the only person who knew how to send Jason Voorhees to Hell permanently. Later, Williams almost got to play a superhero when Fox was casting for the lead role in *M.A.N.T.I.S.* Scheduling problems meant that Williams couldn't take the role, however, and it went instead to Carl Lumbly (who later guest starred on *The X-Files*). In a way, the loss of the role was a positive thing for Williams. *M.A.N.T.I.S.* didn't even last a whole season, and the role would have meant Williams wouldn't have been free for *The X-Files*.

In 1995, while still playing the recurring role of Mr. X on *The X-Files*, Williams was offered a role in a new action series, *L.A. Heat*. Williams accepted the lead role of Detective August Brooks, an LAPD detective who's been on the force for sixteen years. Brooks' partner is Detective Chester "Chase" Mc-Donald, played by ex-*Tarzan* Wolf Larson. Brooks is a dedicated family man, and is married to Kendra Lee Brooks (played by Renee Tenison), his childhood sweetheart. When he's off-duty, he runs a boxing gym for underprivileged youths, allowing Williams to display the boxing abilities from his days in the army.

L.A. Heat is currently filming its second season in California. So, why haven't you seen it on television? Because the series has not been syndicated in the U.S. It airs in Europe but is not yet slated to run in the U.S. or Canada.

During his time off, Williams is an active supporter of a variety of youth-oriented causes, volunteering his time and energy to the Make-a-Wish Foundation, Alta Bates Hospital, Children's Cancer Center, and many other charities. He is also a member of a celebrity committee for the Center to Prevent Hand-gun Violence and an avid proponent of gun control legislation. "When I was nineteen, my friends and I were held up at gunpoint. Two of my friends and I were shot," Williams says in his web site interview. "I still carry the bullet in my shoulder. Thankfully, we all survived the shooting. Then, when I was twenty-six, I was held at gunpoint again and robbed. Those two experiences have made a lasting impression on me."

In his time off from filming, Williams enjoys life in Los Angeles. He has been married twice, but is currently single, and he has two daughters (with his first wife), and one granddaughter. His second wife was Ann Geddes, who is still his agent. Steven enjoys singing and loves jazz music, particularly Joe Williams and Shirlie Horn. He also likes shooting pool and playing backgammon with friends, and he returns to the boxing ring regularly.

As for more directing, after his *21 Jump Street* job, Williams feels he has learned quite a bit about the process. "The most important thing is having that vision of what you want to put on the screen," he said in *Dreamwatch*. "I'm interested in writing, eventually, and in producing, eventually. But I'm not ready to do that yet . . . I think once I'm satisfied as an actor, if I feel I've hit a pinnacle of some sort, then I can concentrate on directing or producing or writing."

Meanwhile, there's one role that he plays at all time, as he reveals in his Web site interview: "To be the best Steven Williams that I can be to my friends and family, and the greatest granddad in the world to my granddaughter."

For more information on Steven Williams, check out his official Web site at http://www.celebrity-network.com/actors/stevenwilliams/ or write his official fan club at The Friends of Steven Williams, 105 East Jefferson Blvd., Suite 800, South Bend, IN 46601.

With the violent dispatch of Deep Throat at the end of the first season of *The X-Files*, a second informant was needed. Originally, the part was intended to go to a woman, but the dynamics of the character did not work out. Glen Morgan and James Wong remembered one commanding actor from *21 Jump Street* and *Black Jack Savage*, and called on their old friend Steven Williams to try out for the role of Mr. X, the informant.

"I went in and read for the role, like everybody else, and I simply nailed it," said Williams in the British *X-Files* magazine. "I nailed it with the intensity, the persona, my acting ability—all of that, combined with the fact that these guys knew me and were comfortable with me. I was X. When I entered that room and when I left that room, I was X."

That isn't to say that landing the mysterious role was easy, as Williams went explained in *Fangoria*. "I really knew very little about him. It was very frustrating. The information they gave me was more about his attitude than about the character. When you audition, they give you sides [script pages] to read, and it was a certain demeanor they were looking for. He was kind of icy, cold, bureaucratic and very businesslike, but with a little tinge of compassion. The one connective thread he has with Mulder is through the Deep Throat character who got killed. They both knew this man. Deep Throat was either a good friend or a mentor to Mr. X. I'm there because I feel the responsibility to carry on Deep Throat's work with Mulder."

However, Mr. X was quite different from his predecessor, Deep Throat. Even more mysterious and enigmatic, Mr. X stood in the shadows, his contact and warnings to Agent Mulder often conveyed with an element of threat. But that threat was largely carried by Mr. X, who "has something to live for," said Williams in *Dreamwatch*. "We do know he is a survivor. We do know he is in danger. And each time he exposes himself to Mulder, he exposes himself to some other unknown element, and he can be taken off by a sniper's bullet at any moment. That's what his nervousness comes from. It's like 'you're going to get us both killed here, pal,' and he's not ready to go yet!"

Additionally, to the end, nothing about Mr. X or his background was ever known. Unlike Deep Throat who had connections to Cigarette-Smoking Man and Bill Mulder, Mr. X seemed a complete rogue agent, unanswerable to anyone. Even when it appeared Mr. X was working with CSM, the viewer was never quite sure who was working with whom.

Williams relished the enigma, as he explained in *Cult Times*. "I always wanted to be naive about the character. I never did any type of research for the role. I deliberately went in, read the words and left. X has become ambiguous, cloudy, and very mysterious to the public because he is that way to me. That's always been the most attractive part about playing the character. To this day nobody knows who X works for, who his boss is, what he's up to or whether he's human, alien, android, or humanoid. It all began as a giant mystery and that's how it's remained."

That mystery allowed Steven Williams great latitude with his character, and an interesting perspective on the elusive "Truth" that Mulder is searching for. "X wants Mulder to learn the truth from A to Z. I think for a long time the fans were frustrated because whenever X would come on and give these clues to Mulder they would think, 'Why don't you just tell him what the hell you want him to know?' " Williams said in *Cult Times*. "X can't do that. He needs Mulder to learn each component. X knows what's going on and wants the truth out there but if he reveals what he knows it would also expose him to the very people who are trying to cover things up. He's always protecting his own butt and I think that's the basis of the relationship between him and Mulder. I think X just needs for the truth to *happen* and for Mulder and the public to know."

In contrast to the dark, brooding, violent Mr. X, Steven Williams has a laugh that comes easily and a gregarious nature that wins fans over. "People tend to think that the person they see on the screen is the person in real life," Williams said an interview on his official Web site. "I throw them off guard and enjoy watching their reactions when they meet me in person!"

So what exactly is known about Mr. X? His exact position in the government is unknown, though he appeared at times to have been in a higher position than Deep Throat was. He provided information to Mulder reluctantly, eventually showing in several circumstances that he did so solely to reach his own goals. He is intensely paranoid and edgy, aware that his predecessor ended up executed in the middle of the night on a dark road.

Unlike the benign Deep Throat, Mr. X is also capable of violence—and always seems to be on the edge of it—with little apparent provocation. The resonance of Williams's deep voice lends his every statement a barely controlled quality that, combined with his steely gaze and imposing size, magnify the element of danger. It's clear that Mr. X is not a man to mess with, although both Mulder and A.D. Skinner have come to blows with him, and even Scully has had him at gunpoint.

Mulder can only contact Mr. X by putting a masking tape "X" on his apartment window and shining a light behind it, implying that Mr. X has some kind of surveillance on Mulder's apartment. This kind of covert attitude is part of the character's appeal. "Secrecy makes a better plot device," said Williams in *Unofficial Channels*. "Look at the controversy surrounding the character. No one knows if he is a good guy or a bad guy and it is the controversy that stimulates conversations about X. I think that once we learn too much about X, he will no longer be a mysterious character. If we learn too much about X, he could end up like Deep Throat: dead." Prophetic words, and ones that would become true in the opening of the fourth season.

Despite his bloody demise in "Herrenvolk," Mr. X's presence in *The X-Files* is still felt. It was Mr. X that led Mulder to the office of Marita Covarrubias. And behind the scenes, Steven Williams has been active in other *X-Files* projects. He performed the adaptation of "Squeeze" for an audiotape and had his voice sampled for the second *X-Files* CD, *The Truth and the Light.* He was also a presenter at the Annual Sci-Fi Universe Readers' Choice Awards in October 1995 and October 1996.

There will be another chance to see Williams as Mr. X again. A return engagement in the televised world of *The X-Files hasn't* been ruled out, though he won't appear in the movie. Mr. X will appear in *The X-Files* interactive CD-ROM game, set for release in early 1998. The actor filmed the footage in 1997, and this time, players will control whether the man from the shadows lives or dies!

And then there's the *real* mystery of Mr. X. Spotted in a window at the J. Edgar Hoover building, the FBI headquarters, were three masking-tape Xs. Are the Federal Agents trying to summon their own informants, or are they just fans of the popular series? The Truth Is Out There . . .

X26 The Host X28 Sleepless X30 Ascension

"The Host" marks the debut of Mr. X, Mulder's second government informant, though we only see brief glimpses of the character. Mr. X warns the agents that this case is very important if they want the X-Files reopened, and tells him he "has a friend at the FBI."

Mr. X finally makes his first visit to Mulder in "Sleepless," giving him data about the secret military experiments. "The Truth is still out there, but it's never been more dangerous," Mr. X warns Mulder. Later, Scully questions Mulder about whether or not he trusts his new informant.

After Duane Barry's death and Scully's abduction, Mulder tries to see Senator Matheson in "Ascension," but is stopped by Mr. X, who tells him that "They have something on everyone, Mr. Mulder."

The scenes with Steven Williams's hands and the phone in "The Host" were actually filmed during production on "Sleepless," and inserted before airing. That's because the role of Mr. X was originally written for—and filmed with—a woman. Actress Natalya Nigolitch was originally cast in the role of Mr. X, and she actually filmed a set of scenes, but the producers were dissatisfied with the dynamics between the actress and David Duchovny. "We wanted someone who had a much different persona than Deep Throat," said Chris Carter in *Cinefantastique*. "And when you choose to go with a strong, very powerful actor (like Williams), you get quite a different feel."

Coincidentally, Williams knew Nigolitch from his acting days in Chicago theater. "She is a fine actress," Williams said in the British *X-Files* magazine. "It was just that the marriage of the actress and the role was not a good one, (and) no reflection on her acting abilities whatsoever."

In "Sleepless," the shots of Mulder reacting to the woman from the originally-filmed scene were kept. The scenes with Williams were edited in later, with voice-overs smoothing the transitions. Thus, Williams did not actually *work* directly with Duchovny until "Ascension."

X32 One Breath X39 Fresh Bones X41 End Game

Mr. X shows just how formidable an opponent he can be in "One Breath." When a mysterious operative steals a vial of Scully's blood and Mulder gives chase, Mr. X angrily executes the man in front of Mulder. He also tells Mulder that he won't allow himself to be killed like his predecessor, Deep Throat, adding that Mulder is his tool, not the other way around. Later, Mr. X gives Mulder the opportunity for revenge on the people responsible for Scully's abduction, but Mulder stays by the bedside of Scully instead.

In "Fresh Bones," Mr. X appears only to offer Mulder some information about the Folkstone INS Processing Center.

Mulder receives more information from Mr. X, and the rest of the cast meets the shadowy character in "End Game." When Scully tries to contact Mr. X from Mulder's apartment, he leaves upon seeing it's Scully, rather than Mulder, who has signaled him. He's met in the elevator by Assistant Director Walter Skinner. The two scrap in a brutal, bloody, fight in the elevator, with Mr. X getting the upper hand and warning Skinner that he has "killed men for far less." Nevertheless, he gives Skinner Mulder's location.

As an actor, Williams was really able to let loose in "One Breath," which remains one of his favorite episodes of the series. "That was a very intense episode for me," he said in *Cinefantastique*. "[Mr.] X went all the way from a scared, frantic, sweaty character with a gun in Mulder's face to this icy killer when he pops this guy in the head. It was a nice little range for me as an actor to work through."

In the same episode, Mr. X delivered the ready-made plans to execute Mulder's revenge to the agent. "I told Mulder, 'Go wait for these guys,'" Williams continued. "Now that was interesting because it indicated that [Mr.] X was a manipulator, an evil son of a bitch. He was setting Mulder up to kill these guys. I was thinking in terms of what I was telling Mulder. 'You're not quite hard, pal. You're too soft. You're going to have to learn to kill or be killed.' I think that was the lesson that [Mr.] X was trying to teach Mulder."

Williams was unavailable for the establishing shot of Mr. X's night at the opera at the Kennedy Center in Washington, D.C. in "End Game." The scene was shot two days before the episode aired and featured the tuxedoed Washington, D.C. assistant film commissioner standing in for Williams as he walks from the front of the building to a series of columns.

That thrill-packed episode also featured a major brawl between Mr. X and A.D. Skinner, when the FBI boss happens upon Mr. X coming out of the elevator in Mulder's apartment building. "Mitch Pileggi and I talked about this," said Williams in *Cinefantastique*. "Do [Mr.] X and Skinner know each other? Why would we have this confrontation? All of these questions went unanswered, because we don't know." Williams helped choreograph the fight scene with Pileggi, using moves he knew from boxing, as well as from martial arts.

As the scene ends, Mr. X has a gun trained on Skinner, but Skinner warns Mr. X that if he kills him, he'll really be killing two men (himself and the missing Mulder). "We never really resolved that ambiguity that was going on," Williams mused in *Dreamwatch*. "In the next scene you see Skinner showing up looking kind of beat up and he's got the information about Mulder . . . I think what happened is that Skinner talked and convinced X that they are both on the same team, that they both need to save Mulder." Still, he acknowledges that the scene may have been therapeutic for fans. "I think the audience wanted X to get beat up because they were so frustrated with X by then. They were glad somebody kicked his butt and made him give out some information!"

X47 Soft Light   X58 Nisei   X59 731   X72 Wetwired

In "Soft Light," when Mulder reveals to Mr. X the bizarre powers of a scientific researcher, Dr. Banton, Mr. X attempts to abduct the man. Later, Mr. X manipulates Mulder into revealing where Banton is, murders Banton's partner (who is working for Mr. X), and escapes with Banton. Mulder realizes that Mr. X can be just as much a foe as he is a friend.

Mr. X only makes a brief appearance in "Nisei," warning Scully not to let Mulder board a train or his life will be in danger. His role is much larger in "731," when Scully pulls a gun on him and demands to know how to help Mulder and what the microchip implant in her neck is for. Later, Mr. X kills the assassin on the train with Mulder and carries the unconscious Mulder out of the boxcar seconds before it explodes in a huge fireball.

The Plain-Clothed Man (actor Tim Henry), a subordinate agent of Mr. X, delivers news about a mind-control experiment to Mulder in "Wetwired." When Mulder tracks down two conspirators who are involved, Mr. X kills the men. Later, Mr. X reports to the Cigarette-Smoking Man, telling him about the operation, but not revealing to him that it was he and his agent that tipped Mulder off in the first place!

"Soft Light" gave Williams and the writers a new direction for the character to grow in, adding an edge to Mr. X. "It had been a long time since X had done anything," said Frank Spotnitz in *The Truth Is Out There*. "The character really needed to grow." Thus, the concept of Mr. X as the nightmare government operative that Banton is paranoid about was created, and Mr. X suddenly became a little more sinister and ruthless in the pursuit of his own agenda.

When Williams read the "Soft Light" script, he thought that the new direction might have gone too far. "The first thing, X has lost his mind! He's gone crazy," the actor said in *Cinefantastique*. "He was very deceptive. There was an aura of evil, of lying and conniving. X is supposed to be Mulder's friend, Mulder's confidant. But all of a sudden he's using Mulder to find this other guy, which I thought was very, very tricky and sort of strange for X."

Mr. X had a redemption of sorts in the "Nisei/731" two-parter, when he physically saved Mulder's life. "That endeared X to a lot of fans," said Williams in *SFX*. "They finally got a clearer picture of whose side X is on, because nobody ever knows whose side he's on or who he works for. And given the choice between saving this alien on the train, and saving Mulder, X chose Mulder. It made him a little more popular."

The train explosion sequence was easier to film than it looked, but only for one of the stars. The man slung across Williams' shoulder was not David Duchovny, but a double! The explosion was done as a blue screen optical effect, which meant Williams just had to run away from the boxcar carrying the Duchovny double. "We did ten or twelve takes," Williams said in *SFX*. "I'm lugging this kid on my shoulder, take after take, and running away from this train. That was a grueling day, because I'm an old man these days! I can't do it like I used to as a youngster," he said, laughing.

But it was "Wetwired" that really shocked the public, with its scenes of Mr. X meeting with Cigarette-Smoking Man! Williams would have had more scenes in the episode, but he was tied up with filming another project in Los Angeles. Thus, the Plain-Clothed Man was created as a messenger for Mr. X, and Mulder was essentially given an assignment by Mr. X. The agent chafed at the idea, but Williams explained the motivation in the *SFX* interview. "X gets his directives from somewhere, and his job is to get Mulder to discover as much information as he can before he has to take the source of information away. . . . There are certain things that X doesn't know, but he knows that Mulder will ferret around and answer some of those questions. X is in no position to spend the time doing the detective work himself."

So, what about those scenes with CSM? "I knew that scene would create all kinds of questions in the audience's mind as to why these two guys are together," Williams continued. "The way we wanted to play it was that you don't know who is working for whom. I don't know if it came off or not, because the Cigarette-Smoking Man has such authority that you assume he's the boss."

X73 Talitha Cumi   X74 Herrenvolk

Mr. X appears at the old Mulder summer home to warn Mulder about the connection between CSM and Mrs. Mulder in "Talitha Cumi." Later, Mr. X tries to get the alien stiletto from Mulder, but the two have a brutal brawl, pulling their guns on each other and backing up in a stand-off. "You're a dead man, Agent Mulder. One way or another," Mr. X warns him.

Cigarette-Smoking Man leaks word that Mrs. Mulder is in danger in "Herrenvolk," but it's a ruse to find out who the traitor in the conspiracy is. Mr. X warns Scully and reveals a few details of the smallpox conspiracy as well. Later, lured to Mulder's apartment, the shadowy informant is shot to death by one of Cigarette-Smoking Man's assassins. Mr. X drags himself to Mulder's door, and scrawls "SRSG" in his own blood before he dies.

Williams was told to soften up his character some for "Talitha Cumi," an order that he followed but that he doesn't think was successful. The scene between Mulder and Mr. X at the Mulder summer home "didn't work. I knew it wouldn't work from the very beginning," the actor said in *SFX*. "They thought it might work because they wanted to humanize X a bit and not make him such a cold killing machine." Once the producers saw the results, they weren't happy with them. "I spent the whole day looping, trying to make X harder. But you can't do that—it doesn't work physically if your eyes are doing one thing and your voice is doing another."

A desperate Mr. X, perhaps sensing that the game was coming to an end, attacked Mulder in the parking garage, allowing Williams and David Duchovny to have a knock-down-drag-out fight. Williams was disappointed in how much of their fight ended up on the cutting-room floor. "They couldn't find a stunt double for me in Vancouver, so I took a young man named William Washington who is my stunt man on *L.A. Heat* up there with me, and he ended up staging most of that fight," said Williams in *Dreamwatch*. Generally, fight scenes are done with stunt doubles and the principal actors are then brought in for the close-up shots, but Williams and Duchovny were intent on doing much of the brawl close up. "The crew was fascinated with the work David and I did—they kept asking if we were sure we were all right. We really went at it! David is *very* athletic and very good. We did a wonderful fight scene. I was disappointed when I saw the end product because they used the stunt double stuff more than they used my and David's stuff."

With Mr. X's murder in "Herrenvolk," the question fans screamed was why would Chris Carter decide to kill off one of the series' most popular characters . . . *again*? The true answer has not been revealed, but it is most likely a combination of factors, not the least of which was Carter's desire to bring in another woman to the series, a woman who could perhaps be used as a romantic interest for Mulder; with the new character, Marita Covarrubias, he got both an informant *and* a woman who created sparks with Mulder.

Still, Mr. X's death was quite a surprise for fans. "It was such a well-kept secret, but I was so surprised that the internet or the trades or someone hadn't mentioned it beforehand," Williams said in the British *X-Files* magazine. "I had literally not told a soul—I wasn't even going to tell my agent! [Mr.] X going was a big surprise for everyone. I think everyone had assumed it would be Krycek who went."

The "Herrenvolk" scenes between Gillian Anderson and Williams—and the death scenes—had to be reshot. "I went to Vancouver and filmed my scenes with Gillian Anderson and the whole shooting sequence, then went back to Los Angeles," Williams said in *Dreamwatch*. The actor then "got a call about a week later asking me to come back and reshoot it. They were not satisfied with the lighting. *The X-Files* is a show which has a very distinctive look and special lighting, and they did not feel that it looked right in what we had shot . . . but the reason we reshot was just technical; there [were] no changes in the scenes."

"When we first shot it, we had this long, long trail of blood where I drag myself down the hallway from the elevator to the doorway and scrawl out some letters. It was a rather elaborate thing and they wanted to make it as dramatic as possible. . . . It was a sad demise; I don't think a lot of people wanted to see X go, and that was part of the nature of how we filmed that scene."

As for whether or not he'll ever be back on the series, Williams said in the British *X-Files* magazine that "we don't know if he is a clone, or a drone, or what; we don't even know if the man is human. In fact, we don't even know if that was really X gunned down in that hallway, so you don't know if he's really gone. And because I love the show, and I love being on the show, my hope is that somehow that old soap opera thing will happen, and we will see X again."

With resurrection a common theme in the world of *The X-Files*, perhaps someday the fans and Steven Williams will both get their wish, and the mysteries of Mr. X will be explored.

ACTOR CREDITS

STEVEN WILLIAMS

AMERICAN TELEVISION

The A-Team (NBC) #41—"Double Heat," aired October 23, 1984 (third season). Role: Eddie Devane.

Booker (Fox) Steven Williams reprises his *21 Jump Street* role as Capt. Adam Fuller. #1—"Booker," aired September 24, 1989 (first season). #11—"The Red Dot," aired January 14, 1990 (first season).

Dallas (CBS) #138—"Ray's Trial," aired November 11, 1983 (sixth season). Role: unknown.

Diagnosis Murder (CBS) #34—"Standing Eight Count," aired December 9, 1994 (third season). Role: Butch.

Disney Presents: The 100 Lives of Black Jack Savage (NBC) Steven Williams plays the ghostly role of Black Jack Savage as of the second episode (Stoney Jackson played the role in the pilot). Some of the episodes were directed by Kim Manners and David Nutter, and series cocreators Glen Morgan and James Wong wrote several episodes. #2—"A Pirate Story," aired April 5, 1991. #3—"A Day in the Life of Logan Murphy," aired April 12, 1991. #4—"Deals Are Made to be Broken," aired April 19, 1991. #5—"Look for the Union Label," aired May 12, 1991. #6—"The Not-So-Great Dictator," aired May 19, 1991. #7—"For Whom the Wedding Bell Tolls," aired May 26, 1991 (series finale).

The Dukes Of Hazzard (CBS) #85—"Dukes in Danger," aired April 2, 1982 (fourth season finale). Role: Leeman. #119—"High Flyin' Dukes," aired December 9, 1983 (sixth season). Role: Percy.

Encounters: The Hidden Truth (FOX) Steven Williams was the host for a second season relaunch of this "reality" series. #1—"Psychics Among Us," aired November 11, 1995. #2—"Future Fear," aired November 18, 1995. #3—"Mysteries of the Mind," aired January 23, 1996.

The Equalizer (CBS) Steven Williams played the recurring character of Lt. Jefferson Burnett, a police officer who worked with private detective Robert McCall, the title character. #1—"Pilot," aired September 18, 1985 (first season). #2—"China Rain," aired September 25, 1985 (first season). #3—"The Defector," aired October 2, 1985 (first season). #5—"Lady Cop," aired October 16, 1985 (first season). #6—"The Confirmation Day" (working title: "The Family"), aired October 23, 1985 (first season). #9—"Mama's Boy," aired November 13, 1985 (first season).

Gimme a Break! (NBC) "Getting to Know You," aired March 29, 1986 (sixth season). Role: Harvey.

Hangin' With Mr. Cooper (ABC) #11—"Unforgettable," aired January 5, 1993 (first season). Role: Chip Dumars, Robin's overprotective father. Williams also sings in this episode.

Hill Street Blues (NBC) #51—"Moon Over Uranus: The Final Legacy," aired February 10, 1983 (third season). Role: Sonny Freeman.

Hunter (NBC) #1—"Hunter," aired September 18, 1984 (first season premiere). Role: King Hayes. #15—"The Beach Boy," aired April 6, 1985 (first season). Role: Parker LeMay.

L.A. Heat (Syndicated overseas) A syndicated series airing in forty-five countries, but not planned for U.S. airing at this time. Steven Williams plays Detective August Brooks, an LAPD detective, and colead of the series.

L.A. Law (NBC) #21—"Oy Vey, Wilderness," aired April 2, 1987 (first season). Role: Detective Sgt. Phipps. #109—"Spleen It to Me, Lucy," aired November 7, 1991 (sixth season). Role: Merrill, an attorney who's made his reputation coming into death row cases at the eleventh hour and arguing against the death penalty.

Martin (FOX) #50—"I Don't Have the Heart," aired March 27, 1994 (second season). Role: Simon, an impulsive and rich marriage-minded older man.

MacGyver (ABC) #14—"Countdown," aired February 5, 1986 (first season). Role: Charlie Robinson, an old Army buddy of MacGyver's who must help him find a hidden bomb.

Me and the Boys (ABC) #3—"Your Cheatin' Heart," aired October 4, 1994 (first season). Role: Richard.

Models, Inc. (FOX) Williams has a recurring role as Marcus Ballard. #4—"Skin Deep," aired July 20, 1994 (first season). #9—"Old Models Never Die," aired September 7, 1994 (first season).

Murder Among Friends (network unknown) #1—"Pilot," aired 1985. (First season pilot.) Role: unknown.

NYPD Blue (ABC) #45—"E.R.," aired October 24, 1995 (third season premiere). Role: Lt. Nathan Stackhouse, a prison guard who is doing bar stick-ups on the side.

Remington Steele (NBC) #51—"A Pocketful of Steele," aired November 20, 1984 (third season). Role: Police Lt. Balcom. (The episode also guest starred Jerry Hardin.)

Renegade (Syndicated/USA Network) #36—"South of the '98," aired January 17, 1994 (second season). Role: Danny, a man who runs a gym that helps under-privileged kids. #85—"Hard Evidence," aired February 24, 1996 (fourth season). Role: Major Peter Flood, an ex-Air Force man who claims to know of evidence of a crashed UFO in a military base outside Reno.

Sammy and Friends (Fox) #1—"Pilot," aired circa 1994. Role: Malik.

SeaQuest DSV (NBC) #13—"Better Than Martians," aired January 2, 1994 (first season). Role: the first African-American President of the United States.

Sister, Sister (ABC) "Twins Get Fired," aired October 11, 1995 (third season). Role: Gregg.

Stingray (NBC) #11—"The Greeter," aired January 9, 1987 (second season premiere). Role: Tommy Miller, a mentally disturbed Vietnam veteran known as "Greeter," who communicates using baseball jargon.

Street Justice (Syndicated) #38—"Countdown," aired February 22, 1993 (second season). Role: Greg Tyson Sr.

21 Jump Street (FOX/Syndicated) Steven Williams played the regular series role of Captain Adam Fuller, the by-the-book commander of a group of undercover police officers. Williams also made his directorial debut with the final series episode, "Second Chances." Many episodes were directed Kim Manners, Rob Bowman, and David Nutter. Glen Morgan and James Wong wrote almost a dozen episodes and were executive story editors for the series. The series ran five seasons, with Williams debuting in the seventh episode, "Gotta Finish the Riff," airing May 17, 1987, and finishing with the one hundred third episode series finale, "Second Chances," which aired the week of May 19, 1991.

Wiseguy (CBS) #40—"The One That Got Away," aired May 3, 1989 (second season). Role: unknown.

Wizards and Warriors (CBS)   #2—"The Kidnap," aired March 5, 1983 (first season). Role: The Aide.

TELEVISION MOVIES

Dummy (CBS),   Aired May 27, 1979. Role: Julius Lang.
The Marva Collins Story (CBS),   Aired December 1, 1981. Role: Mr. McCloud.
The Lost Honor of Kathryn Beck (CBS),   Aired January 24, 1984. Role: Les Averback.
International Airport (ABC),   Aired May 25, 1985 (pilot telefilm). Role: Frazier.
Silent Witness (NBC),   Aired October 14, 1985. Role: D.A. Ted Gunning.
Triplecross (ABC),   Aired March 17, 1986 (pilot telefilm). Role: Kyle Banks.
Northstar (ABC),   Aired August 10, 1986 (pilot telefilm). Role: National Security Agent.
Dreams of Gold: The Mel Fisher Story (CBS),   Aired November 15, 1986. Role: Mo.
The Court Martial of Jackie Robinson (TNT),   Aired October 15, 1990. Role: Satchel Paige.
The Whereabouts of Jenny (ABC),   Aired January 14, 1991. Role: Mick
Heroes of Desert Storm (ABC),   Aired October 6, 1991. Role: Specialist Alston.
Revolver (NBC),   Aired April 19, 1992 . Role: Ken.
Legacy of Sin: The William Coit Story (FOX),   Aired October 3, 1995. Role: Det. Sexton.

FEATURE FILMS

Cooley High. Released June 1975. Role: Jimmy Lee, a pimp.
Mahogany. Released 1975. Role: unknown.
Monkey Hustle. Released December 1976 . Role: unknown.
Big Apple Birthday: Alice in Wonderland. Released 1978. Role: "More Fairy Tale Folk."
The Blues Brothers. Released June 1980. Role: Illinois State Trooper Mount, who pursues the Blues Brothers throughout the entire film.
Continental Divide. Released September 1981. Role: a bar patron who appears an hour and twenty minutes into the film. (If you blink, you'll miss him.)
Doctor Detroit. Released April 1983. Role: pimp Junior Sweet, who appears in the final four minutes of the film, dragging a woman from a party.
Twilight Zone: The Movie. Released May 1983. Role: Bar patron in the prologue sequence.
The Adventures of Buckaroo Banzai Across the Eighth Dimension. Released August 1984. Role: An alien.
Better off Dead. Released 1985. Role: Tree trimmer with one of the film's best lines: "Man, that's a real shame when folks be throwing away a perfectly good white boy like that."
Missing in Action 2: The Beginning. Released March 1985. Role: Nester.
House. Released January 1986. Role: Cop #4, who questions the lead character about a shooting at his house.
Under the Gun. Released December 26, 1989. Role: Gallagher.
Jason Goes to Hell: The Final Friday. Released August 13, 1993. Role: Tough bounty hunter Creighton Duke, who has the secret to send Jason to his final fate.
Deep Red. Released 1994. Role: Sergeant Eldon James, who wears the largest police badge in movie history.
Corrina, Corrina. Released July 1994. Role: Anthony T. Williams, the suave suitor of Whoopi Goldberg's lead character.
Bloodfist VII: Manhunt. Released 1995. Role: Captain Doyle.

THEATER

The Magic City. Pilot II Theatre. Role: Nelson Shakers.

The Mighty Gents. L.A. Inner City Cultural Center, Los Angeles, California. Role: Braxton.

All Honorable Men. St. Nichols Theatre, Chicago, Illinois. Role: Johnson C. Whittaker.

Joplin. St. Nichols Theatre, Chicago, Illinois. Role: all eight male roles. Nominated for the prestigious Joseph Jefferson Award.

Warp (1979–1980). Organic Theatre, Chicago, Illinois. Role: Ensemble member.

Ceremonies in Dark Old Men. Victory Gardens Theatre, Chicago, Illinois. Role: Blue Haven.

Black Picture Show. Amistad Productions. Role: J. D.

Medal of Honor Rag. Milwaukee Repertory, Milwauke, Wisconsin. Role: Dale Jackson.

Don Juan (1977). Goodman Theater, Chicago, Illinois. Role: La Violet.

Taming of the Shrew. Travel Light Theatre. Role: Lucentio.

Cinderella Brown. Forum Theatre, Chicago, Illinois. Role: Godfrey. Nominated for the prestigious Joseph Jefferson Award.

Purlie. IBC Theatre, Chicago, Illinois. Role: Purlie.

Slow Dance on the Killing Ground. Chicago, Illinois.

The Letter (1995). The Hudson Theatre, Los Angeles, California. Role: William P. Bryant. Reprised the role in March 1997 in New York City.

OTHER CREDITS

Area 51: The Alien Interview (Rocket Pictures). Released 1997. Williams is the host of this direct-to-video docudrama purporting to have footage of an interview with a live alien. Documentary footage is mixed with "dramatic recreations of alleged government interaction with E.B.E.s at Area 51."

The X-Files: "Squeeze" (Harper Collins Audio). Running time: 90 minutes on one cassette tape. Williams is the narrator-performer in this audio adaptation of Ellen Steiber's paperback adaptation of the original script by Glen Morgan and James Wong.

The X-Files: The Truth and the Light (Warner Brothers). Running time: 48:36. Soundtrack available on CD and tape. Composer Mark Snow's themes from various episodes of *The X-Files* are woven together with interspersed dialogue from several of the series actors. Williams's dialogue is used in conjunction with music from "The Erlenmeyer Flask," an episode he was not even in!

The X-Files CD-ROM Game (Fox Interactive). Interactive game with new scenes filmed with Williams. The premise for the story was written by Frank Spotnitz. Players will play a third FBI agent who works with Scully and Mulder, exploring and deducing clues to the conspiracy. Both David Duchovny and Gillian Anderson have filmed scenes, as has Williams, who returns as Mr. X. The real sets from the series have been utilized, although player interactive scenes use full-motion video shot at Vancouver and Seattle locations and in front of blue screens. The CD-ROM is due out in spring 1998 on a PC platform, though other game formats are being developed.

X50 The Blessing Way

Case Number: 3.01/ #50 (#3X01)
First Sighting: September 22, 1995
Directed by: R. W. Goodwin
Written by: Chris Carter

GUEST CAST	CHARACTER
Mitch Pileggi	Assistant Director Walter S. Skinner
Peter Donat	William Mulder
Floyd Red Crow Westerman	Albert Hosteen
Melinda McGraw	Melissa Scully
Sheila Larken	Margaret (Maggie) Scully
Nicholas Lea	Alex Krycek
William B. Davis	Cigarette-Smoking Man
John Neville	Well-Manicured Man
Tom Braidwood	Frohike
Jerry Hardin	Deep Throat
Alf Humphreys	Dr. Mark Pomerantz
Dakota House	Eric Hosteen
Michael David Simms	Senior FBI Agent
Rebecca Toolan	Mrs. Mulder
Don S. Williams	Elder #1
Forbes Angus	Scully's M.D.
Mitchell Davies	Camouflage Man
Benita Ha	Tour Guide
Victor Ian	Minister
Ernie Foort	Security Guard
Lenno Britos	Hispanic Man (Luis Cardinal)

UNCREDITED
Stanley Walsh	Elder #2
John Moore	Elder #3
Martin Evans	Major Domo

FIELD REPORT

Farmington, New Mexico/Washington, D.C. Cigarette-Smoking Man and his "black ops" soldiers break into the home of Albert Hosteen and beat him and his grandson, looking for Mulder and the DOD tape. Shortly afterwards, Scully arrives, but when she checks the wreckage of the boxcar she doesn't find any trace of

her partner. Later, mysterious men stop her and take all the DOD printout documents Scully had with her. Back in Washington, Scully is fired by Skinner, and she soon discovers the DAT tape is missing as well. To make matters worse, Frohike visits her to tell her that The Thinker—the hacker who downloaded the DOD files—has been executed by persons unknown.

Meanwhile, back at the wreckage in New Mexico, Mulder is found, barely alive, by Hosteen and his people. They start him on a mystic road of healing, during which time he hallucinates and sees Deep Throat and his father telling him to go on with his search for the truth. Scully is pulled deeper into the conspiracy as she catches Skinner leaving her apartment, and discovers an implanted computer chip in her own neck. When she's met by a Well-Manicured Man at Bill Mulder's funeral, he warns her that she may be killed soon, by someone she knows. Scully guesses that the "someone" is Skinner, and she goes with the Assistant Director to Mulder's apartment where she pulls a gun on him. Meanwhile, Melissa Scully has gone to her sister's apartment, where she is executed by a Hispanic Man, as Alex Krycek watches from the shadows. And at Mulder's, when a sound distracts Scully, Skinner pulls his gun on her, forcing a stand-off.

WITNESS NOTES

This episode features only Tom Braidwood as Frohike, cutting out both of the other two Lone Gunmen.

This episode is also the first appearance of "The Consortium," the mysterious cabal that seems to be behind the main conspiracies we have witnessed thus far on *The X-Files*. Members include Cigarette-Smoking Man, Well-Manicured Man, Major Domo, and Elders #1,

#2, and #3. Confused over who is who in the group? Of the four latter men, Major Domo (played by Martin Evans) has a goatee, and Elder #1 (played by Don S. Williams) is more heavyset. In *Trust No One*, the Consortium is also called "The Shadowy Syndicate."

Navajo Code Talkers were a real part of World War II, so the DOD files written in code are not stretching the truth too far. A specially adapted version of the Navajo language was used by the Code Talkers; it was impenetrable by not only Americans and Japanese but also by other Navajo! One of the Marines at Iwo Jima was a New Mexican Code Talker, and he had a familiar name: Dennie Hosteen. Albert Hosteen, the Code Talker in the *X-Files* trilogy, was named after the brave Marine.

Floyd Red Crow Westerman (Albert Hosteen) most recently appeared in Johnny Depp's feature film directorial debut, *The Brave* (1997), which also featured a lead role for fellow *X-Files* actor Marshall Bell. Westerman's other film credits include the award-winning *Dances With Wolves* (1990), Oliver Stone's *The Doors* (1991), *Clearcut* (1992), *Lakota Woman: Siege at Wounded Knee* (1994), and *Renegades* (1989), which costarred *Millennium's* Bill Smitrovich. Westerman starred in the excellent ABC miniseries *Son of the Morning Star* (1991) as Sitting Bull, and in the recent CBS miniseries *Buffalo Girls*. He played Ezekial on the recent "Shadow Fall" episode of *Poltergeist: The Legacy* and has a recurring role as Raymond Firewalker on *Walker, Texas Ranger*.

Alf Humphreys (Dr. Mark Pomerantz) appeared in "Powers, Principalities, Thrones, and Dominions," an episode of Chris Carter's *Millennium*.

Michael David Simms (Senior Agent) first appeared in "Ascension." He also had roles in the original film version of *Alien Nation* (1989) and Fox's telefilm *Doctor Who* (1996) and played Ike Turner's lawyer in *What's Love Got to Do With It* (1993).

Mitchell Davies (Camouflage Man) later appeared as Rick Scammel in "Paper Dove," the first season finale of *Millennium*.

Lenno Britos (Hispanic Man / Luis Cardinal) appeared in the "Officer April" episode of *The Commish* with actor Nicholas Lea, making it their first on-screen team-up. Britos played an obnoxious Cuban diplomat in an episode

written by Glen Morgan and James Wong. He also starred alongside William B. Davis in "Do Not Go Gently," an episode of *Poltergeist: The Legacy*. Hmmmm. Do we spy a conspiracy?

X51 Paper Clip

Case Number: 3.02/ #51 (#3X02)
First Sighting: September 29, 1995
Directed by: Rob Bowman
Written by: Chris Carter

GUEST CAST	CHARACTER
Mitch Pileggi	Assistant Director Walter S. Skinner
Walter Gotell	Victor Klemper
Melinda McGraw	Melissa Scully
Sheila Larken	Margaret (Maggie) Scully
Nicholas Lea	Alex Krycek
William B. Davis	Cigarette-Smoking Man
John Neville	Well-Manicured Man
Tom Braidwood	Frohike
Dean Haglund	Langly
Bruce Harwood	Byers
Floyd Red Crow Westerman	Albert Hosteen
Rebecca Toolan	Mrs. Mulder
Don S. Williams	Elder #1
Robert Lewis	ER Doctor
Lenno Britos	Hispanic Man (Luis Cardinal)

UNCREDITED
Stanley Walsh	Elder #2
Peta Brookstone	ICU Nurse
Martin Evans	Major Domo
Tony Morelli	Skinner's Hallway Man

FIELD REPORT

West Virginia / Washington, D.C. Mulder enters his apartment, gun drawn, to find Scully and Skinner in a tense stand-off. The two of them force Skinner to lower his weapon, whereupon he admits that he has the DAT tape to keep it from Cigarette-Smoking Man. Later, the Lone Gunmen identify the men in an early seventies picture, including Bill Mulder and a Nazi scientist! The agents track down the Nazi, who tells them to visit a mining site in West Virginia. Meanwhile, Skinner plays a dangerous game with Cigarette-Smoking Man over who has the stolen DAT tape.

Mulder and Scully find tunnels underneath the mine that are filled with miles of filing cabinets. In each cabinet, smallpox vaccination records have been kept, perhaps on everyone in the U.S. Military men arrive to kill the agents, and Mulder witnesses a UFO above the mining site. Back in Washington, Mulder and Scully meet with Skinner and agree to make a trade: the DAT tape for their lives and Bureau reinstatements. At the hospital where the critically injured Melissa Scully has been taken, Skinner is severely beaten by Krycek and two others. Later, betrayed by Cigarette-Smoking Man, Krycek barely escapes with his life and the DAT tape. As the episode ends, Melissa Scully dies, Well-Manicured Man explains a part of the conspiracy, Mulder questions his mother about his father's involvement in Samantha's abduction, and Skinner plays a trump card on Cigarette-Smoking Man.

WITNESS NOTES

The "aliens" in the mine scenes were all played by young boys, though the experience of working with problematic and fidgety boys so unnerved director Robert Goodwin that he vowed to only use young girls in alien roles in the future. In *The Truth Is Out There*, makeup man Toby Lindala notes that the children are "excited at first. Then you get these costumes on them and about a half-hour later they're saying 'Can I go home now?' "

Walter Gotell (Victor Klemper) is a familiar face to fans of the James Bond film franchise. He played General Anatol Gogol, the chief of the KGB in *The Spy Who Loved Me (1977)*, *Moonraker* (1979), *For Your Eyes Only* (1981), *Octopussy* (1983), *A View to a Kill* (1985), and *The Living Daylights (1987)*. He had earlier appeared as a minor villain, Morzeny, in *From Russia With Love* (1963). Despite a reference in *The X-Files Declassified* to him appearing in *Dr. No* (1962), he did not. His weirdest credit? How about his role as Nazi General Mueller in *Puppetmaster III: Toulan's Revenge* (1991)?

Martin Evans (Major Domo) has appeared in an episode of *MacGyver*, the miniseries *Titanic* (1996), and the telefilm *National Lampoon's Dad's Week Off* (1997).

Tony Morelli, who plays the mysterious man Skinner finds in the hallway outside Melissa's room, is the stunt coordinator for the series. Morelli's character teamed with Hispanic

Man and Alex Krycek to brutalize Skinner in the hospital stairwell.

John Neville appears in *The X-Files* as "Well-Manicured Man."

WITNESS INTERVIEW
JOHN NEVILLE

Born: May 2, 1925, Willesden, London, England

No other actor in this book has quite the theatrical pedigree that John Neville has. The distinguished actor now calls himself an "ex-British actor. I've been a Canadian for twenty-five years. I had a huge career in England as a classical actor." Neville first appeared on the London theater scene in 1946, when he attended the prestigious Royal Academy of Dramatic Art. He worked in every theater in London during the fifties and sixties, starring in and directing plays. He is, perhaps, best known for his role as the tile character in *Alfie*, which opened in mid-1963 and garnered much critical notice. Two years later, in 1965, he would be granted the Order of the British Empire, a high honor in England.

While in England, Neville's film career began with classic films like *The Life of Henry V* (1957), *Oscar Wilde* (1959), *Hamlet* (1959), Peter Ustinov's *Billy Budd* (1962), and the miniseries *The First Churchills* (1970), in which he played John Churchill. Neville had even earned a handful of genre credits at the time, including Disney's *The Shaggy Dog* (1968) and *A Study in Terror* (1965), in which Neville played Sherlock Holmes on the trail of the elusive Jack the Ripper. And then there was the low-budget science fiction film *Unearthly Stranger* (1963), in which Neville had the lead role of a husband who had to deal with a wife from another planet!

Neville came to Canada in 1972, and has worked—or run—some of the most prestigious theaters in that country. He also stopped off on Broadway for *Ghosts* in 1981 with actress Liv Ullman, and played Professor Henry Higgins in the 1991 U.S. National Tour of *My Fair Lady*.

As of 1989, Neville began dividing his time between theater, film, and television productions. Neville played the title role in Terry Gilliam's fantastical masterpiece, *The Adventures of Baron Munchausen* (1989), which unfortunately failed to catch on with audiences due to its rather odd plot and even odder characters. Since *Munchausen*, Neville has appeared in a variety of prestigious projects, although a few credits belong squarely in the "how did this get on his resume" category. In the former are the telefilm *Dieppe* (1993), *The Road to Wellville* (1994), *Little Women* (1994), and the recent eye-candy science fiction film *The Fifth Element* (1997). In the latter category are roles in *Baby's Day Out* (1994), which Neville did as a favor to director John Hughes, and *High School High* (1996). Neville also appeared in one episode of *Star Trek: The Next Generation*, as Sir Isaac Newton.

Neville earned his *X-Files* role as Well-Manicured Man when the casting directors contacted his agent and requested him for the role. "I didn't audition. I guess the casting director in Vancouver knew about me, and what I did, and I was cast in this role with the approval of the bosses." Neville was warned that the role might be a recurring role but didn't have a problem with that. "That's part of the attraction of doing it . . . one can do other things. I did a sitcom in Hollywood for two seasons [*Grand*] and you are trapped. You can do nothing else at all, except in hiatus. But [Well-Manicured Man] being a recurring role, one *can* do other things. In fact, all [the producers] ask is that if you get an offer to do something

interesting, 'Let us know and we will work around it.' It is very attractive in that way."

Well-Manicured Man is probably the most human and sympathetic of the characters in the Consortium, and yet his motives remain an enigma. Even the actor has not been given much information on his back story. "All I know is that he is powerful, so I play 'powerful' out of my lexicon of acting. I am still not quite sure whether he is good or evil, but I suspect evil. I do know he is very, *very* powerful. And that's what I try to do. The only background [is when you] hear the director say to other actors 'Now remember, this is the most powerful man in the world.' So, I listen to that, too. I guess all will be revealed eventually."

Neville's sobriquet is Well-Manicured Man, and yet the character is never shown clipping his nails or going to visit a nail salon. "I don't know how the name came up," Neville admits. "I think that they'd already got the Cigarette-Smoking Man, and I think Well-Manicured Man was the title they gave me. He appears to be more powerful than Cigarette-Smoking Man, and indeed, his *boss*, I suppose. In the very first episode that I ever did I had my hands arched like a church steeple in front of my face just to be sure that they knew [that my hands were well-manicured]. But I don't think anyone has taken any note of it."

The Consortium is clearly involved in a multinational government cover-up, conspiring to cover the existence of extraterrestrials. Does Neville believe in alien life and UFOs? "I am simply not sure about it, to be absolutely honest."

Neville will appear in *Blackwood*, the *X-Files* feature film that is shooting this fall. The film will follow the ending of the fifth season (May 1998), meaning Well-Manicured Man will be surviving the next season of *The X-Files*. "I'm in the script [for the film]," Neville admits. As to how far the conspiracy will progress prior to the film, he can only speculate. "I don't know what may happen. . . . They have an arc that they know where they are going roughly. That arc will end with the movie, which is very hush-hush at the moment."

Neville is sometimes surprised by the recognition the series brings him. "The extraordinary thing about *X-Files* is that no matter where you go, no matter how few episodes you've done, you get recognized. I was doing a movie a couple of weeks ago in Toronto and two technicians came up to me and said 'Is she going to die?' and I said 'Is who going to die?' Because I hadn't watched it for a few episodes and had no idea that Scully had cancer. There is an avid kind of attention paid to this [series] by people who are fans."

As for working on the series itself, Neville wraps up by saying "I think that some of us actors sometimes have to pass on quality in order to make a living, but one *isn't* ashamed of doing *The X-Files.*"

X52 D.P.O.

Case Number:	3.03/ #52 (#3X03)
First Sighting:	October 6, 1995
Directed by:	Kim Manners
Written by:	Howard Gordon

GUEST CAST	CHARACTER
Giovanni Ribisi	Darren Peter Oswald
Jack Black	Bart "Zero" Liquori
Ernie Lively	Sheriff Teller
Karen Witter	Sharon Kiveat
Steve Makaj	Frank Kiveat
Peter Anderson	Stan Buxton
Kate Robbins	Mrs. Oswald
Mar Andersons	Jack Hammond
Brent Chapman	Traffic Cop
Jason Anthony Griffith	First Paramedic

UNCREDITED
Cavan Cunnigham	Second Paramedic
Bonnie Hay	Night Nurse

FIELD REPORT

Connerville Oklahoma. Lightning has struck more than once in this sleepy burg. In fact, it's struck and killed four young men in the last year. Mulder and Scully arrive to investigate, and soon find clues that lead them to Darin P. Oswald, a young slacker who works at an auto repair garage and who is the survivor of a lightning strike. Mulder's eventual theory is that Oswald has the ability to harness the power of lightning, and he's right. Oswald has already used his powers to kill the people who've stood in his way, not to mention a cow or two.

After Mulder and Scully question him, Oswald thinks his friend, Zero, has betrayed him. After killing Zero, Oswald sets his sights on Mrs. Sharon Kiveat, the wife of his boss. Oswald has a crush on the woman, and will stop at nothing—including killing the FBI agents and the Sheriff—to get her.

WITNESS NOTES

Sheriff Teller was named after comedian-magician Teller of the duo Penn and Teller. The pair had approached Chris Carter about appearing in the series.

The dead cow in the field is a real dead cow, borrowed from a slaughterhouse. A fake cow looked . . . well, too *fake*, so the producers prevailed upon the local animal rights watchdog group to let them use a previously deceased bovine. Or maybe it was just sleeping.

Giovanni Ribisi (Darren Peter Oswald) appeared as a regular character on *The Wonder Years* and *Family Album.* In an episode of the popular series *Friends*, he played "Condom Boy." Ribisi also played the son of *Millennium* star Lance Henricksen in Wes Craven's *Mind Ripper* (1995).

Ernie Lively (Sheriff Teller) has been active in Hollywood since the mid-eighties. His credits include the role of the warden in *Shocker* (1989), with Mitch Pileggi, and a part in the telefilm *Legacy of Sin: The William Coit Story* (1995), with Steven Williams.

Karen Witter (Sharon Kiveat) was the March 1982 *Playboy* "Playmate of the Month." Two years later, she appeared as Ms. February in the telefilm *I Married a Centerfold* (1984). She later lost clothes again for the video release *Playmates at Play* (1990). Witter had a regular role on *One Life to Live*, and appeared in the horror film *The Vineyard* (1989), directed by and starring future *X-Files* guest James Hong, as well as Edgar Allan Poe's *Buried Alive* (1990) and *Popcorn* (1991). She has had guest roles on *Sliders, Hercules: The Legendary Journeys, Fortune Hunter*, and *Flipper.*

Bonnie Hay (Night Nurse) is Gillian Anderson's stand-in. She also appeared in "Powers, Principalities, Thrones, and Dominions," an episode of Chris Carter's *Millennium.*

Jack Black starred in "D.P.O."

WITNESS INTERVIEW
JACK BLACK

Born: August 28, 1969, Santa Monica, California

California-born actor Jack Black was a commercial star when he was young, getting his Screen Actor's Guild card because of a commercial for the Atari video game *Pitfall*. In his early teens, Black appeared in a play directed by Tim Robbins, then, after he dropped out of UCLA, Black ended up joining a theater company called The Actor's Gang, also run by Robbins. "I went to the Edinburgh Festival and did a play called *Carnage*. We took that to New York in the public theater, and then Tim Robbins cast me in *Bob Roberts* (1992) directly from that production. He was one of the founding members. He gave me my break. I got an agent after that, and everything has come from that."

Recently, Black has had roles in a pair of high-profile films. In *Waterworld* (1995), "I was the pilot who flew the plane that got harpooned. I was in *Dead Man Walking* (1995), as the oldest brother of Sean Penn, and I go and visit him in prison." Black also had a two-part role on *Picket Fences*. In his first episode, he plays a struggling actor who wears a hot dog costume and gets shot by Deputy Maxine Stewart (Lauren Holly). In the second episode,

Maxine is trapped in a trailer with Black, who is now slightly more successful with a role in *Cats*, which he obsesses over in the most mind-bogglingly hilarious case of method-acting seen on screen for a long time. Black also played Matthew Broderick's best friend in *The Cable Guy* (1996), and, more recently, had a featured role in Tim Burton's gonzo *Mars Attacks!* (1996), as a dopey marine who gets vaporized and turned into a red skeleton at the ceremony to welcome the Martians. Black can also be seen in the remake of *Day of the Jackal*, titled *Jackal*, with Bruce Willis.

During the filming of "D.P.O.," Black stayed away from his costar Giovanni Ribisi. "I was scared of Giovanni. Somebody told me—and I don't even know if it's true—that he was hard-core Dianetics. . . deep, deep in. And then on the set, he was constantly 'Jack, you should come over to my hotel. I got some things I want to talk to you about.' And I was like 'Sure, sure,' and then I flaked on him every time. I tried to avoid him," Black laughs. "I was afraid he was going to try to do some scary Dianetic hypnotism. For some reason that whole thing has always creeped me out . . . It's amusing and scary."

Black had actually auditioned for both the role of Darren Peter Oswald and for the role of Zero. "I wanted some special powers. To be the sidekick of the guy with the power is so clearly inferior," he laughs again. Even without the special powers, Black did get one cool stunt scene, where he was zapped by Oswald's lightning powers. "Those electric bolts were added later. I did have some pyrotechnics on me. It felt [like] they were strapping on some sticks of dynamite but I know it wasn't anything that big. I had a couple of squibs on me that exploded. We did it in one take because it would have been too time-consuming to go back and do it again. There was a nice comfortable foam padding that I fell down on."

What does exploding feel like? "There is no heat, there is no pain. There is a little metal protector under the clothing to protect you, but there is a danger of the sparks flying into your hair. They actually put some ointment in your hair to prevent flame, but there is always the outside chance that you can get burned. Like on *Mars Attacks!*—that scene where I get killed—there was some stuntmen exploding out of their tanks that really got burned. One guy got burned really badly and was sent immediately to the nearest hospital. I heard later that he did not file any complaint or anything because that would be the end of his stunt career."

Black enjoyed his death scene in "D.P.O." even though it wasn't his first. " *Jackal* will be the *third* time that I get killed. I'm starting a trend actually. I didn't do it in *The X-Files*, but in *Mars Attacks!* and [*Jackal*], I say something stupid, I show a little butt crack, and then I get exploded. So that's what they are hiring me for now. I have found my niche!"

Given that this episode of *The X-Files* took place largely in a video arcade, the cast and crew were quite distracted. "The whole crew was interested in playing, and everyone wanted to play this one game. *Virtual Fighter* was the new game at the time and it was highly coveted. It was kind of funny because the actual shooting of the scenes was just an interruption of the playing of the video games," Black laughs.

X53   Clyde Bruckman's Final Repose

Case Number: 3.04/ #53 (#3X04)
First Sighting: October 13, 1995
Directed by: Rob Bowman
Written by: Darin Morgan

GUEST CAST	CHARACTER
Peter Boyle	Clyde Bruckman
Stu Charno	The Killer ("Puppet")
Frank Cassini	Detective Cline
Dwight McFee	Detective Havez
Alex Diakun	Tarot Dealer
Karin Konoval	Madame Zelma
Ken Roberts	Liquor Store Clerk
Jaap Broeker	The Stupendous Yappi
David McKay	Mr. Gordon (Young Husband)
Greg Anderson	Police Photographer

UNCREDITED
Doris Rands   Mrs. Lowell

FIELD REPORT

St. Paul, Minnesota. A killer who considers himself a "puppet" is brutally murdering psychics, and Mulder and Scully are soon on the case. The police have brought in a renowned TV psychic known as The Stupendous Yappi, but the charlatan offers very little of substance. The breakthrough in their case comes from an insurance salesman named Clyde Bruckman who has strong psychic powers; unfortunately, those powers only allow him to see visions of death.

Bruckman is reluctant to help the agents, especially as the troubling visions he's receiving lately show his own rapidly decomposing body. Eventually, Bruckman himself becomes the target of the killer, another psychic who stalks those who claim to be psychic but can't give him the answer to why he does what he does. Will Mulder be killed by the "puppet" killer as foreseen by Bruckman?

WITNESS NOTES

Clyde Bruckman is the name of a real screenwriter who worked in the days of silent films with Buster Keaton and Harold Lloyd, among others. A few of his pictures include *The General* (1927, codirected with Keaton), *Leave 'Em Laughing* (1928), *The Man on the Flying Trapeze* (1935), and *Moon Over Las Vegas* (1944). He later committed suicide. One of his films is glimpsed in an episode of Glen Morgan and James Wong's *Space: Above & Beyond*. That episode, written by Glen Morgan and entitled "R&R," also guest starred David Duchovny in an uncredited role.

The old movie references don't end with Bruckman. Detective Havez is named after Bruckman's sometimes collaborator, Jean C. Havez. Detective Cline is named after another 1920s–40s movie director, Eddie Cline. And the dead man under the car is named Claude Dukenfield, which happens to be the real named of another Bruckman associate, W. C. Fields, who was directed in many of his most famous films by Cline.

Actor/writer **Stu Charno** (The Killer/"Puppet") is married to Sara B. Charno, who wrote the second season *X-Files* episodes, "Aubrey" and "The Calusari." The Charnoses cowrote three episodes of *Star Trek: The Next Generation*: "The Wounded," "New Ground," and "Ethics." Stu has appeared in *Friday the 13th Part II* (1981), *The Chosen* (1981), and Stephen King's *Christine* (1984), as well as the telefilm *Sleepwalkers*, and has had roles in episodes of *Beauty and the Beast* and *Freddy's Nightmares*. Charno visited the Fox offices often when his wife was a staff writer on the series, and met Darin Morgan there. Morgan "had this idea of using someone who looked like me—a person with a fairly benign face—as a serial killer," says Charno in a *Cult Times* interview. "It was really his idea to cast me, and he wrote the story with me in mind. I still had to audition for Chris Carter and Howard Gordon and everyone else, but they all agreed I was right for the part."

Frank Cassini (Detective Cline) had the role of Agent Devlin in "Paper Dove," the first season finale to Chris Carter's *Millennium*. He was partnered with Arlen Jones as Agent Emmerlich. The two were named for Dean Devlin and Roland Emmerlich, the writer and director of *Independence Day* (1996).

Alex Diakun (Tarot Dealer) appeared as Dr. Ephraim in "Lamentation," an episode of Chris Carter's *Millennium*. He was also a victim in *Friday the 13th Part VIII* (1989).

Jaap Broeker, who appears here as The Stupendous Yappi, is David Duchovny's stand-in. The role was created for him by writer Darin Morgan. Broeker was born in Holland.

WITNESS PROFILE
PETER BOYLE

Born: October 18, 1933, Philadelphia, Pennsylvania

Peter Boyle had never intended to be an actor. He decided to pursue acting while he was a monk in the Christian Brothers order, and he moved to New York, where he studied with Uta Hagen. Off-Broadway plays followed, as well as a tour with *The Odd Couple* and work with the Chicago troupe Second City. His earliest roles were small, but in the title role of *Joe* (1970), Boyle moved into the bigger leagues, as his portrayal of the hard-hat bigot garnered him critical notice. He later amused audiences with the role of Frankenstein's monster in Mel Brooks's *Young Frankenstein* (1974). Boyle led the film *Crazy Joe* (1974) and had memorable roles in *Taxi Driver* (1976), *Outland* (1981), *The Dream Team* (1990), and *The Shadow* (1994). Recently, as Dan Breen, Andy Sipowicz's AA buddy on the series *NYPD Blue*, Boyle has created another memorable and tragic character.

Initially, Boyle was not enthusiastic about appearing on the series. In *X-Files Confidential*, producer Robert Goodwin says "Peter is not really interested in episodic television. I don't know whether it was a combination of coercion and bribery or what, but when he first arrived, you could tell he didn't want to be there." By the end of the shoot, Boyle had apparently changed his mind. "He was very exuberantly thanking me for the wonderful experience and asking for t-shirts."

"The part wasn't written for Peter Boyle because it was based on my father, and I had a guy in mind who looks like my father. I always thought of Peter Boyle as too powerful an actor to be this guy," said writer Darin Morgan in *Sci Fi Universe*. Morgan had originally written the role with Bob Newhart in mind "but I saw (Boyle's) stuff last year on *NYPD Blue*, and I thought he was great. Very understated, and I knew he could do it."

"I wasn't at all familiar with the show, but I had to get a crash course in what it is about," Boyle said in a *Dreamwatch* interview. Now that he's done the series, he prefers it to films like *Independence Day*. "I think filmmakers are underestimating the audience a little bit! I am pleased to be a member of the *X-Files* family, but I have never seen a flying saucer, I don't know if there are any good restaurants in Area 51, and I believe that we are the aliens."

Peter Boyle won an Emmy Award as Outstanding Guest Actor in a Drama Series for his role as Clyde Bruckman. But he wasn't the only Emmy-award winner for this episode. Writer Darin Morgan won for Outstanding Writing for a Drama Series. Morgan's was presented to him at a ceremony on September 8, 1996, by none other than Peter Boyle!

X54 The List

Case Number:	3.05/ #54 (#3X05)
First Sighting:	October 20, 1995
Directed by:	Chris Carter
Written by:	Chris Carter

FIELD REPORT

Leon County, Florida. A death row inmate named "Neech" Manley is about to be executed. As his executioners prepare, Manley promises to avenge his death from beyond the grave. Soon after the execution, a guard is found dead in a cell, his body being eaten by maggots. Mulder and Scully are dispatched to investigate, and they hear rumors that Manley had a list of five people he was going to kill. The person who has that list now is an inmate named Roche, and he tries to make a deal with the tough warden—a transfer from the prison in exchange for the remaining names on the list.

The warden and his guards beat Roche to death, but that doesn't stop the killings from continuing. Another guard is killed, followed by the executioner and Manley's lawyer. The last name on the list is the warden's. Mulder believes that the ghost of Manley is responsible for the gruesome revenge murders, but Scully thinks the real killer is a guard named Parmelly, who is having an affair with Manley's wife.

WITNESS NOTES

The executioner, Perry Simon, was named for an NBC executive whom Chris Carter worked with while at the network.

The *X-Files Declassified* lists both Don McKay as "Oates" and Micheal Andaluz as "Tattooed Prisoner" as cast members for this episode, but neither are evident on screen. It is unclear whether or not this is the Don MacKay

who has appeared in several other *X-Files* episodes.

Bokeem Woodbine (Sammon Roque) studied at the LaGuardia High School of Music and Art and the prestigious Dalton School, both in New York City. He was the lead singer for the band Mazard!, and has appeared in some very high-profile films, including *Jason's Lyric* (1994), *Crooklyn* (1994), *Panther* (1995), *Dead Presidents* (1995), and *The Rock* (1996).

Badja Djola (Napoleon "Neech" Manley) debuted in the prison film *Penitentiary* (1979). He later appeared in *Night Shift* (1982), the voodoo film *The Serpent and the Rainbow* (1988), and *Mississippi Burning* (1988). He had a role in the film *A Rage in Harlem* (1991), which was written by John Toles-Bey, who also appears in this episode of *The X-Files*.

Ken Foree (Vincent Parmelly) has a host of horror credits, including the zombie film *Dawn of the Dead* (1978), *Phantom of the Mall: Eric's Revenge* (1989), *Leatherface: Texas Chainsaw Massacre III* (1990), *Death Spa* (1990), and *Sleepstalker* (1995). He also starred with Steven Williams in the telefilm *The Heroes of Desert Storm* (1992).

Actor **Denny Arnold** (Key Guard) was in a bit of discomfort for his "key" scene in this episode. The makeup department hadn't had time to make a body cast of him, so he was covered with special makeup and live maggots for the scene in which Scully examines his corpse on an autopsy table.

Joseph Patrick Finn, the line producer for the series, appeared in this episode's teaser opening as the prison chaplain.

WITNESS PROFILE

J. T. WALSH

Born: September 28, 1943, San Francisco, California

J. T. Walsh is another perfect embodiment of the character actor, and, like many of the others profiled in this book, he was never intended for that role. Walsh was born in San Francisco, but his family moved to Europe when he was five. When he was grown, he enrolled at the University of Rhode Island and graduated with a B.A. in sociology. Walsh worked as a social worker in the South Bronx and wrote for an underground newspaper.

Eventually Walsh moved back to Rhode Island, where he worked as a salesman and a restaurant manager, doing community theater on the side. The theater work paid off, and in 1984, Walsh had his big break in the role of a realty manager in *Glengarry Glenn Ross*, a prestigious David Mamet play running on Broadway. The role won him critical notices, and soon he had embarked on a career in Hollywood. Walsh's film career includes roles in over fifty films, most of them high-profile star vehicles such as *Hannah and Her Sisters* (1986), *Good Morning, Vietnam* (1987), *The Russia House* (1990), Stephen King's *Misery* (1990), *Backdraft* (1991), and *A Few Good Men* (1992). In most of these films, Walsh played either a slightly corrupt white-collar character or a slightly corrupt military man. A second Stephen King movie, *Needful Things* (1993), came the same year as a small independent film, *Some Call It a Sling Blade* (1993), in which Walsh played Charles Bushman, a lead character. He would reprise the role for the award-winning feature film version, *Sling Blade*, in 1996. Walsh recently appeared in the Kurt Russell film *Breakdown* (1997).

Walsh came to do *The X-Files* at a request from Chris Carter. As the actor said in a *Cult Times* interview, "He was directing this particular episode, and it was because of this that I accepted. When Chris directs something it's as if he's filming a movie. He's obsessive-compulsive about getting exactly what he wants, so, you work a lot longer than you would on any television episodic thing, but it's worth it." According to Walsh, Carter also donates his directing fees back to the production's catering budget, meaning anyone working on a Carter-directed episode is fed very well.

For the car crash scene at the episode's close, J. T. Walsh was stunt-doubled by the series' stunt coordinator Tony Morelli. Stunts weren't much of a concern for Walsh though; a fly was. In one scene, a fly had to land on Walsh's face. "The fly was near the end of its life and moved very slowly, almost like it was on Quaaludes," related Walsh to *Cult Times*. "It was moving so sluggishly that as soon as they dropped it into frame it landed the first place it could, which wasn't necessarily the right place."

Last year, Walsh was cast as the malevolent

Frank Bach, head of the top-secret government agency Majestic-12, in NBC's new series *Dark Skies*. Many fans (and critics) railed that the series was an *X-Files* rip-off, but those who watched it discovered that while it was akin to *The X-Files* (aliens, conspiracies and the like), the serialized way it handled the story and the historical context it put events into actually made it an excellent show in its own right. In fact, as the series was set in the fifties and sixties, it could almost have functioned as a prequel to *The X-Files*. Walsh's character was killed in the first season finale.

With his experience on two series that deal with extraterrestrial life, what is Walsh's stance on the subject? "I think there are other forms of life in the universe," he said in an NBC press kit. "I'm just not sure how they would get here."

X55 2Shy

Case Number:	3.06/ #55 (#3X06)
First Sighting:	November 3, 1995
Directed by:	David Nutter
Written by:	Jeffrey Vlaming

GUEST CAST	CHARACTER
Timothy Carhart	Virgil Incanto
Catherine Paolone	Ellen Kaminsky
James Handy	Detective Alan Cross
Kerry Sandomirsky	Joanne (Jo) Steffen
Aloka McLean	Jesse
Suzy Joachim	Jennifer
Glynis Davies	Monica
Randi Lynne	Lauren MacKalvey
William MacDonald	Agent Kazanjian

UNCREDITED	
Brad Wattum	Patrolman
P. J. Prinsloo	Graffiti Tagger
Jan Bailey Mattia	Second Hooker
Lindsey Bourne	Second Hooker's John
Dean McKenzie	Lieutenant Blaine

FIELD REPORT

Cleveland, Ohio. Danger lurks in the internet chat rooms, where an online predator named "2Shy" targets overweight women. Detective Cross calls in the FBI after a woman's body is found in her car, partially decomposed. Mulder and Scully link the death to similar deaths in

Mississippi, where women who had placed "lonely hearts" ads had met with a very dangerous suitor. When Scully attempts to examine the woman's body later, she discovers that a digestive enzyme has liquefied the corpse. More tellingly, most of the fat tissues from the body have disappeared.

A warning is released onto the internet, but Mulder and Scully may be too late to stop Virgil Incanto, a man who feeds on adipose tissue (body fat) to survive. While Mulder tracks down suspects from a list of academics, the fat vampire stalks Ellen Kaminsky. In a surprising showdown, Scully almost becomes one of Incanto's victims.

WITNESS NOTES

Timothy Carhart (Virgil Incanto) may never have played a fat-sucking vampiric serial killer before this episode of *The X-Files*, but he has played a few smarmy villains in his career. He played Geena Davis's redneck rapist-to-be Harlan Puckett in *Thelma and Louise* (1991) and also the villain in *Beverly Hills Cop III* (1994). And he was a victim of fellow *X-Files* guest star Tony Todd in *Candyman II: Farewell to the Flesh* (1995).

The actor had previously auditioned for another role on *The X-Files*, though he didn't become a fan until after "2shy." Carhart saw his character as shy, like his internet screen name, and tried to take some acting cues from Tony Perkins's performance in *Psycho*. But the one thing Perkins didn't have to deal with was vomiting mucus onto his victims. "There was a lot of goop in that episode, said Carhart in *TV Zone*, "and I was the one gooping people. They used three different types of professional goop that they got from a special effects house down in Los Angeles. It had to be exactly the right consistency and stringiness." Before each take, Carhart would wait until the last moment, then an assistant would spoon the goop into his mouth, and he would spit it out on cue once the cameras were rolling.

Catherine Paolone (Ellen Kaminsky) has a number of genre guest-star credits, including appearances in the *Alien Nation* pilot, episodes of *Misfits of Science* and *The Twilight Zone*, and two episodes of *Hard Time on Planet*

Earth, where she had a recurring role as Mrs. Rosetti.

James Handy (Detective Alan Cross) actually costarred with Catherine Paolone in the *Hard Time on Planet Earth* episode "The Way Home." He also appeared in the *Quantum Leap* episode "Temptation Eyes" and feature films such as *Arachnaphobia* (1990), *Guarding Tess* (1994), and *Jumanji* (1995).

Randi Lynne, who played hapless victim Lauren MacKalvey in the opening teaser sequence, had a difficult time with her scene. Her mouth was full of slimy Jell-O, making it tough to breathe. When she was finished filming, the producers sent her flowers.

X56 The Walk

Case Number:	3.07/ #56 (#3X07)
First Sighting:	November 10, 1995
Directed by:	Rob Bowman
Written by:	John Shiban

GUEST CAST	CHARACTER
Thomas Kopache	General Thomas Callahan
Willie Garson	Quinton "Roach" Freely
Don Thompson	Lt. Colonel Victor Stans
Nancy Sorel	Captain Janet Draper
Ian Tracey	Sgt. Leonard 'Rappo' Trimble
Paula Shaw	Ward Nurse
Deryl Hayes	Army Doctor
Rob Lee	Amputee
Andrea Barclay	Frances Callahan
Beatrice Zeilinger	Burly Nurse

UNCREDITED	
Pat Bermel	Therapist in group session
Brennan Kotowich	Trevor Callahan
Paul Dickson	Uniformed Guard
D. Harlan Cutshall	Guard

FIELD REPORT

Ft. Evanston, Maryland. Lt. Colonel Stans has made three suicide attempts, but none have been successful; his latest attempt leaves him horrifyingly burned, but still alive. Stans tells Mulder and Scully that the ghost of a soldier he once knew will not let him die, but the two agents are ordered to suspend their investigation by General Callahan. The military hospital holds many secrets though, including angry

Gulf War veteran and quadruple amputee "Rappo" Trimble.

The death toll mounts as an unseen killer drowns Captain Draper and buries General Callahan's son in his backyard sandbox. Veteran "Roach" Freely is initially blamed, but he, in turn, blames Trimble. Mulder thinks that Trimble might be able to leave his body and kill others with his astral spirit, and his theory is supported in a tense confrontation in the hospital's basement. But how can Mulder fight someone who's invisible?

WITNESS NOTES

Throughout the episode, Lt. Col. Victor Stans is referred to as "Lieutenant Colonel." According to Army regulations, the proper way to address Stans would be "Colonel."

Makeup secrets no. 1: For the scenes featuring Ian Tracey as a quadruple amputee, the actor's legs and arms were hidden inside a specially constructed bed, while makeup effects by Toby Lindala provided realistic "stumps" which took three hours to apply.

Makeup secrets no. 2: For the scene in which actor Don Thompson is submerged in boiling water, Toby Lindala and his crew covered Thompson in gelatin and latex that would flake off as if it were blistered skin.

Thomas Kopache (General Thomas Callahan) really is a Vietnam veteran who served in the U.S. Navy. After leaving the service, he began acting in theater and film. He has had four *Star Trek* appearances: *Star Trek: The Next Generation* ("The Next Phase" and "Emergence"), the feature film *Star Trek: Generations* (1994), and *Star Trek: Voyager* ("The Thaw"). Kopache had previously auditioned for *The X-Files* in early 1995 and was cast in this episode at the last minute, when the previously cast actor was unable to play the role. "When playing General Callahan I tried to draw from the memories of people whom I had met during that time, as well as think of the loss that we all shared because of the war," Kopache said in a *TV Zone* interview. "My character goes on this amazing arc which takes him from being someone pretty much in control of eveything around him to having his life completely devastated."

Willie Garson (Quinton "Roach" Freely)

has been involved with a major U.S. conspiracy twice in Hollywood; he played Lee Harvey Oswald in the feature film *Ruby* (1992) and in the 1992 *Quantum Leap* episode "Lee Harvey Oswald." Recently he appeared in two hit films: *The Rock* (1996) and Tim Burton's *Mars Attacks!* (1996). His weirdest credit would probably be the character "Leech Boy" in the 1993 *Flying Blind* episode "The Bride of Marsh Man 2: The Spawning."

Don Thompson (Lt. Col. Victor Stans) has the feature films *Overboard* (1987) and *Knight Moves* (1992) to his credit.

Ian Tracey (Sgt. Leonard "Rappo" Trimble) was a regular supporting character on *The Commish*, another series that was shot in British Columbia. Coexecutive producer Robert Goodwin had been trying to cast Tracey in a role all three seasons before settling on the role of Trimble.

X57 Oubliette

Case Number:	3.08/ #57 (#3X08)
First Sighting:	November 17, 1995
Directed by:	Kim Manners
Written by:	Charles Grant Craig

GUEST CAST	CHARACTER
Tracey Ellis	Lucy Householder
Michael Chieffo	Carl Wade
Jewel Staite	Amy Jacobs
Ken Ryan	Special Agent Walter Eubanks
Dean Wray	Tow-Truck Driver
Jacques LaLonde	Henry
David Fredericks	Mr. Larken
Sidonie Boll	Myra Jacobs
Robert Underwood	Paramedic
Dolly Scarr	Fast-Food Supervisor
Bonnie Hay	Woman
David Lewis	Young Agent Kreski

UNCREDITED	
Alexa Mardon	Sadie Jacobs

FIELD REPORT

Seattle, Washington. Mulder's emotions are put to a very personal test when he must investigate the abduction of a high school girl named Amy Jacobs. He links her to a waitress named Lucy Householder, a girl who had been abducted at the age of eight years and had escaped her captor (Carl Wade) after five years. Her captor has never been found, and Mulder thinks it might be the same man. Indeed it is, and Lucy appears to have some sort of psychic connection to the captive Amy.

Mulder struggles to get Lucy to help him find Amy before it's too late, but the waitress doesn't want to relive the horror of her childhood. Unfortunately, mounting evidence found by Scully implicates Lucy herself as the abductor, or at the very least an accomplice. Unless she can help the agents find Amy, Lucy may be imprisoned by more than her past. But if she faces her abductor again, will Lucy survive?

WITNESS NOTES

Tracey Ellis (Lucy Householder) was most recently seen on film as the haunting Sybil, the blind seer in *The Crow: City Of Angels* (1996), a contrast to her role as Mother Jane Bux in *The Neverending Story III* (1994). Ellis also appeared in the horror film *Necromancer* (1988).

Lucy Householder was more hard-boiled in the original script, but that changed due to the casting of Ellis in the role. "Then you find an actor like Tracey Ellis," says Chris Carter in *Cinefantastique*, "and the hurt plays on her face. So the character had the same lines of dialogue, but the take on them, by virtue of Tracey's casting, was very interesting. Tracey played a more wounded person."

Michael Chieffo (Carl Wade) has appeared in such genre offerings as *Transylvania Twist* (1990), *Child's Play 3* (1992), and *The Last Action Hero* (1993).

Jewel Staite (Amy Jacobs) was a child model, but she soon grew bored with runway work and began taking acting lessons. At six, she appeared in her first professional job: a commercial for Safeway. She began working regularly in television in the early 1990s, appearing in many telefilms and series, including two episodes of *Are You Afraid of the Dark?*, and two episodes of the Canadian science fiction series *The Odyssey*. Staite has appeared on two series as a regular cast member: Nickelodeon's *Space Cases*, where she played the sonic-screaming rainbow-haired girl from Sat-

urn, Catalina, and the Disney Channel's *Flash Forward*, on which she played Rebecca Fisher.

The original actress cast for the role of Amy Jacobs was deemed too young by the Fox Network, whose executives were uncomfortable with the episode's parallels to the highly publicized Polly Klaas abduction-murder case. They wanted the character and the actress to be fifteen or sixteen years old. Staite was barely thirteen when the role was recast but looked old enough for Fox to approve her.

X58 Nisei

Case Number:	3.09/ #58 (#3X09)
First Sighting:	November 24, 1995
Directed by:	David Nutter
Written by:	Chris Carter, Howard Gordon, Frank Spotnitz

GUEST CAST	CHARACTER
Mitch Pileggi	Assistant Director Walter S. Skinner
Stephen McHattie	The Red-Haired Man (Assassin/Malcolm Gerlach)
Raymond J. Barry	Senator Richard Matheson
Robert Ito	"Dr. Shiro Zama" / Dr. Takeo Ishimaru
Tom Braidwood	Frohike
Dean Haglund	Langly
Bruce Harwood	Byers
Steven Williams	Mr. X
Gillian Barber	Penny Northern
Corrine Koslo	Lottie Holloway
Lori Triolo	Diane
Paul McLean	Coast Guard Officer
Brendan Beiser	Agent Pendrell
Yasuo Sakurai	Kazuo Takeo

UNCREDITED	
Carrie Cain Sparks	Train Station Clerk
Warren Takeuchi	Man killed at train station
Bob Wilde	Limo Driver
Roger Allford	Harbormaster

FIELD REPORT

Knoxville, Tennessee/Allentown, Pennsylvania/ Queensgate, Ohio. Mulder watches a tape of a supposed alien autopsy, which Scully decries as an obvious hoax. When the two agents investigate the man Mulder got the tape from, they find him murdered. Skinner forces the agents to release the murder suspect, a high-ranking

Japanese diplomat, but Mulder keeps a satchel from the crime. Inside it Mulder finds photos of a ship and a list of "Mutual UFO Network" members. When Scully investigates the list, she finds a house full of women, all of whom claim to have been abducted, and all of whom have the same implant Scully had in her neck.

Mulder's own investigations lead him to a ship—which he believes was transporting a UFO—and later to the office of his supposed patron, Senator Matheson. Mulder and Scully are stunned to uncover evidence of a secret group of Japanese scientists who performed experiments under the auspices of clandestine government operatives. Mulder pursues the evidence to a train car he believes is carrying aliens, while Scully discovers a secret about her own abduction and receives a warning from the mysterious Mr. X.

WITNESS NOTES

To add an element of realism, real rangers were used in the "Alien Autopsy" video sequence.

The aliens were played by a set of ten-year-old fraternal twins; the brother played the alien in the autopsy video, while his sister played the alien on the train car.

Robert Ito ("Dr. Shiro Zama" / Dr. Takeo Ishimaru) was a regular on *Quincy, M.E.*, where he played Jack Klugman's assistant coroner, Dr. Sam Fujiyama, the assistant Medical Examiner. And talk about embarrassing films to debut in; the earliest role found for Ito is as "Tang" in *Women of the Prehistoric Planet* (1966), which did not feature *any* women who were actually from the prehistoric planet in question! Ito has roles in most projects that cast Asians, though in typically inaccurate Hollywood fashion, he has been cast as Chinese, Japanese, North Korean, or Vietnamese depending on the project needs. Notable roles include guest spots on *Kung Fu, Highlander,* and *The Outer Limits,* as well as appearances in *Rollerball* (1975), the telefilm *Helter Skelter* (1976) with *X-Files* guest Brad Dourif, *The Adventures of Buckaroo Banzai Across the Eighth Dimension* (1984), and *The Vineyard* (1989) with several other future *X-Files* guests. Recently, Ito was the Godfather in the telefilm of

John Woo's *Once a Thief*, a Fox pilot that co-starred Nicholas Lea. Over the years, Ito has also performed a variety of cartoon voices for *Batman: The Animated Series* (Kyodai Ken/ The Ninja), *Disney's Aladdin* (Xin/Xang), *The Karate Kid* (Miyagi Yakuga), *Rambo* (Black Dragon), and *My Little Pony 'n' Friends*, which does not feature any prehistoric women either.

WITNESS PROFILE
BRENDAN BEISER
Born: April 17, 1970, Boston, Massachusetts

This episode introduced Brendan Beiser as Agent Pendrell, a member of the FBI's Sci-Crime lab. Pendrell was named after Pendrell Street in Vancouver. As the character developed, it was clear that he had a crush on Agent Scully, but that she did not reciprocate his interest. Pendrell would appear in eight more episodes before his unfortunate shooting at the hands of Scott Garrett in "Max."

As an actor, Beiser has done a lot more work on stage than in front of a camera. He graduated from Concordia University and has attended the William Davis Centre, where he worked with Davis himself and advanced acting teacher Marc Bauer.

Beiser has had roles in six films, most of which are independent Canadian productions. These include *Dirty*, in which he plays a computer salesman, *Changes,* and *New Comby* (all years unknown). In *The Vigil*, he plays one of six characters who travel to Seattle to stand vigil for Kurt Cobain. He recently had a principal role in Columbia Pictures' Alicia Silverstone film *Excess Baggage* (1997). He also appeared in the 1996 Hallmark telefilm remake of *Harvey*, in which he played a cop who pursued Harry Dean Anderson's lead character.

X59   731 a.k.a. Nisei (Part 2)

Case Number:	3.10/ #59 (#3X10)
First Sighting:	December 1, 1995
Directed by:	Rob Bowman
Written by:	Frank Spotnitz

FIELD REPORT

Perkey, West Virginia / Washington, D.C.. Mulder enters the moving train in search of Japanese scientist Dr. Zama, while Scully has a tense confrontation with Mr. X. Scully takes her implant to Pendrell, who tells her that it contains circuitry that duplicates the brain's mental processes and memory functions. Scully traces a shipment of the implant's circuitry to the Hansen's Disease Research Facility in West Virginia, where leprous creatures huddle in darkness, fearing the military death squads that have been killing them. Later, Scully is warned by the First Elder from the Shadowy Syndicate that the creatures were the only remaining subjects of Zama's inhuman experiments.

Meanwhile, Mulder has found Zama dead and has gotten trapped in the quarantined boxcar carrying what he believes to be the surviving alien. Unfortunately, Zama's assassin is aboard the boxcar as well, and he's determined to kill Mulder. And if that wasn't enough, the car is wired to explode if anyone tries to open the doors from the inside. Scully races to find the answers that will free Mulder, even as help comes from a very unexpected source.

WITNESS NOTES

Most of the twenty-five experiments/creatures who were executed in scenes at the research facility were children in masks. The open grave contained another twenty-five prop bodies.

Stephen McHattie (Red-Haired Man) has been a busy player in Hollywood since the early seventies, with a rather unique and checkered career. The telefilm *Look What's Happened to Rosemary's Baby* (1976) is counterbalanced by *Mary and Joseph: A Story of Faith* (1979); he played a killer in *Death Valley* (1982), James Dean in the telefilm *James Dean* (1976), and Red Henry in the flop Madonna musical *Bloodhounds of Broadway* (1989). And don't even ask about his role in *Pterodactyl Women From Beverly Hills* (1994)! McHattie is best remembered by genre fans for his role as the villainous Gabriel, the man who murdered Catherine in the third season premiere of *Beauty and the Beast,* and continued his reign of terror through most of that season. Some of those episodes were written by Howard Gordon and Alex Gansa; Gordon chose McHattie for this *X-Files* role based on that association. Oddly enough, despite his sobriquet in this episode, "The Red-Haired Man" clearly does not have red hair.

Michael Puttonen (Conductor) has had two other transportation roles: he was a cab driver in both *Pure Luck* (1991) and the telefilm *The Halfback of Notre Dame* (1996).

Colin Cunningham (Escalante, the leper leader) played the role of Walter Nottingham in *Robin of Locksley* (1996), and recently had roles in the telefilms *Captains Courageous* (1996) and *Volcano: Fire on the Mountain* (1997).

Roy MacGregor, who played a leper in this episode, is one of the makeup men working with Toby Lindala's crew. MacGregor was the leper with the bushy black hair. "We used Roy for that one because his nose is really malleable," Lindala revealed in an interview with *Shivers* magazine. "We taped it right down to his face and it looked almost gone. We put a prosthetic over the top and it disappeared."

X60 Revelations

Case Number:	3.11/ #60 (#3X11)
First Sighting:	December 15, 1995
Directed by:	David Nutter
Written by:	Kim Newton

Hayley Tyson	Susan Kryder
R. Lee Ermey	Reverend Patrick Findley
Lesley Swan	Carina Maywald
Fulvio Cecere	Priest
Nicole Robert	Mrs. Tynes

UNCREDITED
Selina Williams   School Nurse

FIELD REPORT

Loveland, Ohio. After a supposedly stigmatic reverend is killed, Mulder and Scully begin an investigation. He's the eleventh alleged stigmatic to have been killed in the last three years, and a series of religious serial killings may be underway. When young Kevin Kryder begins to bleed from his palms, he may be the next victim. Mulder and Scully visit the boy's father in a mental hospital, where he warns Scully that she will be the one who must come full circle to find the truth.

Kevin is abducted by the strange looking gardener, Owen Jarvis, who later tells Mulder and Scully that he is the boy's guardian angel. Later, Jarvis is killed while trying to protect Kevin, and Scully traces the fingerprints of the killer to powerful executive Simon Gates. Despite the agents' best efforts, Gates kidnaps Kevin and takes him to a recycling plant in nearby Jerusalem, Ohio, to kill him. Gates believes that the true stigmatic child must die for the "New Age" to begin. Will Scully, always the skeptic, allow her faith in God to aid her to rescue Kevin?

WITNESS NOTES

Kevin Zegers (Kevin Kryder) was eleven years old when he landed the role in "Revelations." His family had been in Vancouver to take Kevin to an audition for the role of young Anakin Skywalker in George Lucas's *Star Wars* prequel trilogy. Although he wouldn't know if he would be cast in the trilogy for some time to come, Zegers was cast in *The X-Files*. The young actor had previously appeared as the young Michael J. Fox in *Life With Mikey* (1993), *In the Mouth of Madness* (1995), and in the upcoming science fiction film, *The Specimen*.

Sam Bottoms (Michael Kryder) is the brother of actors Joseph and Timothy Bottoms. His early work includes *The Last Picture Show*

(1971), *The Outlaw Josey Wales* (1976), and Francis Ford Coppola's *Apocalypse Now* (1979). His two genre credits are the horror film *Dolly Dearest* (1992) and the cyborg film *Project Shadowchaser III* (1995).

Kenneth Welsh (Simon Gates / "Millennium Man") is another alumni of *Twin Peaks*, where he played a mad genius named Wyndham Earle, who was FBI agent Dale Cooper's former partner. The busy actor has appeared in over seventy films and telefilms, including *Timecop* (1994) and *Hideaway* (1995).

Michael Berryman (Owen Lee Jarvis) is a familiar face to horror film fans and is best known for his roles in *One Flew Over the Cuckoo's Nest* (1975), *The Hills Have Eyes* (1977), *The Hills Have Eyes II* (1984), and *The Guyver* (1991). He has appeared in over thirty films, usually as a villain or creepy character, due mostly to his size and bizarre looks. Other film credits include *Doc Savage: The Man of Bronze* (1975), *Weird Science* (1985), *My Science Project* (1985), *Star Trek IV: The Voyage Home* (1986), *Double Dragon* (1993) and the espionage spoof *Spy Hard* (1996).

The producers were dissatisfied with the voice of Fulvio Cecere, the actor playing the priest in the final scenes with Scully in a confessional. An uncredited Los Angeles actor looped the lines during post production, and they were digitally inserted.

WITNESS PROFILE
RONALD LEE ERMEY
Born: March 24, 1944, Emporia, Kansas

R. Lee Ermey makes a break with military roles for his appearance on *The X-Files*. The actor was a marine who served in Vietnam and retired on full medical disability. He went to Hollywood, where he first served as a military consultant/technical advisor and starred as a marine boot camp drill instructor in *The Boys in Company C* (1978). He followed that with an uncredited role as a helicopter pilot in Francis Ford Coppola's *Apocalypse Now* (1979), then starred in and advised for *Purple Hearts* (1974).

It was his breakout role as sadistic drill instructor Gunnery Sergeant Hartman in Stanley Kubrick's *Full Metal Jacket* (based on Gustav

Hasford's novel *The Short Timers*) that won the actor critical raves. Ermey began to be offered roles other than military men, such as a mayor in *Mississippi Burning* (1988), a detective in *Hexed* (1993), a police captain in *Seven* (1995), and a judge in *Murder in the First* (1995). On television, he played Brisco County Sr. in an episode of the cult western *The Adventures of Brisco County, Jr.*

Still, the lion's share of Ermey's roles have been military men. He ranked as a general in *Toy Soldiers* (1991), another general in *Body Snatchers* (1993), and a lieutenant colonel in *Under the Hula Moon* (1995). Most recently, Ermey parodied his *Full Metal Jacket* role in Peter Jackson's 1996 ghost film, *The Frighteners*, where he appeared as a ghoulishly rotting drill instructor. Ermey also appeared as the voice of "Sarge" in Disney's computer-animated 1996 film, *Toy Story*, and as Gunnery Sergeant Frank Bougus in the pilot for Glen Morgan and James Wong's *Space: Above & Beyond* series. Finally, he was the voice of Colonel Hapablap in *The Simpsons* episode "Sideshow Bob's Last Gleaming."

Ermey is a friend of Chris Carter's and a fan of *The X-Files*, and was specifically asked to appear in this episode.

X61 War of the Coprophages

Case Number:	3.12/ #61 (#3X12)
First Sighting:	January 5, 1996
Directed by:	Kim Manners
Written by:	Darin Morgan

GUEST CAST	CHARACTER
Bobbie Phillips	Dr. Bambi Berenbaum
Raye Birk	Dr. Jeff Eckerle
Dion Anderson	Sheriff Frass
Bill Dow	Dr. Rick Newton
Alex Bruhanski	Dr. Bugger
Ken Kramer	Dr. Alexander Inanov
Nicole Parker	Chick
Alan Buckley	Dude
Tyler Labine	Stoner
Maria Herrera	Customer #1
Shaw Allan	Customer #2
Norma Wick	Reporter
Wren Robertz	Orderly
Tom Heaton	Resident #1
Bobby L. Stewart	Resident #2
Dawn Stofer	Customer #4
Fiona Roeske	Customer #5

UNCREDITED	
Tony Marr	Motel Manager

FIELD REPORT

Miller's Grove, Massachusetts. Mulder has come to a small town to investigate unidentified colored lights in the sky, but he's soon caught up in an investigation of what appears to be cockroach-related deaths. Back in Washington, D.C., Scully finds her evening continually interrupted by Mulder, whose theories about killer cockroaches keep getting wilder and wilder. Even as the death toll mounts and Mulder finds a metallic cockroach exoskeleton, Scully finds rational explanations.

Investigating a government research facility, Mulder is creeped out by a home full of cockroaches, but his unease is put to rest by the beauteous Dr. Bambi Berenbaum, the scientist in charge of a project studying cockroaches. As a terrified town faces pandemonium due to rumors of killer cockroach attacks, Mulder, Dr. Bambi, a just-arrived Scully, and wheelchairbound robotics expert Dr. Ivanov must find the truth. Are the cockroaches really alien invaders?

WITNESS NOTES

Name that character: TV news reporter Skye Leikin is named for Leikin Skye, a fan who won an *X-Files* trivia contest on American Online, the prize for which was to have her name appear on the series. Phillips's character, Dr. Bambi Berenbaum, was named after a wellrespected authority on insects; Dr. May R. Berenbaum, the head of entymology at the University of Illinois. Dr. Alexander Inanov is a nod to famed biochemist-turned-sciencefiction-author Dr. Isaac Asimov, who, in addition to writing hundreds of books, also created the Three Laws Of Robotics.

In the scene where Scully is bathing Queequeg in the sink, actress Anderson had some problems. In *Entertainment Weekly*, she recounted that the dog had *very* bad gas. "I had to hold my breath while saying my lines. Something was dying inside that dog."

Raye Birk (Dr. Jeff Eckerle) is most easily recognized as the hapless Pahpshmir in *Naked*

Gun: From the Files of Police Squad! (1988) and *Naked Gun 33 1/3: The Final Insult* (1994). Earlier, Birk did have a role in one film that relates directly to this episode: *Martians Go Home* (1990).

Dion Anderson (Sheriff Frass) appeared early in his career in the telefilm *Roe vs. Wade* (1989), which costarred Jerry Hardin. He also appeared alongside this episode's costar Raye Birk in the recent telefilm *Columbo: A Trace of Murder* (1997).

Bill Dow (Dr. Rick Newton) is a Saskatchewan-born actor who has directed and starred in stage productions on the Vancouver theater scene. He has served as the associate artistic director for the Blyth Festival, the Belfry Theatre, and the Vancouver Playhouse in past years, and has over thirty-five theater roles to his credit. He had a role in *The Fly II* (1989), *Legends of the Fall* (1994), and the seal movie *Andre* (1994), in which the seal is actually played by a sea lion. He's had guest roles on *The Commish, 21 Jump Street, The Marshall, Strange Luck, Two,* and *Highlander.*

Alex Bruhanski (Dr. Bugger) was a regular on *The Commish* as Irv, a role which brought him into constant contact with future *X-Files* stars Nicholas Lea and Melinda McGraw.

WITNESS PROFILE
BOBBIE PHILLIPS

Born: January 29, 1968, Charleston, South Carolina

Beware the rage of the X-Philes! Bobbie Phillips touched off a firestorm when fans thought her character, Dr. Bambi Berenbaum, was going to become romantically entangled with Fox Mulder. Fans needn't have worried. Phillips was too busy with her own career to stay with *The X-Files* as a regular.

When Phillips entered college, she intended to be a trial attorney. She decided to take an acting course to better her courtroom skills and, soon after, decided to quit college and move to Los Angeles. Once in town, in 1990, she landed guest roles on episodic television series and in low-budget futuristic science fiction and action films like *TC 2000* (1993) and *Ring of Fire III: Lion Strike* (1994). She also appeared on Showtime's *Red Shoe Diaries.*

After Phillips dyed her naturally blond hair to a darker brown, her career seemed to move

Bobbie Phillips was the beautiful Dr. Bambi in "War of the Coprophages."

forward more quickly. She became a favorite guest on *The Dennis Miller Show* in 1992, though that gig ended when Miller's show *like tanked, baby.* Phillips landed the *X-Files* role, then the role of Julie Costello, the sister of the murder victim in the first season of ABC's critically acclaimed *Murder One.* Following that, she was the female lead in UPN's short-lived Las Vegas anthology series *The Watcher,* after which she was cast as astronaut candidate Lt. Commander Barbara De Santos on the syndicated NASA-based series, *The Cape.*

X62 SYZYGY

Case Number:	3.13/ #62 (#3X13)
First Sighting	January 26, 1996
Directed by:	Rob Bowman
Written by:	Chris Carter

GUEST CAST	CHARACTER
Dana Wheeler-Nicholson	Detective Angela White
Wendy Benson	Margi Kleinjan
Lisa Robin Kelly	Terri Roberts
Garry Davey	Principal Bob Spitz
Denalda Williams	Madame Zirinka
Gabrielle Miller	Brenda Jaycee Summerfield
Ryan Reynolds	Jay "Boom" DeBoom
Tim Dixon	Dr. Richard W. Godfrey

Ryk Brown	Minister
Jeremy Radock	Young Man (Basketball player Eric Bauer)
Russell Porter	Scott Simmons

FIELD REPORT

Comity, Carol County, Utah. Something very unharmonious is happening in Comity, the place known as "The Perfect Harmony City." Three young men have been killed in the last three months, and the town fears that a cult may be responsible. Mulder and Scully arrive in town, bickering and sniping at each other all the way, and are faced with two teenaged girls, Margi and Terri, whose claims of satanic ceremonies and sacrifices is too pat to be believed.

An astrologer, Madame Zirinka, tells the agents that the whole town has gone nuts and that the cause is a rare planetary alignment of Mars, Uranus, and Mercury. Indeed, more deaths follow, but the real cause is Margi and Terri, two girls born on the same date. When the girls hold hands and wish the same curse, it comes true. Mulder and Scully must overcome their constant disagreements to figure out a way to stop the crimes, but it's hormones and a cute teenage boy that turn Margi and Terri against each other . . . for better or for worse.

WITNESS NOTES

Note the similarity of Dr. Richard W. Godfrey's name to that of coexecutive producer Robert W. Goodwin. Since Godfrey was a crossdresser, perhaps this was also a nod to star David Duchovny's time in drag as a character on *Twin Peaks*.

Dana Wheeler-Nicholson (Detective Angela White), who amorously jumped atop Duchovny in one scene during the show, may not have been acting. Duchovny had recently split from girlfriend and onetime *X-Files* actress Perrey Reeves ("3") when he asked Dana to accompany him as his date to the 1996 Golden Globe Awards. That was the year that Duchovny was nominated for Outstanding Performance by an Actor in a Drama Series. Wheeler-Nicholson has had roles in *Circuitry Man* (1990), *My Life's in Turnaround* (1993), and *Tombstone* (1993). She also played opposite Dennis Franz as a regular on his short-lived *Hill Street Blues* spin-off *Beverly Hills*

Buntz, and again in the *N.Y.P.D. Mounted* telefilm (1991).

Wendy Benson (Margi Kleinjan) was a regular on *Muscle*, a *very* short-lived WB series in 1995, on which she played Cleo, an actress with a secret past.

Lisa Robin Kelly (Terri Roberts) screamed loud in the low-budget horror sequel *Amityville: Dollhouse* (1996).

X63 Grotesque

Case Number:	3.14/ #63 (#3X14)
First Sighting:	February 2, 1996
Directed by:	Kim Manners
Written by:	Howard Gordon

GUEST CAST	CHARACTER
Mitch Pileggi	Assistant Director Walter S. Skinner
Levani Outchaneichvili	John Mostow
Kurtwood Smith	Agent Bill Patterson
Greg Thirloway	Agent Greg Nemhauser
Susan Bain	Agent Sheherlis
Kasper Michaels	Young Agent
Zoran Vukelic	Model (Peter)

UNCREDITED	
John Milton Brandon	Aguirre
James McDonnell	Glass Blower
Paul J. Anderson	Paramedic
Amanda O'Leary	Doctor

FIELD REPORT

Washington, D.C. After posing for an art class, a nude model is horribly slashed. Later, the FBI, led by agent Bill Patterson, arrests young Soviet immigrant John Mostow. Looking over the case, Mulder finds that Mostow had been a suspect in seven Russian deaths, claiming that the spirit of a gargoyle had possessed him. Now, Mostow says that the gargoyle spirit has entered someone else; when another dead body is found that bears the same slashing, it appears that Mostow might be right. Patterson, Mulder's ex-mentor from the Investigative Support Unit at Quantico, teases his protege, asking him if he believes the "hounds of Hell" are responsible.

Scully's concerned as Mulder is pulled into the case ever more deeply, "becoming" a monster to catch the monster. After Mulder's prints are found on a bloody murder weapon, Scully and Assistant Director Skinner become even more worried, but they don't know exactly how deep into the monster's head Mulder has gone. In Mostow's studio, Mulder discovers a secret room with hideous gargoyle sculptures, each of which hides a grisly secret. And, he discovers that he has now become the prey of someone very close to him.

WITNESS NOTES

Agent Greg Nemhauser is named after the postproduction supervisor on *The X-Files*, Lori Jo Nemhauser.

Actor **Levani Outchaneichvili** (John Mostow) only lists his first name on screen in this role and in the other three roles we could find him credited for. However, his surname is listed on the official *X-Files* Web site and in official print sources. He also played the Russian killer Yaponchik in the "Maranatha" episode of Chris Carter's *Millennium.* He appeared in the second season episode of *The Sentinel* entitled "Red Dust" as a Russian, and had a role in *Independence Day* (1996) as a Russian pilot. Hmmm, do we sense a theme here?

Outchaneichvili does indeed hail from Russia, and when he was cast for *The X-Files*, he was working on his own independently produced film. Called in to the show on the final day of casting, Levani was reading for the casting director, who stopped him midway and enthusiastically spoke with the writer and producer. "Then they came out and asked if I would mind shaving my head for the part," said Outchaneichvili in an *Xposé* interview. "If I shaved my head and was skinnier than normal, it would help communicate the man's almost religious fanaticism." He agreed, got the part, and went on a crash diet to lose ten pounds. Levani later filmed the scene where Mulder hits him on his birthday.

WITNESS INTERVIEW
KURTWOOD SMITH

Born: July 3, 1943, New Lisbon, Wisconsin

Kurtwood Smith laughs when I read him his description in Leonard Maltin's *Movie Encyclopedia*: "Short, feral-looking actor with a knack for playing slimy villains." "How funny,"

Kurtwood Smith starred as Agent Mulder's mentor, Bill Patterson, in "Grotesque."

Smith says. "You know how tall I am? I'm 6'1", and I weigh 185 lbs. I don't think there's anyone who'd describe me as feral looking." Then there's the fact that they got his birthday and place of birth wrong; although he eventually lived in the Bay Area, he was born in Wisconsin, and—not to pick on Maltin too much— Smith notes that *Entertainment Tonight* lists his birthday a year earlier as well. At least Maltin got the "knack for playing slimy villains" right, though Smith insists that he hasn't played as many villains as people think. He's just made the bad guys he has played memorable. . .

He's played the sadistic cop-killer Clarence Boddicker in *Robocop* (1987), the murderous CIA agent in *Flash Point* (1984), Dr. Josef Goebbels in the miniseries *The Nightmare Years* (1989) the father who drives his son to suicide in *Dead Poets Society* (1989), the government lawyer (two words that always scream "villain") Robert Reynard in *True Believer* (1989) . . . maybe he *has* played a lot of villains! The first of those films listed is what Smith blames for the inaccurate representation of him in Maltin's book. "That all comes from *Robocop*. In *Robocop*, they wanted me to look shorter because I'm about the same height as Peter Weller. So I spent a lot of time crouched down doing that part, and some people just thought I was shorter. Then when I did Goebbels they had to make the other people look taller. They had them on boxes and things. They built little curbs of apple boxes for actors to walk along beside me. I have had a lot of people come up to me and say 'Oh! You're taller than I thought.' Usually it's the other way around. Most actors are shorter than they appear."

Kurtwood's Hollywood break was in a telefilm called *The Renegades* (1982) and the resulting series, in which he played a bureaucratic bad guy who went up against hero Patrick Swayze. He would play that type of role dozens of times in the future, from the aforementioned films to television series such as *The A-Team* and *The Paper Chase*. Smith appeared in the genre films *Star Trek VI: The Undiscovered Country* (1991) as the Federation president, *Fortress* (1993) as a prison warden, and had a role as a Cardassian in an episode of *Star Trek: Deep Space Nine*.

Recently, Smith did voices for the *Eek! The Cat* animated series. He was the Brain in "Eek!'s International Spy Adventure," and in "Eek! Goes to Hell," he played Fido, the devil's dog. A portion of that series was called *The Terrible Thunderlizards*, and Smith regularly voiced General Galapagos, the surly boss of the Thunderlizards. Coming this fall, he just completed voicing an episode of the new *Men in Black* animated series, in which he played a psychotic alien taxi driver. Back in the live-action realm, Smith has just completed work on a feature film called *Shelter*, due out soon, and a telefilm remake of *The Magnificent Seven*, in which he plays a Southern villain.

Smith doesn't mind playing the bad guy. "Usually the villain roles are more interesting than the kind of good guy roles that I get. The villains get the good lines and fun things to do, and you create a strong reaction, a strong impression with audiences. People remember them." Smith says that while he was in a courthouse researching his role in *True Believer*, a prisoner got hold of a gun. As the police hurriedly evacuated the building, one of them stopped Smith, blurted out "You were great in *Robocop*!" then ran off to help apprehend the gun-toting convict.

Smith had not really been a fan of *The X-Files* when he was offered the role of Lt. Col. Marcus Belt in the first season episode "Space," which he turned down. "That was when I first became aware of the show. When they sent me ["Grotesque"], I thought it looked pretty interesting. [Agent Patterson] was based loosely on John Douglas, who has been making the rounds of the talk shows the last few months, and he's had a couple of books out. He's the guy who set up the profiles department for the FBI."

"I read [Douglas's] first book, *Mind Hunter*, and was pretty familiar with who the guy was, so I knew what they where talking about. Of course, although Douglas experienced sort of a mental and physical collapse at one point in his career, he didn't go off the deep end and start killing people. At least not that we know of. Nor does it seem that he has the kind of temperament that Bill Patterson has. It doesn't seem to me that Douglas has that strict authoritarian quality that was necessary for Patterson because of what they were trying to establish between him and Mulder."

Although for most of the episode Agent Patterson seems rather sane, in the end, it is revealed that he has gone too deep into the killer's head, and has become the killer himself. In a tense wrap-up, Mulder chases Patterson across the rooftops, a scene that was difficult to shoot. "There was a lot of running around on rooftops and smashing into Mulder. Some of it was done second unit by the stuntman because my face was in shadow; you weren't supposed to know who was doing it at that time. I had to do some running around later on when I was transformed. [Patterson] freaks out and then he knocks the gun out of Gillian's hand and then takes off. They chase him, and as he's running he starts transforming into the gargoyle. Then when he's up on the rooftops running around having the gun battle with Mulder he is in full gargoyle mask. . ." Smith pauses, then laughingly adds "looking very short and feral."

X64 Piper Maru

Case Number: 3.15/ #64 (#3X15)
First Sighting: February 9, 1996
Directed by: Rob Bowman

Written by:	Frank Spotnitz & Chris Carter

GUEST CAST	CHARACTER
Mitch Pileggi	Assistant Director Walter S. Skinner
Robert Clothier	General Christopher Johansen
Jo Bates	Jeraldine Kallenchuk
Morris Panych	Gray-Haired Man
Nicholas Lea	Alex Krycek
Stephen E. Miller	Wayne Morgan
Ari Solomon	Bernard Gauthier
Paul Batten	Dr. Seizer
Russell Ferrier	Medic
Lenno Britos	Hispanic Man (Luis Cardinal)
Kimberly Unger	Joan Gauthier
Rochelle Greenwood	Waitress
Joel Silverstone	Engineer #1
David Neale	Navy Base Guard
Tom Scholte	Young Christopher Johansen
Robert F. Maier	World War II Pilot
Tegan Moss	Young Dana Scully

UNCREDITED

Darcy Laurie	Engineer #2
Richard Hersley	Capt. Kyle Sanford
Peter Scoular	Sick Crewman
Christine Viner	Young Melissa Scully

FIELD REPORT

San Diego, California / San Francisco, California / Hong Kong / Washington, D.C. A French deep sea diver named Gauthier returns from the depths with an oily black substance covering his eyes. Gauthier pilots the ship, the *Piper Maru*, into a port in San Diego; the rest of the crew have severe burns. When Scully and Mulder arrive on the scene, they discover that the burns come from radiation levels not found in nature. Mulder suspects that the *Piper Maru's* crew may have come in contact with a sunken UFO, but Scully finds clues that point to a downed World War II fighter plane carrying an atomic bomb.

While Scully tracks down leads about the plane, Mulder goes to Gauthier's home, but he's too late; the oily substance has transferred to Gauthier's wife. Mulder is able to track the cargo of the *Piper Maru* to an international salvage broker. He follows the broker to Hong Kong, where he accuses her of selling government secrets. Mulder's triumph is short-lived, however, when he's attacked by Alex Krycek, who is waiting in the broker's office. Meanwhile, A.D. Skinner, who is investigating the

murder of Melissa Scully, is shot in a restaurant by Hispanic Man. Back in Hong Kong, Mulder manages to capture Krycek, but the double agent is taken over by the oily black film, which has traveled to Hong Kong inside Joan Gauthier's body.

WITNESS NOTES

Robert Clothier (Gen. Christopher Johansen) is a noted Vancouver stage actor who was also a regular on the Canadian television series *The Beachcombers*. He also appeared in two episodes of *Ray Bradbury Theater* and the sole modern *remake* episode of *The Outer Limits*, "I, Robot."

Jo Bates (Jeraldine Kallenchuk) has only a handful of noteworthy on-camera credits including roles in the films *Deadly Sins* (1995) and *Fear* (1996), as well as the "Under the Bed" episode of *The Outer Limits*.

Stephen E. Miller (Wayne Morgan) is a writer and theatrical actor who began acting in films in the mid-eighties. He appeared in two projects with *X-Files* costar William B. Davis: the horror film *Midnight Matinee* (1989) and the telefilm *The Little Match Girl* (1987).

Robert F. Maier (World War II Pilot) is the construction coordinator for *The X-Files*.

WITNESS INTERVIEW
ARI SOLOMON

Born: July 12, 1965, Vancouver, British Columbia

Ari Solomon's credit list is rather fun to peruse. On the one hand, he has serious theatrical credits such as *The Diary of Anne Frank* and *Talk Radio*, but on the other hand, he was the dentist in a summer theater version of *Little Shop of Horrors*, and the star of *The Puppetmaster of Lodz*. He's been in a few commercials, one for Campbell's soup, and another for Pass the Pigs.

The 1991 graduate of University of British Columbia has trained with *X-Files* guest Linda Darlow and was in the play *The Beggar's Opera*, directed by another of this episode's guests, Morris Panych. Solomon has appeared on numerous television shows, including *The Black Stallion*, *Hawkeye*, the pilot telefilm for *Two*, and UPN's *Breaker High*. He was also recently featured in the Jason Alexander musi-

Ari Solomon starred as Bernard Gauthier in "Piper
Maru."

cal remake telefilm of *Bye-Bye Birdie*, and did
a voice-over reading a Hebrew scroll for an episode of *Poltergeist: The Legacy*.

Solomon's facility for languages is one of the
things that got him cast in *The X-Files*. "The
character is French, and, while I do speak
French, I wouldn't say that I'm fluent." At the
audition "they gave us the sides [script pages]
in English. We were supposed to come in
knowing them in French. I probably could've
got by translating them myself, but I decided to
go to a guy who was a French teacher, and
some people who've lived in Quebec—so I got
a couple of different versions. So I had it all
ready to go, and I go in there, and of course
everyone else there was French-Canadian. It
was very intimidating. And I went in there and
I did my thing, and I left, and kind of lingered,
because that's what you do, thinking that they
might want to call you back in. Sure enough,
they did."

That's where the hitch in Solomon's plan
came up. He hadn't auditioned for the role of
Gauthier; he had auditioned for the role of one
of the engineers who keeps contact with
Gauthier while he's underwater! "They said,
'How about reading Gauthier?' Well, then I
was screwed. It was in English, and I had to
come in saying it in French! So I thought, *Oh,
what am I going to do?* I translated whatever I

could out of my head and the rest I just made
up. So, I went in there and I did it, and then I
did the English part with the accent. They
seemed to like it and I went home. It's a very
quick casting process because half an hour after I got home, I got the call." Solomon never
told the producers he had faked some of the
French dialogue. He laughs, and says "Once in
a while you have to do that. You have to be
bold."

The diving scenes in the episode were shot
in two or three principal locations, and much of
Solomon's work was in a huge, bulky "Newt
Suit," so named because depth—or more specifically atmosphere absolute pressure (ATA)—
is measured in metric Newtons. "The Newt
Suit is basically a self-contained submarine. It's
a very expensive suit—it costs $500,000—so
that makes it a *lot* more expensive than the
Armani suit I wore in *The Black Stallion*. It can
go to one thousand feet, it's fully self-contained, and self-propelled. It's basically like
your personal submarine. So what they do is
they have a crane lower it into the water, and
then from there on, the person inside is completely on their own. There's no cable or anything once you get to the water. When you're
on the ship, the crane kind of hangs you up on
a stand."

According to Solomon, director Rob Bowman and special effects coordinator Dave
Gauthier (who his character is named after) are
both avid divers. The factory that makes the
Newt Suits is right across the street from the
production studios for *The X-Files*. "The guy
who ran [the company] did the ocean shots. I
wasn't qualified to go in the suit for that, but,
when we shot the close-ups with the plane and
such, that was all done in a tank in their factory
that they use for testing the Newt Suit, so I was
in the suit for that. That was a lot easier, because I got to move around. These suits are
made out of steel, and they're very heavy.
When they're hanging out of the water, there's
no way you can put your hands in the arm part
of the suit, because they're too heavy—you
need the buoyancy of the water to raise the
arms so that you can slip your arms in. So when
you're just hanging in the suit, not in the water,
you have to cross your arms kind of 'tomb-
style.' It really did feel like being in a coffin."

While that might not have been a big issue,

the long hours of hanging, and one other factor made it difficult: Solomon is claustrophobic. "They asked me kind of casually at the callback 'Oh, uh, incidentally you're not, uh, claustrophobic are you?' That was another special challenge for me during this shoot—not to freak out. I just kept repeating to myself, 'You're okay, nothing's gonna happen.' I find, also, that money is a very good incentive—it helps cure claustrophobia!"

One of the other big scenes in the episode is where Mulder finds Gauthier on the floor of his home, covered in black oily residue from the alien substance. "You'll never guess what that stuff is . . . *nobody* would ever guess! That goo, which he refers to as an oily substance, is something that's used with studs in horsing. It's basically . . . it's *horse lubricant!* So I had horse lubricant all over my face." He laughs, adding "That was quite a treat. It's kind of a gray-black substance. They had to keep reapplying it because it does dry up, unlike human lubricant. But again, there's that incentive: the paycheck!"

The scene was filmed on the first day of shooting, and Solomon recalls that David Duchovny was quite a cut-up. "He was in a kind of playful kind of mood that day—maybe it was the horse lubricant, I don't know—and he was goofing around. We got into that kind of twentysomething TV trivia sort of thing, and he was doing the scene from *I Dream of Jeannie*, like how her head and her body separates. [David] was doing a little wiggle, in between takes."

Solomon doesn't expect Gauthier to return on the series, though he wants to make one thing clear. "A lot of people mistakenly thought that I'd died. They say, 'Oh I saw you die on *The X-Files*.' I didn't die. I was just a little *disoriented*. Hosts don't die."

X65 Apocrypha

Case Number: 3.16/ #65 (#3X16)
First Sighting: February 16, 1996
Directed by: Kim Manners
Written by: Frank Spotnitz & Chris
                    Carter

GUEST CAST	CHARACTER
Mitch Pileggi	Assistant Director Walter S. Skinner
John Neville	Well-Manicured Man
William B. Davis	Cigarette-Smoking Man
Tom Braidwood	Frohike
Dean Haglund	Langly
Bruce Harwood	Byers
Nicholas Lea	Alex Krycek
Kevin McNulty	Agent Brian Fuller
Barry Levy	Navy Doctor
Dmitry Chepovetsky	Government Man #1 (Young William Mulder)
Sue Mathew	Agent Caleca
Don S. Williams	Elder #1
Lenno Britos	Hispanic Man (Luis Cardinal)
Frances Flanagan	Nurse
Brendan Beiser	Agent Pendrell
Peter Scoular	Sick Crewman
Jeff Chivers	Armed Man
Martin Evans	Major Domo

UNCREDITED	
Harrison R. Coe	Government Man #3 (Young Deep Throat?)
Craig Warkentin	Government Man #2 (Young Cigarette-Smoking Man)
Eric Breker	Ambulance Driver
Richard Hersley	Captain Kyle Sanford
David Kaye	Doctor
Stanley Walsh	Elder #2

FIELD REPORT

Washington, D.C. / Black Crow, North Dakota. In 1953, a Navy crewman who was sent to salvage a downed plane is dying of radiation burns. He tells a trio of government agents about the black oil that overtook their captain and makes the men promise to find the truth. A young Bill Mulder promises the crewman that he can trust them.

Back in the present, Scully is with the wounded Skinner, while Mulder and Krycek come to Washington. Forced off the road, Mulder and Krycek are separated, with Mulder waking up in the hospital and Krycek showing up at the Cigarette-Smoking Man's office with the stolen DAT tape. Krycek, his eyes swimming with the black fluid, wants to know where the salvaged UFO is, and CSM tells him. The Syndicate members are alarmed by Cigarette-Smoking Man's actions, especially when Mulder unexpectedly calls them in their private sanctum.

Mulder finds out that his suspicions are correct—that the World War II plane was a cover story for a downed UFO salvage. Scully finds the man who shot her sister and A.D. Skinner. Mulder pursues the truth to a missile silo in North Dakota, but Cigarette-Smoking Man is already there. Krycek has been reunited with the UFO that the fluid came from, but many secrets are buried by the mysterious government men as Mulder is forcibly taken away.

WITNESS NOTES

The scene in which The Lone Gunmen ice skate was a lot of work for the three actors. Although Bruce Harwood had trained as a professional ice skater before turning to acting, Tom Braidwood had not skated for years, and Dean Haglund had never skated at all.

X66 Pusher

Case Number:	3.17/ #66 (#3X17)
First Sighting:	February 23, 1996
Directed by:	Rob Bowman
Written by:	Vince Gilligan

GUEST CAST	CHARACTER
Mitch Pileggi	Assistant Director Walter S. Skinner
Robert Wisden	Robert Patrick Modell/ "Pusher"
Vic Polizos	Agent Frank Burst
Roger R. Cross	SWAT Lieutenant
Steve Bacic	Agent Collins
Don MacKay	Judge
Bret J. D. Sheppard	Prosecutor
D. Neil Mark	Deputy Scott Kerber
Meredith Bain-Woodward	Defense Attorney
Julia Arkos	Holly
Ernie Foort	Lobby Guard
Darren Lucas	Lead SWAT Cop

UNCREDITED

Henry Watson	Bailiff
Janyse Jaud	Nurse
Dave Grohl	Man in FBI lobby
Jennifer Youngblood-Grohl	Woman in FBI lobby

FIELD REPORT

Loudoun County, Virginia. A suspect has called the FBI, telling them that he committed a string of murders and made them look like suicides. When the agents capture him at a grocery store, he taunts them, promising that they

won't be able to hold him. Sure enough, he escapes, after causing the driver of the FBI car to crash. Mulder and Scully are soon on the case, aiding Agent Burst. Mulder theorizes that Robert Modell, who calls himself "Pusher," has the power to talk people into doing anything he tells them to do.

After forcing another FBI agent to immolate himself, Modell is caught and is brought to a court hearing. The judge is seemingly controlled by Modell's voice, and frees him, after which Modell taunts Mulder. Deciding to make Mulder his biggest target, Modell fakes his way into the FBI headquarters to gain access to Mulder's records. In the process, Modell "pushes" a secretary into macing and attacking Skinner. Finally, Mulder and Scully must have a tense stand-off with Modell in a hospital, where Mulder may be forced to kill Scully!

WITNESS NOTES

Two *X-Files* staffers appear on prop magazines for this episode: production assistant Danielle Faith Friedman is the cover model for an issue of *American Ronin*, while prop master Ken Hawryliw appears in an inset photo on top of the *Weekly World Informer*.

Robert Wisden (Robert Patrick Modell/ "Pusher") was a semiregular on the Canadian science fiction series *The Odyssey*. He played the role of Brad Ziegler, the mysterious leader of a parallel world who ruled the anarchy-filled planet from his abode in a tower. In *X-Files Confidential*, director Rob Bowman says he "thought Robert Wisden was great as 'Pusher.' He is a very energized kind of confident actor with lots of ideas of his own. It took me about a day and a half to get it into him, and then I never had to speak to him again because he had that look in his eyes."

Vic Polizos (Agent Frank Burst) is a burly actor who has appeared on many popular shows, including *St. Elsewhere, MacGyver, Picket Fences,* and *The Pretender*. The actor also appeared in three horror films: *C.H.U.D.* (1984), *Night of the Creeps* (1986), and Stephen King's *Graveyard Shift* (1990), with future *X-Files* guest Brad Dourif. Polizos previously portrayed an FBI interrogator in *The Falcon and the Snowman* (1984), and he holds the distinction of being the only actor in this book (that we're aware of) to have appeared in a Muppet movie: *The Muppets Take Manhattan* (1984).

Don MacKay (Judge) showed up as a pathologist in the "Lamentation" episode of Chris Carter's *Millennium*. MacKay has over thirty films and telefilms to his credit, and has guest starred on many Vancouver-based series. He costarred in *American Boyfriends* (1989) with Nicholas Lea.

Dave Grohl and his (then) wife, **Jennifer Youngblood-Grohl**, were two extras who passed behind "Pusher" as he moved through the FBI headquarters lobby. Dave is leader of the alternative rock band Foo Fighters, which recorded the song "Down in the Park" for the first *X-Files* CD. Prior to that band, Dave was the drummer in the popular grunge band Nirvana.

X67 Teso Dos Bichos

Case Number: 3.18/ #67 (#3X18)
First Sighting: March 8, 1996
Directed by: Kim Manners
Written by: John Shiban

GUEST CAST   CHARACTER
Vic Trevino   Dr. Alonzo Bilac
Janne Mortil   Mona Wustner

Gordon Tootoosis   Shaman
Tom McBeath   Dr. Lewton
Ron Sauve   Security Guard Tim Decker
Alan Robertson   Dr. Carl Roosevelt
Garrison Chrisjohn Dr. Winters
Frank Welker   Special Vocal Effects

FIELD REPORT

Boston, Massachusetts. An Amaru urn, excavated in the Ecuadorian highlands, unleashes a curse on those who dug it up. The urn holds the remains of a powerful female shaman who is seemingly protected by the spirit of the jaguar. The cursed object is imported to Boston Museum of Natural History, where it is to be part of an exhibit at the Hall of Indigenous Peoples. Unfortunately, from the moment the urn arrives, savage deaths begin to occur, in-

cluding those of the researchers working on the project.

Mulder and Scully investigate, with Mulder siding squarely on the "curse" theory. Scully thinks that Alonso Bilac, who has accompanied the urn from Ecuador, may be responsible for the deaths, especially after she finds a hallucinogenic liquid at his house. Back at the museum, Mulder has found another dead body, as well as a dead dog and quite a variety of dead rats. Mulder and Scully enter the tunnels beneath the museum to search for the missing Bilac and Dr. Lewton, not knowing that dozens of deadly feral cats await them in the darkness.

WITNESS NOTES

In one of the series' regular in-jokes, Dr. Lewton is named after the producer of the original *Cat People* film (1942), Val Lewton.

Actress Gillian Anderson is allergic to cats, so the cat that attacked her was actually a puppet covered in rabbit fur. Many of the cats in other scenes, particularly those looking through grates, were computer generated by Mat Beck.

Vic Trevino (Dr. Alonzo Bilac) is a regular sight in such direct-to-video fare as *Beastmaster 2: Through the Portal of Time* (1991), *Kill Zone* (1993), *Firehawk* (1993) and *Night of the Running Man* (1994).

Janne Mortil (Mona Wustner) has an early appearance in the ghost story *The Changeling* (1980), and later appeared dressed in mud and furs in *Clan of the Cave Bear* (1986). She was a regular on the series *Street Justice* as Officer Tricia Kelsey.

Gordon Tootoosis (Shaman) is one of the United States' most respected Native American actors. His work includes the telefilms *Lakota Moon* (1992) and *Call of the Wild* (1993), as well as the feature films *Black Robe* (1991), *Legends of the Fall* (1994), and *Lone Star* (1996). In 1995, he was the voice of Chief Powhatan in Disney's *Pocahontas* and was one of the narrators of the TV series *500 Nations*. Tootoosis was also a regular character on the Canadian television series *North of 60*.

Tom McBeath (Dr. Lewton) pops up in a lot of Vancouver-filmed projects, including *Timecop* (1994) and *Hideaway* (1995), as well as the *Outer Limits* episode "If These Walls Could Talk."

Frank **Welker**, who is credited for "Special Vocal Effects," was the voice of the cats, the rats, and the jaguar spirit. Welker is one of the biggest talents in animation and voice-overs. He has been the voice of literally hundreds of animated characters; in fact, it's hard to find a series that hasn't used Welker at one time or another, and many times, Welker plays several characters at once. Industry veterans have marveled over his ability to argue with himself in two completely different voices, as well as his uncanny ability to produce both animal sounds and sound effects. Frank has done special sound effects for many science fiction productions, including computer sounds for the various *Star Trek* series, the voice of Darwin the dolphin on *SeaQuest DSV*, the Martian vocals for *Mars Attacks!* (1996), and most of the Gremlin voices for *Gremlins* (1984) and *Gremlins 2: The New Batch* (1990), just to name a few.

A brief listing of a few of Welker's animation voices follows: *Animaniacs* (Ralph, Buttons, Runt, Flavio Hippo, and Thaddeus Plotz), *Beauty and the Beast* (Footstool), *Bobby's World*, *Bruno the Kid*, *Chip and Dale: Rescue Rangers* (Zipper), *Disney's Aladdin* (Abu, Rajah, Faisal, and Xerxes), *Gargoyles* (Bronx), *Muppet Babies* (Kermit, Skeeter, and Beaker), *Pocahontas* (Flit the hummingbird), *The Real Adventures of Jonny Quest* (Bandit), *The Real Ghostbusters* (Ray Stantz and Slimer), *Scooby-Doo* (Freddy), *The Simpsons* (Santa's Little Helper), *Spider-Man and His Amazing Friends* (Iceman), *Superfriends* (Marvin and Wonder Dog), *Superfriends: The Legendary Super Powers Show* (Darkseid and Kalibak), and *Tiny Toons Adventures* (Gogo, Uncle Stinky, Furrball, Calamity Coyote, Dodo, Byron Basset, and Little Beeper).

X68 Hell Money

Case Number:	3.19/ #68 (#3X19)
First Sighting:	March 29, 1996
Directed by:	Tucker Gates
Written by:	Jeffrey Vlaming

GUEST CAST	CHARACTER
B. D. Wong	Detective Glen Chao
Lucy Alexis Liu	Kim Hsin
James Hong	Hard-Faced Man
Michael Yama	Mr. Shuyang Hsin
Doug Abrahams	Detective Lt. Neary
Ellie Harvik	Organ Procurement Staffer
Derek Loke	Johnny Lo
Donald Fong	Vase Man
Diana Ha	Dr. Wu
Stephen M. D. Chang	Large Man
Paul Wong	Wiry Man (Li Oi-Huan)
UNCREDITED	
Ed Hong-Louie	Money Man
Graham Shiels	Night Watchman

FIELD REPORT

Chinatown, San Francisco, California. A young Chinese immigrant is burned alive in a crematory oven by three black-garbed ghostly figures. Mulder and Scully come to the case aided by Detective Glen Chao, and they find the word "ghost" scratched into the oven and burnt evidence of hell money. Chao explains that hell money is burned during the Festival of Hungry Spirits by those who owe debts to ghosts. Elsewhere in Chinatown, an elderly man, Mr. Hsin, cannot afford to pay for an important operation for his daughter, so he goes to a gambling den.

In the smoky room, Chinese men vie for a satchel full of money; if they choose the one white tile from a jar full of red tiles, they get the money; if they choose a red tile, they are taken to a doctor, and a body part is removed. Mulder and Scully soon realize that a black market body parts ring is being run from Chinatown, but when Chao is badly beaten and Hsin loses an eye, the stakes get tougher. Is Detective Chao involved in the ring? And when Hsin plays again, will he lose everything?

WITNESS NOTES

Neither Michael Yama nor Lucy Alexis Liu spoke the Cantonese dialect needed for the episode so their dialogue was looped in post-production. Yama is Japanese, and Liu is Chinese, but she speaks with a Mandarin accent.

Lucy Alexis Liu (Kim Hsin) had a powerful role in the early 1997 *NYPD Blue* episode "A Wrenching Experience," as a Chinese babysitter whose actions had possibly killed the child she was caretaking.

James Hong (Hard-Faced Man) appeared in the classic science fiction movie *Blade Runner* (1982). His character, Chew,—who made eyes for replicants—uttered the line "I only do eyes!" In this episode of *X-Files*, Hong plays a doctor who takes people's eyes out (among other organs) and a jar of eyes is visible in one scene. Hong has appeared in over one hundred films and telefilms, and another three hundred-plus television shows. Like Kurtwood Smith, he is often cast as a villain. Hong was a regular on the series *The New Adventures of Charlie Chan* (1957), and once auditioned for the role of Mr. Sulu on a then-unknown science fiction series called *Star Trek*. Hong was the villain in *Big Trouble In Little China*, and has appeared in such genre fare as *Colossus: The Forbin Project* (1969), *The Golden Child* (1986) in which he played "Dr. Hong," *The Shadow* (1994), *Tank Girl* (1995), the pilot telefilm of *The Adventures of Brisco County, Jr.* (1993), and the horror film *The Vineyard* (1989), which he not only appeared in (with several future *X-Files* guests), but also coproduced and co-wrote. In an interview with *Starburst*, Hong said of his *X-Files* character that "Playing that evil doctor and extracting people's organs made me think of what it was like being that evil man. He had his reasons for doing it—he was doing good for humanity because he was going to give those organs to someone else who needed them. Even a mad doctor has a good side!"

Michael Yama (Shuyang Hsin) appeared in the films *Indiana Jones and the Temple of Doom* (1984) and *The Hidden* (1987), as well as an episode of the time travel series *Voyagers!*

WITNESS PROFILE

B. D. (BRADD) WONG

Born: October 24, 1962, San Francisco, California

B. D. Wong was born and raised in San Francisco, and later acted in theater in New York and Los Angeles. Wong appeared in the west coast company of the musical *La Cage aux Folles* for eight months and took a small role in *The Karate Kid Part II* (1986) before a teacher encouraged him to try out for the title role in *M. Butterfly*.

The rest, as they say, is history. Wong not only won the role of Chinese opera performer

B. D. Wong played a police detective in "Hell Money."

Song Liling and made his debut on Broadway in *M. Butterfly*, but he won the 1988 Tony Award for Best Featured Actor. He also won the Drama Desk Award, Theater World Award, Outer Critics Circle Award, and the Clarence Derwent Award, an unprecedented haul for such a young actor in his first Broadway show.

Hollywood was much more receptive to the now-feted actor, and the next several years saw his film credits multiplying. He was a scientist in *Jurassic Park* (1993) and played a role in the historical AIDS drama *And the Band Played On* (1993). He reprised his role as gay wedding coordinator Howard Weinstein from *Father of the Bride* (1991) in its sequel, *Father of the Bride Part II* (1995). On television, Wong was Margaret Cho's older brother in *All American Girl*, and had a recurring role as "Dr. Sing" on *Sesame Street*. He is now appearing as the prison chaplain in HBO's *Oz* series, which debuted this summer, from producers Barry Levinson and Tom Fontana.

Coming up, Wong will be seen opposite Brad Pitt and David Thewlis in *Seven Years in Tibet* (1997), and also has a substantial role in *The Substitute II* (1997). Wong also voices the lead male character, Shang, in Disney's next full-length animated film, *Mulan*, scheduled for release in summer 1998.

When not acting, Wong is active in political causes; he speaks on college campuses about his awakening as a fourth-generation Asian-American artist, and works in advocacy causes for Asian American actors; Wong also attends and participates in a large number of AIDS-related charity events.

X69 Jose Chung's 'From Outer Space'

Case Number:	3.20/ #69 (#3X20)
First Sighting:	April 12, 1996
Directed by:	Rob Bowman
Written by:	Darin Morgan

GUEST CAST	CHARACTER
Charles Nelson Reilly	Jose Chung
William Lucking	Roky Crikenson
Daniel Quinn	Lieutenant Jack Schaeffer
Jesse "The Body" Ventura	Man in Black #1
Sarah Sawatsky	Chrissy Giorgio
Jason Gaffney	Harold Lamb
Alex Trebek	Man in Black #2
Alex Diakun	Dr. Fingers
Larry Musser	Detective Manners
Allan Zinyk	Blaine Faulker
Andrew Turner	CIA Man
Michael Dobson	Sergeant Hynek
Mina E. Mina	Dr. Hand
Jaap Broeker	The Stupendous Yappi

UNCREDITED	
Terry Arrowsmith	Air Force Man
Mike Fields	Thin Alien #1
Doug Morrow	Thin Alien #2
Chris Waddell	Thin Alien #3

FIELD REPORT

Klass County, Washington. How best to describe this purposely incoherent episode? Famed author Jose Chung is writing a book about alien abductions, and is questioning Scully, a fan of his work. She asks that he report the truth, and he scoffs. "Truth is as subjective as reality." And what a reality! Teenagers are in the process of being abducted by aliens when another alien arrives to confront their all-too human abductors. The teenagers are questioned by police, and while Scully de-

duces that it is a case of date rape, the girl and boy both remember being aboard an alien ship.

Roky, a witness comes forward, even though the "Men in Black" told him not to talk. Another witness, science fiction fan Blaine, says that Mulder and Scully were the ones in black, and that Scully threatened him. Blaine even has a videotape of the incident, entitled *Dead Alien: Truth or Humbug?* Meanwhile, Mulder has encountered a missing Air Force pilot, who later turns up in the wreckage of a crashed top-secret plane. And when Mulder asks Chung not to write his book, his concern is justified. Months later, Jose Chung's *From Outer Space* is released, and Scully is shocked to see just how twisted reality can seem from other points of view.

WITNESS NOTES

The giant monster which appears from the UFO is called "Behemoth from the Planet Harryhausen" in the episode's script. It was a tribute to legendary special effects man Ray Harryhausen, whose stop-motion effects delighted audiences for years. Some of his greatest accomplishments are *The Seventh Voyage of Sinbad* (1958) and *Jason and the Argonauts* (1963). *Clash of the Titans* (1981) was one of the last stop-motion movies Harryhausen has worked on. The Behemoth was actually stunt coordinator Tony Morelli in a seven-foot-high suit. The footage was digitally altered to give it the *appearance* of stop-motion!

William Lucking (Roky Crikenson) acted in a number of mid-eighties genre series, including *The Incredible Hulk, The Greatest American Hero, Voyagers!,* and *Tales of the Gold Monkey.* More recently he has appeared in *Star Trek: Deep Space Nine* and *The Pretender.* Recent genre credits include the cloning telefilm *Duplicates* (1992), *Sleepstalker* (1995), and *The Trigger Effect* (1996). He both starred in and directed the low-budget science fiction telefilm *Humanoid Defender* (1985).

Daniel Quinn (Lieutenant Jack Schaeffer) was the title character in *Scanner Cop* (1994) and *Scanners: The Showdown* (1994).

Jesse "The Body" Ventura, an ex-pro wrestler, appears in the episode as one of the mysterious "Men in Black." He appeared with Arnold Schwarzennegger in both *The Running*

Man (1987) and *Predator* (1987), and with fellow überman Sylvester Stallone in *Demolition Man* (1993). He also appeared in the exorcism spoof *Repossessed* (1990) as himself, and played the title role in the low-budget film *Abraxas, Guardian of the Universe* (1990). In 1984, he released a twelve-inch picture disc rock record. The disc featured two pictures: one of him in military camouflage with guns and the other of him in Cleopatra eye-makeup, beaded headdress, and feather boa with a guitar. Ventura, whose real name is James Janos, is one of two politicians who have guest-starred in *The X-Files* (Ruben Blades from "El Mundo Gira" is the other); he served for a one-year term as mayor of Brooklyn Park, Minnesota, in 1990–1991. He is also a sports commentator, and once cohosted *The Grudge Match*, a syndicated physical combat series. Look for Ventura as a goofy guard at Arkham Asylum in the recent feature film *Batman & Robin* (1997).

Sarah Sawatsky (Chrissy Giorgio) was a regular character on ABC's *Murphy's Law*.

Alex Trebek, who played the other the mysterious Men in Black, was sharing the small screen for the second time with David Duchovny. The *X-Files* star had appeared on a popular charity episode of *Celebrity Jeopardy*, where he played against Stephen King and Lynn Redgrave. Reportedly, Trebek was actually second choice for the role, after singer Johnny Cash. Trebek began hosting *Jeopardy* in 1984, but he has other game show hosting experience including *The Wizard of Odds* (1974), *High Rollers* (1974), *The $128,000 Question* (1977), and *Classic Concentration* (1987).

Larry Musser, whose character was the much-bleeped Detective Manners is, of course, named for director Kim Manners. Kim was originally going to play the character, but his directing duties left him too worn out to do so.

The Unauthorized Guide to the X-Files states that actor **Allan Zinyk** is really episode writer Darin Morgan, but this is untrue. Actor Zinyk *did* play Blaine Faulker, the man wearing a *Space: Above & Beyond* t-shirt, but he is *not* this episode's writer. A comparison of Darin Morgan on screen in season four's "Small Potatoes" will clearly show the two are different people.

Mike Fields, Doug Morrow, and **Chris**

Waddell who played the three chief aliens in this episode are makeup men on Toby Lindala's crew. "Three of our guys . . . played the main aliens in 'Jose Chung,' because they're very thin," Lindala revealed in an interview with *Shivers* magazine.

Charles Nelson Reilly.

WITNESS PROFILE

CHARLES NELSON REILLY

Born: January 13, 1931, New York, New York (or Connecticut)

"We were looking at either Rip Taylor or Charles Nelson Reilly to play Chung," said episode writer Darin Morgan in *Sci Fi Universe*. "With Charles Nelson Reilly you know that's who he is—he plays eccentric—and so you just accept it and start paying attention to what he's saying."

Reilly is a theatrically-trained actor who appeared on Broadway in the original *How to Succeed in Business Without Really Trying* (for which he won a Tony Award) and *Bye, Bye Birdie*. Reilly was mainly a comedic actor, and he was first introduced to television audiences in the 1962 CBS variety show *Talent Scouts* (an early version of *Star Search*). Reilly would be a regular on variety and game shows throughout the sixties and seventies, and appeared as the owner of the haunted cottage in *The Ghost and*

Mrs. Muir, a 1968 spinoff from the feature film. On the Sid & Marty Krofft children's series *Liddsville*, Reilly was the villainous magician Horatio J. Hoodoo who lorded over of an alternate dimension where the citizens were all hats.

In the last few years, Reilly has returned to Broadway and the theater, often directing both plays and opera. In fact, in 1997, he received a Tony nomination for Best Director of a Play for *The Gin Game* at the Lyceum Theater. Reilly has also taught acting for years as well; he currently teaches at The Faculty in Los Angeles.

Unlike Peter Boyle, the last big-name actor in an episode written by Darin Morgan, Charles Nelson Reilly was excited about appearing on *The X-Files*. In the book *X-Files Confidential*, producer Robert Goodwin recalls that he "couldn't wait to watch the dailies, because [Reilly] is hysterical when he is doing the dialogue, but even funnier when he goes off it. He forgets his lines. If you saw the dailies, you would die. I don't know how Gillian could continue to act because it was so funny."

"I have been a fan of this show since the beginning," said Reilly in a *Dreamwatch* interview. About his episode, he remarks "I thought it was so good, so clever—like a play within a play—I have had to watch it several times to get everything. Now I show it to my friends and explain it to them—'Don't you get that? This isn't happening!' "

Coming this fall, Reilly will reprise his role of Jose Chung, twice! First he'll appear in a second season episode of *Millennium*, where he needs the Millennium group's help after he writes a Satanic Verses type of book. Later in the year, he'll make another appearance on the fifth season of *The X-Files*. Both episodes will be written by Darin Morgan.

X70 Avatar

Case Number:	3.21/ #70 (#3X21)
First Sighting:	April 26, 1996
Directed by:	James Charleston
Story by:	Howard Gordon and David Duchovny
Telepay by:	Howard Gordon

GUEST CAST	CHARACTER
Mitch Pileggi	Assistant Director Walter S. Skinner
Tom Mason	Detective Waltos
Jennifer Hetrick	Sharon Skinner
William B. Davis	Cigarette-Smoking Man
Amanda Tapping	Carina Sayles
Malcolm Stewart	Agent Bonnecaze
Morris Panych	Gray-Haired Man
Michael David Simms	Senior Agent
Tasha Simms	Jay (Jane) Cassal
Stacy Grant	Judy Fairly
Jamie Woods-Morris	Lorraine Kelleher
Brendan Beiser	Agent Pendrell

UNCREDITED	
Bethoe Shirkoff	Old Woman/Succubus
Piper Maru Anderson	Girl on Bus
Cal Traversy	Young Detective

FIELD REPORT

Washington, D.C. Assistant Director Skinner's wife is divorcing him after seventeen years, but a bitter Skinner won't sign the divorce papers. That night, he picks up a woman at a bar and sleeps with her. The next morning, she's lying in bed next to him, her head twisted around backwards . . . very dead. Skinner doesn't want Mulder and Scully involved, but they investigate anyhow. The woman was a prostitute hired by Skinner, according to her madam. Later, after his wife is involved in an accident, Skinner is suspected of further wrongdoing and is relieved of his duties at the FBI.

When Skinner continues to act irrationally and insist he's seeing an old woman from his near-death experience in Vietnam, Mulder suspects a succubus. But the truth is more down-to-earth, as the agents discover, when they identify the man who was driving Skinner's car when his wife was run off the road. The same man kills the madam, and his next target is another prostitute who knows the truth. As Mulder and Scully try to entrap the real killer, Skinner visits his comatose wife in the hospital and receives a warning from the old woman who appears in his dreams.

WITNESS NOTES

Although *The Unofficial X-Files Companion II* notes that Pendrell's role was originally supposed to have been a "new character named Dr. Rick Newton," this seems unlikely, as Dr.

Rick Newton was actually a character in the earlier episode "War of the Coprophages."

The character of Judy Fairly is named after Judith A. Fairly, who was Howard Gordon's assistant from 1993 to 1995, and a script coordinator for Chris Carter from 1995 to 1996. In September of 1996, five months after this episode aired, Fairly filed a lawsuit in Los Angeles, accusing Fox and Gordon of sexual harassment, discrimination, and sexual assault and battery. The outcome of the lawsuit is unknown.

Tom Mason (Detective Waltos) has been a series regular in more television shows than almost anyone else in this book, though not many of the shows lasted terribly long. He starred in *Freebie and the Bean, Two Marriages, Our Family Honor, Jake and Mike, DEA, Grandpa Goes to Washington*, and the recent *Party of Five*. Film credits include *Apocalypse Now* (1979), *F/X 2* (1991) and Robert A. Heinlein's *The Puppet Masters* (1994).

Jennifer Hetrick (Sharon Skinner) is most familiar to science fiction fans as Vash, the lover of Jean-Luc Picard on *Star Trek: The Next Generation* ("Captain's Holiday" and "QPid") and in *Star Trek: Deep Space Nine* ("Q-Less"). The Ohio-born actress was a regular for two seasons on *L. A. Law* as Corrine Hammond and was in the cast of the 1989 series *Unsub*, a show about catching serial killers. In a 1995 interview in *TV Zone Special*, Hetrick made a wish for her future: "I would really like to do an *X-Files*!" Looks like she got her wish.

Malcolm Stewart (Agent Bonnecaze) appeared in the "Progenitor" episode of *M.A.N.T.I.S.*

The uncredited old woman/succubus is played by **Bethoe Shirkoff**, who can be seen as the art teacher in *Little Women* (1994).

Gillian Anderson's daughter, **Piper Maru**, makes her first appearance on the series. She's a little girl on a passing bus in the scene where Skinner runs across the street to catch the raincoat-wearing woman.

X71 Quagmire

Case Number:	3.22/ #71 (#3X22)
First Sighting:	May 3, 1996
Directed by:	Kim Manners
Written by:	Kim Newton

GUEST CAST	CHARACTER
Chris Ellis	Sheriff Lance Hindt
Timothy Webber	Dr. Paul Farraday
R. Nelson Brown	Ansel Bray
Mark Acheson	Ted Bertram
Peter Hanlon	Dr. William Bailey
Tyler Labine	Stoner
Nicole Parker	Chick
Terrance Leigh	Snorkel Dude

UNCREDITED
Murray Lowry	Fisherman

FIELD REPORT

Blue Ridge Mountains, Georgia. Dr. Paul Farraday is concerned about the extinction of a species of frogs in the area surrounding Heuvelman's Lake, but the answer to their disappearance may not be what anyone suspects. Mulder arrives in town to investigate a missing Boy Scout leader, which he tells Scully may be the work of Big Blue, a monster that supposedly lives in the lake. Indeed, when the half-eaten lower half of the Scoutmaster turns up, it appears something hungry may be lurking in the water.

Soon, bloody bodies are bobbing up all over the place, although the Sheriff refuses to close the lake despite Mulder's warnings. Later, Queequeg, Scully's Pomeranian dog, is eaten in the woods. The two FBI agents rent a boat to check out the lake at night but something crashes into their boat, stranding them on a mist-encircled rock. They discuss cannibalism, *Moby-Dick*, and Mulder's obsession with the truth before they're "rescued" from the rock— only a few feet from the shore—by Dr. Farraday. Shortly thereafter, Faraday is bitten by something large in the woods, and Mulder heads out to face the monster. But what's trapped in the cove surprises everyone!

WITNESS NOTES

Photographer Ansel Bray was most likely named after Ansel Adams, a world-renowned nature photographer. Dr. Paul Farraday was named after Dr. Michale Farraday, a physicist and chemist whose work included the discovery of the basis for generating electric power.

Chris Ellis (Sheriff Lance Hindt) appeared in a number of early episodes of Chris Carter's *Millennium* as Pensayres, including "Gehenna," "Dead Letters," and "The Judge." He also recently guested on *The Pretender* episode "Mirage."

Tyler Labine reprises his Stoner character from "War of the Coprophages." Still on a search for the ultimate high, Stoner tries licking frogs, then freaks out when his buddy's head pops up in the lake, the body missing! Labine has had guest roles on *The Odyssey, The Commish,* and *Poltergeist: The Legacy,* as well as parts in the Showtime telefilm *Sabrina, the Teenage Witch* (1996) and the feature film *Robin of Locksley* (1996) as Little John.

WITNESS INTERVIEW
NICOLE PARKER

Born: December 28, Victoria, British Columbia

For such a young actress, Nicole Parker has racked up an impressive list of credits. On *The X-Files,* you may only know her as "Chick," the teenager who accompanies "Stoner" on his cross-country search for the ultimate high. But this fall, Parker will be seen in a very different role: she'll be climbing into the costume of Venus de Milo in Fox's new live-action *Ninja Turtles: The Next Mutation,* a role that finds her in a very heavy costume. In fact, when we did the phone interview, the young actress was lying in bed with a hurt back from the weight of her costume's fake shell!

On stage, Parker has appeared in productions of *West Side Story, A Chorus Line, My Fair Lady, Les Miserables, Cats,* and *The Music Man.* In television, she had recurring roles in *The Odyssey* and *Neon Rider,* plus an appearance in the *Sliders* episode "Gillian of the Spirits." Telefilms include *She Stood Alone: The Tailhook Scandal* (1995), and *Ebbie* (1995), while features include *The Neverending Story III* (1994) and *Hard Core Logo* (1997).

Parker was called in to audition for *The X-Files* because local casting directors are so familiar with her. Discussing the role, she'd first like to dispel a persistent rumor that dogs

Nicole Parker appeared in "Quagmire" and "War of the Coprophages."

the actors who portrayed Stoner and Chick. Tyler Labine and Nicole were *not* under the influence of anything when they shot their scenes. "We were drinking water that tasted like beer but that is about it," she says, then adds "He really did lick the frogs [though]. When the stunt guy got hurt and fell under the water, all the ambulance guys were there. Tyler went running up to the paramedics, and he was like 'I licked a toad! Am I gonna die?' He kept licking the toad by mistake. It was pretty gross, but we were not under a *real* influence." She laughs, and adds "Am I ruining a rumor now?"

Nicole notes that director Kim Manners "liked what we were doing with our characters right away. He just explained how he thought it would be like to be stoned. We talked about that for a while, then about what kind of stoned we were going for: whether it was a high-energy or a freak-out or whatever. Kim was actually quite inspiring to work with. Some directors are cool, and some are nightmares, [but] he was really cool."

Parker's first episode, "War of the Coprophages," had a lot of cockroaches in it. Did Parker like the crawly creatures? "Absolutely not! And they used real ones. They were huge! Hundreds of them . . . they were disgusting." The shot where Alan Buckley's character, "Dude," freaks out and thinks cockroaches are crawling under his skin was a little difficult to film. "I did end up with quite a bruise on the side of my head from that shot. Tyler was told to wrap his arm around Alan's waist as we pull him down, and he instinctively kept going for his head. My head was right there, and he repeatedly kept punching me upside the head. So, I had a really nice shiner after that!"

Parker lets me in on another embarrassing secret, in which the scourge of youth caught up with her. "When we were filming the cockroach episode, I had a huge pimple in the middle of my forehead. Huge, like the biggest I ever had in my whole life! I *never* break out, but this time I did, and it all went to one place." She groans, recalling the scene. "The director of photography had to light it so that you couldn't see this huge zit protruding from my head. I notice it because I know exactly where it is, but you really can't see it."

Her worst secret out of the way, Parker talks about Alan's scene where cockroaches come out of his arm. "That was all prosthetics. He had to go in a couple hours before us and get all that done. He showed up, and we're like 'Yuk!' He had these crater holes in his arm and it looked real."

After Tyler's daring adventures, did Nicole try licking a frog herself in this episode? "Absolutely not. People were staying clear of that. [Tyler] kept throwing the frog at me though. I was not happy about that. Something would happen, and he would throw the frog and it would whack me in the face." [Laughs.] "We had to loop a lot of the frog episode because the sound had a lot of problems. We added a lot of screams and stuff for when we see the head floating there."

Stoner and Chick may be back for future episodes. "Kim told us that they liked the response they are getting from the Stoner and Chick thing, and the fact that we could show up in other places is kind of neat. We're like vagabonds. We just show up wherever and just kick around. We're traveling the world looking for ways to get high."

Parker worked with Chris Carter and his crew again when she appeared in the *Millennium* episode "Blood Relatives." "I think that was by far one of my favorite projects I have ever worked on. The episode is pretty dark. In

a way, I feel pretty weird about that, like I don't want my mom watching that one. I didn't tell too many people that I was in that just because it is such a dark show."

Whether or not she tells her friends and family about her appearances, Parker is often recognized on the street. "Especially on Granville Street. Granville is where the skaters and the alternative people hang out. I can walk down that street and people are like 'Yeahhh dude, you're cool!' " Not every fan experience is quite so predictable though. After her *Millennium* episode had aired, a man came up to her who recognized her from the episode and specifically remembered that her character had been crying. "He goes 'Did they hit you to make you cry?' I was like 'Excuse me?' and he goes 'Well, you looked like you were really crying. It didn't look like it was just tears that they put on you. Do they hit you to make you cry?' I said 'No, that is acting.' This from a *grown man . . .*"

It seems not even the strangest of exchanges can daunt Parker's infectious enthusiasm. But then again, what else could one expect from an actress who happily works with cockroaches, frogs, and now turtles!

X72 Wetwired

Case Number:	3.23/ #72 (#3X23)
First Sighting:	May 10, 1996
Directed by:	Rob Bowman
Written by:	Mat Beck

GUEST CAST	CHARACTER
Mitch Pileggi	Assistant Director Walter S. Skinner
Sheila Larken	Margaret (Maggie) Scully
William B. Davis	Cigarette-Smoking Man
Tom Braidwood	Frohike
Dean Haglund	Langly
Bruce Harwood	Byers
Steven Williams	Mr. X
Colin Cunningham	Dr. Henry Stroman
Tim Henry	Plain-Clothed Man
Linden Banks	Joseph Patnik
Crystal Verge	Dr. Lorenz
Andre Danyliu	County Coroner
Joe Maffei	Motel Manager
John McConnach	Officer #1
Joe DoSerro	Officer #2 (Jimmy)
Heather McCarthy	Duty Nurse

FIELD REPORT

Braddock Heights, Maryland / Washington, D.C. In the dark woods, Joseph Patnik buries a body of a man but upon returning home, he finds the same man, alive, in his kitchen. He kills him again, but when the police arrive on the scene, they're the same man as well! After getting a tip from a mysterious Plain-Clothed Man, Mulder and Scully arrive on the case, discovering that it's the second bizarre murder spree in the same area in a short time, and that both killers had been watching a lot of television lately.

Scully and Mulder watch Patnik's mammoth collection of videotapes of cable news programs. After several hours, Scully begins to hallucinate that Mulder is betraying her to the Cigarette-Smoking Man. When a housewife hallucinates and kills her husband, Mulder finds a strange-looking device hooked to the cable wires. The Lone Gunmen confirm that the device emits a signal, but that doesn't help Scully, who is convinced that Mulder is out to kill her. Someone is conducting mind control experiments through the television, but will Mulder be killed by his own partner before he finds out who?

WITNESS NOTES

Among the photos on Mrs. Scully's bedside table is one of her holding a baby. That's actually not a prop photo; it's actress Sheila Larken holding her own child.

Sheila Larken (Margaret Scully) was introduced in the first season episode "Beyond the Sea," as the mother of Dana Scully. The actress is the wife of *X-Files* producer Robert W. Goodwin. A New York native, Larken acted for many years in theater and television. Her television debut was in 1967 in *Judd, for the Defense*, and she went on to appear in numerous detective shows of the seventies as well as playing the lead in the short-lived series *The Storefront Lawyers* (renamed *Men at Law*) in 1970–71, and a recurring role in *Medical Center*.

Larken had left acting for some time to get a master's degree in clinical social work, but once she and Goodwin moved to Washington, she began receiving acting offers again. She now alternates her time between social work and acting. Goodwin suggested his wife for the role of Margaret Scully to director David Nutter, who had seen the actress in auditions for his 1985 film *Ceasefire*. In an interview with *Cinefantastique*, Larken describes her role as "a military wife, married before I graduated college, someone who never gets to finish her college degree or find a career for herself, but mainly gets enmeshed in her family. You know, the Everymother . . . I think Margaret is ever-evolving."

Tim Henry (Plain-Clothed Man), appears for the first time here as a presumed messenger from Mr. X. Plain-Clothed Man was not in the original script. Due to conflicts in his shooting schedule while filming *L.A. Heat*, Steven Williams had to give up three scenes as Mr. X, though he was able to shoot the climactic revelatory scene between Mr. X and Cigarette-Smoking Man.

X73 Talitha Cumi

Case Number:	3.24/ #73 (#3X24)
First Sighting:	May 17, 1996
Directed by:	R. W. Goodwin
Story by:	David Duchovny & Chris Carter
Teleplay by:	Chris Carter

GUEST CAST	CHARACTER
Mitch Pileggi	Assistant Director Walter S. Skinner
William B. Davis	Cigarette-Smoking Man
Peter Donat	William Mulder
Jerry Hardin	Deep Throat
Roy Thinnes	Jeremiah Smith
Brian Thompson	The Bounty Hunter/Pilot
Angelo Vacco	Man shot at restaurant door
Steven Williams	Mr. X
Hrothgar Mathews	Galen Muntz
Rebecca Toolan	Mrs. Mulder
Stephen Dimopoulos	Detective
John MacLaren	Doctor Laberge
Cam Cronin	Paramedic
Bonnie Hay	Night Nurse
UNCREDITED	
Brian Barry	Last Man
Ross Clarke	Pleasant Man

Washington, D.C. / Quonochontaug, Rhode Island / Arlington, Virginia. After a gunman shoots up a fast-food restaurant and is consequently shot by police snipers, he is healed by a mysterious man who disappears into the crowd. Mulder's mother meets with Cigarette-Smoking Man at the family's old summer home, and they argue about a past they seem to have shared together. Later, Mulder's mother is hospitalized after having a stroke, and she tries to tell Mulder something in a note. Cigarette-Smoking Man's minions capture the healer, Jeremiah Smith, and take him to a special prison cell for a strangely metaphysical interrogation.

At the summer home, Mulder is surprised to see Mr. X, who shows him pictures of his mother and Cigarette-Smoking Man arguing. Inside the house, Mulder finds a hidden alien stiletto, like the one the alien bounty hunter used to kill the clones of Samantha Mulder and the Gregors. Mulder asks for Skinner's help, confronts Cigarette-Smoking Man, and has a brutal brawl with Mr. X over the stiletto. Meanwhile, Scully finds out that there are dozens of men who look just like Jeremiah Smith, and when the healer comes to her for protection, she calls Mulder. The three of them meet, unaware that the alien bounty hunter has followed them to kill Jeremiah Smith.

WITNESS NOTES

Most of the children used as background extras in the opening sequence shoot-out at "The Brothers K" restaurant are the offspring of *X-Files* staffers; they include Tom Braidwood's daughter, cinematographer John Bartley's daughter, key grip Al Campbell's daughter, and Tony Morelli's three children.

Melinda McGraw was supposed to appear in the scene where Thinnes's character morphs into three of the people Cigarette-Smoking Man has had killed: Deep Throat, Bill Mulder, and Melissa Scully. McGraw's schedule did not permit the time for filming, so Thinnes did not do any genderbending.

Hrothgar Mathews (Galen Muntz) had to juggle filming schedules of an independent film to appear in this episode. He later appeared in "Loin Like a Hunting Flame," the sex-themed episode of Chris Carter's *Millennium*. Mathews grew up in Ottawa and studied theater in Montreal before moving to Vancouver and becoming a part of the creative scene there. He had a role in *The Neverending Story III* (1994) and the telefilm *Ebbie* (1995), which was a feminized version of *A Christmas Carol*.

Brian Thompson appears as the Alien Bounty Hunter in many episodes of *The X-Files*.

WITNESS INTERVIEW

BRIAN THOMPSON

Born: August 28, Ellensburg, Washington

He's clearly the *biggest* star to have ever appeared on *The X-Files*—not in terms of star power, though Brian Thompson has plenty of that, but in terms of sheer size. The 6'2" granite-jawed actor's imposing stature has been a boon to him throughout his career, landing him a cadre of villain roles. As *The X-Files*'s only known recurring alien, The Bounty Hunter/Pilot, Thompson is in a unique position of knowing *some* of the truth that is out there. After all, if Cigarette-Smoking Man is in his debt, he must have some powerful secrets!

Thompson's background isn't much of a secret though. He grew up in Washington, playing sports and taking part in other school activities. But in his senior year, when he landed a role in a production of *You Can't Take It With You*, Thompson's interest in acting was sparked. Acting "seemed to be the one where when you did all your homework and did all your preparation, that the fire you built at the end was a little brighter than the rest. Part of your quest is to find out where your talents are and then to foster those talents. I felt, ignorantly or not, that I had a real talent for this."

In 1983, after studying acting for several years at the University of California–Irvine, Thompson headed to a casting call at Universal Studios, where auditions were being held for a live *Conan the Barbarian* show. Given that notices had been put up in gyms all over the country, Thompson was sure he'd never have a chance against a bevy of Schwarzennegger wannabes. "I went to the audition and I was absolutely right. They wouldn't even consider me to play Conan. They asked me to [audition for] the evil villain who fights Conan." Thompson got the role of the villainous Paras Mordar, a role he played off and on for three years.

During that time, Thompson began acting in some major action films. In *The Terminator* (1984) he squared off against Arnold Schwarzennegger, while in *Cobra* (1986) he sparred with Sylvester Stallone, and in *Lionheart* (1990) he faced Jean-Claude Van Damme. "Chuck Norris, Bruce Willis . . . all the action adventure stars I've taken a swing at at one time or another," Thompson chuckles.

Thompson's genre film credits include a role in *Alien Nation* (1988), director Roland Emmerich's debut film *Moon 44* (1989), *Nightwish* (1989), *Fright Night Part II* (1989), *Doctor Modred* (1992), *Star Trek: Generations* (1994), and the recent *Dragonheart* (1996). In the upcoming *Mortal Kombat: Annihilation*, he plays the lead villain, Shao Kahn. But lest anyone think that playing villains is always a piece of cake, Thompson describes how in one scene in the latter film "I had to stand on top of this mountain in Wales in the dead of winter with no shirt on for a two-minute monologue. It was raining, it was 35 degrees outside, and the wind was blowing easily 30 knots. I had just conquered the world. It was my victory speech . . . and tears are blowing out of my eyes!"

The actor has had a full slate of genre television appearances too, with guest roles in *The Adventures of Superboy, Something Is Out There, Otherworld, Alien Nation, Knight Rider, Star Trek: The Next Generation, Star Trek: Deep Space Nine*, and *Babylon 5*. He was a regular as the two thousand-year-old werewolf Nicholas Remy in the latter part of the season on Fox's *Werewolf*, and also had a major role in the *Buffy, The Vampire Slayer* pilot telefilm (1997). And then there was his regular role on Fox's short-lived *Kindred: The Embraced*, where he played Eddie Fiori, leader of the Brujah vampire clan.

Thompson had worked on *Star Trek: The Next Generation* with Rob Bowman, who was also the director of *The X-Files* episode "End Game." This helped the actor make a decision to take a role on *The X-Files*, a series he hadn't known anything about when he was offered the role. Once he took the role, Thompson wasn't aware just how closely his character would tie in to the main conspiracy and the abduction of Samantha Mulder until filming progressed. "The scene where I told him that I knew that his sister was alive was not in the original script. I'm pretty sure that was David Duchovny's idea. For him to have had me say that one line was, I'm sure, the reason that I was brought back. The fact that I told him 'Yes, your sister is alive,' but I wouldn't tell him any more."

With the rough-and-tumble background he's had, Thompson has performed most of his own stunts on *The X-Files*. "I *was* doubled for the falling off the bridge. In the scene where they pull me out of the water, that was another guy also. I think those are the only two shots. Any time they had to pull the guy out or put him in cold water . . . that was the dead of winter in Vancouver! Yeah, stuntman, go ahead. [Laughs.] The hand-to-hand stuff I feel most comfortable doing."

On the series, Thompson's Bounty Hunter is the only character viewers can be reasonably certain is an alien, largely due to his powers of healing, morphing, super strength, and relative invulnerability. Roy Thinnes's character is probably connected, though the alien-human hybrids and the clones have muddied the issue. "We live amongst you," intones Thompson, noting that his "alien personae" has never been clearly defined by the producers or Chris

Carter. "I honestly haven't felt the need to ask him. I have in my own imagination reasons why it is, and that's all I need as an actor. I haven't felt the need for him to be literal with me because I like my own reasons as to why I am doing what I am."

Not to sound too Hollywood, but what is the character's motivation then, according to Thompson? "My reasons are [that] I work for a benevolent but sometimes very cruel alien force that has adopted their own set of rules for the amount of interference that they allow on the planet Earth. My alien being is capable of many things, like the Terminator, but also has the power to heal, has the heightened sense of ESP, has this heightened sense of smell and touch. He probably has the maximum sense capability of all the animals on the planet, as opposed to just human beings. I haven't defined the name of my boss, but I do believe it to be benevolent because they have tried to keep earth clean of other aliens. They are not allowing them to habitate. Because of my association with the Cigarette-Smoking Man, we are ultimately involved in some type of—I wouldn't want to call it a teaching program and I don't think it is just as cruel as an experiment—but I would like to believe that we are helping mankind work things forward."

That sounds very much as if Thompson sees the Bounty Hunter and CSM as heroic, which is something viewers might not agree with. "They don't know that the CSM is a villain. They don't know what he's trying to do. What's his ultimate goal? It is so easy to say that because he follows the rules he is a bad person. We all want to be the person who doesn't have to follow the rules. What has the CSM done that is viciously cruel? I believe our presidents have had people killed. Definitely the people who run the CIA have. The bloodiest wars are the Holy Wars. So, define *benevolence*, define a *kind* creature."

That's quite a different interpretation of two of the series' villains. So if he means no harm, why would the Bounty Hunter taunt Mulder with the knowledge that his sister is alive and then leave him to die? "He didn't leave him to die," Thompson says. "He knew that he would

be safe. He has the ability to know that. He does know that a search-and-rescue team is on the way. But he's not a machine. He felt the need from this person—who only wanted to know whether or not his sister was alive—to at least let him know that. Now that is *not* a cruel person. I think a crueler person would have said *nothing*. But that probably was a break in the rules for him to say that. His boss didn't tell him that he could tell Mulder that his sister was alive. That was something he chose to do on the spot, which does make him more human than machine."

Thompson brings his unique interpretation of his character to a close, discussing the ending to both "End Game" and "Herrenvolk." "Before he healed Mulder's mother he asked the Cigarette-Smoking Man 'I need to know the reasons why this should be.' It wasn't something that he was going to do just because the CSM said so. He wasn't following the CSM's orders. He was in a *conference* with him." And what about the clones of Samantha Mulder? "Did he kill them all? Were they clones? Did they really die? Did they really live? You don't know what happened, so I am not gonna say. Did I need to know whether I killed the Samantha clones when I went in there for the final scene with the CSM? No. That would have been important if my character had been a person who had never killed someone before. This is the 'man' who just got off of work. His work happens to be ridding the planet of unauthorized clones, which is a very beneficial job in his eyes. Quite possibly a very benevolent job toward the human race."

So will Thompson and the Bounty Hunter be back in season five of *The X-Files*? "Absolutely. I can say that I am contractually guaranteed to be back." He won't reveal how many episodes, nor any plot details he has been informed about . . . or not informed about. "Everyone's calling you and asking you what is going to happen. If you don't know you don't have to lie." Thompson is currently not scheduled to appear in *The X-Files* movie, *Blackwood*. "At this point it is unclear, but doubtful. But Chris Carter said I would be in the second one."

THE NICHOLAS LEA FILE

Name: Nicholas Christopher Lea (born
              Nicholas Herbert)
Born: June 22, 1962, New Westminster,
              British Columbia
Height: 6′ 1″
Weight: 180
Hair: Brown
Eyes: Green (or blue)
Marks: Small hoop earring or stud in left ear

Nicholas Lea speaks at *The X-Files* convention in Burbank, California on 24 August 1996.

Any other actor might see the nickname "Ratboy" as a liability, but Nicholas Lea earned the name playing Agent Alex Krycek, one of the most mysterious characters of *The X-Files*. When introduced, Krycek was the fresh-faced junior agent assigned to help Agent Mulder, but it was soon revealed that he was in fact working for Cigarette-Smoking Man. And in an even stranger twist, Krycek went rogue, and has been revealed as a triple agent who appears to be working for Russia.

Nicholas Lea was born Nicholas Herbert in New Westminster, British Columbia. Watching films at the local theaters, Lea was entranced by the characters and the actors. Companions at the Prince of Wales Secondary School in Vancouver don't recall that he was involved much in the drama department, though they do recall his ambition to be a rock star. He sang with a Canadian alternative band called Beau Monde for five years, beginning in high school.

Lea's road to the stage and screen was not without its side trips. He flirted with pursuing careers in archeology or advertising, and played soccer and rugby. He attended art school for three years, did a stint in the Canadian Navy, and worked in a clothing store. While at that clothing store, he met an acting coach and decided to take the plunge. So, at twenty-five years old, Lea quit his job and began studying acting the next day. Over the years, he trained at the Beverly Hills Playhouse, Charles Conrad Studios, and the Gastown Actor's Studio. He considered auditioning for London's Royal Academy for the Dramatic Arts but decided against it.

In 1983, when he was 21, Nick had a small role in the film *Star 80*, though the part mainly ended up on the cutting room floor, and he went uncredited as yet another "extra." It would be 1989 before he had another film role, in *American Boyfriends*, followed by a guest shot on the Canadian series *E.N.G.* and a role in the low-budget science fiction film *Xtro II*.

In 1991, Lea had his first major break when he was cast as a recurring police officer, Enrico "Ricky" Caruso, in ABC's *The Commish*, which was filmed in British Columbia. Lea was in seventeen of the first season's twenty-two episodes, and at least another seventeen over the course of the next two seasons. "I guess what was a big crack for me was three years on *The Commish*," Lea said in *Cinefantastique*. "That really gave me a lot of exposure in front of the camera, and I studied all the way through that."

Lea also met his long-time girlfriend while filming *The Commish*. Melinda McGraw began as a regular character on *The Commish* in the second season. Nick and Melinda first worked together on the second episode, and they became romantically involved soon after. They were together from 1992 to sometime in 1995. As of December 1996, during an IRC chat, Nick described himself as "very single."

Since his first exposure on *The X-Files*, Lea's profile has risen among casting agents. His largest role was in the film *The Raffle* (1994), which he top-lined, and he has had meaty guest roles on *Highlander* and *Lonesome Dove: The Outlaw Years*. A two-part guest appearance on *Sliders* in 1995 and 1996 led to speculation that Lea might join the cast of that series, though the producers and Lea mutually decided against it; Lea was sure that *The X-Files* would bring him a higher profile.

Before he landed the regular role on *Once a Thief* (see page 166), Lea was a regularly seen booster of *The X-Files*. He appeared at almost every official *X-Files* convention and did two summer promotional tours for *The X-Files* in Europe with Mitch Pileggi. His disarming sense of humor often takes bizarre turns; when asked on a *Fox World* IRC chat whether he wore boxers or briefs, he replied "I wear an old piece of leather strapping that I found on a recent hiking trip to Buenos Aires. The problem is, I can't wash it because it's leather and it really needs to be dry cleaned." To another question on a *People Online* chat, he quipped that in his spare time he indulged in "masturbation. A lot of masturbation."

In actuality, when he isn't working in front of the camera, Lea enjoys practicing guitar and learning new songs, though he doesn't sing much in public these days. He also enjoys drawing, running, and playing golf with co-star Mitch Pileggi.

X14 Genderbender

In his first appearance on The X-Files, *Lea played Michael, a studly nightclub patron who picks up what he thinks is a girl named Marty. During an intense sex scene in Michael's car, the two of them are interrupted by a cop. When Marty gets out of the car, she decks the cop and morphs into Martin, a man! Michael is left behind in the car, shocked and debilitated by the hormone-absorbing succubus Marty/Martin. Later, in the hospital, Michael relates the story to Mulder and Scully. "The club scene used to be so simple," Michael admits ruefully.*

Lea admitted in *Scarlet Street* that he wasn't concerned about the potential subtext to the scene. "I never thought of the homophobic ramifications of it. I suppose some people could say, 'The guy freaked out because he thought it was a man.' But he didn't freak out because he was making out with a girl and then found out it's a guy; he freaked out because she changed directly in front of him. It was also an interesting angle, that the guy was so macho and then he's lying in a hospital bed scared out of his life."

Krycek

When the producers were casting the role of Mulder's new partner for a three-episode story arc that would explain away Scully's brief disappearance from the series (so that Gillian Anderson could have her baby), director Rob Bowman remembered Lea from his role in "Genderbender." Several Los Angeles area actors were called in to audition, as well as Toronto actor Paul Gross (who would go on to fame as the squeaky clean Mountie Benton Fraser on *Due South*), but it was Lea—the only Vancouver actor asked to audition—who won the role. Little did Lea know that the three-episode part would be expanded to several seasons of recurring work, nor that the role would garner him such fan nicknames as "Ratboy," "Skippy," and "Weasel," as well as a death threat or two.

Lea worked with the production staff to make Krycek look the part, getting a bad haircut, and wearing drab suits and tacky ties, which contrasted the true nature of the turncoat agent. "That's what I liked about the character when I got the first script," Lea said in *Freetime*. "He was leading a double life . . . he was all polish and shine on the outside and all bad on the inside, all very devious on the inside. I wouldn't say he was bad, but he was lying his way through the very first episode. I though that was very interesting, because it gives you the opportunity to play the good guy but then hopefully let little bits of things come out between the cracks, just little indications here and there."

The writers had not specified a background for Krycek, so Lea created one for him, to work from as an actor. "What I tried to inject into it was the guy is young and in way over his head. I made the decision that he came from a military background; his father was in the military, and he was trying very, very hard to fill some big shoes," Lea said in *Scarlet Street*. "I can draw on my own life about my relationship with my own father, and how you're constantly trying to live up to somebody's image of what they think you should be. Krycek doesn't know he's being bad; he's just trying to get ahead and trying to please all these people in the past. He's just doing what he has to to survive."

This moral ambiguity fits in closely with Lea's preferences as an actor, as he said in the *Fox World* IRC chat. "I don't like playing just good characters, and I don't like just playing bad characters. I like to find the balance in between that makes a person. And you never know whether to trust them or not. I like playing complex characters. I like to try to find the psychology behind people." To play the bad side of Krycek, Lea notes further that he finds "the angry, cheating, ugly, reprehensible, moralistically deprived, sexually deviant side of myself and go from there."

With developments in the fourth season, it's unlikely a redemption for

Krycek will come any time soon, and Lea sees Krycek as firmly entrenched in the middle of the conspiracy. "There is no such thing as just good and just bad. In between that, that's where everybody sits. Maybe the guy will go back and forth a little bit. That's what people are speculating a lot: Am I going to be a good guy now? Am I going to go over to their side? I don't think that's going to happen. I think that the day that I become a good guy is the day that I die on that show."

X28 Sleepless   X29 Duane Barry   X30 Ascension

With the first appearance of Krycek, in "Sleepless," the young fresh-faced FBI agent seems straight out of the Academy, clean-cut and eager to please. He even managed to gain some of Mulder's trust by expressing his eagerness to learn from the senior agent and a willing-ness to believe and to explore Mulder's extreme possibilities. Krycek even seems convincingly shaken when he is forced to shoot the sleepless Augustus Cole. But by the episode's end, it's clear that Krycek is working for the Cigarette-Smoking Man and that plans are in the works to dispose of Scully.

In "Duane Barry," Krycek takes a secondary role, trailing Mulder and fetching coffee for the FBI hostage-negotiating team who are attempting to talk Duane Barry into releasing his hostages.

Krycek finally shows his true colors in "Ascension," when he aids in the abduction scenario to get rid of Agent Scully. First, he kills a tram operator, stranding Mulder halfway up the side of a mountain on a treacherously swaying tram. Then, he is implicated in the death of Duane Barry, who dies after being privately questioned by Krycek. Later, Mulder finds cigarette butts in Krycek's car, and he realizes that the agent is working with Cigarette-Smoking Man. But when Mulder and Skinner call for Krycek, the double agent has disappeared!

Writer Howard Gordon actually created the character of Krycek for the episode "Sleepless," though he worked with Chris Carter to make sure Krycek's story fit in seamlessly into the "mythology" story arc in the following two-parter. Lea's disarming puppy-dog appeal charmed fans and Mulder alike, so his turncoat actions were doubly surprising. The scene in "Ascension," where Krycek casually killed the tram operator stood in stark contrast to the scene where Krycek had been "forced" to shoot Cole in "Sleepless." "The way it was originally written was that I bring up my gun and whack the tram operator. You see the guy get knocked over instantly, and the camera cuts to the gondola," said Lea in *Scarlet Street*. "What I decided to do was whack him and then shake it off and fix my hair a little bit. I thought it would say something about Krycek, that he was trying to keep himself together and that he was very cool."

A scene in "Ascension" between Krycek and Cigarette-Smoking Man was used to explain the often-asked question of why the Consortium didn't just kill Mulder and get him out of the way. Another scene was rewritten at the last minute, when the producers realized they had a loose cannon—and some wicked story ideas—in Krycek. "I originally thought it was just going to be three [episodes]," Said Lea in *Starburst*. "Originally they had written a different ending, where the three of us, Mitch, David, and I have a real confrontation. Then in the final draft, which was really disappointing to me, it just kind of vaporized. You didn't know what happened to him."

But as we saw in the finale for the second season, Krycek didn't exactly disappear into thin air . . . he was just obscured by smoke from the Cigarette-Smoking Man.

X49 Anasazi   X50 The Blessing Way   X51 Paper Clip

Krycek returns, still in the employ of Cigarette-Smoking Man, and seemingly kills Bill Mulder, framing his son, Fox, for the crime. Later, Fox gets the drop on Krycek and holds him at gunpoint, demanding the truth. Krycek's life is spared by Scully, who shoots Fox in the shoulder to stop him from murdering the double agent.

Dispatched on another assassination mission, Krycek and another killer, the Hispanic Man, hide in Scully's apartment in "The Blessing Way." Unfortunately, in the dark, they mistake Melissa Scully for her sister and the Hispanic Man kills her instead.

Things take a turn for the worse for Krycek in "Paper Clip," when Cigarette-Smoking Man, thinking Fox Mulder has been killed, sees no more use for the double agent. He sends Krycek, the Hispanic Man, and a third agent to the hospital, where the trio ambushes Assistant Director Skinner in a stairwell, beating him badly and taking an important DAT tape from him. Later, when the other two agents go into a service station for beer, Krycek realizes he's been set up. He escapes the car as it explodes into a fireball, and later calls Cigarette-Smoking Man. "I'm alive, you double-crossing sonofa-bitch," he spits into the phone. Make that alive, in possession of the stolen DAT tape, and without anyone on his side.

Although it initially appears that Krycek is the one who shoots Melissa Scully, a frame-by-frame viewing of the scene will reveal that it is actually Hispanic Man who pulls the trigger. Behind the scenes, actor Nicholas Lea and Melinda McGraw were still dating, which imbued the scene with an odd shading. The official guidebooks (and most of the *X-Files* books for that matter) list Krycek as Melissa's killer, but they are incorrect. Even Lea has referred to the shooting as his doing. Perhaps they filmed the scene with both men shooting, and then decided to use the Hispanic Man's scene?

For the scene at the end of "Paper Clip" where Krycek escapes from the exploding car, the plan was to originally have been filmed with Krycek standing outside the car when he started to run. In *XPosé*, Lea says he asked "Wouldn't it be more interesting if I was actually sitting in the car when the shot starts because then there's a little more energy and excitement behind it?" The producers talked to the demolitions experts and agreed to do the shot, and the scene was rehearsed several times while crowds gathered at the perimeter of the set. Then filming began, and Lea hit his marks. "It was scary. I could feel the literal push from behind and I could feel the heat on the back of my head and the back of my jacket" as the car exploded in flames behind him.

X64 Piper Maru   X65 Apocrypha

Krycek seems to pop up in the strangest places, and his appearance in "Piper Maru" is no exception; he previously showed up in Scully's apartment and Mulder's shower, and now he's in Hong Kong, where Mulder has gone to track down information about the cargo of the Piper Maru. After several scuffles, Mulder manages to capture Krycek, but when the rogue agent goes into a bathroom, he is attacked by a woman and possessed by a black, oily, body-hopping alien!

In "Apocrypha," Krycek is Mulder's prisoner on a flight back to the U.S., but once they get back to Washington, D.C., Krycek escapes. He shows up at the Cigarette-Smoking Man's office, offering him the stolen DAT tape in exchange for being reunited with the salvaged UFO that the black oily alien possessing him came from. As the episode ends, Krycek is vomiting up the alien from within, but the unfortunate agent has been locked up in the bowels of a missile silo, with no food or water and no means of escape!

Lea's downward spiral continued in this two-parter, as he has to resort to selling government secrets to survive. "It really wasn't what I expected," he said in *Shivers*. He notes happily that he had further "input into what I was going to look like physically . . . the black leather and the chopped haircut and the bags under the eyes and everything. I really wanted to make him look like a man on the run."

Krycek's brutal fight scene with David Duchovny in "Piper Maru" was jointly choreographed by the two actors. "The first time that we did a fight [in "Anasazi"], the stunt man turned up late, so David and I choreographed that one," Lea explained in *Shivers*. "Then this time . . . they just let us go ahead and do it ourselves. We added all kinds of things; his hitting me with the phone was something we also thought of while we were there . . . when I walked past him on one of the takes, he actually whacked me on the head with the phone and I had a big egg on my forehead!"

Lea found it difficult to play the possessed Krycek with the right amount of alien attitude. "It was kind of hard, because they wanted me to play it like an automaton, and how do you research that?" he asked in the British *X-Files* comic magazine. "How do you go about playing someone who has absolutely nothing going on?" A quick viewing of Robert Patrick's steely performance in *Terminator 2* helped cue Lea along the right track, but the end scenes in "Apocrypha" demanded more emotion. "In the end, in the hangar, I got to just go crazy—on the first take, I actually broke the door down hammering on it!"

The black oily alien swimming in Krycek's eyes was an effect added in postproduction, but the scene at the end where the alien evacuates itself from Krycek was all on-set makeup special effects. "It was a prosthetic mask that I had to wear," said Lea in *XPose*. "Putting it on and taking it off a couple of times—horrible! At first I was excited about it, and then after an hour it became really tedious because I couldn't see, I couldn't breathe properly, tubes all running through my hair and everything."

X81 Tunguska   X82 Terma

When an anonymous tip leads the FBI to stop a right-wing bombing in "Tunguska," Agent Mulder doesn't feel terribly grateful to the tipster, Krycek. The militia men had freed Krycek from the silo, and the rogue agent wants revenge against Cigarette-Smoking Man. Krycek leads Scully and Mulder to intercept a Russian courier carrying a piece of rock of extraterrestrial origin. After storing Krycek at Skinner's place for a while (where the Assistant Director takes his revenge by beating the captive Krycek), Mulder tracks down the courier's point of origin as Tunguska and sets out for there, dragging the Russian-speaking Krycek along as translator. The two are captured and put into a gulag, but Mulder soon learns Krycek is working with their captors.

Then, in "Terma," Mulder escapes, taking Krycek with him, but not before Krycek, calling himself "Comrade Arntzen," has sent an Russian assassin out on a mission to the U.S. Krycek is caught in the woods, and his left arm is amputated by villagers who think they're saving him from a black plague. As the episode ends, Comrade Krycek/Arntzen, wearing a prosthetic left arm, meets his Russian assassin and commends him for a job well done.

In "Tunguska," Lea decided to do one of the most dangerous stunts himself: dangling from Skinner's balcony sixteen stories above the ground! A platform was built for Lea to practice on, but when it came time to film, the actor pressed for the platform to be removed. "They were going to shoot me down to the knees so it would look like I was hanging there, but you wouldn't be able to see my feet," Lea said in *The X-Files* magazine. "I won't kid you, it was pretty frightening." Lea was wearing a harness and cables underneath his clothes, but as special effects coordinator Dave Gauthier recalls, "When you take everything away and you step into nothingness and hang from a cable, you're trusting your entire life on that piece of cable. I held Nick's hands as I let him down in the cable, and he said [in a grim whisper], 'Okay, I'm ready.' "

Although it sounded as if Lea was fluent in Russian in the episodes, the actor had to learn all of his dialogue with Russian coaches. "It was brutal to learn—it's a language with no connection to English at all," he said in *The X-Files* magazine. "And it takes three or four Russian sentences to say one short English sentence." On a *Fox World* IRC chat, he elaborated, saying, "It was akin to speaking English backwards. It took me a long time to memorize it and then get it up to speed and then act it."

One of the most shocking things to fans—besides the clear-out-of-left-field revelation that Krycek was somehow a Russian double agent—was that Krycek's left arm was amputated. "They called me and suggested the idea, and I immediately fell in love with it," Lea said in the *Fox World* chat. "The one-armed man will always be remembered, and it takes the character in a totally different direction. Plus, didn't you feel just a little sorry for him?"

For the scene in which the lopped-off limb is shown, or rather not shown, Lea pressed for a rather unrealistic-looking prosthetic arm. "They had bought what looked like a Frankenstein glove you'd buy at Thrifty's for a dollar," he said in *TV Guide*. "I suggested that I put on a surgical glove that would fit skintight and paint it with makeup to make it look shiny and plastic. I was psyched. I thought it was beautiful, so over the top. It really extracts that pound of flesh for all Krycek's evil work in the world."

With season five about to start, and Lea having confirmed that Krycek will appear in at least two episodes the fan community is buzzing with discussions about the latest developments with Krycek. Most everyone is under the same opinion; that Chris Carter's decision to make Krycek a Russian agent comes completely out of thin air, and that it seemingly invalidates all established history for the character. If Krycek was a Russian agent, why didn't Cigarette-Smoking Man know about it, or discover it? Why didn't Krycek return with the DAT tape to Russia rather than try to sell it in Hong Kong? And if he recently became a Russian agent, how is he so well-connected that he can command top Russian assassins? These newest developments with Krycek are perhaps more unexplainable than many of the other mysteries on *The X-Files*. Did Chris Carter make a big mistake, or does he have a road map for where Krycek is going?

The truth will be out there soon enough, but meanwhile, Nicholas Lea has become yet another kind of agent . . .

Once a Thief

In 1996, Lea was cast in a lead role in John Woo's *Once a Thief*, a pilot telefilm remake of a 1991 Woo film from Hong Kong. Woo is probably the most successful of the Hong Kong action directors, and he was hot off the feature film *Broken Arrow* when *Once a Thief* went into production.

The story followed the adventures of of former prostitute Li Ann Tsei (Sandrine Holt) and former street thief Mac Ramsey (Ivan Sergei) who have escaped the clutches of Hong King's criminal underworld and have been chosen to be a part of an elite international crime-fighting unit. The two work with maverick ex-cop Victor Mansfield (played by Lea), who has designs on Li Ann. "He is the good guy who is reluctant to be the hero, the good guy with a few pieces missing," said Lea about Mansfield in press materials for *Once a Thief*. "He tries to be good, but can't always do it, which is really the way it is." As with all of John Woo's films, *Once a Thief* is action-oriented to an extreme, requiring the entire cast to do tremendous amounts of stunt work. "Physically it was pretty tough. This is one of the first jobs I've had where I show up every day with elbow pads and knee pads," Lea said in a *Toronto Sun* interview.

Fox aired the telefilm in September 1996, and when it posted good ratings, the network agreed to further development. They ordered six episodes for a possible mid-season series. After Fox dropped development of the series, Alliance Communications, the Canadian producer, quickly locked up a deal with Woo to produce *Once a Thief* as a weekly syndicated series, with twenty-two one-hour episodes filmed in Toronto. The series debuted in late September 1997 on Canada's CTV, and in twenty other countries. No American companies have bought the series for syndication yet, though it's likely that the series will be picked up by a U.S. network or in syndication before 1997 is through.

Lea has a five-year contract for *Once a Thief*, and a three-month hiatus from January through March 1988 will allow him to film his fifth-season *X-Files* reappearances. "No matter where my career goes in the future, I will always be proud to be on the show" said Lea in a *People* IRC chat. "Any time they ask me."

ACTOR CREDITS

NICHOLAS LEA

AMERICAN TELEVISION

The Burning Zone (UPN) #8—"Hall of the Serpent," aired November 12, 1996 (first season). Role: Philip Padgett, a charismatic leader of a cult in the rain forest.

The Commish (ABC) Nicholas Lea played Officer Enrico "Ricky" Caruso, a recurring character who appeared in thirty-four episodes of the first three seasons. Many of his episodes were directed by David Nutter or Kim Manners, and several were written by Glen Morgan and James Wong. Lea appeared in the series premiere on September 28, 1991, and recurred until the third season finale on May 14, 1994.

The Hat Squad (CBS) #8—"Lifestyles of the Rich and Infamous," aired January 2, 1993 (first season). Role: Night club owner Brett Halsey. The episode was directed by Kim Manners.

Highlander (Syndicated) #34—"The Fighter," aired week of January 31, 1994 (second season). Role: Rodney Lange, the alcoholic brother of a main character. #93—"Money No Object," aired week of November 4, 1996 (fifth season). Role: Cory Raines, a fun-loving Immortal bank robber.

Lonesome Dove: The Outlaw Years (Syndicated) #34—"Lover's Leap," aired week of December 18, 1995 (second season). Role: Tom Andrews, the town's school teacher, who is hiding a dark past.

The Marshal (ABC) #1—"The Marshal," aired January 31, 1995 (first season premiere). Role: Ray Turner.

Moloney (CBS) #12—"Damage Control," aired January 30, 1997 (first season). Role: Anson Greene, a crazy gunman who takes a criminal psychiatric ward hostage.

Robin's Hoods (Syndicated) #7—"Double or Nothing," aired October 6, 1994 (first season). Role: Faber.

Sliders (Fox) Lea played the recurring role of Ryan, who is attracted to Wade Wells and accompanies the Sliders. #10—"Luck of the Draw," aired May 17, 1995 (first season finale) #11—"Into the Mystic," aired March 1, 1996 (second season premiere).

CANADIAN TELEVISION

E.N.G. (CTV) #96—"Cutting Edge," aired 1990 (fifth season). Role: Jeffrey Leggett, a young broadcasting producer.

Jake and the Kid (Syndicated) #3—"Grand Plans" or "The Final Pitch," aired 1995 (first season). Role: an escaped convict named Tony Edwards who used to be a minor league baseball player.

Madison (network unknown) "Not Just Anybody," aired 1994 (first season). Role: Jack, the friend of a high schooler who is starting an interracial relationship.

North of 60 (CBC) "Out of the Blue," aired early 1993 (first season). Role: Hillard.

Once a Thief (CTV) A spin-off from the FOX telefilm, this is not planned for U.S. airing at this time. Lea plays the regular role of Victor Mansfield, an ex-cop who works with an international crime-fighting agency. Premiere date: September 15, 1997.

Taking the Falls (CTV) "Easy Money," aired early 1995 (first season). Role: Mac Stringer, the boyfriend of one of the lead characters.

TELEVISION MOVIES

Once A Thief (Fox), Aired November 29, 1996. Role: Victor Mansfield, an ex-cop who works with an international crime-fighting agency.

Their Second Chance (Lifetime), Aired February 9, 1997. Role: Roy, the annoying boyfriend of Laurie.

FEATURE FILMS

Star 80. Released 1983. Role: Mickey, a male dancer friend of Dorothy Stratten's. His scene mostly ended up on the cutting room floor.

American Boyfriends. Released September 1989 (Canada) /direct-to-video in U.S. Role: Ron.

Xtro II: The Second Encounter. Released November 1990 (Canada) / direct-to-video in U.S. Role: Lt. Baines, a space marine.

The Raffle. Released 1994. Role: David Lake, a womanizing creative director of an advertising agency who hatches a scheme with his friend to raffle off the woman of every man's dreams.

Bad Company. Released January 20, 1995. Original title was *The Tool Shed.* Role: Jake, a male secretary barely glimpsed near the film's end.

Guts to Glory. Released 1996. This is a small, independent Canadian film, directed by Don Williams for I.T.C. Role: unknown

From Pig to Oblivion. Release date unknown. This is a small, independent Canadian film, directed by Simon Barry for Pygmy Productions. Role: unknown.

THEATER

At Home. Gastown Theatre
Bloody Business. Western Canadian Theatre Co./New Bastion Theatre
Fair Game. Arts Club Theatre
For What We Reap. Station Street Theatre

X74 Herrenvolk

Case Number:	4.01 / #74 (#4X01)
First Sighting:	October 4, 1996
Directed by:	R. W. Goodwin
Written by:	Chris Carter

GUEST CAST	CHARACTER
Mitch Pileggi	Assistant Director Walter S. Skinner
William B. Davis	Cigarette-Smoking Man
Roy Thinnes	Jeremiah Smith
Brian Thompson	The Bounty Hunter/Pilot
Steven Williams	Mr. X
Laurie Holden	Marita Covarrubias
Garvin Cross	The Repairman
Don Williams	The Elder
Morris Panych	Gray-Haired Man
Rebecca Toolan	Mrs. Mulder
Brendan Beiser	Agent Pendrell
Ken Camroux	Second Senior Agent
Michael David Simms	Senior FBI Agent

UNCREDITED	
Vanessa Morley	Young Samantha Mulder Clones

FIELD REPORT

Washington, D.C. Mulder helps Jeremiah Smith escape from the Bounty Hunter, but the alien killer follows. Smith takes Mulder to a strange farm where he sees clones of young Samantha Mulder working as drones alongside clones of an unidentified young boy. The bounty hunter arrives to kill them, forcing Mulder, Smith, and a Samantha clone to hide in a giant beehive. Back in Washington, Skinner and Scully discover that there are five Jeremiah Smiths, all of whom are cataloguing humanity based on protein tags placed in them during the Smallpox Eradication Program.

Meanwhile, Mulder's mother is still in a coma, and word has been leaked to Mr. X that she is in danger. The "danger" is a ruse to flush out Mr. X as Mulder's informant, and he is killed, but not before he scrawls "SRSG" in blood outside Mulder's apartment. The clues lead Mulder to the United Nations, where he meets the beautiful Marita Covarrubius, an assistant to the Special Representative of the Secretary General. She covertly gives him files about the farm and the Samantha clones. Back at the hospital, Cigarette-Smoking Man instructs the alien Bounty Hunter to heal Mulder's mother.

WITNESS NOTES

Unlike those in other episodes, the bees in this episode were almost all computer-generated. Also, Vanessa Morley and the unidentified boy who worked with her in the farm were photographed and manipulated in the computer to create the clones of Samantha and the young boy.

Garvin Cross (The Repairman) is a stuntman and an actor. He's performed stunts for films such as *White Tiger* (1996) and *Unforgettable* (1996) and as an actor, he's been in the stunt-heavy films *Cyberjack* (1995), *Mask of Death* (1996), and the pilot telefilm for John Woo's *Once a Thief* (1996).

Morris Panych (Gray-Haired Man) is well-known in Vancouver's theater scene, having played the lead roles in *Amadeus*, *Torch Song Trilogy*, *Children of a Lesser God*, *Pal Joey*, *The Importance of Being Earnest*, and *The Glass Menagerie*, among others. On television, he has guested on almost every Vancouver-based action series, including *MacGyver*, *Wiseguy*, *Airwolf*, *J.J. Starbuck*, *21 Jump Street*, and *Booker*. He's also been in the feature films *Look Who's Talking Too* (1990) and *Mystery Date* (1991). His two genre credits are an appearance in an episode of *M.A.N.T.I.S.*

("Faces in the Mask," directed by *X-Files* director Kim Manners) and a starring role in the pilot for Fox's *Strange Luck* series.

Rebecca Toolan (Mrs. Mulder) has, like most Vancouver actresses, been in a *21 Jump Street* episode ("The Education of Terry Carver,") with *X*-actor Steven Williams. She guested in the "V.V." episode of *The Commish*, which guest starred fellow *X-Files* regulars Nicholas Lea and Dean Haglund. She also appeared in the Canadian film *Urban Safari* (1996), which guest starred such future *X-Files* guests as Donnelly Rhodes, Jay Brazeau, Teryl Rothery, Anthony Harrison, and David Palffy!

Roy Thinnes was a shape-changing healer in "Talitha Cumi" and "Herrenvolk."

WITNESS PROFILE
ROY THINNES

Born: April 6, 1938, Chicago, Illinois

It's ironic that Roy Thinnes is playing the part of a man who may be an alien in *The X-Files*. After all, for two years he was architect David Vincent on *The Invaders*, one of the few humans that knew that the aliens were among us and that they were intent on world domination. Then there was his role as an investigator of supernatural events in the pilot telefilm *The Norliss Tapes* (1973). With a pedigree like that,

how could he not become a guest star on *The X-Files*?

With critics calling him "the new Paul Newman," Thinnes landed the 1967 series *The Invaders*. In the series, the aliens were as hard to discern as they are in *The X-Files*. Because they could take human shape, one had to look for clues: a rigid little finger, no blood or heartbeat, a glow around their bodies when they need to regenerate. Thinnes's character was constantly on the run, trying to convince authorities—or anyone—that the aliens lived among us. In *Science Fiction Television Series*, Thinnes notes the questions his character had at the time: "I think we all share that kind of paranoia. Is the government telling us the truth? Does the government want to hear the truth?" Sounds suspiciously like *The X-Files*, doesn't it?

After the series ended, Thinnes went on to a role in the aforementioned *The Norliss Tapes* (1973). The latter production was created by Dan Curtis, the creator of *Dark Shadows*. Curtis would later cast Thinnes in his television revival of *Dark Shadows* in 1991, in the dual role of Roger Collins and Reverend Trask.

In 1985, Thinnes began to develop *The Invaders* as a project for ABC. Sam Rolfe, the creator of *The Man From U.N.C.L.E.*, wrote the script based on Thinnes's story, and the project was sold to ABC for a three-hour pilot and six episodes. Internal politics scuttled the project, but Thinnes did end up starring in the 1995 Fox miniseries remake of *The Invaders*, in which he co-starred with Scott Bakula.

R. W. Goodwin met actor Thinnes on a plane and remembered him from his work in *The Invaders*. He suggested that Carter use Thinnes for a role in the third season, leading to Thinnes's casting in "Talitha Cumi." Given the nature of his role in the series, it's very likely that Thinnes will be seen again.

X75 Home

Case Number:	4.02 / #75 (#4X03)
First Sighting:	October 11, 1996
Directed by:	Kim Manners
Written by:	Glen Morgan & James Wong

FIELD REPORT

Home, Pennsylvania. A hideously malformed child is born and buried in a field but is later found by young boys playing a game of baseball. Sheriff Andy Taylor requests the FBI's aid and Mulder and Scully arrive to investigate. What they begin to uncover is the disturbing story of the Peacock clan, a family that lives in a house on the outskirts of town. Rather than mix with the other townspeople, they have been inbreeding for years and the current three Peacock boys are all deformed and animalistic.

Thinking the Peacock boys have kidnapped and impregnated a woman, Mulder and Scully investigate, while something watches them from inside the house. That night, the Peacocks retaliate by brutally killing Sheriff Taylor and his wife. The agents set free the Peacocks' pigs to distract them, then enter the house to free the "imprisoned woman," only to find that the mother of the baby is Mrs. Peacock herself. The woman, a multiple amputee, is kept under the bed, where she cares for her three boys as only an insane, but proud, mother can.

WITNESS NOTES

This is the first episode of The X-Files to feature a pre-show warning. The title card reads "Due to some graphic and mature content, parental discretion is advised."

Clearly, Sheriff Andy Taylor and Deputy Barney were named after the lead characters in the long-running Andy Griffith Show. The Peacock brothers were named after children who lived next door to the grandparents of writer Glen Morgan. The actual storyline of this episode was inspired by an event comedian Charlie Chaplin recounted in his autobiography about a bizarre British family that kept their multiple-amputee son underneath a bed.

Sebastian Spence (Deputy Barney Paster) appeared in the telefilms Family of Cops (1995) and Breach of Faith: Family of Cops II (1997), and can be seen in the Dead Man's Gun episode "My Brother's Keeper."

Judith Maxie (Barbara Taylor) appeared in "The Sea Wasp" episode of M.A.N.T.I.S. as well as in "Powers, Principalities, Thrones, and Dominions," an episode of Chris Carter's Millennium.

Adrian Hughes (Sherman Nathaniel Peacock) is the only "Peacock" actor that credits could be found for: the telefilm National Lampoon's Dad's Week Off (1997) and the Outer Limits episode "The Light Brigade." However, he's much more famous for his off-camera role than for his screen time. In mid-January 1997, Vancouver police began investigating Hughes (real name Stanley Adrian Hockey) on five charges of sexual assault involving three women. The alleged assaults took place between December 1991 and September 1995; the alleged victims were in their twenties, and all worked in the acting or modeling industry. The media was all over the case, as it involved not only an X-Files guest, but, possibly, an X-Files star. Hughes was not being accused by the press of assaulting Gillian Anderson; rather, he was accused of having an affair with her!

Gillian Anderson and husband Clyde Klotz officially announced their amicable separation in January 1997, but things had reportedly been over for quite a while before that. The Sun, a British tabloid, had reported that Klotz had moved out of their home in October and that Gillian had been seen with a younger man in and around London over the Christmas vacation. Anne Hockey, Adrian Hughes's mother, told the British Express newspaper that Anderson had spent the Christmas holiday with their family in Yorkshire, England. Oddly, while Hughes denied any type of affair with Anderson, insisting that they were only friends, she didn't deny or confirm the relationship in an US magazine interview. "I have learned so many lessons," she says. "Three times in the past couple years, I have been in a completely open, trusting situation with a friend and just been in shock that they were a different person than I knew."

Tucker Smallwood appeared in "Home."

WITNESS INTERVIEW
TUCKER SMALLWOOD

Born: February 22 (and September 14), Washington, D.C.

Tucker Smallwood's voice is rich and deep—not quite James Earl Jones-deep, but resonant nonetheless. Given his beliefs, it's appropriate that Smallwood has guest starred on *The X-Files*, though it's unfortunate that the episode he appeared in had nothing to do with alien life. But we're getting ahead of ourselves here . . .

First some background. Tucker was born in Washington, D.C., grew up in Greece, Washington, and Antioch, Ohio, before embarking to Munich, Germany, for two years of college. He returned stateside to attend classes at the University of Maryland, graduating with a B.A. in television production. He went on to become the first African-American director for WBAL-TV in Baltimore.

Drafted into the U.S. Army in 1967, he was sent to Vietnam in 1969, where he served as a senior advisor to a Vietnamese Army unit for six months. Smallwood was wounded six months after his service began in the Mekong Delta and spent quite a bit of time in various hospitals. Tucker celebrates two birthdays now, because "there's another day that a doctor in a hospital in Vietnam gave me back my life. He believed that I should live when other's decided that I was toast."

It was while recovering, Smallwood says, that he decided to retire from the service and change focus. "I spent six months in the hospital after Vietnam, and I had the time to reflect upon what it was before me. I decided to discover more about the process of acting to be a better director. And I fell in love with the process of acting." For the last twenty-two years, Smallwood has been active in theater and on film and television. He has been in over a hundred commercials and done over a thousand commercial voice-overs. He's had recurring roles on the soap operas *One Life to Live* and *Guiding Light* and smaller roles in *Texas, Search for Tomorrow,* and *Somerset.* His role as the host of the public affairs series *Channel 2, The People* earned him an Emmy Award nomination, while his role as Tucker the Writer on the WCVB children's television series *Jabberwocky* inspired children to explore their imaginations and to develop stronger reading habits.

Smallwood's film roles have included parts in *S.O.B.* (1981), *The Cotton Club* (1984), *The Secret of My Success* (1987), the critically acclaimed cable documentary *Dear America: Letters Home From Vietnam* (1988), *Presumed Innocent* (1990), and *Bio-Dome* (1996). Telefilms include *Adventures of a 2:00 Werewolf* and *For Ladies Only* (1981), in which he played Tornado, a male stripper. The versatile actor has had guest roles on the short-lived *Get Smart* revival and the equally short-lived *Mr. and Mrs. Smith,* as well as *Babylon 5, Murphy Brown, Wings, Reasonable Doubts, Silk Stalkings,* and *Flipper.*

It was while appearing in filmed segments for the Sony Playstation CD-ROM game *Agile Warrior* that Smallwood made an important connection. Glen Morgan and James Wong were casting for their new series *Space: Above & Beyond,* and Smallwood auditioned for the part of Commodore Ross, the commander of a space carrier in the future. "Ross was not supposed to be black. He was just supposed to *be,* and [Morgan and Wong] said, 'It wasn't even close, Tucker. It was real clear who was supposed to be Ross, and it was you.' " The part on the series was initially a guest role, but it eventually blossomed into a regular role on the Fox series.

When Morgan and Wong returned to *The X-Files*, they brought many of their *Space* actors with them, including Smallwood. "They created the character of Andy Taylor for me, and they created a character for James [Morrison] on *Millennium*." When he read the script, Tucker recalls thinking it was *so* dark. He did, however, like several things about it. "I got to die on television—that's the first time I got to die on TV. [Also] he has a wife. He has a relationship. He was not macho. He was a man that said, 'I have a weapon, but I have an existence here, I've made an agreement, a pact with my wife [and] I don't carry my piece.' There's a moment when I'm sitting at my desk after having loaded my revolver, and I look off to a picture of my wife and myself. They didn't cut to that picture—I was a little regretful about that."

The script also showcased a bizarre symbiosis between the sheriff and the Peacock clan. "The pact was, 'You don't [expletive] with them, they don't [expletive] with us.' It was so interesting to die in that show because I shot my death scene that first night. It was incredibly physically exhausting, because I'm swinging a baseball bat with all my *might* at these people, and then I have to break it at the last instant and not hurt the actor. So I got the intensity, and I've got a stunt-bat and they've got protection, but I'm wailing! After about forty takes, my wrist and forearms were just *throbbing*!" Unfortunately, a problem cropped up. "It turned out we didn't use any of that footage, because they fired the director of photography. The DOP was fairly new, and he wasn't comfortable shooting as darkly as Chris [Carter] liked. And so they said, 'You've got bad guys who look like Shirley Temple, and that won't work!' So I had to stay another five days and shoot it again!"

As for his actual death scene, Smallwood decided to forgo a stuntman. "I thought, *I'm gonna die. I don't want them to cut away from me, I'm gonna do my own stunts*! So I'm diving backwards, I forgot to tuck my head, I whacked my head against the floor, and I'm seeing double." After the camera ran over Tucker's foot and he suffered a few other bruises and aches, he relented. "I said, 'Let the stunt man

earn his money. He knows what he's doing.' " The scene also required Tucker to lie in a pool of blood as he died. "I had lain in a pool of my own blood [in Vietnam]. I know what it's like, but movie blood is not the same thing. It's cold! It's not warm, it's sticky, and it's unbelievably uncomfortable. When my hands fall back in the pool of blood, it's just a single shot, and in Europe they cut the scene. Fox had to fight for that shot because [the censors] thought it was his brains flying! It was such a hoot! It was dark, so it's really abstract."

"Home" was one of the most shocking episodes of the series, but Smallwood received critical acclaim for his role in it. There has even been talk of an award nomination, but a video must be submitted for the Emmy committees to review. Apparently, despite the benefits the series receives from nominations, *The X-Files* producers require actors to pay the fees involved, arguing that the actors can write the costs off on their taxes. *The X-Files* production offices "asked me to pay a hundred-some dollars to submit a tape of that show for Emmy consideration. I was prouder of the work I did on *Space*," Smallwood says. "I would have been more happy to have spent that money saying, 'Consider *this* work. You might not vote for it, it's not on the air [any more], but it's good work and you should look at it.' "

Recently, Smallwood has returned to theater, and he has a large role in *Contact* (1997), based on Carl Sagan's book about the search for extraterrestrial life. Which brings up the topic of aliens and military cover-ups, an *X-Files* mainstay. Does Smallwood believe that there is extraterrestrial life visiting us on Earth? "There's no question in my mind," he states emphatically. He poses the question "What do you find more compelling? A, that all this is going on? or B, that all this is going on and our government or whoever has managed to make it so unpopular or so uncomfortable that it's not in the *Wall Street Journal* or whatever? My gut says B is more compelling . . . more fascinating. There's no question that it's going on. I think it's more amazing for them to say, '*It's not happening*.' We're convinced that it's bull."

Indeed, Smallwood has been a witness to something that he considers to be extraterrestrial in origin. On a 1991 trip to the area around "secret" Nevada Base, Area 51, Tucker and five other men (four were pilots, three were Vietnam veterans) saw a "yellowish-white" light slowly rise up in the sky, its color and intensity varying as it maneuvered in a manner that seemed otherworldly. "What I've seen there transcends physics, transcends aerodynamics. We saw what we saw. I don't expect you to accept it because you didn't see it. You're not supposed to accept it. If I hadn't seen it, I wouldn't accept it. What you believe is a lie, what you *experience* is the truth. I know what I've seen, okay? I am at peace with it, and I'm looking forward to the years to come."

Tucker feels that shows like *The X-Files* and *Dark Skies*, and movies *Independence Day* and *Contact* are helping people become comfortable with the concept of alien visitation. "I don't know who to believe, or when to believe, I just know that there's *more* out there than I know. The millennium is an interesting time to come. Let's wait and see."

Karin Konoval starred in "Home" and "Clyde Bruckman's Final Repose."

BONUS WITNESS INTERVIEW
KARIN KONOVAL

Born: Baltimore, Maryland

You'd never know that under the makeup of Mrs. Peacock was a vivacious theater star from Vancouver, but that is indeed Karin Konoval

beneath the latex. Konoval has appeared in over thirty theatrical productions in Vancouver, including *Godspell*, *A Midsummer Night's Dream*, *Side by Side by Sondheim*, *Dads in Bondage*, *Gypsy*, *West Side Story*, and *Brigadoon*. She won the Jessie Richardson Award for her role in *When We Were Singing*. "I spend about half my time in theater," she says. She is also a familiar face on television, with roles as diverse as "prostitutes, fortune tellers, hot dog vendors, nurses, and evil hijackers." Konoval appeared in *21 Jump Street*, *Wiseguy*, *The Commish*, *The Marshall*, and the Canadian series *Danger Bay* and *Max Glick*. Her genre credits include the film *The Neverending Story III* (1994) and episodes of *Poltergeist: The Legacy* ("Town Without Pity"), *Two* ("A.D."), and an episode of Chris Carter's *Millennium* ("Weeds"). You may also remember her as a fortune teller in the *Sliders* episode "Into the Mystic."

In her first *X-Files* episode, "Clyde Bruckman's Final Repose," Konoval played another fortune teller, Madame Zelma. "The first time [it was] the standard audition process for a fortune teller. They liked my take on it, so I got the part. That was a really quick shoot. We just got that down in a morning." Konoval only did the scene with the killer; when her body was found in the dumpster, the actress was not required. "That wasn't even me. That was just mocked-up body parts. They did the fake hand before they did my hand, so they had to make my hand to look like the fake one when I came to the set that day."

Konoval would have a lot more experience with makeup by the time she had finished her second *X-Files* episode. Mrs. Peacock "stands out as one of the most interesting things I have ever done to date. I am really glad that I did it." But when her agent showed her the synopsis for the auditions, she didn't believe it. "I just laughed hysterically because I had a few other auditions that day and I thought she was throwing this in as a *joke* audition. I am a thirty-five-year-old slightly exotic-looking brunette, and I can't imagine where a woman with no arms and no legs who's rotting under a bed [was] going to come from!"

"From the moment I read the script I was incredibly disturbed by it. Something about it really got to me. The audition process alone was a huge mountain to climb because you look at this and say, 'How the hell do you prepare for this? How do I dress? What do I do?' All I did was put on a black jumpsuit and no makeup whatsoever and pulled my hair tight back from my face." Next, Konoval worked to find what the voice of Mrs. Peacock might sound like, and explored her thoughts about her "bizarre love for her sons. I felt this character is pretty much based in love, strangely enough."

When she showed up to audition, she put herself in pain. "I had incredible pains all through my body just from trying to achieve the physicality of this person. I decided all I would have to work with on screen would be my eyes and my voice. I just sat in the chair and didn't use my arms, didn't use any part of me but my eyes and my voice. I didn't even move my neck around very much. I put the whole character through there, and didn't use the rest of my body at all. So, I was in great physical pain all week long and had some very strange dreams!"

Once she got the role, Konoval was fitted for fake teeth. The teeth initially gagged her, but helped her find the voice for her character. "I just found that I had to relax my throat a lot so that I would not gag. It took a lot of focus." Her other makeup was "just one prosthetic piece that sort of went across my nose and over one ear. I was amazed at how little makeup there actually was. Toby [Lindala] blended it so well into my face and then put very subtle makeup around my eyes, but there was nothing else on my face. The special effects team were just amazing. I feel like we worked in tandem to create that grotesqueness."

The rest of Mrs. Peacock's body was not so easy to get used to. "They did do a full body cast of me. I am rather a petite woman, and Mrs. Peacock is sort of falling apart from lying on a board all these years. So they did a full body thing on top. The most frightening thing about it for me was in order to hide my body, they had to build a sort of a coffin box that was based on my body but a bit larger. Mrs. Peacock was over the top of me, so that my body was hidden. Just getting into that box and being pushed under that bed . . . I have incredible claustrophobia, and it took every ounce of courage that I had to do that every day that I came in.

"The first day was the worst," Konoval continues. "I almost didn't think that I was going to be able to do it because there was this pitch-black room and this old iron bedstead no higher off the ground than a regular bed. I was pushed under the bed, and of course they would have brought me out for air whenever I wanted, but the more they had done that, the more time it would have taken. So I spent several hours under the bed with the bed right in front of my face in the dark, and I am so claustrophobic it just scared the [expletive] out of me. They made it such a very dark episode, and the lights were so specific, that the smallest movement of your head could make the shot come to life or wreck it. I had to move infinitesimally, and it was funny because I found that what I had done in the audition—by kind of pushing all the passion through my eyes and my voice—was all I had to work with under that bed."

She remembers that star David Duchovny was "so sweet the day they did that scene where they pull me out and I am shrieking. There's people under the bed operating the [fake stump] legs and arms and they really wanted to get that shot over and over. [David] didn't say very much, but just his presence being there . . . he would reach down every once in a while and just pat my shoulder and ask if I was okay. I have to say that got me through the day. I think my spirit sort of hung onto his spirit."

The Mrs. Peacock bodysuit was created by makeup effects man Toby Lindala and his crew. "What Toby had built for me was this apparatus that fit under this little dress—sort of fake stumps. They built a harness for my upper body with these [stumps] off of it. Those were operated, I suppose, at the end of a wire. The rest of the body, with the leg stumps attached to it, were radio-controlled. My stomach muscles got very tired because every time Mrs. Peacock would use any part of her, I could [only] use my upper body as much as the shoulders and the neck, because that part of Mrs. Peacock was me. But anything I wanted to do, we sort of worked in tandem. The special effects team and I worked as a team."

In one scene, Mrs. Peacock asks her boys to disrobe so she can see them, but the actress was able to read her lines from offscreen and didn't have to endure the under-the-bed coffin. "The boys take off their clothes and revolve for me so that I can check them over. Those poor boys had to have hair put on them from neck to toe. When they left the special effects truck, all you could hear was 'Ow! Ow! Ow!' because they would have those hairs applied to them. They were such good sports about it. I felt quite isolated within the episode—except of course Kim Manners was wonderful. I did feel like quite a freak walking around with all this apparatus and a deformed face and the teeth and everything. Some people didn't want to sit with me at dinner. The day we shot the teaser, when she is giving birth, several people had to leave the building during the birthing. I was screaming my lungs out. And then they cut the umbilical cord and had the sugar water for the blood and everything. I even thought 'I can't believe I am doing this.' That day *really* nobody wanted to sit with me at dinner. Nobody wanted to *eat* dinner that day."

Given the amount of makeup Konoval had on in the episode, it seems a far cry that somebody would recognize her, but it happened recently. "My boyfriend's cousin had the opening of a pool hall and somebody there knew who I was, and that I played Mrs. Peacock. They happened to tell this young woman who was there, and all of a sudden this woman started screaming at the top of her lungs! About a hundred people are looking around at her like 'What on earth? What's happened?' She grabbed me and she said 'It's you! It's you!' and screamed again. She *wasn't* screaming in glee. I mean people were disturbed by my very *presence* for a while after I was found out. And that happened more than once." Was Konoval herself disturbed after filming? "No," she laughs. "I just felt kind of *exhausted* for a little bit."

X76 Teliko

Case Number:	4.03 / #76 (#4X04)
First Sighting:	October 18, 1996
Directed by:	Jim Charleston
Written by:	Howard Gordon

GUEST CAST	CHARACTER
Mitch Pileggi	Assistant Director Walter S. Skinner
Carl Lumbly	Marcus Duff
Willie Amakye	Samuel Aboah
Laurie Holden	Marita Covarrubias
Brendan Beiser	Agent Pendrell
Zakes Mokae	Minister Diabira
Bob Morrisey	Dr. Simon Bruin
Danny Wattley	First Officer
Maxine Guess	Flight Attendant
Bill Mackenzie	Bus Driver
Michael O'Shea	Lieutenant Madson

UNCREDITED	
Geoffrey Ayi-Bonte	Seat Mate
Dexter Bell	Alfred Kittel
Don Stewart	Businessman

FIELD REPORT

Philadelphia, Pennsylvania. On an airplane, a West African black man goes into the bathroom. He's later found, quite dead, and drained of all pigmentation. Later, in Philadelphia, four other African-American men have seemingly vanished, but when another body is discovered lacking its pigmentation, Scully is brought in to investigate. Mulder compares this to the case on the airplane, and the agents eventually find their way to recent West African immigrant Samuel Aboah, who lacks the pituitary gland used to produce the melanin that helps make up skin color.

Mulder is given a tip by Marita Covarrubias which leads him to Minister Diabira, a diplomat from Burkina Faso in West Africa. Diabira tells him the myth of the Teliko, vampiric night spirts which drain color from their unfortunate victims. Mulder theorizes that the Teliko are a real clan that lack pituitary glands and thus hunt others for their hormones. But when Aboah escapes and captures Mulder, the agent may be the next victim of the Teliko.

WITNESS NOTES

The Official *X-Files* Web site lists actor Sean Campbell in the role of Lieutenant Madsen (with an 'e'), but the on-screen credit is for Michael O'Shea as Lieutenant Madson (with an 'o').

Zakes Mokae (Minister Diabira) was born in Johannesburg, South Africa. His credits include *Cry Freedom* (1987), the voodoo film *The Serpent and the Rainbow* (1988), and the horror films *Body Parts* (1991) and *Dust Devil* (1992). Recently, he played Pram in *Waterworld* (1995), had a role as a doctor in *Vampire in Brooklyn* (1995), and played another doctor in the virus film *Outbreak* (1995).

WITNESS PROFILE
CARL LUMBLY
Born: August 14, 1952, Minneapolis, Minnesota

The son of Jamaican immigrants, Carl Lumbly worked as a reporter for the Associated Press and as a public relations executive for the 3M Company prior to his career in acting. He won several awards for his impressive theater work, and later had roles in the films *Escape From Alcatraz* (1979), *Caveman* (1981), *The Adventures of Buckaroo Banzai Across the Eighth Dimension* (1984), the time-travel slave film *Brother Future* (1991), and *Nightjohn* (1996). In *To Sleep With Anger* (1990) he starred alongside his wife, actress Vonetta McGee.

Lumbly has guest starred on the critically acclaimed series *L.A. Law* and *Tribeca* and had a regular role for the entire six-year run of *Cagney & Lacey*, where he appeared as Detective Mark Petrie. He followed that up with a role in the series *Going to Extremes*, then was cast in the new Fox science fiction series *M.A.N.T.I.S.* in which Lumbly starred as Dr. Miles Hawkins, a wheelchair-bound scientist who donned a black exo-skeleton that gave him superhuman powers and allowed him to fight crime. The series lasted one season and was actually the Friday-night lead-in for *The X-Files* in 1994–1995. Lumbly was the only actor who remained from the high-rated *M.A.N.T.I.S.* telefilm that Fox had aired in January 1994 as a test pilot. Interestingly enough, the second choice for the role of Hawkins was Steven Williams, who went on to become the mysterious Mr. X on *The X-Files*.

X77 Unruhe

Case Number: 4.04 / #77 (#4X02)
First Sighting: October 27, 1996
Directed by: Rob Bowman
Written by: Vince Gilligan

GUEST CAST	CHARACTER
Pruitt Taylor Vince	Gerry Thomas Schnauz
Walter Marsh	Druggist
William MacDonald	Officer Trott
Sharon Alexander	Mary Louise Lefante
Ron Chartier	Inspector Puett
Michael Cram	Officer Corning
Christopher Royal	Photo Technician
Michele Melland	ER Doctor
Scott Heindl	Boyfriend (Billy)

UNCREDITED
Angela Donahue   Alice Brandt

FIELD REPORT
Traverse City, Michigan. After taking photographs for her passport, a young woman is kidnapped and her boyfriend is murdered. Mulder receives the photographs, which show the woman screaming in a nightmarish whirl. He believes they are examples of psychic photography, but Scully thinks they were faked. When the girl is found, she has been given a partial lobotomy by the killer, and she repeats the word "unruhe" over and over. The word means "unrest" in German, and when the killer/kidnapper strikes again, the agents realize they only have a short amount of time to find the victim.

Scully puts the clues together to find that the same construction company has been working in the area near each crime scene, and when she confronts the drywall-stilt-wearing foreman, Gerry Thomas Schnauz, she knows she has her man. But after Schnauz is arrested, he kills a guard and escapes. Mulder finds photos that show his next victim will be Scully, whom Schnauz immobilizes and captures. Mulder must find Schnauz's lair, while the captive Scully must get inside the killer's head before he gets inside hers and gives her a lobotomy.

WITNESS NOTES
Walter Marsh (Druggist) specializes in playing judges, sitting on the bench in the films *Bingo!* (1991) and *Man of the House* (1995) and in the telefilms *Hands of a Stranger* (1987), *Assault and Matrimony* (1987), *Whose Child Is This? The War for Baby Jessica* (1993), *The Amy Fisher Story* (1993), and *Heads* (1994). He appeared in the horror film *Midnight Matinee* (1988) with William B. Davis and several fu-

ture *X-Files* guests and had a role in the 1991 telefilm *The Girl From Mars.*

William MacDonald (Officer Trott) appeared in the *Outer Limits* episode "Under the Bed" and worked with this episode's co-star Walter Marsh in both the feature film *Pure Luck* (1991) and the telefilm *Sin and Redemption* (1994).

Michael Cram (Officer Corning) was a paramedic in the "Maranatha" episode of Chris Carter's *Millennium.*

Scott Heindl (Boyfriend), who has very few scenes in this episode, was utilized to much stronger effect in "The Thin White Line," an episode of Chris Carter's *Millennium.* There he played Jacob Tyler, the ex-cellmate of a Hannibal Lecter-like killer.

Angela Donahue (Alice Brandt) earned a credit as Amy Lee Walker in the season finale episode of Chris Carter's *Millennium,* "Paper Dove."

Pruitt Taylor Vince was the stilt-wearing killer in "Unruhe."

WITNESS PROFILE

PRUITT TAYLOR VINCE

Born: 1960, Baton Rouge, Louisiana

Pruitt Taylor Vince is certainly making a big splash in Hollywood these days. He recently showed up as the vigilante killer Clifford Banks, a.k.a. "The Street Sweeper," on the second season of ABC's *Murder One* and received a "Cheers" from *TV Guide* for special-guest synchronicity in his roles for *The X-Files* and *Murder One.*

Vince is a Southern boy who suffers from a birth defect which sometimes causes his eyes to jiggle. "It's supposed to stop me from doing what I do, but I haven't let it," Vince told *Entertainment Weekly.* He worked in theater before getting his Hollywood break in the film *Down by Law* (1986). His scenes in *that* film were cut, but he went on to appear in *Red Heat* (1988), *Mississippi Burning* (1988), and *K-9* (1989). While filming that latter film, he was bitten in the crotch by the canine co-star.

The actor has had an amazing streak of big-name films to his credit, including *Wild at Heart* (1990), *Jacob's Ladder* (1990), *JFK* (1991), *Natural Born Killers* (1994), *Nobody's Fool* (1994), and *Heavy* (1995), in which he played the lead role. Vince also played Hank Pilcher, the husband of a wacked-out woman who wants to kidnap a soap star to impregnate her on the *Quantum Leap* episode "Moments to Live."

Vince is a fan of *The X-Files,* and was enthusiastic about appearing on the series. "It was so cool to be on my favorite show," the actor said in *Entertainment Weekly.* "It was like actors who got to be on *The Twilight Zone.*" Not everything went smoothly on the episode though. One of the scenes between Gillian Anderson and Vince had to be reshot, at the request of writer Vince Gilligan. "When dailies were coming back, the acting was a little off in a very crucial scene," Gilligan explained in a *Fangoria* interview. "I tried to figure out what was wrong and realized that it was in my screen direction in the script; I mentioned that Agent Scully is drugged by this guy. Gillian was playing the scene drugged, because she's very good and tries to do what the script asks of her, but the scene was getting too drugged, so to speak, and therefore the energy was sort of down." The writer made some calls, and because Pruitt Taylor Vince was still on-set, the scene was reshot. "I felt bad asking [them to reshoot], but they did it and just knocked it out of the ballpark. That scene played just great in the reshoot."

X78 The Field Where I Died

Case Number:	4.05 / #78 (#4X05)
First Sighting:	November 3, 1996
Directed by:	Rob Bowman
Written by:	Glen Morgan & James Wong

GUEST CAST	CHARACTER
Mitch Pileggi	Assistant Director Walter S. Skinner
Kristen Cloke	Melissa Riedal-Ephesian
Michael Massee	Vernon Warren a.k.a. Vernon Ephesian
Anthony Harrison	FBI Agent Riggins
Doug Abrahams	Harbaugh
Donna White	Therapist
Michael Dobson	BATF Agent

UNCREDITED	
Douglas Ray Dack	Mighty Man
Les Gallagher	The Attorney

FIELD REPORT

Apison, Tennessee. Sidney, a member of a doomsday cult, the Temple of the Seven Stars, calls the FBI to warn them that the cult members are involved in child abuse and weapons stockpiling. The FBI and the BATF (Bureau of Alcohol, Tobacco, and Firearms) carry out a joint raid on the cult compound, fearing that they might have another Waco or Jonestown in the making. They don't find the weapons or Vernon Ephesian, the cult's charismatic leader. Mulder feels something calling to him from a field, and the agents find an underground Civil War bunker, where Ephesian and his seven wives are preparing to commit suicide.

Ephesian is taken into custody along with his wives, but the FBI must release them the next day, lacking proof of either weapons or child abuse. Mulder is strangely drawn to one of the wives, Melissa, who reveals multiple personalities under intense questioning. As they soon find, she is also Sidney, and Mulder thinks Sidney is one of the woman's past lives. When Melissa shifts into the personality of Confederate Civil War nurse Sarah Kavanaugh, the agents get an even bigger shock. Her dead fiancé, Sullivan Biddle, is one of Mulder's past lives! In search of the truth, Mulder undergoes regression hypnosis, and Scully finds an old photo that seems to confirm the story of Sarah

and Sullivan. But once Ephesian and his wives are released, the cult rushes to commit suicide. Will Mulder's reincarnated love die once again before he can rescue her?

WITNESS NOTES

Michael Massee (Vernon Warren, a.k.a. Vernon Ephesian) is not well-known to television audiences. He is a friend of David Duchovny, and played a role in Duchovny's 1997 film, *Playing God*. This *X-Files* role was filmed after that film was shot, when the actor told the producers that he wanted to do an episode with Duchovny. Massee grew up in Europe, but graduated from Hunter College in Manhattan, where he earned a degree in theater and writing. An early film credit was as a transsexual in *My Father is Coming* (1991), followed by roles in the horror film *Tales From the Hood* (1995), *Seven* (1995), and David Lynch's *Lost Highway* (1996).

Massee is best remembered for his role as Funboy in the gothic horror film *The Crow* (1994). While his onscreen time is memorable, an event during filming was much more historical. Massee's character was part of a gang that terrorized and killed Eric Draven (played by Brandon Lee). Shortly after noon on March 31, 1991, cameras were rolling as Lee came through a door carrying a bag of groceries. Massee, playing Funboy, was supposed to shoot a prop .44-caliber revolver, filled with "blanks", at Lee. A squib was set to detonate in the grocery bag, simulating a bullet strike. Unfortunately, the prop gun contained a lead bullet tip, which was propelled from the gun by the force of the blank. Lee crumpled to the ground, and it was only after the shooting finished that the crew realized that Lee had really been shot. The actor died later that day. Filming was halted, and Massee went into seclusion. When production began again, Massee did return to finish his scenes. He was cleared by the police of all wrongdoing.

To prepare for his role in *The X-Files*, Massee studied cult leaders Jim Jones and David Koresh. "What really impressed me with Koresh was that when he was interviewed he seemed so normal and relaxed," said Massee in *XPosé*. "I tried to make the character as normal as possible. In all the scenes, except where he's preaching at the end, I didn't want the character to appear paranoid or schizophrenic." Ephesian, he says, "had to be in such control of his life and everyone around him, to make sure that he wasn't losing it. He drove the cult to suicide at the end to stay in control, even if it meant a betrayal of his faith."

Anthony Harrison (FBI Agent Riggins) is an actor who has been pegged as an authority figure. He played cops in the telefilms *Shadow of a Stranger* (1992) and *The Only Way Out* (1993) as well as in an episode of *The Commish*. He played a paramedic in the cable telefilm *Incident at Deception Ridge* (1994) and a firefighter in the Canadian film *Urban Safari* (1996).

WITNESS PROFILE
KRISTEN CLOKE

Born: September 2, Van Nuys, California

A California native, Kristen Cloke landed her first film role in the futuristic thriller *Megaville* (1990). She went on to roles in such films as *Stay Tuned* (1992), *Caged Fear* (1992), and *The Rage* (1996), and had a small role in *Mistress* (1991), a film cowritten and directed by *X-Files* guest Barry Primus. In 1994, Cloke became a regular on the short-lived prime-time NBC flesh-fest *Winnetka Road*, and also had a recurring role on *Silk Stalkings* as Annie Overstreet. She won over critics with her performance in the ABC Afterschool Special *The Long Road Home*.

In 1995, Cloke was cast as Marine Corps Air and Space Cavalry squadron member Shane Vansen on Glen Morgan and James Wong's new Fox science fiction series *Space: Above & Beyond*. "Kristen Cloke, who plays Shane, is a dark figure. She's pretty, but not overtly beautiful. She had a toughness to her—when she auditioned, it was clear that she had a dark past that she was really sad about," said Glen Morgan in a *Starlog* interview.

Space: Above & Beyond only lasted one season on Fox, but when Morgan and Wong returned to *The X-Files*, they retained a loyalty to the stars of their previous series. Just as they had used *X-Files* actors David Duchovny, Doug Hutchison, and R. Lee Ermey on *Space*, many of that series' players were cast in *X-Files* episodes, including Cloke, Morgan Weisser, Rod-

ney Rowland, and Tucker Smallwood. James Morrison was also utilized in an episode of Chris Carter's other series, *Millennium*.

"The role [of Melissa] was actually written for me by Glen Morgan, with whom I worked on *Space: Above & Beyond* and who is now my fiancé," revealed Cloke in an *Xposé* interview. The multiple personalities on the episode were written to allow Cloke an acting tour de force, though when the episode ran twenty minutes over, many scenes, including many "past regression" scenes were trimmed. "It's a shame since many of these scenes were extremely gut-wrenching and grueling in nature," continued Cloke. "Playing her was emotionally taxing in that you had to rip your ego down to the absolute minimum. You had to be someone whose life was worth so little that you would give your heart and soul to a man who believed it was in your best interest to die."

Cloke recently had a major role in "Monster," a second season episode of *Millennium*, and may become a recurring supporting actor.

X79 Sanguinarium

Case Number: 4.06 / #79 (#4X06)
First Sighting: November 10, 1996
Directed by: Kim Manners
Written by: Valerie Mayhew & Vivian Mayhew

GUEST CAST	CHARACTER
Richard Beymer	Dr. Jack Franklyn
O-Lan Jones	Rebecca Waite, R.N.
Arlene Mazerolle	Dr. Theresa Shannon
Gregory Thirloway	Dr. Mitchell Kaplan
John Juliani	Dr. Harrison Lloyd
Paul Raskin	Dr. Eric Ilaqua
Andrew Airlie	Attorney
Marie Stillin	Dr. Sally Sanford
Norman Armour	ER Doctor
Martin Evans	Dr. Hartman

UNCREDITED
Nancy J. Lilley	Liposuction Patient
Celine Lockhart	Skin Peel Patient
Nina Roman	Jill Holwagerm

FIELD REPORT

Chicago, Illinois. Patients at Chicago's Greenwood Memorial Hospital who check in to the

Aesthetic Surgery Unit get more than a little plastic surgery. A doctor gets a little too into his work, liposuctioning a patient to death. The doctor claims an out-of-body experience, and Mulder and Scully arrive to investigate what could be a case of demonic possession. Scully is skeptical, blaming the crazy behavior on drugs, but Mulder finds a pentagram on the operating room floor and another marked on the flesh of another patient who is lasered to death.

All of the evidence seems to point to Nurse Waite, a practicing witch who worked at the clinic ten years ago, when another string of similarly bizarre murders were committed. The agents find all sorts of unsettling magical materials at Waite's house, but the bewitching nurse is at Dr. Franklyn's where she attacks him with a knife. She's stopped and arrested, but dies an awful death, leading Mulder to suspect Dr. Franklyn might be a warlock. He's right, but can the agents stop him before he casts one final evil spell?

WITNESS NOTES

Richard Beymer (Dr. Jack Franklyn) is another in a long line of *Twin Peaks* veterans, having played the role of scheming developer Benjamin Horne. The Iowa-born actor started acting in his early teens, appearing in the films *So Big* (1953) and the acclaimed *The Diary of Anne Frank* (1959). He also played the role of Tony in the original film version of *West Side Story* (1961), though his singing voice was dubbed by Jimmy Bryant. Beymer has appeared in some other classy films, such as *The Longest Day* (1962) and *Hemingway's Adventures of a Young Man* (1962), but by the eighties his career had changed to television guest roles and appearances in such low-budget movies as *Silent Night, Deadly Night III: Better Watch Out!* (1989). Beymer now has a recurring role as Li Nalas on *Star Trek: Deep Space Nine*. In 1996, Beymer starred in a telefilm that had a title reminiscent of the role he played in this episode: *A Face to Die For*.

Arlene Mazerolle (Dr. Theresa Shannon) has appeared in the films *Switching Channels* (1988) and *Cocktail* (1988), as well as the telefilms *Acts of Vengeance* (1986) and *Beyond Betrayal* (1994).

Paul Raskin (Dr. Eric Ilaqua) also had a role in "Paper Dove," the first season finale episode of Chris Carter's *Millennium*.

O-Lan Jones appeared in "Sanguinarium."

WITNESS INTERVIEW

O-LAN JONES

Born: May 23, Los Angeles, California

She's an actor. She's a writer She's a composer. And she's best known by genre fans as either the trailer trash mom in Tim Burton's eclectic *Mars Attacks!*, or as the pin-spitting witch on *The X-Files'* goriest episode. O-Lan Jones's triple-threat status in Hollywood makes her a valuable addition to any project she's involved in. Her roll-with-the-punches sense of humor doesn't hurt either.

Jones' film credits include *Married to the Mob* (1988), *Miracle Mile* (1989), *Pacific Heights* (1990), *Edward Scissorhands* (1990), *Beethoven* (1992), *Shelf Life* (1993), and *Natural Born Killers* (1994). In contrast to her character in *Mars Attacks!* (1996), where she played a shotgun-toting trailer park mom, Jones jumped to the other side in *Martians Go Home* (1990), in which she played a medley-singing Martian. On television, she was a regular on *Harts of the West*, and has guested on *Nash Bridges*, *Chicago Hope* (twice), *John Laroquette*, and *Lonesome Dove*.

Jones has also done a lot of theater, including such interestingly-titled off-Broadway plays as *Women in High Heels Moving Heavy Equipment, Forensic and the Navigators, Back Bog Beast Bait,* and *Sprintorgasmics.* Jones wrote the simple musical hymn her church-going character plays on the organ in *Edward Scissorhands.* As an award-winning composer she's mostly written for theater. "I write opera. In fact, I'm having a one night stand at Carnegie Hall on June 30th, 1997. And, I've got a company called Overtone Industries. We make up new operas, based on myths mostly, or *made-up* myths. Things that have big themes. It's not like people stand around with a cup of coffee singing for no reason," she laughs. "They're singing because they *mean* it." Jones has won the Bay Area Critic Circle Award for an original score, as well as *Dramalogue* awards for composing and sound design. She has scored one movie, *Siren Moon,* a short film.

Jones had previously auditioned in *The X-Files* offices for the role of Willa Ambrose on the second season episode "Fearful Symmetry." She didn't get that role, but won the part of Rebecca Waite in "Sanguinarium." "Yeah, it was a fun, wild role! There were fights and everything. I think it was one of their bloodiest ones. That's what Kim [Manners] was saying . . . that and the woman they slid out from under the bed ('Home')."

The script for "Sanguinarium" was undergoing rewrites even as filming began. "In fact, I didn't know I was a witch until I got up there, and then they handed me some hoodoo words to say. It looked like they'd lifted it from somebody's real live spell. As it turned out, I only remembered half the spell, and they only wanted me to repeat thirty impossible words rather than a hundred. So it would only have raised up a half-baked spirit anyhow!"

Jones found the fight scenes in *X-Files* much more fun than her recent shooting scenes on *Nash Bridges.* "It's just when you're doing it, it takes like two hours [to film] and then on the screen it's ten seconds! There was some leaping around in blood-drenched clothing, and howling and shrieking and knocking each other around. The fight scenes are fun to a certain extent. It's choreographed, it's playing. Gun scenes are not fun to me. Because I grew up on the 'mean streets,' guns mean something to me. I've been caught in the cross fire too many times. My body recognizes it as a real live thing. When I was doing the *Nash Bridges* thing, it was an Uzi. I had to yell out at the same time like Rambo or something, just so I felt like the bullets were coming *from* me and going out somewhere else, rather than coming *at* me."

Still, violent stunt scenes do need to be choreographed. The fight coach for *The X-Files* went over the scene with Richard Beymer and Jones in detail before they ever practiced. "He said 'Before any of these blows are supposed to happen, make eye contact. And that just sort of focuses the whole thing up so that your timing is good. Cause if somebody slugs you they can hurt you.' I just did a movie where there wasn't anybody really paying attention to that, and I was supposed to be fighting with a woman who hadn't really done anything like that before. All of a sudden she just started hitting me, which was like . . . 'Nooooooo . . .' " [Laughs.]

In the fight, a knife is used, but it wasn't always a harmless prop. The crew told Jones that they couldn't "use the play knife for this one. 'We need the real one cause it's got a better gleam.' Well, if it has a better *gleam*, no matter for my skin," the actress laughs. Later, she was covered with fake blood. "When I was just simply drenched in it, I was kind of resisting embracing the impression of it, because people would walk by and be like *Yuuuccch.* So in my witch role, I was thinking I am covered in power," she laughs, "rather than I am covered in blood and none of the crew can look at me."

Being nude on the set was not a big issue for Jones. "I had a piece of something to throw over me when people came through, but I was nude on set. I had some black material over my lap. You can't help but notice that the guy on the dolly or whatever is sort of taking a look. I had done partial make-out scenes [in other roles] but not where I am just nude on-set with a bunch of people I don't know. They were all very considerate about it, and they had done it before, so they know to come in and kind of cover you up. I wasn't just walking around nude—I did have some acting, and some impossible words to remember. So that helped."

Speaking of the set, Jones remembers that in the set for Nurse Waite's room, "they did have real chicken feet strung up like a chandelier from the middle to the corners of the room, and that you could smell after a while." That wasn't the grossest thing she had to deal with though. Another scene had leeches in it! "Another very amazing incident for me was wrangling the damned *leeches*. Those were real live leeches. And the squirm factor is *high*. The grown grips—those guys would be going by just shuddering looking at me because leeches don't just sit there. They're on a mission. They had their marks. They were supposed to be on a pentagram, and they wouldn't stay, of course."

Jones shudders at the memory. "The only thing that kept me together with that one— probably the hardest of the episode—was that there was this actress lying there and she had a prosthetic stomach for the leeches to be on. As soon as no one was paying attention to them, the leeches would just dive under the sheets to get at her. She was completely freaked. And so I thought her position is so much worse than mine just to be lying there with leeches on you. So I kind of got it together to make sure people had taped the sheets down for her. It was easier if I was thinking that I was preventing *her* from losing her mind, than just preventing *myself* from losing my mind.

"Even the girl who was the leech wrangler—and they are usually tough as anything— was squirming and shuddering being around them. I think it is a primitive instinct." Did any of the leeches ever get to the table-bound actress? "No. There is one that you can see in the scene that they used that is trying to make a big escape, and I catch it a couple times. They were looking for the real stuff."

In an episode full of extraordinarily weird things for one actress to be put through, Jones was put through one more for her big death scene: A bewitched Waite coughs up a bloody bunch of straight-pins. "They had all these pins that I think someone had gone to the trouble of taking the points off. For my own protection, they wanted to fit my mouth with this *ghastly* contraption that would prevent the pins from going down my throat, and still allow me to breath through my nose. It was like some den-tal dam. They also took impressions of my teeth like the dentist does when you need a crown. But it was not a dentist. It was in the special effects shop, where it is a very different atmosphere than the hygiene of the dentist.

"So they had these awful things that they were sticking in my mouth plus [I was] surrounded by alien corpses and fetuses. The guys who work in the shop are these perfectly angelic Botticelli-curl kind of guys that are surrounded with this horror. Whenever they would come onto the set they would be bringing one ghastly *bleeding* thing after another. They put this dental dam thing together that was so awful, and it didn't really work. I was saying that I was willing to put pins in my mouth and trust that my tongue was smart enough to keep them away from my throat, but they wouldn't have it. There's this thing that happens in the movies sometimes when they just want to get something done . . . they forget that there is a real live person there. I said I wanted to have a demonstration of how it would work by another *human*. So the poor special effects guys had to take an impression of their own mouth and have one of these dams in their mouth and show me liquids of varying viscosity and how the pins would work therein. And I actually felt quite connected to this other poor soul who had gone through the whole thing. It was still an awkward horrible thing, but *possible* once I knew there was a fellow creature who had gone through it."

That wasn't the end of the indignities though, as Jones laughingly says, "Then I also had to learn to puke in rhythm with the guy who was working the puke machine. They had some piping-thing set up with ghastly gurgling and whole lot of pins coming out of it cause I could only have a few coming out of my mouth. We had to be like in sync with when he would push the plunger and I would make the heaving—it was like another strangely intimate relationship."

Jones agrees that the *X-Files* experience taught her things she never thought she would have to do when she was taking acting lessons. Now her resume can list in the special skills category "Can puke pins." "It comes in handy," she laughs. "You never know."

X80 Musings of a Cigarette-Smoking Man

Case Number: 4.07 / #80 (#4X01)
First Sighting: November 17, 1996
Directed by: James Wong
Written by: Glen Morgan

GUEST CAST	CHARACTER
William B. Davis	Cigarette-Smoking Man
Morgan Weisser	Lee Harvey Oswald
Chris Owens	Young Cigarette-Smoking Man
Donnelly Rhodes	General Francis
Tom Braidwood	Frohike
Bruce Harwood	Byers
Jerry Hardin	Deep Throat
Dan Zukovic	Agent
Peter Hanlon	Aide
Dean Aylesworth	Young Bill Mulder
Paul Jarret	James Earl Ray
David Fredericks	Director
Laurie Murdoch	Lydon

UNCREDITED

Anthony Ashbee	Corporal
Marc Baur	Matlock
Gonzalo Canton	Cuban Man
Colin Lawrence	Troop Leader
Peter Mele	Mob Man
Steve Oatway	Supervisor
Michael St. John Smith	Major General
Jude Zachary	Jones

FIELD REPORT

Washington, D.C. Frohike and the Lone Gunmen have unravelled the secret past of the Cigarette-Smoking Man, and they call in Mulder and Scully to fill them in on the conspiracy. In a building nearby, Cigarette-Smoking Man eavesdrops on them with an electronic listening device, even as he targets the front door with a sniper's rifle. The conspiracy begins back when CSM was an Army Captain who is drafted by right-wing conspirators to assassinate JFK and set up Lee Harvey Oswald.

Through the years, CSM gives orders to J. Edgar Hoover, aids in the assassination of Martin Luther King Jr., rigs elections and sporting events, and helps start wars. When an alien is found in wreckage from a UFO and is killed by Deep Throat, CSM discovers a reborn purpose and sets off on a path that leads to the opening of the X-Files. All the while, CSM is writing pulp espionage stories and novels under the name of "Raul Bloodworth." When he finally gets a story accepted, he plans to quit the shadowy conspiracy and smokes his last cigarette. But after the story is serialized in the sleazy magazine *Roman á Clef,* he is disillusioned, buys a fresh pack of cigarettes, and resumes his malevolent activities. As the story concludes, will he kill Frohike, or is the truth still out there?

WITNESS NOTES

At one point, Lee Harvey Oswald refers to Cigarette-Smoking Man as "Mr. Hunt." While this name is surely as fictitious as CSM's writing *nom de plume,* Raul Bloodworth, it *is* a reference to Howard Hunt, a CIA agent who was involved in the Watergate scandal. Conspiracy theorists also link him to the Kennedy assassination.

Neither David Duchovny nor Gillian Anderson actually filmed any original scenes for this episode. All scenes with them are flashbacks to the pilot episode. They did, however, record their voices for the opening sequence.

Morgan Weisser had a small role in this episode as conspiracy-favorite and possible-President-killer Lee Harvey Oswald. Weisser is a second generation actor whose father is Norbert Weisser. Morgan has appeared in the post-apocalypse flick *City Limits* (1985), the bleakly futuristic *Prayer of the Rollerboys* (1991), and the horror film *Mother* (1996). He's also had a handful of guest appearances on *Crime and Punishment, China Beach, Law & Order,* and *Quantum Leap.* Weisser was also a lead in Glen Morgan and James Wong's Fox science fiction series, *Space: Above & Beyond,* where he played Marine fighter pilot Nathan West, whose quest for his lost girlfriend drives him dangerously forward into unknown territory.

Chris Owens (Young Cigarette-Smoking Man) appeared in the movies *The Big Town* (1987), *Cocktail* (1988), and *Sabotage* (1996).

Michael St. John Smith (Major General) appeared as Gil in "Paper Dove," the first season finale episode of Chris Carter's *Millennium.*

He also appeared in "Monster," the second season episode of *Millennium.*

X81 Tunguska

Case Number: 4.08 / #81 (#4X09)
First Sighting: November 24, 1996
Directed by: Kim Manners (Rob Bowman?)
Written by: Chris Carter & Frank Spotnitz

GUEST CAST	CHARACTER
Mitch Pileggi	Assistant Director Walter S. Skinner
William B. Davis	Cigarette-Smoking Man
Nicholas Lea	Alex Krycek
Laurie Holden	Marita Covarrubias
John Neville	Well-Manicured Man
Brendan Beiser	Agent Pendrell
Fritz Weaver	Senator Sorenson
Malcolm Stewart	Dr. Sacks
David Bloom	Stress Man
Campbell Lane	Committee Chairman
Stefan Arngrim	Prisoner
Brent Stait	Terry Edward Mayhew

UNCREDITED

John Hainsworth	Gaunt Man
Olesky Shostak	Bundled Man
Robin Mossley	Dr. Kingsley Looker
Jessica Schreier	Dr. Bonita Sayre
Eileen Pedde	Angie
Lee Serpa	Swarthy Man

FIELD REPORT

Tunguska, Siberia / Washington, D.C. A man claiming diplomatic immunity is carrying a pouch but a customs agent insists on searching it. Moments later, the agent is the victim of a strange black oil that pierces his skin. In Washington, D.C., Mulder receives a tip from Alex Krycek about a bombing by a right-wing militia group and Krycek tells Mulder he wants revenge on Cigarette-Smoking Man. On Krycek's word, Mulder and Scully capture a Russian courier whose diplomatic pouch carries an extraterrestrial rock that is suffused with the black oil. A scientist attempting to study the rock is attacked by the oil, and seemingly killed.

Taken to Skinner's apartment, a captive Krycek is beaten, then handcuffed to a balcony ledge. Even so, Krycek manages to kill a man who's searching Skinner's place, leaving Skinner with some sticky questions to answer when the cops arrive. Mulder and Krycek travel to Tunguska, Siberia, where Mulder knows a meteor crashed in 1908. There, the two men find a gulag where prisoners are forced to mine the rock containing the deadly black oil. They're both captured, and Mulder soon finds out that Krycek is working with the Russians. That night, Mulder is wired to a table and the black oil is dripped onto him.

WITNESS NOTES

The official *X-Files* Web site lists Jan Rubes appearing in this episode as Vassily Peskow, but he does not appear until the next episode.

The blue biohazard suits used in this episode and the next were on loan from the technical advisor of *Outbreak*, the 1995 Dustin Hoffman film about a viral disaster. Real biohazard suits used by the Centers for Disease Control are not nearly so interesting looking.

Fritz Weaver (Senator Sorenson) is an industry veteran, having appeared in over forty movies and dozens of television series since the fifties, where he was in many live television productions. Also a stage actor, Weaver won Broadway's Tony Award in 1970 for his performance in *Child's Play*. Some of his most impressive on-camera credits are *Marathon Man* (1976), Thomas Harris' *Black Sunday* (1977) in which he played FBI Agent Corley, the *Holocaust* miniseries (1978), and the telefilm *Citizen Cohn* (1992). Genre credits include the horror film *Demon Seed* (1977), Ray Bradbury's *The Martian Chronicles* miniseries (1980), the execrable *Jaws of Satan* (1981), and Stephen King's *Creepshow* (1982). On television, he appeared in two episodes of the original *Twilight Zone* and one of the eighties *Zone* revival episodes, as well as episodes of *Rod Serling's Night Gallery*, *The Invaders*, *Mission Impossible*, *Tales From the Darkside*, *Monsters*, *Friday the 13th*, and *The New Adventures of Wonder Woman*.

Malcolm Stewart (Dr. Sacks) has science fiction credits that include episodes of *The Twilight Zone*, *Ray Bradbury Theater*, *My Secret Identity*, and the movies *Timecop* (1994) and *Jumanji* (1995).

Stefan Arngrim (Prisoner) was born in 1955 in Canada, and became an actor in the mid-sixties. In 1968, he played the role of Barry Lockridge, a twelve-year-old dog owner, on the television series *Land of the Giants*, which ran for two seasons on ABC. He appeared in other shows of the period, but basically disappeared from Hollywood in the seventies, when he was the lead singer of a punk rock band. He returned to acting in the eighties with roles in such low-budget horror films as *Fear No Evil* (1981) and *Class of 1984* (1982). Arngrim recently appeared on *Highlander*, in *The Sentinel* episode "Payback," and in the futuristic film *Strange Days* (1995). He wrote the screenplay for the film *Cold Front* (1989) and is reportedly working on a pilot for a possible series.

WITNESS PROFILE
LAURIE HOLDEN

Born: 1971 or 1972

Who is Marita Covarrubias, and whose side is she on, anyway? Those answers aren't due any time soon, but as seen in the fourth season's "Zero-Sum," things are not as they seem with Mulder's latest informant. Covarrubias may be working for Cigarette-Smoking Man and the Syndicate, or she may be playing both ends against each other. So, if we can't answer that first question, how about "Who is Laurie Holden?"

The simple answer is that Holden is the actress that plays the sultry blond Covarrubias, known by fans as the "UNBlond." Raised in Toronto, Holden migrated to California to attend the UCLA School of Theater, Film, and Television, graduating with a B.A. in 1993. She made her feature film debut in the Canadian film *Separate Vacations* (1986). Soon thereafter she was seen in the interactive live-action children's show *Captain Power and the Soldiers of the Future* in the episode "Gemini and Counting," which was about a virus spreading throughout the land.

Feature credits for Holden include *Physical Evidence* (1989), *Expect No Mercy* (1995), and *Past Perfect* (1996). The blond actress has also had roles in the telefilm *TekWar: Tek Lab* (1994), as well as the TNT miniseries *Young Catherine* (1991). Television appearances include guest shots on *Due South, Murder, She Wrote*, and *Edison Twins*.

Holden has appeared in a number of genre projects, including episodes of *Highlander* ("Homeland"), *Poltergeist: The Legacy* ("The Thirteenth Generation" with fellow *X-Files* star Vanessa Morley), and *Two*. She'll be seen in an upcoming episode of Showtime's *Dead Man's Gun*, and is a regular cast member on the CBS mid-season replacement for 1997–1998, *The Magnificent Seven*.

Holden landed the role of Marita Covarrubias in the summer of 1996, when she went to a very hush-hush audition. Secrecy was so tight that she was unable to get a script to prepare for her scene before she arrived at the audition. "All I knew was that it was a woman who worked at the U.N. who had an air of 'intelligent seriousness.'" Holden said in *Entertainment Weekly*. "They've always said to me 'Keep the mystery.'" The actress thinks of Covarrubias as a treacherous Mata Hari. "You can't really read what she's saying or what her intentions are."

As to the development of the character, "I thought it was more interesting for Mulder's next contact to be a woman," said Chris Carter in *TV Guide*. "I wanted there to be some suspicion about whether Mulder would be involved with her romantically. And she [works] in the United Nations as the conspiracy [is] expanding globally."

Will Covarrubias become involved with Mulder? The future will tell, but Holden admits in *Entertainment Weekly* that "He *is* very attractive. But any attraction would be overridden by the greater task at hand . . . so far."

X82 Terma

Case Number: 4.09 / #82 (#4X10)
First Sighting: December 1, 1996
Directed by: Rob Bowman
Written by: Frank Spotnitz & Chris Carter

GUEST CAST	CHARACTER
Mitch Pileggi	Assistant Director Walter S. Skinner
William B. Davis	Cigarette-Smoking Man
Nicholas Lea	Alex Krycek
John Neville	Well-Manicured Man
Stefan Arngrim	Prisoner
Jan Rubes	Vassily Peskow
Fritz Weaver	Senator Sorenson

Brent Stait	Terry Edward Mayhew
Malcolm Stewart	Dr. Sacks
Campbell Lane	Committee Chairman
Robin Mossley	Dr. Kingsley Looker
Jessica Schreier	Dr. Bonita Chung-Sayre
Brenda McDonald	Auntie Janet
Pamela MacDonald	Nurse
Eileen Pedde	Angie

UNCREDITED

John Hainsworth	Gaunt Man
Olesky Shostak	Bundled Man

FIELD REPORT

Tunguska, Siberia / Washington, D.C. Scully and Skinner are forced to appear before the Senate Select Subcommittee on Intelligence and Terrorism to explain the death of the Russian diplomat at Skinner's apartment and to explain the whereabouts of the missing Mulder. Back in Tunguska, Mulder escapes from the camp, managing to drag Krycek along with him. Former KGB assassin Vassily Peskow is brought out of retirement to kill Dr. Bonita Chung-Sayre, the physician (and lover) of the Well-Manicured Man. Chung-Sayre has also apparently been experimenting with benificial uses of the black oil.

Scully won't reveal Mulder's whereabouts, and is jailed for contempt of Congress. Peskow kills the scientist who was infected by the black oil within the rock, then takes the Tunguska rock with him. In Tunguska, Krycek escapes from Mulder and is rescued by a band of one-armed men who live in the woods. Krycek finds out too late that they amputate the left arm of everyone they save to keep them from being infected by the black oil virus. Mulder returns to Washington, D.C. in time to save Scully from testifying before the committee, and the two agents race to find evidence of the black oil before Peskow can destroy all of it. In the end, Cigarette-Smoking Man suppresses the evidence about the black oil, while Krycek, now with a prosthetic left arm, welcomes Peskow back to St. Petersburg.

WITNESS NOTES

The official *X-Files* Web site lists Brendan Beiser appearing in this episode as Agent Pendrell, but he only appears in the previous episode.

The riders who appeared in this episode as Russian prison guards were world championship riders from nearby Calgary. Stunt coordinator Tony Morelli said in *The Official X-Files* magazine that "All of those riders have been in movies before, so whenever I need a cowboy I go to Calgary." The horses were from Vancouver, and were specially trained to work in front of the cameras and not be skittish around gunfire.

Jan Rubes (Vassily Peskow) worked in Hollywood in the late sixties and seventies, but most of his larger roles came in the eighties. He appeared in such films as *Charlie Grant's War* (1980), *Blood Relations* (1987), and *D2: The Mighty Ducks* (1994). He has appeared in the genre projects *War of the Worlds* (the "Choirs of Angels" episode), the direct-to-video *The Amityville Curse* (1990), and the telefilm *The Birds II: Land's End* (1994).

Brent Stait (Terry Edward Mayhew) made one of his earliest professional acting appearances in *Captain Power and the Soldiers of the Future*, in the episode "The Eden Road." He later appeared in the telefilms *Omen IV: The Awakening* (1991), *I Still Dream of Jeannie* (1991), and the *Titanic* miniseries (1996).

Campbell Lane (Committee Chairman) played the role of Frank Jewett in Stephen King's *Needful Things* (1993) and appeared in the feature film *Look Who's Talking Now* (1993) and the telefilms *Deadlocked: Escape From Zone 14* (1995) and *In Cold Blood* (1996). He has also done voices for the animated series *Captain N: The Game Master* and *Stone Protectors*.

X83 Paper Hearts

Case Number:	4.10 / #83 (#4X08)
First Sighting:	December 15, 1996
Directed by:	Rob Bowman
Written by:	Vince Gilligan

GUEST CAST	CHARACTER
Mitch Pileggi	Assistant Director Walter S. Skinner
Tom Noonan	John Lee Roche
Byrne Piven	Robert Sparks
Rebecca Toolan	Mrs. Mulder
Jane Perry	Day Care Operator

Vanessa Morley	Young Samantha Mulder
Edward Diaz	El Camino Owner
Paul Bittante	Local Cop
Carly McKillip	Caitlin Ross

UNCREDITED
| Sonia Norris | Young Mother |
| John Dadey | Local Agent |

FIELD REPORT

Manassas, Virginia/Hollyville, Delaware. When Mulder's dreams lead him to the hidden grave of a murdered child with a heart shape cut out of her clothing, he is taken back to one of his first cases, wherein he profiled serial killer John Lee Roche. The killer had abducted thirteen young girls, strangled them, and kept a heart-shaped piece of fabric cut from their clothes. Those trophies of his killings were never found, and Mulder becomes convinced Roche killed more girls than he has admitted to. Led by clues in his dreams, Mulder finds sixteen cloth hearts, meaning Roche still has two more undiscovered victims.

After questioning the killer, Mulder dreams about his sister's abduction; this time, instead of the aliens taking Samantha, it's Roche who is stealing her away. Scully is alarmed at Mulder's anger towards Roche, and Skinner removes him from the case for hitting the killer. Even as Roche taunts him with clues, Mulder finds more evidence that Roche may indeed be Samantha's abductor. In a desperate bid to find the truth, Mulder takes Roche out of prison and back to the Mulders' home in Martha's Vineyard. Mulder tricks the killer, but Roche later escapes and abducts another girl. Will Mulder have her blood on his hands?

WITNESS NOTES

Tom Noonan (John Lee Roche) was most memorable when cast in Michael Mann's feature film *Manhunter*, the adaptation of Thomas Harris's *Red Dragon*, the first novel to feature Hannibal Lecter. Noonan played Francis Dollarhyde, the spacey killer who is pursued by FBI profiler Will Graham. Noonan also appeared in *The Monster Squad* (1987) as Frankenstein and in *The Last Action Hero* (1993) as the Ripper. For more on the career of Tom Noonan, visit his official Web site at http://www.tomnoonan.com/

Byrne Piven (Robert Sparks) is the father of actor Jeremy Piven of *Ellen* fame. Byrne has been working in Hollywood since the mid-seventies and has appeared in the films *Creator* (1985), the remake of *Miracle on 34th Street* (1994), and $E=mc^2$ (1996). He also appeared in the telefilm *Dreams of Gold: The Mel Fisher Story* (1986) with Steven Williams and in the miniseries *Pandora's Clock* (1996) with Jerry Hardin.

Vanessa Morley made her first appearance as Young Samantha Mulder in the second season episode "The Blessing Way." The young actress does not have many credits yet, though she did appear in *Look Who's Talking Now* (1993) as a little girl in the schoolyard. In the "Corner of the Eye" episode of Showtime's revival of *The Outer Limits*—in which a man who gains healing powers may be possessed by aliens—she starred in the role of Miranda. She also appeared in "The Thirteenth Generation" episode of *Poltergeist: The Legacy*.

X84 El Mundo Gira

Case Number:	4.11 / #84 (#4X11)
First Sighting:	January 12, 1997
Directed by:	Tucker Gates
Written by:	John Shiban

GUEST CAST	CHARACTER
Mitch Pileggi	Assistant Director Walter S. Skinner
Ruben Blades	Conrad Lozano
Raymond Cruz	Eladio Buente
José Yenque	Soledad Buente
Simi	Gabrielle Buente
Lillian Hurst	Flakita
Susan Bain	County Coroner
Robert Thurston	Dr. Larry Steen
Michael Kopsa	Rick Culver
Marcus Hondro	Barber
Janette Munoz	Village Woman
Pamela Diaz	Maria Dorantes
Fabricio Santin	Migrant Worker
Jose Vargas	INS Worker
Tony Dean Smith	Store Clerk

UNCREDITED
| Tina Amayo | Older Shanty Woman |

FIELD REPORT

San Joaquin Valley, California. A hot yellow rain pours down on a migrant worker camp after which a young girl, Maria Dorantes, and a goat are found mutilated. Mulder and Scully arrive, Mulder claiming that the yellow rain is a Fortean event. Things become stranger still when an old migrant woman says the deaths were the work of the mythical El Chupacabra (the Goatsucker), a hairless grey creature with big eyes and a large head that feeds on goats and unlucky humans.

Suspicion for the girl's death falls on Eladio Buente, who had been flirting with Maria shortly before her death. Eladio's accuser is his jealous brother. After Eladio is arrested and later escapes, Scully finds that he may be carrying a highly contagious fungal enzyme that can kill people very quickly; anyone exposed to Eladio may be in danger. With the aid of Immigration agent Conrad Lozano, Mulder and Scully attempt to find Eladio before his own brother can kill him, unaware that Eladio has indeed become something less than human . . . and that his brother may be changing into a Chupacabra as well.

Ruben Blades starred in "El Mundo Gira."

WITNESS NOTES

The actor whose face is rotting off due to the curse of the "Chupacabra" (Raymond Cruz) is actually wearing a special makeup mix comprised of K-Y Jelly lubricant, glue, and instant potato flakes.

Raymond Cruz (Eladio Buente) has had major roles in *Vietnam War Story III* (1989) and Tom Clancy's *Clear and Present Danger* (1994). He also appeared in *Gremlins 2: The New Batch* (1990), *Dead Again* (1991), and *Alien: Resurrection* (1997).

Simi (Gabrielle Buente) is presumably actress Simi Mehta, whose only other known credit is in the telefilm *Grand Avenue* (1996).

Lillian Hurst (Flakita) had a role in the direct-to-video horror film *Sleepstalker: The Sandman's Last Rites* (1994).

WITNESS PROFILE
RUBEN BLADES

Born: July 16, 1948, Panama City, Panama

"There's a Hispanic actor of note, Ruben Blades, who is a big fan of the show," said Chris Carter in *Sci Fi Universe* prior to the filming of this episode. "We're trying to figure out a way to put him on. He's called with several suggestions, something that would be indigenous [to his Hispanic culture]."

As Carter states above, Blades is a Hispanic actor of note, though he's also done quite a bit more than acting. He was a Panamanian pop star whose specialty was salsa music when he began acting in films in the early eighties. He cowrote and starred in *Crossover Dreams* (1985), earning critical acclaim for his portrayal of an egocentric salsa singer.

Blades is best known by genre fans for his role as a cop in *Predator 2* (1990), one of his only genre roles. More current roles include *Color of Night* (1994) and the recent *The Devil's Own* (1997). In the summer of 1997, Blades was one of eighteen Hollywood personalities to be awarded a star on the Hollywood Walk of Fame for his work as a musician.

A graduate of Harvard Law School, Blades ran for president of Panama in 1994 as the founder and leader of the Papa Egaro party. He came in third behind the two leading parties, winning twenty percent of the vote. His party is still active, having gained enough seats in the Panamanian Legislature to ensure that its voice is heard. Speaking of being heard, despite what's written in other books, Ruben's surname is pronounced not "Blaidz," but "Blah-dess."

X85 Leonard Betts

Case Number: 4.12 / #85 (#4X14)
First Sighting: January 26, 1997
Directed by: Kim Manners
Written by: Frank Spotnitz, John Shiban
                    & Vince Gilligan

GUEST CAST	CHARACTER
Paul McCrane	Leonard M. Betts, a.k.a. Albert Tanner
Marjorie Lovett	Elaine Tanner
Jennifer Clement	Michele Wilkes
Bill Dow	Dr. Charles Burks
Sean Campbell	Local Cop
Dave Hurtubise	Pathologist
Peter Bryant	Uniformed Cop
Laara Sadiq	Female EMT
J. Douglas Stewart	Male EMT
Brad Loree	Security Guard

UNCREDITED	
Lucia Walters	EMT
Ken Jones	Bearded Man
Greg Newmeyer	New Partner
Don Ackerman	Night Attendant

FIELD REPORT

Pittsburgh, Pennsylvania. When an ambulance is hit by a truck, one of the EMTs, Leonard Betts, is decapitated. Later, his headless corpse seems to walk out of the hospital on its own, and the security tapes show a strange fog around the head of the person leaving. Mulder and Scully look in the hospital's bio-disposal unit for clues, where they recover the missing head. During Scully's autopsy on the head, it exhibits signs that it's not quite dead!

Betts's tissues are analyzed, and his body is full of cancer. Mulder thinks Betts may be able to regenerate his body parts, and when the agents search Betts's car, they find bags full of human tumors. Apparently, Mulder is right, and Betts needs tumors to survive. He kills a bearded man and eats his cancerous lung, then gives "birth" to another Leonard Betts! Mulder and Scully think they've killed Betts in self-defense, but it's actually only the previous host body. They track Betts to his mother's house, then inadvertently give Betts a ride to the hospital aboard the ambulance. There, Betts menaces Scully, telling her she has something he needs to survive. Later, the ordeal over, Scully's nose begins to bleed and she wonders whether she has cancer herself.

WITNESS NOTES

A warning at the beginning of the episode reads "This episode may contain sequences too intense for younger children. Parental discretion is advised."

Paul McCrane (Leonard M. Betts/Albert Tanner) is a Philadelphia-born actor whose most famous role was as the sensitive gay student, Montgomery MacNeil, in the musical film *Fame* (1980). Other memorable films he appeared in include *Robocop* (1987), the cable film *Strapped* (1993) with fellow *X-Files* guest Bokeem Woodbine, and Stephen King's *The Shawshank Redemption* (1994). He was also a regular on Stephen Bochco's failed musical TV series, *Cop Rock*.

Marjorie Lovett (Elaine Tanner) has had roles in two major drag movies—*Tootsie* (1982) and *The Birdcage* (1996)—as well as in a movie most critics called "a drag"—*The Fan* (1996).

Jennifer Clement (Michele Wilkes) co-starred with Nicholas Lea in *The Raffle* (1995), and appeared in *The Crush* (1993) and the Christmas telefilm *Ebbie* (1995).

X86 Never Again

Case Number: 4.13/ #86 (#4X13)
First Sighting: February 2, 1997
Directed by: John Shiban
Written by: Glen Morgan & James Wong

GUEST CAST	CHARACTER
Rodney Rowland	Ed Jerse
Jodie Foster	The voice of "Betty"
Bill Croft	Comrade Svo
Jay Donahue	Detective Gouveia
B. J. Harrison	Hannah
Jillian Fargey	Kaye Schilling
Jan Bailey Mattia	Mrs. Hadden
Igor Morozov	Vsevlod Pudovkin
Ian Robison	Detective Smith

UNCREDITED	
Carla Stewart	Judge
Barry "Bear" Hortin	Bartender
Rita Bozi	Ms. Vansen
Marilyn Chin	Mrs. Shima-Tsuno
Natasha Vasiluk	Russian Store Owner

| Peter Nadler | Ed's Lawyer |
| Jen Forgie | Ed's Ex-Wife |

FIELD REPORT

Philadelphia, Pennsylvania. Newly divorced and hurting from the settlement, handsome Ed Jerse gets drunk and heads into a tattoo parlor. When he leaves he's got a vampy cartoon woman on his arm with the words "Never Again" scrolled across her. Soon, Ed starts hearing a female voice that denigrates him, and his behavior becomes erratic and angry. And speaking of anger, Scully has had about enough of Mulder's theories and is glad he's being forced to take a vacation. She goes to Phildelphia to investigate a potential X-File involving a Russian; the case leads nowhere, except that Scully meets Jerse at the tattoo parlor where he's begging to have his tattoo removed.

Despite her better judgement, Scully accepts a date with Jerse, then gets a tattoo of her own and accompanies him back to his apartment. Before the two can become intimate, Ed's tattoo warns him that if he kisses Scully, she's dead. Jerse sleeps on the couch that night, and the next morning, Scully is rousted by detectives investigating the death of Jerse's downstairs neighbor. Scully soon finds that one of the chemicals used in her and Ed's tattoos has hallucinogenic properties; later, taunted by his tattoo and the knowledge that Scully is an FBI agent, Jerse tries to kill Scully. As he's about to stuff her into the incinerator, Jerse decides to take control, and burns the tattoo off by thrusting his arm into the flames instead.

WITNESS NOTES

Rodney Rowland (Ed Jerse) was a star of Glen Morgan and James Wong's Fox science fiction series, *Space: Above & Beyond*, where he played Cooper Hawkes. Rowland is a surfer and the rebellious son of a minister and was a print model in Europe before moving to acting. The sparks flying between Anderson and Rowland in this *X-Files* episode may have lit a fire between the two. Gillian Anderson has been out on at least two dates with Rowland, showing up on his arm (or was he on her arm?) at the spring ceremony where Fox unveiled its fall 1997 schedule to the press and again on June 7th for the MTV Movie Awards ceremony.

Bill Croft (Comrade Svo) played Broadface in the "Maranatha" episode of Chris Carter's *Millennium*.

WITNESS PROFILE

JODIE FOSTER

Born: November 19, 1962, Los Angeles, California

Although she only appears in this episode as a disembodied voice, actress Jodie Foster's husky voice was recognizable and she was also the biggest name cast member *The X-Files* had seen so far.

Foster was born Alicia Christian Foster, and her brother, Buddy, was a child actor as she grew up. A fluke audition at an interview for Buddy led to Jodie's becoming the "Coppertone girl" with a puppy pulling down her swimsuit to show an untanned cheek. Foster worked through the sixties on television and film, appearing in many Disney projects and as a regular in the series *Paper Moon*.

In 1976, Foster made a big splash, appearing in Martin Scorcese's *Taxi Driver* in the role of a teenage prostitute, for which she received an Oscar nomination for Best Supporting Actress. That role also brought her her first stalker, John Hinckley, who fixated on the young star and years later attempted to assassinate President Ronald Reagan to prove his love for her.

Foster continued to act while attending Yale University. In 1988, she played a lower-class rape victim in *The Accused*, filmed in Vancouver, a part that won her the Best Actress Oscar. She captured the award again for her role as FBI trainee Clarice Starling in *The Silence of the Lambs* (1991). That role was one of the inspirations for the character of *The X-Files'* Dana Scully, both in look and demeanor.

In the past several years, Foster has been quietly gaining power as an actress, a producer, and a director, with all of the attendant publicity that comes with it. She has persistently not commented on the rumors that she is a lesbian, preferring that her private life remain private, and has been the subject of a tell-all biography, *Foster Child*, by brother Buddy. She has continued to win critical acclaim for her roles in such films as *Sommersby* (1993), *Maverick* (1994), and *Nell* (1994), for which she received yet another Oscar nomination. She produces films under the production company Egg Pictures, founded in 1990, and has directed *Little Man Tate* (1991) and *Home for the Holidays* (1995).

In 1997 Foster starred in *Contact*, the feature film based on Carl Sagan's book. She plays Dr. Eleanor Arroway, the first scientist to make contact with extraterrestrial life.

X87 Memento Mori

Case Number: 4.14/ #87 (#4X15)
First Sighting: February 9, 1997
Directed by: Rob Bowman
Written by: Chris Carter, Frank Spotnitz, John Shiban & Vince Gilligan

GUEST CAST	CHARACTER
Mitch Pileggi	Assistant Director Walter S. Skinner
William B. Davis	Cigarette-Smoking Man
Sheila Larken	Margaret (Maggie) Scully
David Lovgren	Kurt Crawford
Gillian Barber	Penny Northern
Tom Braidwood	Frohike
Dean Haglund	Langly
Bruce Harwood	Byers
Morris Panych	Gray-Haired Man
Sean Allen	Dr. Kevin Scanlon
Julie Bond	Woman

FIELD REPORT

Allentown, Pennsylvania / Washington, D.C. Scully admits to Mulder that she has an inoperable tumorous cancer, and the two agents begin an investigation of the female abductees who had implants in their necks (last seen in "Nisei"). The agents discover that all but one of the women are dead from cancerous brain tumors, and they also find a computer hacker downloading all of abductee Betsy Hagopian's computer files. As Mulder searches the files with the hacker, Kurt Crawford, Scully visits the last survivor, Penny Northern. At Penny's advice, Scully begins experimental treatments with Dr. Scanlon.

That night, the Gray-Haired Man kills Crawford, but when Mulder breaks into a fertility clinic, he discovers another Kurt Crawford. With the help of the Lone Gunmen, Mulder accesses a secret research facility, where

he finds the clones of Kurt Crawford working with eggs harvested from the ovaries of the now-dead female abductees. Mulder is almost killed by the Gray-Haired Man, but he escapes and returns to the hospital to join Scully, who has been stopped from taking the treatment due to warnings from Byers. And in the background, Skinner has made a deal with Cigarette-Smoking Man to save Scully's life.

WITNESS NOTES

There is some confusion over the title of this episode. The official Fox *X-Files* Web site lists both "Momento Mori" and "Memento Mori." It seems likely that the latter is correct.

David Lovgren (Kurt Crawford) has yet to have a breakthrough film or television role, though he has appeared in *Cool Runnings* (1993), and six telefilms, including *The Comrades of Summer* (1992) and *Not Our Son* (1994).

Gillian Barber starred in "Nisei" and "Memento Mori" as Penny Northern, and in "Ghost in the Machine" as Nancy Spiller.

WITNESS INTERVIEW

GILLIAN BARBER

Born: February 22, 1958, Coventry, Warwickshire, England

At the age of four, Gillian Barber decided to become an actress. It seemed natural, as her mother was a stage actress and young Gillian often watched her in musicals. After her family moved to Canada, Barber worked in every stage production she could, musical and otherwise, leading to her attendance at London's Guildhall School of Music and Drama. In 1979, she came back from London, lured by the promise of several CBC radio drama jobs.

Barber continued perform in theater through the eighties, becoming one of Vancouver's most respected stage actresses. She played in the Vancouver production (and subsequent tour) of *Angry Housewives* for over a year, and later toured with the Canadian hit play *Talking Dirty*. When Hollywood began doing productions in Vancouver, she was a favorite of casting directors, though she had already had roles in such Canadian fare as *Danger Bay* and *The Beachcombers*, plus a critical role in *Midnight Matinee* (1988), a film which featured many future *X-Files* stars.

Gillian appeared in the films *The Stepfather* (1987), the Oscar-nominated short film *Rainbow Wars*, Stephen King's *Needful Things* (1993) as fellow *X-Files* guest J. T. Walsh's wife, *Jumanji* (1996), and the recent miniseries *In Cold Blood* (1996), in which she played doomed wife Bonnie Clutter, and Dean R. Koontz's *Intensity* (1997). Her television guest appearances have included roles on *The Commish, The Outer Limits, Sliders* ("Gillian of the Spirits"), *The Sentinel*, and *Poltergeist: The Legacy*. She is part of the medieval folk singing group "Willie and the Wassailers," which also includes fellow *X-Files* guest Karin Konoval.

Having appeared on four episodes of *The X-Files*, Barber is clearly a favorite of the casting directors. "The first season I played the head of the FBI who gave Scully and Mulder a dressing down at a board meeting (in 'Ghost in the Machine')," says Barber. "At that point I met Robert Goodwin, and he was so nice to me. He said 'Oh, you did a great job, we will have you back.' Well sure enough, the second season they called me in every second [audition] because they wanted to try and get me a part. That's when I did 'Red Museum.' Then in the third season, I got cast as one of the MUFON women that had been abducted and recognized Scully as one of us."

The role was Penny Northern in the episode "Nisei," and Barber didn't expect her to reap-

pear. But in January 1997, the *X-Files* producers brought her back to film "Memento Mori." "Robert [Goodwin] phoned me two days after I finished shooting and said 'Don't worry. Just because we killed you off doesn't mean you won't be in next season. We'll morph you into something else!' " [Laughs.]

The hospital scenes were emotionally demanding for Barber and Anderson—who were known as 'Gillian A' and 'Gillian B' on the set—because both were going through family brushes with cancer. "It was difficult for both of us, but the director, Rob [Bowman] was extremely sensitive to that and let us go. They never cut. They would always let us go all the way through the scene rather than stop us mid-emotion. And it was not a closed set, but there certainly were not as many people milling around as usual. I just stayed in my hospital bed all hooked up to all the machines. My father had recently had a huge operation for cancer. It took him a long time to recover from it. So that was really present in my mind as I was doing it. Watching him go through it had really informed me of the suffering and the intense feelings that you have . . . how you are desperate to communicate whatever those deep emotions that you are feeling . . . because you just never know when any breath may be your last. [Filming] was quite emotional. I spent a few days crying."

Although it had been emotional during the shoot, the episode was "very cathartic. Because my father was better, it freed me to act my way through it, but then be relieved at the end of the day. I didn't take it home with me. My father phoned me up after he saw it and said that he was very proud of me and glad that he could be of help."

Backtracking a bit, Northern remembers her first *X-Files* role as Nancy "The Iron Maiden" Spiller. "You really want to let the wardrobe and makeup help you, so I asked for the tightest skirt they could find (and) a pair of support panty hose. It just sucks everything in right, so what it does to your carriage when you walk is make you ramrod straight. I also did some reading on the FBI to get that bureaucratic feel. I had gotten them to drag my hair back into a tight bun, and the scene really did the rest. 'The Iron Maiden,' " she laughs. "All I could think about was chastity belts."

Barber finds the attention she's gotten from *The X-Files* "very flattering. I got a piece of fan mail from a very lonely veteran in North Virginia who had been collecting the [cards] and asked me to sign it and send it back to him. I was really touched. You don't think about your work being broadcast to millions—it's not a concept that crosses your mind when you try to do your work. I have always been very proud of my work for *The X-Files* and very glad to work with them. It has done nothing but enhance my career actually. I would say that the *Sentinel* and the *Poltergeist* people are very aware of the fact that I had done several seasons of *X-Files* and that had piqued their interest."

Barber recently appeared as the mother of an evil child in "Monster," a second season episode of *Millenium*.

X88 Kaddish

Case Number:	4.15/ #88 (#4X12)
First Sighting:	February 16, 1997
Directed by:	Kim Manners
Written by:	Howard Gordon

GUEST CAST	CHARACTER
Justine Miceli	Ariel Luria
David Groh	Jacob Weiss
David Wohl	Kenneth Ungar
Channon Roe	Derek Banks
Harrison Coe	Isaac Luria
Jonathan Whittaker	Curt Brunjes
Timur Karabilgin	Tony Oliver
Jabin Litwiniec	Clinton Macguire
George Gordon	Detective
Murrey Rabinovitch	First Hasidic Man
David Freedman	Rabbi

FIELD REPORT

Brooklyn, New York. A Hasidic Jew named Isaac Luria is killed by a trio of teenage hate-mongers shortly before the religious ceremony that will bind him to his already-legal wife, Ariel. At the cemetery on the night of Isaac's burial, a shadowy figure creates a giant man out of mud. When Mulder and Scully begin to investigate the hate crime against Luria, they find Tony Oliver, one of the assailants, dead. He's been strangled, and the dead-and-buried

Luria's fingerprints are on his body! The other two teens (Banks and Macguire) are being protected by anti-Semite copy-shop owner Curt Brunjes, who denies any knowledge of the crime to Mulder and Scully. Rumors begin to swirl around the community that Isaac Luria has returned from the grave to avenge his death.

That night, Banks and Macguire dig up Luria's body, but it's still in the coffin. Shortly after, something kills Macguire. The next day, Mulder finds a book on Jewish mysticism tucked into Luria's shroud, and Mulder soon theorizes that a Golem, a mythical living being created from earth, may be responsible. Banks is hung in the synagogue, and Ariel's father, Jacob Weiss, confesses. Brunjes is killed soon after, by an earthy creature that resembles Isaac. That night, inside the darkened synagogue, Ariel prepares to finally wed Isaac in a religious ceremony, but Mulder and Scully intrude. In a final, desperate act of love, Ariel tells Isaac she loves him, and then erases the spell. The Isaac-Golem crumbles, leaving his new wife alone.

WITNESS NOTES

David Groh (Jacob Weiss) is best known as Rhoda's husband Joe Gerard on the long-running CBS sitcom *Rhoda*. He had appeared in episodes of the original *Dark Shadows* as the Hangman's Assistant and the One-Armed Man, and recently appeared in the Roger Corman cable film *Last Exit to Earth* (1996).

David Wohl (Kenneth Ungar) has appeared in a number of genre projects including the clone film *D.A.R.Y.L.* (1985), the zombie/vampire film *Chillers* (1988), and as the voice of Bob the dinosaur in two episodes of *Dinosaurs*. He also appeared in *Roe vs. Wade* (1989) with Jerry Hardin.

Channon Roe (Derek Banks), when not acting, indulges in Chris Carter's favorite sport: surfing. Recently, he was seen as Cash, the leader of the vampire biker-rocker Gangrel clan on Fox's short-lived *Kindred: The Embraced*; he often tangled with rival vampire gang leaders—and fellow *X-Files* stars—Jeff Kober and Brian Thompson.

Justine Miceli starred as Ariel Luria in "Kaddish."

WITNESS INTERVIEW
JUSTINE MICELI

Born: April 30, Jackson Heights, Queens, New York

The tempestuous world of law enforcement is excellently portrayed on ABC's drama series *NYPD Blue*, where actress Justine Miceli spent two seasons as Detective Adrianne Lesniak. The role was a natural for the New York native, but after two seasons, the writers had written the character into such a depressed and unlikeable being that it seemed better for Lesniak/Miceli to exit the series rather than stay on board. Soon after, she won the role of Ariel Luria, the young Jewish wife whose love for her murdered husband is strong enough to bring him back from the grave.

Miceli always wanted to be an actress, and was enrolled in a local drama/dance school when she was five or six. Later, she was accepted into the prestigious High School of the Performing Arts (made famous by the movie and series *Fame*), after which she attended the California Institute of the Arts on a full scholarship.

"I always wanted to do good work whatever medium that was in," says Miceli, speaking about the difference between theater and film. "Unfortunately, I struggled over the years because I never had representation. If you don't

have [an agent] you just don't get seen. I finally got representation, and from there I started doing plays, and I was doing commercials, and then I got two soaps [*Another World* and *As the World Turns*]." Miceli got a job on the series *Law & Order* as an extra, then was promoted to a stand-in, and was eventually featured in a guest role. After that came a guest shot on *Feds*, the role on *NYPD Blue*, and *The X-Files*.

When she auditioned for the role of Ariel, Miceli "put on a very modest dress, curled my hair, and basically did it." She relied on information from Orthodox Jewish friends with whom she had participated in some religious ceremonies. "A few months before the auditions for *X-Files* came up I was celebrating with them and we wound up going over to the rabbi's house. The rabbi said 'Justine, maybe one day you'll get to play a Jew,' and a few months later I was cast!"

"I did have to learn [some] Hebrew to say the Kaddish. I talked to a rabbi, and Chris Carter's team hired a teacher, to learn the prayer. I think a lot of what I drew from was just how I was raised in a very old family tradition." How traditional were the ceremonies and the spell to bring the Golem back? "It is a very old sort of ceremony. Most Jews when you say 'Golem,' they understand what it is. I don't know how true it is. I think it is a very spiritual thing . . . more mind over matter."

The Kaddish is actually a prayer said to the dead. "That is the prayer that [Ariel] performs when he passes away. Most women do not say the Kaddish traditionally. Usually it is the men that do most of the praying." Miceli didn't have to film the scene where she molds the Golem out of the wet graveyard earth. "I had volunteered actually to be in the rain and do it, but they did not find that necessary. It was very long hours, and it was very wet and cold. They had a stand-in for me do that. They just more or less tried to have the hands match."

Miceli used personal tragedy to help visualize the pain her character was experiencing. "I used the death of my father in lieu of the death of my fiancé on the show. That was the most personal and the strongest parallel for me, so it was a very exhausting two weeks emotionally."

Miceli is now back on the audition circuit, looking for roles in films, series, and even roles on Broadway. "I have played very diverse characters," she says, before adding "I have not played the sexy femme fatale yet. I am hoping to do that one day."

X89 Unrequited

Case Number:	4.16/ #89 (#4X16)
First Sighting:	February 23, 1997
Directed by:	Michael Lange
Written by:	Howard Gordon & Chris Carter

GUEST CAST	CHARACTER
Mitch Pileggi	Assistant Director Walter S. Skinner
Peter LaCroix	Nathaniel Teager
Scott Hylands	General Benjamin Bloch
Laurie Holden	Marita Covarrubias
William Taylor	General Leitch
William Nunn	General Jon Steffan
Larry Musser	Denny Markham
Lesley Ewen	Renee Davenport
Ryan Michael	Agent Cameron Hill
Allan Franz	Dr. Ben Keyser
Jen Jasey	Female Private
Mark Holden	Agent Eugene Chandler
Don McWilliams	P.F.C. Gus Burkholder

UNCREDITED	
Bill Agnew	Lt. General Peter MacDougal

FIELD REPORT

Washington, D.C. An invisible killer is stalking high-ranking government officials, leaving a "death card" with each corpse. The card is tied to the radical paramilitary group The Right Hand and Skinner orders an investigation into its leader, ex-Marine Denny Markham. The man gives the FBI a photo of Nathaniel Teager, a Green Beret captured in Vietnam and kept as a POW for over twenty years. Later, Renee Davenport reports seeing a man appear and disappear at the Vietnam Veterans Memorial after giving the grieving widow her husband's dog tags and telling her he's still alive.

After a well-guarded General is killed and evidence of Teager's visit is captured by cameras, but not by eyewitnesses, Mulder theorizes that Teager may be able to hide himself from people's vision by creating a floating blind spot. Marita Covarrubias warns Mulder that General Benjamin Bloch will be next to die, given his role in a commission that is hiding a terrible secret from Vietnam. The problem is that Bloch is speaking at a rededication ceremony at the Memorial, and the crowds of thousands can easily hide any number of attackers . . . especially if they can also become invisible!

WITNESS NOTES

The scene in the stadium was not quite as full of people as you might have thought from the screen. Five hundred extras were hired to fill out the scene, then new special effects person Laurie George used a process called a "tiling effect" to computer generate duplicates of the crowd, filling in the stadium to make it appear as if there were five thousand people in the crowd.

Scott Hylands (General Benjamin Bloch) is one of two *X-Files* actors to have ever appeared on *Project UFO* ("Sighting 4006: The Nevada Desert Incident"). He was also in an episode of *Powers of Matthew Star* ("36 Hrs.") and *Wonder Woman* ("Judgment From Outer Space Part I").

William S. Taylor (General Leitch) had roles in *The Fly II* (1989), *Beyond the Stars* (1989) with William B. Davis and Don S. Davis, and the telefilm *Omen IV: The Awakening* (1991). He was also a regular cast member on *Neon Rider*.

William Nunn (General Jon Steffan) played Lt. McCormick in the "Maranatha" episode of Chris Carter's *Millennium*, and had another role as Hunziger in the episode immediately following it, "Paper Dove," the first season finale.

Ryan Michael (Agent Cameron Hill) is a classically-trained actor who studied at London's Guildhall School and appeared on stages in London and Vancouver and with a touring theater company in Africa. He is a water and snow ski instructor, a national mountain bike champion, and has had roles in the films *Superman IV: The Quest for Peace* (1987), *Look Who's Talking Now* (1993), the telefilm *Blind Man's Bluff* (1991), and the miniseries of Stephen King's *It* (1990). Guest-star credits include *Highlander, Two, The Outer Limits, MacGyver*, and *Poltergeist: The Legacy*.

Peter LaCroix starred in "Unrequited."

WITNESS INTERVIEW
PETER LaCROIX
Born: October 17, 1953, Hearst, Ontario, Canada

Unlike many actors, Peter LaCroix had been a fan of *The X-Files* since the beginning. "The first year they weren't doing that well, but it had sort of a cult following. I was one of those. And I thought if I could get on *The X-Files* and *The Simpsons*, I could die happy." The actor had already done a lot of theater in Vancouver and would appear on such series as *Wiseguy*, *21 Jump Street*, *The Commish*, *Strange Luck*, *Sliders*, *Poltergeist: The Legacy*, *The Sentinel*, and *Two*.

LaCroix didn't have to audition too many times before he landed the role of Frank Druce in one of the first season's most pivotal episodes, "E.B.E." Was he an innocent trucker, or was he a government employee illegally transporting UFO wreckage and a living alien across the country? The actor recalls one scene from the episode that did not make the cut. "In the original script you're supposed to see, not exactly the alien, but I think there was a note in the script for an extreme closeup of these weird alien eyes. Although you actually did see the alien spacecraft, they made the decision not to show the alien at that point. Everything [on the series] is always left fairly ambiguous."

In the second season, LaCroix played the tram operator who gets ambushed and killed by a traitorous Agent Krycek in "Ascension." Originally, LaCroix's character was to have survived his encounter with Krycek. "It wasn't until I watched the show that I realized I'd been killed! That was a late change."

LaCroix returned to audition in the fourth season, landing the role of Nathaniel Teager, a veteran with the ability to make himself invisible. He had short hair at the audition, which helped the casting director visualize him in the role, and director Michael Lange had worked with him previously on "Ascension." To shoot the scenes where Teager disappeared from view, old-fashioned camera trickery was employed for most shots. "On the actual shooting, I'm weaving through [the crowd], and when the Assistant Director yelled 'Freeze!' all the extras froze. I got the hell out of there as fast as I could and then we started again. Then they digitally faded me out slowly. I thought it was kind of cool—I watched it frame-by-frame and I noticed that the very last thing to disappear was my eyes. No one would notice when it's slowed down, but at full speed it's kind of a nice effect."

Although it appeared the episode was mainly shot outdoors in the evening at a grandstand, it was actually shot in a big warehouse, with over five hundred extras. "It was a loading dock where they unload the cruise ships in Vancouver—a huge building with a very high ceiling—they could light it and make it look like night." Some of the exterior scenes were shot in a park, though, which created problems for stars Duchovny and Anderson. "I think it must be a huge drag for them. Out in the park, there'd be a lot of the public walking around and [security] trying to hold the people back. People were trying to take pictures, and you can't blame them, but [Duchovny and Anderson] are getting tired of it. It can be intrusive. It's difficult for them."

Two scenes were added a week after shooting was finished: the opening teaser scene with Teager and Mulder, and the scene with the veteran behind the grandstands was reshot. "Originally, I just blew [the veteran] off. He sees me, he starts following me, and I turn around and look at him and do my disappearing trick and that was it. At some point they decided to add another scene. It gave me more to do, and it explained my motive a little more. I was working on another job. They flew me back, gave me a fake goatee because I'd shaved by that time, and then went and shot until five in the morning." The other scene filmed that night had Teager "coming out of the crowd and fading toward Mulder, like, 'Is he coming to kill Mulder?' You don't know at that point that I'm trying to kill the General, and I just kind of fade out there."

LaCroix hopes to work on *The X-Files* again in the future, although because this last role was so big, he isn't sure he'll be able to audition for the fifth season. Meanwhile, he's got a lead role in the film *Free Willy III*, (1997), and he's still doing lots of episodic work, and hoping to reach his other television goal. "Next is *The Simpsons*," he says, grinning like the Cheshire Cat.

X90 Tempus Fugit

Case Number:	4.17/ #90 (#4X17)
First Sighting:	March 16, 1997
Directed by:	Rob Bowman
Written by:	Chris Carter & Frank Spotnitz

GUEST CAST	CHARACTER
Joe Spano	Mike Millar
Tom O'Brien	Corporal Louis Frish
Scott Bellis	Max Fenig
Chilton Crane	Sharon Graffia
Brendan Beiser	Agent Pendrell
Greg Michaels	Scott Garrett
Robert Moloney	Bruce Bearfeld
Felicia Shulman	Motel Manager
Rick Dobran	Sergeant Armondo Gonzales
Jerry Schram	Larold Rebhun
David Palffy	Dark Man
Mark Wilson	Pilot
Marek Wiedman	Investigator
Jon Raitt	Father

FIELD REPORT

Great Sacandaga Lake, New York / Washington, D.C. At Scully's birthday celebration, Sharon Graffia approaches Mulder and Scully with the news that she's the sister of alien abductee Max Fenig (last seen in "Fallen Angel"), who was killed in a bizarre airplane crash

hours before. At a meeting of the National Transportation Safety Board investigation team, led by Mike Millar, a recorded radio exchange from the plane talks of an intercept. Mulder believes a UFO forced the plane down. Combing the crash site, Mulder finds that all of the wristwatches have a nine-minute chunk of missing time, and a radiation-burned survivor is found.

After Mulder and Scully question the soldiers who manned the Air Force Reserve air control tower on the night of the crash, one of the men ends up dead, and the other, Corporal Louis Frish, barely escapes with his life. Meanwhile, Sharon Graffia is abducted from her motel room. Frish contacts Mulder and Scully, seeking their protection, and tells them that there were three objects in the sky that night: the plane, an unidentified aircraft, and a third craft, which shot down the second craft. That night, Mike Millar finds Sharon Graffia wandering at the crash site underneath the bright lights of a UFO; Mulder investigates a second crash site, finding an underwater UFO and an alien pilot; and Scully attempts to protect Frish, but a mysterious mustachioed man shoots at them in a pub, hitting Agent Pendrell.

WITNESS NOTES

The official *X-Files* Web site lists Mitch Pileggi as appearing in this episode, but he does not.

Tom O'Brien (Corporal Louis Frish) was a regular cast member on the series *Call to Glory* and later on the short-lived series *Men*. His film credits include *The Big Easy* (1987), *The Accused* (1988), and the excellent miniseries *Son of the Morning Star* (1991). He has had guest roles on *The Twilight Zone* ("The Convict's Piano"), *Early Edition* ("Gun"), and *Dark Skies* ("White Rabbit").

WITNESS INTERVIEW

JOE SPANO

Born: July 7, 1946, San Francisco, California

Although he won an Emmy Award for Best Guest Actor for a role on *Midnight Caller* in 1989, Joe Spano is best remembered for his seven-year stretch as Lt. Henry Goldblume on the critically-acclaimed *Hill Street Blues*. He received an Emmy nomination for Best Sup-

Joe Spano starred as Mike Millar in "Tempus Fugit" and "Max."

porting Actor for that role as well, and later on appeared in the first season of *Murder One* and the series *Amazing Grace*.

A native of San Francisco, Spano graduated from the University of California, with training in classical stage acting and improvisational comedy. He made a "mid-life Broadway debut" in Arthur Miller's *The Price* with Eli Wallach and Hector Elizando. That play received a Tony Award nomination for Best Revival. Later, on the West Coast, Spano was awarded the L.A. Drama Critics Circle Award for his role in *American Buffalo*. He is a founding member of three theatrical companies, including the Berkeley Repertory Theater, and is currently a member of the Antaeus Theater Company.

Spano made his film debut in either *American Graffiti* (1973) or the horror film *Warlock Moon* (1973), which he says "was really bad. That was the first movie I ever had a lead in. The thing was really cheap." Other film credits include *The Incredible Shrinking Woman* (1981), *Terminal Choice* (1985), *Apollo 13* (1994), the suspense film *Primal Fear* (1995), and this year's cable telefilm *A Call to Remember* (1997). He is currently shooting scenes for the independent film *In Quiet Night*.

It was while filming *Apollo 13* that the actor had a discussion with NASA technicians about UFOs. "They had these two guys down from Houston who were part of the control team on Apollo 13, and I asked one of them what he thought about UFOs. I thought they would have as much access to information as anybody. He said, 'Well, I've never seen one, I've never seen evidence of one, but that doesn't mean they don't exist.' So I think I feel the same way. Scientifically there's just no proof, nor have I had any personal experience with it, so there's no reason for me to believe that they exist. Apart from that I don't think the people who make [*The X-Files*] believe that stuff."

So why the overwhelming belief and interest in UFOs that *The X-Files* and other series and films are capitalizing on? "I think it's satisfying a need that we have, for something over and above the everyday reality we live in. Most of us don't have a very strong religious or spiritual background, and as a result we don't have the kind of resources that people who do have spiritual backgrounds have. When we reach out for explanations for the things that bother us or befuddle us or things that hurt us, we don't know where to look. We are easily attracted by explanations of behavior and events that we don't understand, we are attracted to solutions like these. And it serves a purpose. People go on physical rides that scare them at amusement parks, and they do things physically that push them to the limits and they watch horror films and things that scare them because it's fun. And I think the same is true with *X-Files*. Not to mention the fact that a lot of repeat TV viewing is based on the comfortableness, or even *love* we feel for the regular characters. And I think people tune in to a large extent to be with David and Gillian."

Spano had been approached by Chris Carter several times to do roles on *The X-Files*. "He offered me a part once which I didn't want to play in the first or second season. It was sort of a mad professor role—something about hallways and the lights going out. He ends up behind glass and disappears. [Dr. Banton in 'Soft Light'] I think [Chris] just knew me from *Hill Street* and he wanted to use me. It seemed to be a lot of screaming and being weird, which I wasn't too much into doing. So then he called me back and we met again when he started *Millennium*, and he wanted me to read for the partner, Lance's partner in that first episode.

Chris wanted me to come on board *Millennium* as one of the recurring characters, as part of the Millennium group, but by the time he got to me I was on to something else so I couldn't do that. So finally, this part [in *X-Files*] came up and it was a two-parter and I said 'sure.' "

The character of Mike Millar turned out to be a disappointment for Spano, who had only seen the first script when shooting began. "Rob Bowman, who directed one of my episodes, wanted me to pick up the pace at a certain point in my scene with David, and I said, 'OK, I'll pick it up there, but I'd like a little time here, because there's got to be room for one honest skeptic in the world of *X-Files*.' I would think he would have had to [be a skeptic]. Unfortunately the episode didn't deal with it at all. They just kind of said, 'Well, we'll forget about him.' " When the second script came in and Spano's character pretty much disappeared without a trace, the actor mentioned, "I was disappointed. But, you know, the least of their worries is what I think about the character.

"Second unit on the *X-Files* is very difficult because that's often when they shoot all the stuff like . . . in our case out in the middle of this marsh in the middle of night, shooting stuff that's going to be laid over with aliens . . . it seemed a little disorganized on the second unit. You know, I've never worked on any show quite like it, although I've worked in Vancouver and Canada before. I think shows that work in Vancouver are a little bit underfunded. Now one would wonder why *The X-Files* would be underfunded—it's making money hand over fist—but what it boils down to is it *seems* underfunded."

It sounds like Spano has ambivalent feelings about doing the series, but he did find some of it pleasant. "What was enjoyable about it was I got to travel with my wife and new daughter for the first time, and that was really a lot of fun. Vancouver is a great city. It's not particularly a satisfying kind of show for the actor, because you can't ask the kind of questions I think an actor likes to ask, like 'Why am I going here? Why am I doing this? Does this make sense?' That's not what the show's about. The show is not about making moment-to-moment sense, it's about *mystery*. It just has to have enough sense to carry the viewer from the beginning of the show to the end of the show."

With the tragic and only partially-explained crash of TWA Flight 800 last year, the plots for this *X-Files* two-parter seemed suspiciously similar and, perhaps, insensitive. "Somebody else interviewed me about this particular show [*XPosé* magazine], and was wondering whether I was concerned about this show offending the people whose friends and relatives were involved in the TWA airplane disaster. I said it never crossed my mind that it had anything specifically to do with that. Obviously, when we are talking about aliens sucking people out of airplanes it didn't have anything to do with it. Maybe I should have taken [the crash] into account, but it never even occurred to me anybody could take offense at it. You know, it's fantasy, it's totally fantasy."

Does Spano prefer doing guest shots on series or would he rather have ongoing roles such as he had on *Hill Street Blues*? "It totally depends on what the quality of the show is. I got an Emmy for an episode of *Midnight Caller* that I did, which was an extraordinary episode, but it was *about* my character. That's different. *The X-Files* was not, by the slightest stretch of the imagination, about *my* character. I had hoped that eventually there would be some resolution of my character, but there wasn't. You take a job for any number of reasons. You take it because you need the money, or you take it because you respect the people who create the show. In this case, I took it because I respected Chris . . . I respect Chris actually more than I like the show."

Before fans cry sacrilege, Spano explains his position. "It's not my cup of tea. I'm not interested in it. I don't believe it. It doesn't move me anywhere. *Millennium* is very powerful [as well]. They are both well done, but *Millennium* is just too grim for me. It could be that I'm too paranoid, so that kind of stuff isn't entertainment for me."

While filming these episodes of *The X-Files*, *Playboy* magazine wanted to interview Gillian Anderson, David Duchovny, and Chris Carter together. Spano recalls that "they sent a whole sheath of previous interviews, one of which was a *Hill Street* interview. David gave that to me to read and I sat there and read this whole interview that [the cast of *Hill Street*] had done years and years ago. That was pretty bizarre. It brought two eras together. [*Hill Street*] was a very visible show. Everybody watched it who liked television and wanted to see what cutting edge television was about." Sounds like *The X-Files*. "In a sense, though, it's much more popular than *Hill Street* ever was. *Hill Street* was very popular with a certain kind of person, but it was never a ratings bonanza, nor a financial bonanza. *X-Files* on the other hand, I think is a gold mine."

Spano laughs, relating that this is the third interview he's done about his guest role on *The X-Files*. "It is amazing to me that I do one guest shot on TV and get three requests for interviews. It's a cottage industry!"

X91 Max

Case Number:	4.18/ #91 (#4X18)
First Sighting:	March 23, 1997
Directed by:	Kim Manners
Written by:	Chris Carter & Frank Spotnitz

GUEST CAST	CHARACTER
Mitch Pileggi	Assistant Director Walter S. Skinner
Joe Spano	Mike Millar
Tom O'Brien	Corporal Louis Frish
Scott Bellis	Max Fenig
Chilton Crane	Sharon Graffia
Brendan Beiser	Agent Pendrell
Greg Michaels	Scott Garrett
John Destrey	Mr. Ballard
Rick Dobran	Sargeant Armondo Gonzales
Jerry Schram	Larold Rebhun
David Palffy	Dark Man
Mark Wilson	Pilot

UNCREDITED

Robert Moloney	Bruce Bearfeld
Felicia Shulman	Motel Manager

FIELD REPORT

Great Sacandaga Lake, New York / Washington, D.C. Mulder is captured at the site of the UFO wreckage and put under military arrest. In D.C., Pendrell's shooter escapes, despite having taken a bullet in the leg from Scully. Skinner arrives and arrests Frish while agent Pendrell is being taken to the hospital. Later, Mulder is released, and the government has come up with a cover story: "The jet collided with a military fighter jet," though Mulder thinks the fighter jet was pursuing the UFO. Agent Pendrell dies from the gunshot wounds, and Mulder and Scully find out that Sharon Graffia is actually not Max's sister. At Max's mobile home, they find a videotape in which Max claims to have incontrovertible evidence that the military salvaged alien technology to use in their own technological applications.

Mulder tells Mike Millar his theory about the jet crash; that Fenig was carrying the physical proof; that a UFO intercepted the flight to abduct Fenig; and finally that a military jet sent to destroy the alien craft caused the crash of the airliner. Mulder later finds a knapsack containing one-third of the alien "proof" Max had gathered, and takes it on a plane to Washington with him. Unfortunately for him, another passenger on the plane is Scott Garrett, the mustachioed man who shot Pendrell and was, in turn, shot by Scully. Although Garrett gets the knapsack, the plane is intercepted by a UFO, and Garrett is sucked out into the air, clutching the knapsack containing Max's evidence. Later, the plane lands, missing nine minutes of time . . . not to mention Garrett and Fenig's knapsack.

WITNESS NOTES

The song playing on Max's stereo in this episode is "Unmarked Helicopters," by Soul Coughing. It is the second song on the first *X-Files* soundtrack, *Songs in the Key of X*.

Chilton Crane's (Sharon Graffia) rather short list of credits includes the telefilm *The Death of the Incredible Hulk* (1990) and an episode of *The Commish* and *Poltergeist: The Legacy*.

WITNESS INTERVIEW
GREG MICHAELS

Born: June 27, 1948, Butler, Pennsylvania

His character's name is Scott Garrett, but the fans know him best as "Moustache Man," due to Greg Michaels' bushy Tom Selleck–like moustache. He thinks that was a plus when he auditioned for *The X-Files*. "Sometimes you land jobs for different reasons. I do think they wanted my character not only to be mysterious, but memorable. They knew they were going to

Greg Michaels starred as Scott Garrett in "Tempus Fugit" and "Max."

shoot me in part one a few seconds here and a few seconds there, and I think the mustache really helped in this case." It certainly made Michaels easily visible in the scenes on a series that seems to relegate facial hair to bad guys and double-dealing informants.

Michaels is a stage actor, with sixteen major theatrical credits to his name in Denver, Los Angeles, Dallas, San Francisco, and elsewhere. He's been active in film and television since the eighties, appearing in episodes of *Dallas* and *The Dukes of Hazzard* early on, and more recently on *In Living Color, Highlander*, the miniseries *Texas Justice*, and the telefilm *True Confessions*. "I actually played a warrior-elf in a TV pilot called *Wild Space*," Michaels chuckles. "It never took off."

Michaels has done a lot of swordplay, fight choreography, and stunt work, which helped him prepare for the scene at the end of "Tempus Fugit," where he is shot by Scully. "They wanted me to fall when I get shot in the leg by Gillian, and they wanted it to look like it kicked my leg out from under me. I know how to fall in different ways. So I went upstairs by myself and just kind of choreographed how I wanted to fall. They still put a trip wire on me, which I didn't need—but they didn't know that—and it just gave me the impulse for the shot. They put a squib on me for the shot, did a

little trip wire and I told the guy, 'Pull it lightly and I'll take the impulse from that.' And I fell, and they rushed up right after that first take and said, 'Are you okay, are you all right?' It was great. If you do it right, everybody looks good."

Michaels had not worked with a lot of guns prior to the role of Scott Garrett, so he talked with the stunt coordinator and made a specific choice about how to shoot. "I wanted to use just one hand, not hold it with my left hand on the wrist. I made the choice that I'm the old-fashioned professional, and I use one hand. More importantly, I treated the gun like a sword, so when I drew it, I leaned into the gun shot. It's almost like a thrust with the sword. These are kind of actors' secrets you do. You play little head games with yourself. Especially when you don't have dialogue, you try to imbue as many specific choices as you can into your character. That makes that character come alive, even on film for three seconds when you're shooting a gun."

Shooting at not one but two of television's hottest stars was a strange experience for Michaels. "That's strange, pointing a 9 millimeter at a woman [Gillian Anderson] and having her point a 9 millimeter at you. At times we were pointing guns at each other and [firing] point blank." He also had some heavy gun scenes with Duchovny. "David is fun to play off of. I was having some fun with him in the plane when I finally get the drop on him. I was basically yelling, 'David, put down the package you son-of-a-bitch!' I was off camera at that point so I could say any line I wanted to and David was playing along with my stuff. Normally I was pointing a gun at his head but at one of the takes I pointed it right at his crotch to see if he had a different reaction. And he never said a word, he never missed a beat, he just was kind of right there with me!"

At the end of "Tempus Fugit," Michaels's character shoots Brendan Beiser's Agent Pendrell, a favorite character of *X-Files* fans. "I talked to Brendan about it because I hate to kill actors off in a series. He was a real great guy. I hit it off with a few of the actors on the set, and he was one of them. Brendan did a lovely drunken improvisation in two or three of his takes, right as he meets Gillian at the bar, but only about a fourth of it ended up on the actual show . . . which is a shame because it was a beautiful drunk improvisation; cute, funny, and then a moment later he's shot in the chest. I think at that point I wasn't even sure if he was going to die. They didn't confirm his death until part two. He was a real gentleman about it and said 'That's the breaks of the game, and I've had a good run with this character.' You know, actors can eat when they do recurring characters. I hated to kill him off the show and possibly ruin a decent income for the guy.

"*The X-Files* is probably the baddest guy I played on TV, though I played nastier guys in the theater," Michaels recalls. "I'd actually read a couple times for roles in *The X-Files* and I think I was actually playing things a little too big. I was playing a different TV style, a little broader, and it came back to my agent that I needed to tone it down because their style is very low-key. So I dropped the casting woman a card and said, 'I've watched some of your shows now and I understand the style better.' She called me in for another audition, and when it all came down to it they offered me the main bad guy for part one and two."

The role evolved during filming, as the second part was not written when shooting started on the first part. "It was a little more twisted role when it was originally written. There were a few more scenes, and they changed the role quite a bit from the original rendition of the role. Since I literally had only one line of dialogue in part one, when they said be a bad guy, I didn't know if I was on the *psychotic* end of bad, or if I was on the *spanking* end. Right up to the moment we were shooting they were changing the concept of the role and how shadowy they wanted me to be, and how mysterious, and how much they'd shoot me. After they saw the dailies, I remember Rob Bowman, the director, coming back and saying, 'You gave me just the right amount of heat. Not too much, not too little. I want to see more of that.' So that's what I did until part two, and then a different director came on board and we talked about what had happened so far, and where we needed to go with the thing now that it was finally written."

Michaels later worked heavily with David Duchovny on the airplane set, where Garrett and Mulder have an intense confrontation.

Duchovny had to leave the evening of shooting [Friday], to go to the Screen Actors Guild awards on Saturday. "David and I shot our scenes together in the closeup scenes, face to face, nose to nose. Then when he left at 10 P.M. that night, I had to do the scenes when I had the drop on him with the gun—and my reaction scenes to him—with his stand-in. I learned [to work with stand-ins] a long time ago and I was more prepared to project my realities onto David's stand-in."

During that sequence, which took several days to shoot, one of Michaels's favorite lines was cut. "It was at the beginning when I say, 'You know what happens when a plane depressurizes at 30,000 feet?' I can't remember the whole line . . . 'things go flying through the air, including your weapon, uncontrollable mucus discharges from your nose and mouth.' I had talked on the set to the consultant that they had hired. This guy had been doing this stuff for twenty years . . . going to plane wrecks. He said they had been picking his brain about what happens at 30,000 feet before a plane wrecks, and he said what happens is all the mucus starts coming out, as well as a lot of *flatulence*. And he said, 'I don't know how much of this they'll put in the script.' Well, finally, when they wrote the script there's *nothing* about flatulence, but they did have the uncontrollable mucus discharge from the nose and mouth." He laughs. "I love that line, and it is true. I noticed when they edited the scene they cut that line out, for whatever reasons. So for the fans that want to *know* . . ."

Given that *The X-Files* tends to bring characters back—this two-parter was the return engagement for season one's Max Fenig after all—could the abducted Garrett make a return appearance? "They never said a word. However, I wrote Chris Carter a letter and said I was overjoyed to play that role. I said, 'Gee, the possibilities for my character . . . being the government man that he is, if he were abducted and came back, wouldn't he be a great disciple for alien beings?' I treated Garrett basically as a patriot, [not] as a bad guy. From his fanatical point of view, he's doing the right thing, for his world and his government. If he got abducted and came back, I could see some interesting storylines coming out of that."

X92 Synchrony

Case Number: 4.19/ #92 (#4X19)
First Sighting: April 13, 1997
Directed by: Jim Charleston
Written by: Howard Gordon & David
                    Greenwalt

GUEST CAST	CHARACTER
Joseph Fuqua	Jason Nichols
Susan Lee Hoffman	Dr. Lisa Ianelli
Michael Fairman	Older Jason Nichols
Jed Rees	Lucas Menand
Hiro Kanagawa	Dr. Yonechi
Jonathan Walker	Chuck Lukerman
Alison Matthews	Doctor
Norman Armour	Coroner
Patricia Idlette	Desk Clerk
Brent Chapman	Security Cop
Terry Arrowsmith	Uniformed Cop
Aureleo Di Nunzio	Detective

UNCREDITED
Eric Buermeyer	Bus Driver
Austin Basile	Bellman

FIELD REPORT

Boston, Massachusetts. Two researchers at the Massachusetts Institute of Technology are arguing when an old man approaches and warns them that one of them will soon die. The death indeed occurs, and suspicion falls on the surviving researcher, Jason Nichols, who was competing with the dead man for lucrative grant money. When the security guard who detained the old man is found frozen solid and a Japanese researcher, Yonechi, is similarly turned into a popsicle, Mulder and Scully know that they must find out who Nichols's accomplice is.

Nichols's girlfriend, researcher Lisa Ianelli, tells Mulder and Scully that the freezing agent used to kill the guard and Yonechi has not yet been invented, but that it is just now being developed. Later, finding a photograph in the old man's room, Mulder theorizes that the man has come back from the future to stop Nichols from perfecting his rapid freezing agent. As Scully tries to save the life of a flash-frozen Lisa, Mulder rushes to stop the old man—Jason Nichols from the future—from killing his younger self and thus altering the timeline.

WITNESS NOTES

Joseph Fuqua (Jason Nichols) played the role of Confederate cavalry Major General J. E. B. Stuart in the stunning Civil War film *Gettysburg* (1993).

Susan Lee Hoffman (Dr. Lisa Ianelli) appeared in the genre film *Wizards of the Lost Kingdom II* (1985), and appeared as another "Dr. Lisa" (Aronson) in *Outbreak* (1995). In a *Cult Times* interview, Hoffman recalls the most memorable thing about being on *The X-Files* was "the disgusting yellow liquid that I had to be in! Unfortunately, at the time I had the flu along with a 102 degree temperature and I had to lie in that stuff for almost three hours. Luckily they warmed up the liquid for me because it was freezing outside."

Michael Fairman (Older Jason Nichols) was a regular for several seasons of *Cagney & Lacey* as Inspector Knelman. He's had guest roles on *Alien Nation* ("The Takeover"), *Powers of Matthew Star*, and *Quantum Leap* ("The Great Spontini"). Fairman also wrote the 1983 telefilm *Found Money*.

Hiro Kanagawa (Dr. Yonechi) has three genre films to his credit: Dean R. Koontz's *Hideaway* (1995), *Cyberjack* (1995), and the Japanese comic book-based *Crying Freeman* (1995).

X93 Small Potatoes

Case Number: 4.20/ #93 (#4X20)
First Sighting: April 20, 1997
Directed by: Cliff Bole
Written by: Vince Gilligan

GUEST CAST	CHARACTER
Mitch Pileggi	Assistant Director Walter S. Skinner
Darin Morgan	Eddie Van Blundht, Jr.
Christine Cavanaugh	Amanda Nelligan
Lee de Broux	Edward Van Blundht, Sr.
Robert Rozen	Dr. Alton Pugh
Paul McGillion	Angry Husband (Fred Neiman)
Jennifer Sterling	Angry Wife (Mrs. Neiman)
David Cameron	Deputy
Forbes Angus	Security Guard
Peter Kelamis	Second Husband
P. Lynn Johnson	Health Department Doctor
Carrie Cain	Sparks Duty Nurse

FIELD REPORT

Martinsburg, West Virginia. A woman in labor says that her baby's father is an alien; when the child is born with a tail, it seems quite possible. Mulder and Scully travel to the town, investigating the fact that five babies have been born with tails recently. Scully chalks it up to ground water contamination or prescription drug interaction, but then discovers all of the babies have the same fathers. Investigating the mothers' fertility specialist, Dr. Alton Pugh, Mulder and Scully spot a janitor who has a scar at the base of his spine . . . as if he had had a tail removed!

The agents take janitor Eddie Van Blundht into custody, but they are unaware that he has an unusual ability to make himself look like anyone, and he uses it to escape. Later, when Mulder and Scully confront Van Blundht's father, they discover Eddie is masquerading as his father, and he escapes again. Eddie later assumes the form of Fox Mulder, capturing the real agent and locking him in a hospital basement. He begins to live the life of the FBI agent as he imagines it should be, including an attempt to seduce Scully. Van Blundht's efforts are in vain though, when the real Fox Mulder arrives to stop the FBI tête a tête.

WITNESS NOTES

The headlines of the *World Weekly Informer* read "Monkey Babies Invade Small Town: Did West Virginia Women Mate With Visitors From Space?," "Michael Jackson Held Captive by Exotic Pets!," and "ETAP Bigshot Busted." The ETAP bigshot pictured is likely an *X-Files* production staffer.

When Van Blundht is impersonating Mulder, and wanders through his apartment, he listens to the phone message tapes. One of the messages is from the Lone Gunmen, while another breathless message is from Chantal, a phone sex operator, who offers "Marty" (obviously Mulder's phone sex *nom de télé*) lower rates.

Lee Jones de Broux (Edward Van Blundht,

Sr.) has over thirty films and telefilms to his credit including the genre films *Robocop* (1987), *Pumpkinhead* (1988), and the comic-based telefilm *Vampirella* (1996).

Christine Cavanaugh appeared in "Small Potatoes."

WITNESS INTERVIEW
CHRISTINE CAVANAUGH
Born: August 16, Ogden, Utah

Interviewing Christine Cavanaugh over the phone, I get an incredible sense of deja vu. Not because I've seen *Babe* (1995), the movie in which Cavanaugh voiced the talking title pig, but because I have heard her voice everywhere! As a character actress and a popular voice-over actress, Cavanaugh is used to people saying "I can't place you, but you sound familiar."

"I became an actress when I was about fourteen," Christine says, adding that she "didn't do voices. I worked on accents and things like that for acting reasons. I did a lot of theater here in Hollywood when I first got here, fourteen years [ago]. My first professional voice-over job was a Pizza Hut commercial, and I had one line: 'May I take your order please?' I've been with the theater company over nine years, the Playhouse West Acting Company in North Hollywood. Jeff Goldblum is a staff member there and one of the teachers."

Cavanaugh's first on-camera job was on *Cheers*, and she went on to have guest appearances on *Empty Nest*, *Herman's Head*, *Wings*, and the underrated *Bakersfield P.D.* She had a recurring role on Fox's *Wild Oats* and Nickelodeon's *Salute Your Shorts*, and appeared in the feature films *Mixed Nuts* (1994), *Little Surprises* (1995), and *Jerry Maguire* (1996). Her bio sheet even says that she specializes in strange characters. She says her best roles are "crazy people. I play the elderly and the older roles in our theater group because we don't have any older actors. I tend to get the oddball roles. I'm not the 'straight man.' "

Cavanaugh got into voice-over acting as a job for an animator who was doing an animated film at UCLA. "I did voices for quite a few student films at UCLA and USC over the years. I spent several years taking classes and going to workshops. I had fifty-some auditions before I booked a job."

Besides her *Babe* gig and lots of commercials, Cavanaugh did voices for the film *Balto* (1995) and received an Emmy Award nomination for her work on *The Flintstones' Christmas Special*. Among her many regular voice credits are the shows *Rugrats* (Chuckie Finster), Disney's *Darkwing Duck* (Gosalyn Mallard), *Aaahh!!! Real Monsters* (Oblina), *Dexter's Laboratory* (Dexter), *Disney's Aladdin* (Sadira, Bud), *Sonic the Hedgehog* (Bunnie Rabbott), *The Critic* (Marty Sherman and others), *Cathy* (Cathy), *Cave Kids* (Bam-Bam), *Disney's Sing Me a Story* (Carol the Book Worm), and the upcoming *Disney's 101 Dalmatians* series (Dumpling). Viewers may realize that many of those characters are *male*. "Little boy voices are almost always done by women in the voice-over arena. I am one of many women who do it. I have got a quality to my voice that's got a little bit of male edge to it. There's a range there that is a little deeper than other women."

On this episode of *The X-Files*, although her character of Amanda Nelligan is confused and a little wacky, Cavanaugh stresses that she wasn't that weird. Nelligan believes that Luke Skywalker is the father of her baby because the shape-changing Eddie Van Blundht has assumed his form to have sex with her. "You know, I am playing a 'straight man' in *The X-Files*. She comes off crazy, but she is not

crazy because she is telling the truth. She is just a little bit of a fanatic about *Star Wars*, just a little obsessed." So, how many times has Christine seen *Star Wars* herself? "I might have seen it twice."

The opening birth scene took one complete day to film. "I was only there a total of about three days. I spent one entire day in labor, screaming and having labor pains. There was a good nine hours of screaming bloody murder." Most of the day, the actress had her feet up in stirrups. "They had to prop me up for the camera angles, and they had to put sandbags under my feet and weigh my feet down to keep me from sliding." Was her "child" a real baby? Thanks to a crew member who was a new father, yes. "They had two seven-week-old twins for the part. They shared the role. Then they had CGI for the tails. These babies were very good. Calm happy babies."

Now, Christine wants a return engagement on the series. "I begged them to let me come back and recur as a monster," she laughs. Given Darin Morgan's first role on the series, may we suggest a future role for Cavanaugh as the Bride of Flukeman?

X94   Zero-Sum

Case Number:	4.21/ #94 (#4X21)
First Sighting:	April 27, 1997
Directed by:	Kim Manners
Written by:	Howard Gordon & Frank Spotnitz

GUEST CAST	CHARACTER
Mitch Pileggi	Assistant Director Walter S. Skinner
William B. Davis	Cigarette-Smoking Man
Laurie Holden	Marita Covarrubias
Nicolle Nattrass	Misty
Paul McLean	Special Agent Kautz
Fred Keating	Detective Hugel
Allan Gray	Entemologist, Dr. Peter Valedespino
Addison Ridge	Bespectacled Boy
Don S. Williams	First Elder
Lisa Stewart	Jane Brody
Barry Greene	Dr. Emile Linzer
Christopher J. Newton	Photo Technician
Morris Panych	Gray-Haired Man

Theresa Puskar   Mrs. Kemper
John Moore   Second Elder

FIELD REPORT

Desmond, Virginia. When a mail sorter sneaks a cigarette in an employee bathroom, she is stung to death by hundreds of bees. Stranger still, when an e-mail file about the death is sent to Mulder, Assistant Director Skinner intercepts it. That night, he erases all evidence of the attack, including incinerating the girl's body. He even impersonates Mulder when he goes to the police forensics lab, exchanging a vial of blood for the dead girl's blood. When Detective Ray Thomas talks to the man he thinks is Mulder, Skinner tells him there's no investigation to be done. Later, Mulder arrives at Skinner's apartment with news of the apparent impersonation and cover-up, as well as the fact that Detective Thomas was executed that evening.

Skinner soon realizes that he's being used as a pawn by Cigarette-Smoking Man. As Skinner is framed for the detective's murder, Mulder begins to uncover the imposter's identity. Meanwhile, Scully's cancer is getting worse. Skinner has an entomologist study a piece of the honeycomb the deadly bees came from, but the larvae hatch and swarm, killing him. When a bee attack in South Carolina leaves children dying, Skinner warns the hospital that the kids should be treated for smallpox. After being confronted by Mulder with the truth, an enraged Skinner fires several shots at the lurking Cigarette-Smoking Man, accusing him of not helping save Scully's life. And as Mulder seeks answers from Marita Covarrubias, we learn that she too is a pawn of the shadowy Syndicate!

WITNESS NOTES

The scenes in the schoolyard where the children were terrorized by bees was real. Thousands of bees were released on the set, with terrified extras running away from them. In a *TV Guide* interview, director Kim Manners admits that "four or five of them got stung. We had paramedics there who took out the stingers and put on little Band-Aids. But the mother or father would say 'Get back out there! You're on *The X-Files*!' "

Nicolle Nattrass (Misty) appeared in the film *Sleeping With Strangers* (1994).

Paul McLean (Special Agent Kautz) appeared in the telefilm *I Still Dream of Jeannie* (1991) and the *Outer Limits* episode "First Anniversary."

Don S. Williams (First Elder) has over forty years of credits in the entertainment field. As of 1997, he had produced, directed, and/or choreographed 276 theatrical productions, films, and television series (including forty-five episodes of *The Beachcombers*); has had roles in seventeen TV episodes, five feature films, and fourteen plays; and has written three plays, one screenplay, a TV documentary series, and a video drama. He has been the Artistic Director for the Ailanthus Performing Arts Center for Inner-City Youth, and has instructed at a number of film and television schools and colleges. Look for Williams on-screen in the feature film *The Stepfather* (1987), and in episodes of *The Commish, Neon Rider, Wiseguy,* and *Mom P.I.*

X95 Elegy

Case Number: 4.22/ #95 (#4X22)
First Sighting: May 4, 1997
Directed by: Jim Charleston
Written by: John Shiban

GUEST CAST   CHARACTER
Steven M. Porter   Harold Spuller
Alex Bruhanski   Angelo Pintero
Sydney Lassick   Chuck Forsch
Nancy Fish   Nurse Innes
Daniel Kamin   Detective Hudak

Lorena Gale   Attorney
Mike Puttonen   Dr. Martin Alpert
Christine Willes   Agent Karen F. Kosseff
Ken Tremblett   Uniformed Officer

UNCREDITED
Gerry Naim   Sergeant Conneff

FIELD REPORT

Washington, D.C. Angie Pintero, the owner of a bowling alley, finds a bloody girl caught in the carriage of his pinsetting machines, but when he goes for help, he finds the police outside, gathered around the body of the same girl, now dead. Mulder and Scully listen to the man's tale, with Mulder theorizing that the girl's ghost was trying to communicate with Pintero; three similar murders in the area have been reported, all with ghostly apparitions. A 911 call reporting the murder is traced to the New Horizon Psychiatric Center, where one of Pintero's workers, the severely autistic Harold Spuller, lives.

In the bathroom, Scully witnesses another ghost, and a murdered girl is found nearby. Harold is gone from the Center, but Mulder tracks him to a room above the bowling alley, where Harold has posted and memorized hundreds of bowling score sheets. Harold sees Pintero's ghost, and minutes later, Angie is dead, due to a heart attack. Mulder realizes that everyone who saw a ghost died shortly thereafter, implying Harold is in danger; Fox does not realize that Scully has also seen a ghost. Back at New Horizon, the real killer is revealed to be a drug-addicted nurse, and Scully has to defend herself against a deadly scalpel attack. Later, Harold is found dead in an alley, but his ghost appears to Scully. The skeptical agent is left to wonder if the two ghosts are warnings of her own possible demise.

WITNESS NOTES

Original titles for this episode were "Revenant" and "Tulpa."

Autism is a subject that Chris Carter has been concerned with for some time, so it's not surprising an episode was built around the subject. A Fox executive who has an autistic child told Carter about the Eras Center for Autism. Carter decided to support the charity by holding charity auctions at each of the official *X-Files* conventions.

Dr. Martin Alpert is named after the physician of this episode's writer, John Shiban. Coincidentally, Alpert is also the physician of this episode's main guest star, Steve Porter!

Chuck Forsch is the name of Chris Carter's main assistant.

Alex Bruhanski (Angelo Pintero) had a recurring role as Detective Irv Wallerstein on the first season of *The Commish*, often appearing in the same episodes as Nicholas Lea.

Sydney Lassick (Chuck Forsch) was born in Chicago on July 23, 1922, making him seventy-five this year, and the second oldest *X-Files* guest star (after Henry Beckman). Lassick played a similar character in *One Flew Over the Cuckoo's Nest*. *TV Guide* gave *The X-Files* a "Cheer" for casting Lassick in this role, noting "we love it when prime time outcasts are so well cast." Other genre roles for Lassick were in Stephen King's *Carrie* (1976), *Alligator* (1980), and *The Lady in White* (1988). His weirdest film was probably the surreal *Shakes the Clown* (1991), in which Lassick played Peppy the Clown.

Ken Tremblett (Uniformed Officer) appeared as FBI Agent Riley in "The Thin White Line," an episode of Chris Carter's *Millennium*.

Steven Porter starred as Harold Spuller in "Elegy."

WITNESS INTERVIEW

STEVEN M. PORTER

Born: January 23, Erie, Pennsylvania

Steve Porter's memorable portrayal of Harold Spuller, an autistic man in the "Elegy" episode of *The X-Files*, will likely be landing him job offers for some time to come.

Porter has done a lot of theater work, largely in the Los Angeles area with The Actor's Gang (see page 126). He notes that he has "been doing it a long time, but it's only been in the last five years that I've made a living at it." He laughs, and adds "since I quit smoking is when I started making money." Is he saying there's a correlation? "I gained thirty pounds after I quit smoking, so I sort of rounded out more and became more of a character-looking actor. My hairline was receding, so that helped as far as making me more of a character. Just hitting the 'character' age range, mid-thirties, sort of helped out as far as getting me more work."

Although Porter's early work included the low-budget exploitation films *Angel* (1984) and *Avenging Angel* (1985), he later began landing a lot of guest roles, with appearances on *Mad About You, Wings, Murphy Brown, Friends, Party of Five, Bakersfield P.D., Danger Theatre, The Big Easy*, and *3rd Rock from the Sun*. His recent film work includes *Bad Girls* (1994) and *The Scout* (1994), with *Edwards and Hunt* set for release in the fall of 1997.

While at UCLA in the early '80s, Steve Porter made friends with Frank Spotnitz, who would later become producer for *The X-Files*. That association helped him get consideration for a role. Porter originally auditioned for the role of Chuck Forsch, "then all of a sudden they offered me the bigger role. Which was fine with me." Porter got the role of Harold Spuller, while the role of Forsch went to Sydney Lassick, whom Porter admired for his work on *One Flew Over the Cuckoo's Nest*.

Porter was already prepared somewhat for the role. "I had done a play several years earlier about an insane asylum. The character was somewhat similar, and for that I had done some research. I had rented some video tapes about people with mental disabilities and things like that. [Harold's] mannerisms were easy to get into, and the way he spoke and walked just sort of came out. A lot of character actors have many characters within them that they bring out when they are doing a role. Sometimes it just clicks and you don't even have to think about it and it just works. After they cast me, we had a meeting up in Vancouver with Chris Carter and the writers and the director. They just wanted to make sure we were all talking the same language. They had rewritten a lot of the script and they had made it so much better and clearer. When I read the rewrites it was like 'oh my gosh, I *know* this guy.' "

Hollywood has had very little exploration of autism, limited mainly to Dustin Hoffman's portrayal in *Rain Man* (1988) and a recurring character on *St. Elsewhere*. Porter didn't want to sugar-coat his character. "From the research I have done, they can be somewhat tragic people but they can also be very uncommunicative and can be childish and throw tantrums and things like that. It's not just this cute retarded person, which was something that we definitely were not going to go towards."

Was Porter worried about negative reaction from autistic groups and other special interest groups for the mentally challenged? "No, because there was nothing in the character that was bad or anything like that. He actually was a sweet person. He had this disability, and I think that I played him with enough empathy that it wasn't making fun or anything like that. I feel that we played him honestly, and with empathy. After they realized that he wasn't a bad guy, Mulder sort of took him under his wing and showed compassion towards Harold."

Porter admits that one of the fun things about the episode was working in the bowling alley. "It was fun seeing what the bowling alley looked like from a pin's point of view. My biggest fear was that somebody would flip the wrong switch and turn it on. Whenever we weren't shooting, everybody was bowling." And yes, Porter says that Duchovny really did hit the strike seen in the show. "That was one shot and he really nailed it like that. He's a heck of a bowler. He said he grew up bowling."

One of Harold Spuller's fixations in the episode was memorizing everyone's bowling scores, a task that Porter found daunting. "It was a long list of numbers I had to remember, and I was kind of surprised that I was able to do it. I had to settle down and memorize them all. At first we thought that I didn't have to, that I could just randomly spit out numbers, but as I looked at the script more I realized there were different scenes where you are talking about specific people's scores, so they had to match up. Then I realized I really do have to memorize these and get them correct! That was hard work, but hard work is what we're here for anyway."

X96 Demons

Case Number:	4.23/ #96 (#4X23)
First Sighting:	May 11, 1997
Directed by:	Kim Manners
Written by:	R. W. Goodwin

GUEST CAST	CHARACTER
Jay Acovone	Detective Joe Curtis
Mike Nussbaum	Dr. Charles Goldstein
Chris Owens	Young Cigarette-Smoking Man
Rebecca Toolan	Mrs. Mulder
Andrew Johnson	Medical Examiner
Terry Jang Barclay	Officer Frank Imhoff
Vanessa Morley	Young Samantha Mulder
Eric Breker	Admitting Officer
Rebecca Harker	Housekeeper
Shelley Adam	Young Mrs. Mulder
Dean Aylesworth	Young Bill Mulder
Alex Haythorne	Young Fox Mulder

FIELD REPORT

Providence, Rhode Island. Fox Mulder has a vivid dream about his parents fighting and his younger sister, Samantha. When he wakes up, he has blood all over him, and he barely manages to call Scully before he goes into shock. When Scully arrives at the hotel, she discovers that Fox, still in shock, can't remember anything since Friday, two days ago, and that in addition to the blood, two rounds have been fired from his gun. The two agents track down the car Mulder was driving to an Amy Anne Cassandra, and after picking up clues at her house, they visit her childhood home. There, Mulder and Scully find Amy and her husband both shot dead—apparently by Mulder's gun!

As the local detectives try to prove Mulder's guilt in the deaths, Scully tracks down leads to a local doctor who was using experimental treatments on the Cassandras—and Mulder— to help them recover repressed memories. And while Fox can't remember where he was the last two days, his memories of the night his sister disappeared are coming back, and this time they include the involvement of a young Cigarette-Smoking Man! Once he's cleared, Mulder has an intense confrontation with his mother before returning to the doctor for what may be one final treatment. But will Mulder's memories drive him over the edge?

WITNESS NOTES

Jay Acovone (Detective Joe Curtis) played the Deputy DA on *Beauty and the Beast*. His genre credits include *The Stepfather III* (1992), *Doctor Mordred* (1992) with fellow *X-Files* guest Brian Thompson, and *Independence Day* (1996), in which he played a guard at Area 51, the mysterious UFO holding site.

Mike Nussbaum (Dr. Charles Goldstein) appears as an alien in one of 1997's biggest summer hits, *Men in Black*. Nussbaum plays Mr. Rosenberg, an elderly jeweler who is really an alien and who hides a surprising secret inside his head.

Eric Breker (Admitting Officer) had a guest role in "Paper Dove," the first season finale of Chris Carter's *Millennium*.

X97 Gethsemane

Case Number:	4.24/ #97 (#4X24)
First Sighting:	May 18, 1997
Directed by:	R. W. Goodwin
Written by:	Chris Carter

GUEST CAST	CHARACTER
John Finn	Scott Kritschgau
Matthew Walker	Arlinsky
James Sutorius	Babcock
Sheila Larken	Mrs. Scully
Pat Skipper	Bill Scully, Jr.
John Oliver	Rolston
Charles Cioffi	Division Chief Scott Blevins
Steve Makaj	Ostelhoff
Nancy Kerr	Agent Hedin
Barry W. Levy	Vitagliano
Arnie Walters	Father McCue
Rob Freeman	Detective Rempulski
Craig Burnanski	Saw Operator

FIELD REPORT

Yukon Territory, Alaska/Washington, D.C. As the episode begins, Scully identifies a dead body in Mulder's apartment, then makes a report to her superiors at the FBI, including Division Chief Scott Blevins. Flashbacks show us Arlinsky and Babcock, a pair of anthropologists, who arrive by helicopter at a glacial camp in the Yukon Territory. A trek up the mountain reveals a gray alien, perfectly preserved in the ice inside a cave. Mulder calls Scully at her mother's home, where a gathering has become uncomfortable for Scully due to discussions of her health with her brother and pastor.

Mulder and Scully meet Arlinsky at the Smithsonian, where he shows them ice core samples from around the alien that are two hundred years old. Mulder and Arlinsky fly to the camp, where someone has killed nearly everyone. One man, Babcock, has barely survived, and he has hidden the frozen alien. In D.C., Scully is attacked by a mysterious man, who she later finds out is Michael Kritschgau, a Pentagon researcher. When she captures Kritschgau, the man warns her that if he goes to jail, the people who gave Scully cancer will kill him!

Scully arranges a meeting with Mulder, who has returned with Arlinsky, Babcock and the frozen alien. Kritschgau tells Mulder that the alien is a fake, and that he's being used as part of a government conspiracy. When Mulder returns to the warehouse, he finds Arlinsky and Babcock have been murdered, and the alien is gone. Back in the present, Scully admits that the body in Mulder's apartment was his; he died of an apparent self-inflicted gunshot wound to the head.

WITNESS NOTES

John Finn (Scott Kritschgau) is clearly a favorite of Chris Carter's. He also had the lead role in "Covenant," an episode of *Millennium*, where he played a father that confessed to killing his family. Finn was a regular on *EZ Streets*, and had roles in the Civil War film *Glory* (1989) and the recent *Turbulence* (1997).

Matthew Walker (Arlinsky) was a regular on the action series *Supercarrier* and *Lightning Force*. His genre credits include *Halloween 5: The Return of Michael Myers* (1989), *Child's Play 3* (1992), the telefilm *Double, Double, Toil and Trouble* (1993), and an episode of *The Outer Limits* ("The Choice"). He played an Interpol judge in the pilot film of John Woo's

Once a Thief (1996), which also starred Nicholas Lea.

James Sutorius (Babcock) was the lead in the 1977 series *The Andros Targets* and later appeared on four seasons of *Dynasty* as Gordon Wales. He was featured in the Frankenstein-reworking telefilm *Prototype* (1982), and the miniseries of James A. Michener's *Space* (1985).

Pat Skipper (Bill Scully, Jr.) has a number of genre credits, including *Demonstone* (1989), *Memoirs of an Invisible Man* (1992), *Demolition Man* (1993), *Independence Day* (1996), *Hellraiser IV: Bloodline* (1996), the telefilm *The Dreamer of Oz: The L. Frank Baum Story* (1990), as well as two episodes of *Quantum Leap* ("M.I.A." and "The Beast Within").

John Oliver (Rolston) was a regular on the Canadian series *North of 60*, and appeared as a goalie in *The Mighty Ducks* (1992).

Charles Cioffi (Division Chief Scott Blevins) returns here in the role he played in *The X-Files* pilot and "Conduit." He is well-known for his role as NYPD Lieutenant Vic Androzzi in the 1971 blaxploitation film, *Shaft*. He also appeared in *Klute* (1971), the Buzz Aldrin telepic *Return to Earth* (1976), and the cult favorite time-travel movie, *Time After Time* (1979). In 1969, Cioffi appeared on the soap opera *Where the Heart Is*, returning to soaps in 1979 for *Another World* and in 1990 for *Days of Our Lives*. In the mid-seventies he had a lot of television guest roles, and had starring roles in ABC's police/spy series *Get Christy Love* and *Assignment Vienna*. He was also a regular cast member of *Kojak* when that series had a revival on ABC in 1989. Cioffi's superhero credits include guest roles on both *The Six Million Dollar Man* and *The Bionic Woman*, an appearance on *Lois & Clark: The New Adventures of Superman,* and a campy turn as the villainous Raymond Manta on *The New Adventures of Wonder Woman*.

THE WILLIAM B. DAVIS FILE

William B. Davis strikes a familiar pose.

Name: William Bruce Davis
Born: January 13, 1938, Toronto, Ontario,
         Canada
Height: 6′ 2½″
Weight: 180
Hair: Brown with gray
Eyes: Hazel

He was there in the beginning, watching through squinted eyes as Agent Scully was first assigned to the X-Files and told to disprove and debunk Agent Mulder's investigations. His head wreathed in smoke from an ever-present cigarette, he was present at many of Mulder and Scully's reports, often suppressing evidence that *something* was out there. As time moved on and the agents learned more and more of the truth, the Cigarette-Smoking Man took a more active hand in stopping their progress, resorting to beatings, abduction, and murder to keep the truth hidden. Now, having taken away family members and health, and driving devilish bargains with all sides, the Cigarette-Smoking Man is no longer just a keeper of the conspiracy . . . he is an active part of the machinations of evil.

Playing the Faustian role of Cigarette-Smoking Man—commonly known as CSM—is actor William B. Davis, a highly respected Canadian theatrical actor who almost seems born to the stage. Young William was exposed to theater by his cousins, Murray and Donald Davis and Barbara Chilcott. The trio ran a summer stock theater, the Straw Hat Players, in Muskoka, Ontario, which "actually rehearsed in our basement when I was a child ," said Davis from his apartment in Vancouver. "My father, as a lawyer, was often involved in their theater business enterprises as a kind of legal consultant or a board member." Davis's mother was a psychologist.

Eventually, young William began to get involved with his cousins' productions. "When they needed a child actor they used me," he recalls, noting that none of his brothers were similarly bitten by the acting bug. "I was acting when I was only eleven years old. Acting just seemed like a heck of a lot of fun. I seemed to be good at it. I don't know that I knew that much about it . . . it was just kind of an instinctive thing for me at the time, which is partly why I turned to directing [as an adult] because directing seemed to me a more serious pursuit. I wasn't sure acting was something that grown up people would really do; it wasn't really serious work, it was just sort of play. I have since learned a whole lot more about the delicious art of the actor."

Davis's first appearance on stage was in a play called *Portrait in Black*, with a summer stock company. He started taking acting lessons, and had done either one or two summers of plays when another opportunity presented itself. He was cast as "Mickey," the young son in *Life With the Robinsons*, a CBC radio drama which ran for two years in the early fifties. "It was a mental health program," explains Davis. "It was a drama for twenty-five minutes or so that brought up problems that were happening in a family, and then a psychologist [Dr. John Griffith of the Canadian Mental Health Association] would come in at the end and give an analysis of what the difficulties were and [offer] some solutions. It was actually written and narrated by Ted Allen, who is quite a well established writer." Davis made $30 a week for acting on the show.

Davis went on to do several other radio shows, but these jobs dried up after Davis's voice changed and his family moved to the country. Davis continued to do one play a year with the summer stock company, and upon graduation, entered the University of Toronto. Donald Sutherland was one of Davis's classmates. "When I first went there I was still thinking that I would be an actor. So I did quite a lot of acting, but about halfway through is when I started directing and took off in that direction. Directing seemed to be more challenging, and it had more mental work to do. I still hadn't really learned very much about what the actor's process could be; I was still kind of doing my acting pretty much on instinct so I didn't really have a shape or a method of work really."

While majoring in philosophy (he earned his Honors B.A. in 1959), Davis and friend Karl Jaffray recreated The Straw Hat Players, running from 1958 to 1961. They performed an eclectic mix of plays, from comedies to dramas to mysteries. To continue his education, Davis felt that "if I wanted to be a good director I needed to know a whole lot more about what an actor does. The London Academy of Music and Dramatic Art (LAMDA) had this one year program for people who had already a reasonably established background." That one year stretched to five, with Davis staying in England from 1960 to 1965. After he left LAMDA in 1961, he became the resident director at the Civic Theatre in Chesterfield for a year. One of his last roles at Chesterfield was as Don John, the bastard brother of Don Pedro in Shakespeare's *Much Ado About Nothing*.

Davis says that the role "was a rough draft for the Cigarette-Smoking Man. Don John is the villain of the play, and I wasn't quite sure how to go about playing a villain. So after looking at the play fairly carefully I could see some reasons, obscure though they might be to the audience, but reasons that would be valid for me for *why* I was doing the things that I was doing; why I had been unfairly treated; and why it was appropriate to take the actions that I took. Basically, I took the attitude that I was the *hero* of the play and that Pedro, who the audience thinks of as the hero, I took to be the villain. And it worked really well. Every time I came on stage, the high school students hissed at me. I couldn't understand why they would hiss at the hero, but they did. And that seems to be what goes on with the Cigarette-Smoking Man; he plays the *hero* of *The X-Files* and everybody hisses at me." The role of Don John would be Davis's last acting role for almost twenty years.

After Chesterfield, Davis moved to become the artistic director for the Dundee Repertory Theatre for a year. Then, from 1963–64, he worked as a freelance director and an acting teacher. In 1964, Davis became an assistant director at the National Theatre School of Great Britain, auditioning for Sir Lawrence Olivier to get the job. Davis went on to work with Albert Finney and Maggie Smith on plays such as *Miss Julie* and *Black Comedy*. In 1965, Davis was nearing the end of his contract. "When my contract with the National Theatre finished I was to be assistant director to Albert Finney when he directed his first movie (*Charlie Bubbles*, released in 1968). So I had a whole kind of career laid out in front of me. And I was sitting there in my apartment and I got a telephone call from Montreal [asking] would I come and be assistant artistic director at the National Theatre School of Canada? They offered me so much money I could not believe it."

Davis and his second wife (he was married, briefly, as an undergraduate) transplanted themselves back to Canada, where Davis was quickly bumped up from assistant to full-fledged artistic director. He stayed from 1966–1970, then went on to establish the Festival Lennoxville in Quebec (with David Rittenhouse); it was the first mainstage theater company in Canada devoted solely to the production of Canadian plays. He also became the associate professor of drama at Bishops University, where the Festival Lennoxville was based. He taught through the mid-seventies, then directed in Lennoxville and traveled around the country as a freelance director until 1977. That's when he got an offer to work for the CBC (Canadian Broadcasting Corporation). At the time, he was courting the woman who would become his third wife. The two of them planned to have children, and the good monetary offer from the CBC meant stability. (Davis and his third wife did have two daughters, who are now fifteen and nineteen.)

At the CBC, Davis was back in semi-familiar territory, only this time he was on the other side of the desk. He produced—and executive produced— radio dramas. Davis made a major lifestyle change while working at the CBC. Having been a smoker for twenty-five years, Davis decided to quit in 1980. "I vividly remember trying to produce my first radio drama as a *non*-smoker. It was *very* difficult." As a stop-gap, Davis ate chocolate-covered truffles. He wouldn't smoke again until his role on *The X-Files*.

Davis returned to freelancing in 1980, directing, teaching, and finally acting again. "I hadn't really done any acting for close to twenty years. It seems as though I learned something in all that time I had spent telling other people what to do. I had learned something for *me* and I found myself quite excited by it." His first role was in an industrial training film, but he had small roles in films such as *The Dead Zone* (1983), *Daddy's Home* (pre-1986), and *Head Office* (1986). He also did "lunch-time theater" with the Solar Stage company.

In 1985, Davis was offered the job of director of the Vancouver Playhouse Acting School, a prestigious school in Vancouver, British Columbia. The city was just beginning to get the film and television crews, but its theater scene was vibrant. Davis soon fell in love with the area, and the film industry began to boom, offering a new outlet for his acting talents.

Davis opened his own acting space in 1989, called The William Davis Centre for Actors' Studies. He still teaches there, though his time is taken up these days with his own career. The most famous graduate of the school is Lucy Lawless, currently the star of *Xena: Warrior Princess*. Some of the other attendees at the school have included Brendan Beiser (*The X-Files'* Agent Pendrell), and Sarah Jane Redman (who was in the *Millennium* episode "Lamentation").

Although Davis is best known for his work on *The X-Files*, he has done a lot of television, mainly episodic series and movies-of-the-week. He has fond memories of filming the children's show, *Captain Power and the Soldiers of the Future*, though he never saw his finished episode. "It was a completely different look. It was such a western, desert, raw, Clint Eastwood sort of look, and I am not seen that way. Apparently it looked terrific." He also had a recurring role on *Airwolf*, and appeared on many of the other Vancouver-based series such as *21 Jump Street* and *The Commish*.

In his time off from acting and teaching, Davis sometimes retreats to a getaway in Blaine, Washington. He also enjoys water-skiing, horseback riding, and is a certified downhill ski instructor and racer. For the last three years he has held the title of Canadian National Water Ski Champion in the 55–65 age category. He notes that while the announcers are told to announce him as "Bill" Davis, they often tell the crowds that Davis is Cigarette-Smoking Man.

Currently, Davis is single again, though he has been involved for quite some time with Barbara Ellison, a high school English teacher in Vancouver. Davis sometimes drops by her class to lecture on Shakespeare, which the kids think is cool. When the couple recently attended an opening at Planet Hollywood, the reverse happened. "They all recognized my girlfriend. There was a group of kids that suddenly shouted out 'Mrs. Ellison! Mrs. Ellison!' They were more excited to see their high school teacher than they were to see big stars," he laughs.

In fact, that laughter is one of the few disarming things about Davis. During our interview, though his voice was easily recognizable, it was also soft and soothing, with a touch of a Canadian accent. "No. *You* have a touch of an accent," he tells me when I comment on it. Still, as the conversation turns to his most famous role, Davis slips out of his comfortable speech patterns, and without warning, the Cigarette-Smoking Man is on the phone.

Thankfully, Davis slips out of the voice quickly, but I'm sure that I can smell a trace of smoke coming through the phone line.

The X-Files

When Davis auditioned for *The X-Files*, not only did he not know the role *would* be recurring, he didn't know it *could* be recurring, as it was a science fiction pilot, a risky proposition in the early nineties. Then again, he didn't audition for the role of Cigarette-Smoking Man either. "I actually auditioned for senior FBI agent (Third Man) in the pilot and I didn't get it. *I* got the part with no lines. Ken Camroux got the senior FBI agent. So that was fine. It was a gig."

When *The X-Files* continued past the pilot, Davis had made enough of an impression on the producers that they used him again. Gradually, the role of Cigarette-Smoking Man became more prominent, especially as an overreaching conspiracy began to be built into the background of the series. Even from the beginning, it was clear that CSM was covering up something big with the conspiracy, and that he would go to almost any length to keep the coverup going. So, given that the series has not given CSM a history—at least until season four's hypothetical "Musings of a Cigarette-Smoking Man"—what has Davis created internally?

"It keeps changing as I get more information. It's always in flux. I think most of what came out in 'Musings of a Cigarette-Smoking Man' is in the imagination of Frohike and is not actually real. I don't believe that I assassinated Kennedy although I might have been part of it. It used to be part of my [internal] back-story that I was the one on the grassy knoll, but Oswald still fired the shots.

"But the story kind of shifts as the whole question of the project gets clearer. Whatever the opportunity to get involved in this process which we thought was a good idea, or a necessary idea, or the planet's only hope or whatever . . . [I] embarked on it with a certain idealism. The costs of maintaining it keep building; the people that you would have to kill, or see that others were killed . . . Mulder's father jumped out because he couldn't deal with that, but then he couldn't deal with being out either. Cigarette-Smoking Man stayed and had to almost systematically shut down those parts of himself that would interfere with doing what he had to do. Now we have almost a shell of a person who is committed to a track that he can't get off—and he wouldn't have anywhere to go if he *did* get off. [He] has stopped asking questions about it because it would be too painful to consider them."

Some of those questions deal directly with Mrs. Mulder and Fox. It is pretty clear that CSM has some affection for Mrs. Mulder, "and that is all that's left. It's true that I saved her life and that I really did risk a great deal both personally, and in terms of the operation, to do that. And [I] got away with it because the Bounty Hunter believed my story."

Davis has enjoyed his newfound fame as a result of *The X-Files*, and has begun a tour traveling to colleges as a guest speaker. He's also appeared at a number of *X-Files* conventions. "I enjoyed them. I'm sorry they went into hiatus. I was surprised when I first went because I thought they would be sort of freaky in a way—that there would be real fanatics and a lot of strange people. I was quite surprised to find them a lot of real normal people, lots of families." Only one experience, at a British convention, was strange. "They had a couple of people from the paranormal world as guest speakers. And one of them kept coming up to me and trying to interest me in his subject. He kept starting off by saying 'You *obviously* have an interest in the paranormal.' As if I had *chosen* to be on *The X-Files* because I was fascinated with the paranormal. It wasn't because I was a working actor without a job? I finally had to say actually 'I don't.'"

So, how *does* Davis feel about the three main themes of *The X-Files*: aliens, the paranormal, and government conspiracies? "I am glad to see you separate them because aliens keeps getting included in paranormal," he says. "If aliens were here among us it would not really be paranormal. The greatest scientists that we have do not think it impossible that we would find alien life. It does not conflict with our understanding of how the universe and how life works. It's just that there is no evidence that there are aliens *among us.* There aren't aliens among us, but there could be."

Many of the paranormal events the series explores are difficult for Davis to give any credence to as well. "It would mean that everything that science currently works from would be false . . . I don't even feel that I have to defend my position because the onus is really on the person who says that something exists to prove that it *does,* rather than the other way around. I don't see any more reason why I should have to prove that there *are not* aliens among us, or whether channeling doesn't really work, any more than I have to prove that leprechauns don't exist or unicorns don't exist. But because it keeps coming up, maybe I better pay more attention."

As to conspiracies, "I don't think there's any broad-ranged conspiracy, I don't think things work like that. Things appear to be conspiracies when little decisions that have been made—often in the very best of interests or sometimes out of expediency—kind of add up to an effect. People look at the effect and think that it was a conscious plan and it almost never is. If the governments were capable of the conscious plans that the conspiracy theorists credit them with, how come they aren't better at their *other* conscious plans of running the country?" Davis laughs.

So what does Davis think about CSM's far-reaching power? "I don't think that CSM has Machiavellian power. I have power to get people killed," he admits, then adds "although I have terrible help. *Nobody* I hire seems to be able to shoot straight. Apart from that, I think I am caught in a circumstance that I cannot move. I can only go *with* it. I couldn't stop it now if I wanted to."

Speaking of stopping, are there any clues as to CSM's fate? Fans will be glad to know that he survives the entire upcoming fifth season, and will appear in much of the *X-Files* movie, *Blackwood,* though Davis won't confirm or deny that. "I have to tell you it spoiled my fun, and I am not sure how I am going to do these college talks that I am scheduled to do in the fall. One of the joys of the show is that I don't *know* anything. So, when fans ask me questions, I don't know. I can play the fan game with them. But *now* that we have got this movie and I've actually seen a script that is farther ahead than the public knows, I actually now have information that I am not at liberty to disclose." He laughs, and adds "It is very inconvenient and I can't have as much fun!"

In any case, it seems that there's no stopping William B. Davis. After all, he's been voted one of the most hissable villains on television today. And he's recognized worldwide, such as the time a hotel doorman in Milan asked for an autograph from "Il Fumatore," the Italian name for Cigarette-Smoking Man.

X1 Pilot   X16 Young at Heart   X21 Tooms

The date is March 6, 1992, and Dana Scully has just been assigned to the X-Files in "The X-Files," to spy on Agent Mulder. In the background of the office of Section Chief Blevins, a silent Cigarette-Smoking Man watches. Later, when an alien implant is offered by

217

the agents as evidence, CSM takes it to a cavernous warehouse in the Pentagon, where he places it in storage, with several other objects.

Near the end of "Young at Heart," after Mulder shoots the regenerating killer John Barnett, CSM is seen in the background, trying to get Barnett to talk before he dies.

CSM watches as Scully is chewed out by A.D. Skinner in "Tooms," and later, watches as Mulder is also berated. When Skinner reads Mulder's final report on Tooms, he asks CSM if he believes it. "Of course I do," smirks the mysterious man.

Although William B. Davis is identified as "Smoking Man" in the pilot episode, he has no lines. A later memo from Fox network executives asked that Davis no longer smoke in future episodes. Part of the memo read "Fox Television is a non-smoking network." When the villainous nature of CSM was emphasized, the network backed off.

"Young at Heart" marks the first time Mulder actually sees CSM, whom he refers to as "probably CIA." The end credits do indeed list him as "CIA Agent," but it is clear that it is the same character. It has never been revealed whether CSM does work for the CIA, though it is entirely possible.

CSM's brief dialogue at the end of "Tooms" is his first clearly spoken words since his debut on the series. In "The X-Files," he whispers something to Blevins, and in "Young at Heart," he can be heard shouting "Where are they? Can you hear me? Where did you hide them?" to the dying Barnett. Curiously, it sounds as if this dialogue was looped by another actor; it sounds nothing like Davis' voice.

Despite reports elsewhere, Davis says that he smoked real cigarettes for his first several episodes. "They actually gave me a choice. I chose to smoke the real cigarettes for the first two or three episodes that I did, and then I realized that this was not a good idea. I started thinking it would be nice to get to do another one of those shows," he chuckles. "They had offered me the herbal cigarettes right from the beginning but I had been a 'real actor' so I would use real cigarettes." Davis also used his own distinctive way of holding a cigarette—between his thumb and forefinger—for his character. In the time since, Davis has used herbal cigarettes (the Honey Rose brand), which do not have nicotine, but do have a heavy smell. "I've gotten used to them. They smell terrible, but mostly to other people . . ."

X24 The Erlenmeyer Flask   X25 Little Green Men   X28 Sleepless

In a scene in "The Erlenmeyer Flask" that mirrors the closing of the series premiere, CSM puts an alien fetus into storage at the Pentagon.

CSM and Skinner discover that Mulder has left his post in "Little Green Men," but Skinner angrily throws CSM out of his office near the episode's end.

Alex Krycek, Mulder's new partner, reports to CSM in the sur-

prise ending of "Sleepless." When Krycek notes that Scully will be a big problem, CSM says that "Every problem has a solution."

In an amusing sequence in "Little Green Men," CSM discovers that his pack of Morleys (introduced here) are empty. He gives A.D. Skinner a pleading look, but Skinner smirks and answers "I don't smoke." In reality, actor Mitch Pileggi *does* smoke, and has been seen with packs of Marlboros, the cigarettes that Morleys are based upon!

CSM makes his most threatening move to eradicate the X-Files in "Sleepless" with his casual dismissal of Scully as he snubs out a Morley cigarette.

X30 Ascension   X32 One Breath   X46 F. Emasculata

CSM observes when Skinner takes Mulder off Scully's abduction case in "Ascension," but Krycek keeps CSM up to date on Mulder's movements. When Mulder goes to Skyland Mountain to rescue Scully, Krycek calls CSM and tells him he'll keep Mulder occupied "until they locate her," then leaves Mulder hanging in a tram above the mountain. Later, Krycek asks CSM why they don't just kill Mulder, and CSM warns him that the death of Mulder would risk "turning one man's religion into a crusade."

In "One Breath," CSM subtly threatens Skinner, but is later surprised when Mulder shows up at his hotel room at 900 West Georgia Street. Mulder threatens CSM with a gun, but CSM sneers, saying "I've watched presidents die." He talks Mulder down from his anger.

Having disappeared for most of the latter half of the season, CSM reappears in "F. Emasculata" arguing with Skinner and Mulder about whether the potentially deadly disease outbreak should be made public knowledge.

Fans had been questioning why CSM didn't simply kill Fox Mulder if he wanted him out of the way so much, and the scene between Krycek and CSM in "Ascension" was put in as an explanation. Of course, as the series has gone on, it's clear that there is a more personal reason that CSM has not had Fox killed.

Mulder calls CSM "Cancer Man" for the first time in "One Breath," giving rise to a nickname that spread throughout fandom. CSM also reveals for the first time here that he believes what he's doing is right, and tells Mulder he likes him. He also says that he has no wife and no children, and he has empty bottles of Budweiser on his coffee table. An early version of the scene included Mulder knocking a cigarette out of CSM's mouth and saying "Those things are slow suicide," but it slowed the intensity of the scene down and was removed.

X49 Anasazi   X50 The Blessing Way   X51 Paper Clip

The conspiracy begins to show its roots in "Anasazi," when CSM visits his old friend, Bill Mulder. They discuss the stolen government files which carry proof of extraterrestrial life. CSM tells Bill that he's protected Fox Mulder so far. Later, CSM calls Fox on his cellphone while the agent is exploring a boxcar buried in the desert. CSM and his troops show up at the boxcar, but Mulder is apparently gone, and CSM orders the boxcar napalmed.

In "The Blessing Way," CSM is panicked when he believes Mulder may still be alive, but lies to the Consortium, telling them that Fox is dead. He also assures them that all of the files have been recovered. Later, he listens in as Skinner questions Scully about the missing DAT tape, and watches Skinner squirm when he gets an unexpected phone call.

The Consortium comes down on CSM in "Paper Clip," blaming him for the murder of Melissa Scully, and asking that he turn the stolen DAT tape over. He promises they'll have it tomorrow. Later, CSM threatens Skinner, who may have the tape, and sends Krycek and other killers after the Assistant Director to get it. But when CSM double-crosses Krycek and tries to have him killed, the rogue agent threatens to expose him and release the DAT tape now in his possession. To make matters worse, Skinner has trumped CSM as well, trading cover-up of the information for Mulder and Scully's safety. Skinner tells CSM that this is where he should "pucker up and kiss my ass."

Is CSM responsible for Krycek murdering Bill Mulder in "Anasazi," or was the rogue agent acting on his own? CSM tells Mulder he wasn't involved, but it wouldn't be the first time he's lied. Mulder calls him a "black-lunged son of a bitch" in this episode.

"The Blessing Way" is the first appearance of the shadowy Consortium, the mysterious syndicate that seems to be behind the main conspiracies we have witnessed thus far on *The X-Files*. Members include Cigarette-Smoking Man, Well-Manicured Man, Major Domo, and Elder, #1, #2, and #3.

In the old photo that Mulder and the Lone Gunmen examine in "Paper Clip," besides Bill Mulder and Victor Klemper, a young Cigarette-Smoking Man, a young Deep Throat, and a young Well-Manicured Man are obvious; the other three men's identities are not clear.

X59 731   X65 Apocrypha   X70 Avatar

CSM oversees a translator working on Dr. Zama/Ishimaru's journals in "731," then meets up with the rogue agent Krycek in "Apocrypha." CSM recognizes that the black alien goo is controlling Krycek, and reunites the goo with its spaceship in an underground silo in North Dakota. He gets rid of another problem as well, locking Krycek in the silo with no food or water or means of escape.

Is CSM framing Skinner from behind the scenes in "Avatar"? That's never clear, though we briefly see him watching from behind a one-way mirror in an interrogation room.

Young CSM makes his first appearance in "Apocrypha," in a scene in which he, young Bill Mulder, and young Deep Throat visit the bedside of a Navy man who's dying from radiation burns gained in a salvage operation in 1953. "You can trust us," says the young CSM.

In "Avatar," a scene between Cigarette-Smoking Man and Skinner was removed from the episode due to time considerations, meaning actor William B. Davis actually had no lines in the as-aired episode. In the scene, CSM questioned Skinner's allegiance.

X72 Wetwired   X73 Talitha Cumi   X74 Herrenvolk

A tense scene between Mr. X and CSM takes place in "Wetwired," but it's unclear whether Mr. X is reporting to CSM, or whether they're on equal ground. CSM wants to know who Mulder's informant is, unaware that Mr. X himself is the informant.

CSM meets with Mrs. Mulder at the old family summer home in "Talitha Cumi," and they reminisce. He reminds her that he was a better water-skier than Bill Mulder, noting "that could be said about so many things . . . couldn't it?" They argue, and afterwards, she's found suffering from a stroke. Later, CSM questions the shape-changing Jeremiah Smith, and remains unfazed when Smith takes on the face of Deep Throat and Bill Mulder, two of CSM's old friends (and possibly victims). Smith also tells CSM that he's dying of lung cancer. Later still, Fox pulls a gun on CSM in a hospital hallway when CSM goes to visit Mrs. Mulder. CSM tells Fox that he knew Mrs. Mulder before Fox was born, and that she came to him for information.

Fox Mulder's informant is finally identified by CSM and his underlings in "Herrenvolk," and Mr. X is shot to death outside Mulder's apartment. Later, CSM tells the alien Bounty Hunter to heal Mrs. Mulder, saying that it will remove Fox as an obstacle because "The fiercest enemy is the man who has nothing left to lose."

Some scenes in "Talitha Cumi" were reminiscent of Dostoyevsky's *The Brothers Karamazov*, a novel which tells of Christ's second coming during the Spanish Inquisition and the church's refusal to believe he is who he is. They imprison him and the Grand Inquistor questions him, telling Christ that he's no longer welcome on earth. The interrogation scene between Smith and CSM was designed to closely resemble the Inquisitor sequence.

"Herrenvolk" is the first episode to feature an "also starring" designation for William B. Davis.

CSM's caring for Mrs. Mulder is highlighted in "Herrenvolk," when he chooses to let the Bounty Hunter heal her rather than asking him to take the cancer away from himself. However, there had been a strong implication in "Talitha Cumi" that CSM might have freed Smith in order to be healed by the captive shape-changer.

"Talitha Cumi" is Davis's favorite episode so far, "partly because of the mental challenge. I mean I had to go and read Dostoyevsky three times to really understand the debate with Jeremiah. What is my case? What is my point? I had a range of stuff between those kind of intellectual debate scenes to fear I'm going to die to the scene with Mrs. Mulder to the confrontation with Fox. It just had lots of different stuff in it."

So were Cigarette-Smoking Man and Mrs. Mulder lovers, as it has been implied? "Oh yeah," Davis says readily. So does this mean Fox is Cigarette-Smoking Man's son? "I don't know. My theory is that *nobody* knows. My theory is that even Mrs. Mulder doesn't know. Unless we do a DNA test we are not going to know because she was sleeping with both of us at the time. So it *is* possible. It is possible that I am *Samantha's* father . . ."

X80 Musings of a Cigarette-Smoking Man

> In the Lone Gunmen's office, Frohike reveals to Scully and Mulder the past he's supposedly uncovered for CSM, while CSM himself listens with high-tech devices from a building next door, and targets the Lone Gunmen's office with a sniper rifle. What follows is a bizarre laundry list of possibilities, none of which seem impossible, but which, taken together, seem a bit too bizarre.
>
> CSM's father supposedly died in the electric chair for being a Communist spy and his mother died of lung cancer. As an army captain in 1963, rooming with young Bill Mulder, CSM is recruited by a shadowy conspiracy to assassinate President John F. Kennedy. Later, CSM also takes part in the assassination of Martin Luther King Jr., starts wars, drugs a Russian Olympic goalie, fixes the Oscars and the Super Bowl, and even moves the Rodney King trial! Later, he convenes with Deep Throat to murder a living alien.
>
> Despite his power, CSM just can't get his stories published. He's a frustrated author who writes hack detective stories under the pen name "Raul Bloodworth," but when his work is finally accepted, by the skin magazine Roman á Clef, the editors butcher his work. In the present, CSM decides not to kill Frohike, simply because he knows he can do so at any time.

Writer Glen Morgan and director James Wong took the framework for this episode from a DC Comics project called *The Unauthorized Biography of Lex Luthor*. It also examined the past of a villainous character through other people's eyes. While Morgan and Wong contend that the story could be true, Chris Carter has said that it isn't the true background of CSM.

Want to quote that great *Forrest Gump* bit that CSM spouts at the end of the episode? Here it is: "Life is like a box of chocolates . . . a cheap, thoughtless, perfunctory gift that nobody ever asks for. Unreturnable, because all you get back is another box of chocolates. So you're stuck with this undefinable whipped-mint crap that you mindlessly wolf down. Sure, once in a while there's a peanut butter cup or an English toffee, but they're gone too fast, and the taste is fleeting. So you end up with nothing but broken bits filled with hardened jelly and teeth-shattering nuts. And if you're desperate enough to eat those, all you've got left is an empty box filled with useless brown paper wrappers." Gosh, he's *bitter*.

Reportedly, director James Wong actually filmed a scene where CSM shoots Frohike, which is how the episode was originally scripted. Chris Carter overrode the scene, telling them that Frohike must live. Wong planned to edit together a reel of the show with his ending to argue the point with Carter, but the film of Frohike's assassination mysteriously disappeared!

Another scene was shot, but cut in the editing process. It featured CSM coming home on Christmas Eve to a feeble Christmas tree with only one present under it—a lighter with the words "Trust No One" on it. The gift-giver? Alex Krycek. That was "really stretching things," Davis said in *Dreamwatch*. "I mean, what happened to the lighter I'd used for the previous five years? And if I was moving around in circles where I was trying to impress people, would I pull out a lighter that said 'Trust No One' on it?"

As to whether or not Frohike's findings are true, it seems that some of them could be, but others are unlikely. If CSM was really born in Baton Rouge, Louisiana on August 20, 1940, he would have been only thirteen years old in 1953 when he was working with young Bill Mulder and young Deep Throat in "Apocrypha." He would also have been an army captain at the age of twenty-two, which is highly unlikely, though not impossible. Captaincy at that early an age could be the result of a direct field commission during war time or due to medical training; neither explanation fits CSM, which the military-minded Frohike should have known.

The name of CSM was actually revealed in this episode, though fans may never find out what it is. Davis signed his resignation letter with the name he gave CSM, but it isn't seen on screen.

X81 Tunguska   X82 Terma

CSM warns Skinner outside his apartment that he needs a diplomatic pouch that Mulder and Scully intercepted in "Tunguska," then meets with the Well-Manicured Man, who calls him a fool and tells him "this will take more than just a good aim."

In "Terma," CSM meets with Well-Manicured Man who wants him to find out who killed his lover. CSM discovers that it's a Russian agent, and assures his Consortium partner that the man will be taken care of. Later, CSM reads the reports that Scully and Mulder have made to Senator Sorenson.

Fans who want to know whats Davis sounds like in person should listen to the dialogue between CSM and Skinner outside Skinner's apartment in "Tunguska." The voice he is using is closer to his real voice than any other appearance on the series, with even a touch of the Canadian accent slipping in.

Previous episodes have established an animosity between Well-Manicured Man and CSM, but it really flares up in this two-parter. Unfortunately, two scenes were cut before airing. "For time reasons they did not make it into

'Tunguska.' The contention that was going on between Well-Manicured Man and CSM was more developed because he first called me out to his ranch to tell me that there was trouble to be investigated. We did not have that scene in the end, we had the scene in the end where I come and report to him. Then there was a third scene where I am hanging out at night waiting for him, and challenging him for taking it [public at Senator Sorenson's] committee and he is defending that."

X87 Memento Mori   X94 Zero-Sum

> *Scully's cancer takes a turn for the worse in "Memento Mori," and Mulder wants to make a deal with CSM, but Skinner won't let him. Instead, Skinner meets with CSM, who questions him. "You think I'm the devil, Mr. Skinner?" Later, CSM agrees there is a way to help save Scully's life, if Skinner is "willing to pay the price."*
>
> *That price is extracted in "Zero-Sum," when CSM assigns Skinner to steal a body and erase records of a suspicious death. Skinner soon learns that he has been set up for murder by CSM. "I wouldn't get too comfortable on your moral high ground, Mr. Skinner," CSM warns him. Later, in a phone call, he gives Skinner a veiled threat of assassination when the Assistant Director threatens to expose CSM. The Consortium questions CSM about the progress of an experiment using smallpox-carrying bees, and he assures them it's already begun. Later still, Skinner confronts CSM in a hotel room, drawing his gun on him. Angrily, Skinner shoots three times, the bullets ripping into the wall to either side of CSM's head. Shortly after, CSM tell Marita Covarrubias to tell Mulder what he wants to hear.*

The final two Davis episodes of the fourth season added a progressively more sinister element to CSM's character, especially as it related to his control over Skinner. When I mention that CSM has not kept his promise to heal Scully, Davis immediately switches into CSM's voice. "I beg your pardon. You don't know that. She hasn't died yet, has she?" Well, no she hasn't. "All right then. So don't accuse me of not keeping up my side of the bargain. Skinner did not keep *his* side of the bargain. He started to, he tried, and then he quit. And [if] Scully dies, tough. He hasn't done what he said he would do."

Davis notes that in his college talks he jokes about the fact that "then Mulder found out about [Skinner's deal]. So Mulder found out what was needed to do to save Scully because Skinner had tried. So what does Mulder do? Mulder covers his ass. Mulder could have come and offered himself for Scully's life. Does he? No, because he is a chicken."

Does CSM actually control Marita Covarrubias? "I know what you mean and I don't know if I have an answer to that," Davis says, enigmatic once again.

X96 Demons

> *Although William B. Davis is not in this episode, its scenes of a young CSM warrant a closer examination. In season four's penulti-*

mate episode, "Demons," the possibility of CSM's involvement with the Mulder family's past is even more clear. Using experimental treatments involving electrical impulses, and a hallucinogenic drug called Ketamine, Dr. Charles Goldstein helps Mulder flash back to confront the demons of his past.

Mulder recalls his mother and father fighting in the downstairs living room at the summer house in Quonotonug, with his mother yelling "Not Samantha!" Suddenly, the sinister figure of young CSM is behind Fox, saying "You're a little spy," and closing the door to shut the boy off from his parents. The scenes is repeated in several different ways, finally ending when Fox runs upstairs to witness his sister's abduction.

Although Fox did recall things he hadn't before, their validity is easily called into question. First, the other patients of Dr. Goldstein killed themselves, due to the treatment and the things it supposedly showed them about their own alien abductions. Secondly, as Scully points out to Mulder, Ketamine is a powerful hallucinogen. Thirdly, given some of the "truths" Mulder has found out about his sister's abduction, it is entirely possible that his conscious mind has overlaid facts onto his subconscious mind, thus creating CSM and "Not Samantha!" when they weren't really there.

The most telling part of the episode happened when Fox went to his mother's Greenwich home and confronted her about her involvement with CSM. He accused her of having an affair, and asked her if Cigarette-Smoking Man was his father. Through the harrowing questioning, a shocked Mrs. Mulder not only remained defensive, but she also never confirmed or denied anything Fox asked. Finally, she slapped Fox, stormed out of the room and stomped upstairs, refusing to speak to him any more about the subject.

Actor Chris Owens has played the role of Young CSM in two episodes this season: "Musings of a Cigarette Smoking Man" and "Demons." Did Davis work with the young actor at all, or his predecessor, Craig Warkentin from "Apocrypha"? "No. They have worked with my tapes, but they haven't actually worked with me. I know Chris Owens spent a lot of time kind of studying particularly how I smoked."

ACTOR CREDITS

WILLIAM B. DAVIS

AMERICAN TELEVISION

Airwolf (USA)   Davis played a recurring character named Newman in the following fourth season episodes: #65—"Stavograd, Part One," aired March 20, 1987; #66—

"Stavograd, Part Two," aired March 27, 1987; #69—"Rogue Warrior," aired April 24, 1987; #72—"The Key," aired May 15, 1987.

Captain Power and the Soldiers of the Future (Syndicated)   #14—"Judgement," aired January 31, 1988 (first season). Role: Arvin.

The Commish (ABC)   #5 and #6—"Pilot, Part 1 and 2" a.k.a. "A Matter of Life and Death, Parts 1 and 2," aired November 2, 1991 (first season). Role: Dan Chesley.

MacGyver (ABC)   #124—"Trail of Tears," aired April 29, 1991 (sixth season). Role: Judge

Nightmare Cafe (NBC)   #5—"Sanctuary for a Child," aired March 27, 1992 (first season). Role: Doctor who attends at the bedside of a young boy.

The Outer Limits (Showtime)   #13—"The Conversion," aired June 9, 1995 (first season). Role: Ed. #41—"Out Of Body" (original title "Etherically Yours"), aired July 14, 1996 (second season). Role: John Wymer, a religious leader from the group Family Foremost. A creepy threatening figure, he is Cigarette-Smoking Man without the cigarette.

Poltergeist: The Legacy (Showtime)   #10—"Do Not Go Gently," aired June 21, 1996 (first season). Role: Dr. Bill Nagle, a benign doctor who briefly consults with series regular Rachel Corrigan.

Sliders (FOX)   #7—"Eggheads," aired April 26, 1995 (first season). Role: Professor Myman.

Street Justice (Syndicated)   Davis appeared in episode. No information is available.

Jump Street (FOX/Syndicated)   #13—"Mean Streets and Pastel Houses," aired June 28, 1987 (first season). Role: Mr. Weidlin. #30—"Champagne High," aired March 6, 1988 (second season). Role: Mr. Wickenton. #99—"Crossfire," aired week of March 3, 1991 (fifth season). Role: Judge Harrison.

Wiseguy (CBS)   #16—"The Merchant of Death," aired February 1, 1988 (first season). Role: Curant. #51—"People Do It All the Time," aired November 8, 1989 (third season). Role: Inspector #2.

CANADIAN TELEVISION

Backstretch (CBC)   Two episodes. No information available.

Danger Bay (network unknown).   Three episodes. No information available.

North of 60 (CBC)   One episode. No information available.

TELEVISION MOVIES

The Limbic Region (Showtime),   Aired 1996. Role: unknown.

When the Vows Break (Lifetime),   Also known as *Courting Justice*. Aired 1995. Role: Dr. Alexander.

Circumstances Unknown (USA),   Aired April 19, 1995. Role: Gene Reuschel, whose son is murdered.

Dangerous Intentions (CBS),   Also known as *On Wings of Fear*. Aired January 3, 1995. Role: a group leader.

Don't Talk to Strangers (USA),   Aired August 11, 1994. Role: Huddleston.

Heart of a Child (NBC),   Aired May 9, 1994. Role: Vern.

Not Our Son (CBS),   Aired January 31, 1994. Role: unknown.

Diagnosis of Murder (CBS),   Aired January 5, 1992 (pilot telefilm for the series *Diagnosis Murder*). Role: Marvin Parkins.

Omen IV: The Awakening (FOX),   Aired May 20, 1991. Role: unknown.

Stephen King's It (ABC),   Aired November 18, 1990. Role: Mr. Gedreau.

Anything to Survive (ABC),   Aired February 5, 1990. Role: Dr. Reynolds.

The Little Match Girl (NBC),   Aired December 21, 1987. Role: unknown.

Sworn to Silence (ABC), Aired April 6, 1987. Role: Peter Massio.

The Cuckoo Bird (CBC), Air date, unknown. Role: Ted.

FEATURE FILMS

Unforgettable. Released February 23, 1996. Role: Doctor.

The Hitman. Released 1991. Role: Dr. Atkins.

Look Who's Talking. Released October 1989. Role: Drug Doctor.

Midnight Matinee. Released 1989 (Canada). Role: Heath Harris, a B-grade horror-film director who is hanged.

Personal Choice. Released on video as *Beyond the Stars* Released 1989. Role: Hal Simon.

Head Office. Released 1986. Role: University dean.

Daddy's Home. Released pre-1986. Role: unknown.

The Dead Zone. Released October 21, 1983. Role: Ambulance driver.

Beyond Obsession. No information available.

THEATER

Portrait in Black (1950). Straw Hat Players, Ontario.

Picnic (1958–1961). Straw Hat Players, University of Toronto, Ontario. Directed by Davis.

Bus Stop (1958–1961). Straw Hat Players, University of Toronto, Ontario. Directed by Davis.

Robinson Crusoe (1961–1962). Civic Theatre, Chesterfield, England. Role: The Cannibal King.

Two for the Seesaw (1961–1962). Civic Theatre, Chesterfield, England. Directed by Davis.

Much Ado About Nothing (1961–1962). Civic Theatre, Chesterfield, England. Role: Don John (Davis's final role for twenty years).

A Winter's Tale (mid-1960s). Vermont Shakespeare Festival. Directed by Davis.

A Midsummer Night's Dream (1966–1970). National Theatre School, Montreal. Directed by Davis.

A Long Day's Journey Into Night (1971–1974). Neptune Theatre, Halifax, Nova Scotia. Directed by Davis.

Sunrise on Sara (1973). Lennoxville Festiville, Lennoxville, Quebec. Directed by Davis.

The Diary of Anne Frank (1978). Vancouver Playhouse, Vancouver, British Columbia. Directed by Davis.

Stage 2.

RADIO

Life With the Robinsons (CBC). Original Airdates: Tuesdays, 1951–1953. Half-hour radio drama series in which an eleven-year-old Davis played the role of Mickey Robinson. Thirteen episodes were produced in each season. The premiere of season two was February 12, 1952.

Cuckoo Clock House (CBC). Early 1950s children's radio program which featured a young Davis.

Cross Section (CBC). Early 1950s radio program. Davis was in one episode.

Sussex Drive. (CBC). Davis produced the first season of this satirical drama about Canadian political life.

CBC Stage/Sound Stage (CBC). Davis produced the first season of this anthology drama series.

OTHER CREDITS

The X-Files: The Truth and the Light (Warner Brothers). Running time: 48:36. Soundtrack available on CD and tape. Composer Mark Snow's themes from various episodes of *The X-Files* are woven together with interspersed dialogue from several of the series actors. Davis has several dialogue snippets.

THE LONE GUNMEN FILE

onspiracies abound on *The X-Files*, and it only seemed natural that conspiracy theorists would eventually turn up. The character of Max Fenig in the first season episode "Fallen Angel" was actually a dry run for a trio of misfits who would collectively capture the hearts of X-Philes even as they built up bizarre data that sometimes helped Mulder and Scully.

The trio did not initially have a name—the "Lone Gunman" was the name of the small-press conspiracy magazine they published. The name came from the "lone gunman theory" popularly used regarding the assassination of President John F. Kennedy. Eventually, the trio of theorists became known by the name the Lone Gunmen as well, first using that name in "One Breath."

Working from a non-descript office jammed with surveillance equipment and questionable scientific apparatus, the Lone Gunmen trio was introduced in the first season episode "E.B.E.," when Mulder brings Scully to them to find information on recent UFO sightings in the Persian Gulf. Mulder tells Scully that the Gunmen are an "extreme government watchdog group," and he's understating the case.

The Lone Gunmen were actually inspired by three real conspiracy activists whom *X-Files* writers Glen Morgan and Marilyn Osborn saw at a June 1993 UFO convention in Los Angeles. Morgan was fascinated in the paranoid theories of a trio of men behind one table, especially with the hold their ramblings held on the crowd. The secret of the metal strips hidden in ten and twenty-dollar bills used in the "E.B.E." episode actually came from the trio at the convention.

Over the course of the next four years, the Lone Gunmen would aid Mulder and Scully numerous times, whether it meant hacking into classified files, producing bogus government IDs, keeping covert surveillance, or intercepting transmissions and data. Through it all there didn't seem to be anything that the trio didn't have information on, or at the very least an opinion about. Despite their paranoia that the government was out to get them (and in several instances, it was), the Lone Gunmen actively put their lives on the line for several of Mulder's missions.

According to Bruce Harwood, the main reason for the Lone Gunmen's popularity relates directly to the series' exploration of paranoia. "The fear of what's in the water, or why I can't remember last night, or where did this funny mark on my arm come from, and fear of dark places . . . the Lone Gunmen are living on that edge all the time," said Harwood in *Cinefantastique*. "Everything is dangerous. You have to be afraid of everything. They are a pure expression of what the show is about."

The question of whether conspiracy theorists are paranoid with good reason is one that not only can be debated on the series, but also in real life. Harwood used a real-life figure as the basis for his character. "I thought of

Noam Chomsky, the MIT professor, and his theories about the way the media [formulates public opinion]. People who don't like his ideas call him paranoid," Harwood said in the *X-Files* magazine.

"In our first episode we were a little more fringy, said Haglund in the *X-Files* magazine. "Now we're more accessible, and the success comes from people identifying with us." Still, he admits that as far as the characters go, "each one of us believes the other two to be complete freaks. They trust each other because they know the other two are thinking the same thing. So it's sort of like this Mexican standoff on who's the biggest geek."

The Lone Gunmen have proved popular enough that an early fifth season episode, written by Vince Gilligan, will focus solely on them and how they met and got together. They will appear in several episodes of the season, and have a role in the *X-Files* feature film, *Blackwood*.

NAME: TOM BRAIDWOOD

Born: September 27, 1948, Vancouver, British Columbia
Lone Gunman: Frohike

Short and lascivious, the ever-horny Frohike classified Scully as "hot" on their first meeting, but over the years, he proved a valuable protector and helper as well. Clad in rumpled clothing and combat boots, the constantly unshaven Frohike is the trio's specialist in photography and surveillance.

"The character started off as a bit of a lecherous hippie," said Tom Braidwood, who plays Frohike, in the *X-Files* magazine. "But I don't have the same lust for Scully. I've grown to know her and her intelligence and personality." Braidwood was given the role when William Graham, the director of "E.B.E." noted "We need somebody slimy . . . somebody like Braidwood." When the assistant director walked by on his way to the bathroom, he was cast.

Braidwood has appeared in more episodes than any of the other Gunmen for one simple reason; he works behind the camera as well. Since the first season of the series, Braidwood has been one of several First Assistant Directors on the series, alternating between the odd- and even-numbered episodes depending on the season.

Braidwood is a graduate of the University of British Columbia, where he earned a master's degree in film, and a bachelor's degree in theater. He set out to be both an actor and a production person, but although he landed roles every now and then since his debut in the Canadian film *Harry Tracy* (1981), most of his time has been spent on the other side of the camera: as director, story editor, and even producer.

Helping direct such Vancouver-based shows as *Danger Bay* and *21 Jump Street*, Braidwood got to know the area's actors and actresses, as well as production personnel, writers, and producers. He started on *The X-Files* with "The Jersey Devil," and has stayed on ever since.

Braidwood is married and has two daughters, Kate and Jessica. The girls appeared in an unreleased film he produced, *The Portrait*, and at least one of them appeared in the crowd in *The X-Files* third season closer, "Talitha Cumi." In his free time, Braidwood enjoys gardening.

NAME: DEAN HAGLUND

Born: July 29, 1965, Winnipeg, Manitoba
Lone Gunman: Langly

With his long straggly blond hair, rock band t-shirts, and geeky glasses, Langly bears a startling resemblance to Garth of *Wayne's World* fame. If you took the music geekiness away from Garth and added computer geekiness, you'd have Langly, the techno-head hacker of the Lone Gunmen.

Early on, the black-rimmed glasses changed with each show because the prop master was never sure whether or not the Lone Gunmen would ever be used again. "If you look closely, they're a different pair each time," said Dean Haglund, who plays Langly, in *Cinefantastique*. "The prop guy keeps pulling a different pair out of the bag. He's got a bag of all these glasses and we can never remember which ones we used on the show before."

Dean Haglund is best known in the Vancouver area as a stand-up comic, emcee, and member of the improvisational troupe TheatreSports. The group has performed spoofs such as *Star Trick, Star Trick: The Next Improvisation, Free Willy Shakespeare*, and their summer 1997 travelogue hit, *See B.C.*. With several members of his troupe, Haglund wrote the comedy TV pilot *Channel 92*. "My ten years of TheatreSports training has allowed me to go into improv situations and not have to worry about being idiotic, crass, or embarrassing myself," he said in a *Vancouver Sun* profile. "I know I can go into any kind of situation and not blurt something out that I'll regret later." Haglund also performs stand-up comedy routines at many of *The X-Files* conventions.

When he auditioned for Langly's role, Haglund was up against about thirty other actors, most of them reportedly pasty-faced and bearing crew-cuts. The long-haired Haglund went into the audition basing his idea for Langly on computer theory researchers from his days at Simon Fraser University, who, despite their brains, were fans of the best rock bands of the period. "They're certainly not the pocket protector types," Haglund said in *Cinefantastique*. "A lot of these guys who were deep into computer culture have more of that ideal than just the techno end of it."

Haglund comes by his musical interests naturally; when he was growing up in Winnipeg, he played drums in a garage band called the Truncheon Scars. "We considered ourselves repressed youth," Haglund said in the *Vancouver Sun*. "We were four suburban kids in a white, middle-class neighborhood. The only time we saw the police was when a car would drive by on the street. We were just a really awful punk-rock band. Basically, we sucked."

Haglund trained with Prairie Theatre Exchange in Winnipeg, then went on to earn a bachelor of arts degree from Simon Fraser University, where he had studied theater, dance, and video production. And, as seen at his Web site, Haglund does a little bit of amateur cartooning on the side. To find out more about Haglund, check out that Web site at http://www.deanx.com

NAME: BRUCE HARWOOD

Born: April 29, 1963, British Columbia
Lone Gunman: Byers

The most prim member of the Lone Gunmen is Byers, whose neat-as-a-tack suits and ties set him at incongruous odds with the grungy Frohike and Langly. His specialty is military and information systems, and his knowledge of conspiracies and odd facts seems to be unrivaled.

"I used to think Byers was a university professor, but then I decided he's technically smart, but he's not that smart," Bruce Harwood told the *X-Files* magazine, who plays Byers. "I decided he works for Xerox—he's the guy who comes around in a suit and tie and fixes the photocopiers. His whole focus is on maintaining the Lone Gunmen office and the newsletter."

Of the trio, the bearded Harwood is the actor with the most credits on his resume, including a recurring stint on the popular *MacGyver* as an environmentalist. He's also appeared in three episodes of *The Outer Limits*, and other Vancouver-based series such as *21 Jump Street* and *Wiseguy*.

Harwood is a former figure skater and, when not acting, is a clerical worker at one of the Vancouver branch libraries. He is married to a high school teacher, and is another graduate of the University of British Columbia.

CREDITS

TOM BRAIDWOOD

CREW CREDITS

The Portrait (1992). Unreleased film. Producer.
Eyes of an Angel (1991). Feature film. First assistant director: Canada unit.
My American Cousin (1985). Feature film. Production manager.
Low Visibility (1984). Feature film. Producer.
Danger Bay (1984) Series. First assistant director.
Jump Street (1987–1990). Series. First assistant director.
Madison (1991–1994). Series. Story editor.
The Odyssey (1992–1994). Series. Job unknown.

ACTOR CREDITS

Harry Tracy. Feature film. Released 1981. Role: unknown.
My American Cousin. Feature film. Released 1985. Role: Wally.
Eyes of an Angel. Feature film. Released 1991. Role: unknown.
The Portrait. Feature film unreleased. Shot in 1992. Role: unknown
The Only Way Out. Telefilm. Aired 1993. Role: Court Official.
Mom P.I. Series. "Beneath the Pacific," aired 1990. Role: unknown

DEAN HAGLUND

TELEVISION SERIES

Channel 92 (network unknown). "Pilot," aired March 1996. Haglund was the cowriter.
The Commish (ABC). #21—"V.V.," aired May 9, 1992 (first season). Role: Drug Dealer.
   #69—"Working Girls," aired October 8, 1994 (fourth season). Role: Zack

Sliders (FOX). "Fever," aired March 29, 1995. Role: Stockboy

Street Justice (Syndicated). Haglund appeared in one episode. No information is available.

Lonesome Dove: The Outlaw Years (Syndicated). "The Return," aired the week of September 25, 1995. Role: Bounty hunter Nathan Silas, who is hanged.

TELEFILMS

Mask of Death (HBO). Aired 1996. Role: Drug Dealer

FEATURE FILMS

Dangerous Indiscretion. Released 1994. Role: Crackhead

BRUCE HARWOOD

TELEVISION SERIES

MacGyver (ABC). #54—"Blow Out," aired December 21, 1987 (third season). Role: Juice. Harwood had a recurring role as Willis in the following episodes: #117—"The Wasteland," aired January 21, 1991 (sixth season); #124—"Trail of Tears," aired April 29, 1991; #125—"Hind-Sight," aired May 6, 1991.

The Outer Limits (Showtime). Second series. #2—"Valerie 23," aired March 31, 1995 (first season). Role: Technician; #22—"Trial by Fire," aired March 1, 1996 (second season). Role: Dr. Norris; #61—"A Special Presentation," aired July 25, 1997 (third season). Role: Dr. Avery Strong.

Jump Street (FOX). Harwood appeared in one episode. No information is available.

Wiseguy (CBS). Harwood appeared in one episode. No information is available.

TELEFILMS

Beauty's Revenge. Aired 1995. Role: Cameraman
Bye Bye Birdie. Aired 1995. Role: Reporter #1
Earth*Star Voyager. Air date unknown. Role: Scientist

FEATURE FILMS

Bingo! Released 1991. Role: Network Executive
The Fly II. Released 1989. Role: Technician

X-FILES GUEST ACTORS IND-X

235

Brown, Ryk 3.13
Bruhanski, Alex 3.12, 4.22
Brunanski, Craig 2.23, 3.05, 4.24
Bryant, Peter 4.12
Buckley, Alan 3.12
Buermeyer, Eric 4.19
Bunting, Lisa 1.15
Butler, Dan 2.14
Butler, Tom 1.07, 2.16

Call, R. D. 1.18
Cameron, David 1.09, 4.20
Campbell, Sean 4.12
Camroux, Ken 1.01, 2.25, 4.01
Canton, Gonzalo 4.07
Carfra, Gillian 1.21
Carhart, Timothy 3.06
Carlson, Les 2.01
Carlson, Leslie 1.22
Carrington, Grai 1.14
Carter, Chris 2.25
Cassini, Frank 3.04
Cavanaugh, Christine 4.20
Cavanaugh, Michael 1.04
Cavendish, Nicola 2.08
Cecere, Fulvio 2.01, 3.11
Chang, Stephen, M. D. 3.19
Chapman, Brent 3.03, 4.19
Charno, Stu 3.04
Chartier, Ron 4.04
Chauvin, Lilyan 2.21
Chepovetsky, Dmitry 2.19, 3.16
Chieffo, Michael 3.08
Chin, Marilyn 4.13
Chinlund, Nick 2.13
Chisholm, Kathrynn 1.13
Chivers, Jeff 3.16
Chrisjohn, Garrison 3.18
Christmas, Eric 2.11
Cioffi, Charles 1.01, 1.04, 4.24
Clarke, Ross 3.24
Clarkson, Helene 2.21
Clement, Jennifer 4.12
Clothier, Robert 2.10, 3.15
Coe, Harrison R. 3.16, 4.15
Cloke, Kristen 4.05
Coffin, Frederick 1.10
Coghill, Joy 2.12
Conway, Kevin 2.15
Coulson, Bernie 2.25
Cram, Michael 4.04
Crane, Chilton 1.18, 2.22, 4.17, 4.18
Crichlow, Brenda 1.15
Croft, Bill 2.21, 4.13
Croft, Cam 3.24

Cross, Garvin 2.18, 4.01
Cross, Roger R. 2.15, 3.17
Cruz, Raymond 4.11
Cubitt, David 2.19
Cunnigham, Cavan 3.03
Cunningham, Colin 2.17, 3.10, 3.23
Cuthbert, Jon 1.02, 2.11
Cutshall, D. Harlan 3.07
Cygan, John 2.03
Czinege, Franky 2.14

D'Arcy, Jan 1.21
Dack, Douglas Ray 4.05
Dadey, John 4.10
Dandeneau, Jacqueline 2.21
Daniels, Andre 1.21, 2.03
Danyliu, Andre 3.23
Davey, Garry 1.11, 1.23, 2.17, 3.13
Davies, Glynis 1.21, 2.13, 3.06
Davies, Jackson 1.15
Davies, Mitchell 2.25, 3.01
Davis, Don S. 1.13, 2.08
Davis, William B. 1.01, 1.16, 1.21, 1.24, 2.01, 2.04, 2.06, 2.08, 2.22, 2.25, 3.01, 3.02, 3.10, 3.16, 3.21, 3.23, 3.24, 4.01, 4.07, 4.08, 4.09, 4.14, 4.21
Dee, Taunya 1.04
DeMartino, Claude 2.04
Denis, Neil 4.02
DeSalvo, Anne 1.24
DesRoches, Paul 1.09
Destrey, John 4.18
DeYoung, Cliff 1.01
Deveaux, Nathaniel 2.23
Di Nunzio, Aureleo 2.25, 4.19
Diakun, Alex 2.20, 3.04, 3.20
Diaz, Edward 4.10
Diaz, Pamela 4.11
Dickson, Paul 3.07
Dimopoulos, Stephen 2.19, 3.24
Dixon, Tim 2.05, 3.13
Djola, Badja 3.05
Dobran, Rick 4.17, 4.18
Doduk, Alex 1.18
Donahue, Angela 4.04
Donahue, Jay 4.13
Donat, Peter 2.16, 2.17, 2.25, 3.01, 3.24
Dobson, Michael 2.05, 3.20, 4.05
DoSerro, Joe 3.23
Douglas, Robin 1.16
Dourif, Brad 1.13

Dow, Bill 1.05, 2.21, 3.12, 4.12
Driscoll, Roby 2.12
Duborg, Kathleen 2.03, 2.13
Dughi, Mikal 1.21
Duvall, Wayne 1.07

Eastin, Steve 2.10
Ellis, Chris 3.22
Ellis, Tracey 3.08
Ermey, R. Lee 3.11
Estabrook, Christine 1.16
Evans, Martin 3.01, 3.02, 3.16, 4.06
Ewen, Lesley 1.01, 1.14, 3.11, 4.16

Fairman, Michael 4.19
Fargey, Jillian 4.13
Ferguson, Anna 1.06
Ferrier, Russell 3.15
Ferrucci, Frank 2.07
Fields, Mike 3.20
Finck, Bill 1.07
Finn, John 4.24
Finn, Joseph Patrick 3.05
Fish, Nancy 4.22
Flanagan, Frances 3.16
Fleming, Peter 2.12
Fong, Donald 3.19
Foort, Ernie 3.01, 3.17
Foree, Ken 3.05
Forgie, Jen 4.13
Foster, Jodie 4.13
Fox, Kelli 1.06
Franz, Allan 4.16
Fraser, Duncan 1.12
Frazer, Bob 2.10
Frazier, Guyle 2.07, 2.23
Fredericks, David 2.03, 3.08, 4.07
Freedman, David 4.15
Freeman, Rob 4.24
French, Michael Bryan 1.02
Fresco, David 2.11
Fry, Cory 4.02
Fuqua, Joseph 4.19
Furlong, Brian 1.02

Gaffney, Jason 3.20
Gale, Lorena 1.06, 2.08, 4.22
Gallagher, Les 4.05
Ganee, Raoul 2.02
Gann, Merrilyn 1.16
Gardener, Katya 1.01
Gardner, Katya 2.15
Garson, Willie 3.07

Owens, Shelley 1.04

Palffy, David 4.17, 4.18
Palmer, Joel 1.04, 2.21
Pantages, Tony 1.10
Panych, Morris 2.22, 3.15, 3.21, 4.01, 4.14, 4.21
Paolone, Catherine 3.06
Parker, Monica 1.02
Parker, Nicole 3.12, 3.22
Paton, Laurie 1.12
Patterson, Sheila 1.10
Payne, John 1.24, 2.20
Pays, Amanda 1.12
Pedde, Eileen 4.08, 4.09
Perry, Freda 1.10
Perry, Jane 4.10
Petersen, David 1.16
Phillips, Bobbie 3.12
Pickett, Tom 1.06
Pileggi, Mitch 1.21, 2.01, 2.02, 2.04, 2.06, 2.08, 2.16, 2.17, 2.22, 2.25, 3.01, 3.02, 3.09, 3.14, 3.15, 3.16, 3.17, 3.21, 3.23, 3.24, 4.01, 4.03, 4.05, 4.08, 4.09, 4.10, 4.11, 4.14, 4.16, 4.18, 4.20, 4.21
Pinard, Bruce 3.05
Piven, Byrne 4.10
Polizos, Vic 3.17
Pollard, Barbara 2.05
Porter, Russell 3.13
Porter, Steven M. 4.22
Pounder, C. C. H. 2.05
Prentice, Ernie 2.11
Primus, Barry 1.06
Prinsloo, P. J. 3.06
Progish, Tim 2.13
Puskar, Theresa 4.21
Puttonen, Michael 1.02, 2.04, 3.10
Puttonen, Mike 4.22
Pyper-Ferguson, John 2.22

Quinn, Daniel 3.20

Rabinovitch, Murrey 4.15
Rader, Jack 2.18
Radock, Jeremy 3.13
Railsback, Steve 2.05, 2.06
Raitt, Jon 4.17
Rands, Doris 3.04
Raskin, Paul 3.05, 4.06
Redmond, Sarah Jane 2.12
Rees, Jed 4.19
Reeves, Perrey 2.07

Reid, Ric 1.01, 2.21
Reilly, Charles Nelson 3.20
Rennie, Callum Keith 1.15, 2.15
Restell, Kim 2.16
Reynolds, Ryan 3.13
Rhodes, Donnelly 1.19, 4.07
Ribisi, Giovanni 3.03
Ridge, Addison 4.21
Riley, Claire 2.19
Roald, Glen 1.04
Robert, Nicole 3.11
Roberts, Ken 2.16, 3.04
Robertz, Wren 3.12
Robbins, Kate 3.03
Robertson, Alan 1.12, 3.18
Robison, Ian 4.13
Roe, Channon 4.15
Roeske, Fiona 3.12
Rogers, Greg 3.05
Rogers, Michael 1.10, 2.16
Rolfsen, Torben 2.09
Rolston, Mark 2.10
Roman, Nina 4.06
Rose, Gabrielle 1.02, 2.02
Rose, Jim 2.20
Rose, Len 1.13
Rosen, Elisabeth 2.10
Rosseau, Gerry 2.03
Rothery, Teryl 2.11
Rowat, Bill 2.22
Rowland, Rodney 4.13
Royal, Christopher 4.04
Rozen, Robert 2.23, 4.20
Rubes, Jan 4.09
Russom, Leon 1.01
Ryan, Ken 3.08

Saban, Stephen 2.12
Sadiq, Laara 4.12
St. Michael, Jody 2.18
Sakurai, Yasuo 3.09
Sali, Richard 1.22
Sampson, John 2.05
Sampson, Tony 2.10
Sand, Paul 2.10
Sanders, Alvin 1.10, 2.22
Sanderson, William 2.03
Sandomirsky, Kerry 1.23, 3.06
Sargent, Richard 2.16
Santin, Fabricio 4.11
Saunders, Mark 1.15, 2.13
Sauve, Ron 2.02, 3.18
Savage, John 2.19
Sawatsky, Sarah 3.20
Scarr, Dolly 3.08
Schiavelli, Vincent 2.20

Scholte, Tom 3.15
Schombing, Jason 1.15
Schram, Jerry 4.17, 4.18
Schreier, Jessica 4.08, 4.09
Scoular, Peter 3.15, 3.16
Serpa, Lee 4.08
Shalhoub, Tony 2.23
Shaw, Paula 3.07
Sheppard, Brent 3.17
Sheppard, Mark 1.12
Shiels, Graham 3.19
Shimono, Sab 2.11
Shirkoff, Bethoe 3.21
Shostak, Olesky 4.08, 4.09
Shulman, Felicia 4.17, 4.18
Sierra, Gregory 1.05
Silverstone, Joel 3.15
Simi 4.11
Simms, Michael David 2.06, 2.25, 3.01, 3.21, 4.01
Simms, Tasha 1.11, 2.11, 3.21
Simpson, Debis 2.20
Skipper, Pat 4.24
Slater, Blair 2.20
Sloyan, James 1.23
Smallwood, Tucker 4.02
Smith, Charles Martin 2.22
Smith, Douglas 4.02
Smith, Jamil Walker 2.15
Smith, Kurtwood 3.14
Smith, Michael St. John 4.07
Smith, Shawnee 2.09
Smith, Tony Dean 4.11
Snodgress, Carrie 1.04
Solomon, Ari 3.15
Sood, Veena 1.06
Sorel, Nancy 3.07
Spano, Joe 4.17, 4.18
Sparks, Carrie Cain 2.24, 3.09, 4.20
Spence, Sebastian 4.02
Stait, Brent 1.10, 4.08, 4.09
Staite, Jewel 3.08
Stansfield, Claire 1.05
Stebbings, Peter 1.14
Sterling, Jennifer 4.20
Stevan, Diana 2.03
Stewart, Bobby L. 2.06, 3.12
Stewart, Carla 4.13
Stewart, Don 4.03
Stewart, J. Douglas 4.12
Stewart, Lisa 4.21
Stewart, Malcolm 1.01, 2.07, 3.21, 4.08, 4.09
Stillin, Marie 4.06
Stofer, Dawn 3.12

BIBLIOGRAPHY

Books

Brooks, Tim, and Earle Marsh. *The Complete Directory to Prime Time Network TV Shows 1946–Present*. Ballantine, 1995.

Corey, Melinda. *A Cast of Thousands*. Stonesong Press, 1992.

Cornwell, Paul, Martin Day, and Keith Topping. *X-Treme Possibilities*. Virgin, 1997.

David, Nina. *TV Season 74–75*. Oryx Press, 1976.

David, Nina. *TV Season 75–76*. Oryx Press, 1977.

Edwards, Ted. *X-Files Confidential: The Unauthorized X-Philes Compendium*. Little, Brown, 1996.

Erickson, Hal. *Television Cartoon Shows*. McFarland, 1995.

Fulton, Roger. *Encyclopedia of TV Science Fiction*. TV Times Boxtree, 1990.

Genge, N. E. *The Unofficial X-Files Companion*. Crown, 1995.

Genge, N. E. *The Unofficial X-Files Companion II*. Avon, 1996.

Gianakos, Larry James. *TV Drama Series Programming: A Comprehensive Chronicle 1947–1959*. Scarecrow, 1980.

———*TV Drama Series Programming: A Comprehensive Chronicle 1959–1975*. Scarecrow, 1978.

———*TV Drama Series Programming: A Comprehensive Chronicle 1975–1980*. Scarecrow, 1981.

———*TV Drama Series Programming: A Comprehensive Chronicle 1980–1982*. Scarecrow, 1983.

———*TV Drama Series Programming: A Comprehensive Chronicle 1982–1984*. Scarecrow, 1987.

Lenburg, Jeff. *The Encyclopedia of Animated Cartoons*. Facts On File, 1990.

Lovece, Frank. *The X-Files Declassified*. Citadel Press, 1996.

Lovece, Frank. *The Television Yearbook*. Perigree, 1992.

Lowry, Brian. *The Truth Is Out There: The Official Guide to the X-Files*. HarperPrism, 1995.

Lowry, Brian. *Trust No One: The Official Third Season Guide to the X-Files*. HarperPrism, 1996.

Maltin, Leonard. *Leonard Maltin's Movie Encyclopedia*. Dutton, 1996.

Mitchell, Paul. *The Duchovny Files*. ECW Press, 1996

Morris, Bruce B. *Prime Time Network Serials*. McFarland, 1997.

Morton, Alan. *The Complete Directory to Science Fiction, Fantasy and Horror Television Series*. Other World Books, 1997.

Phillips, Mark, and Frank Garcia. *Science Fiction Television Series*. McFarland, 1996.

Prouty, Howard H., editor. *Variety Television Reviews 1923–1988*. Variety, 1989.

Ward, Jack. *Television Guest Stars*. McFarland, 1993.

Scheuer, Steven H. *The Television Annual 1978–79*. Collier, 1979.
Shuster, Hal. *The Unauthorized Guide to the X-Files*. Prima, 1997.
The Official Map of the X-Files. HarperPrism, 1997.
Connors, Martin, Julia Furtaw, and James Craddock, eds. *Videohound's Golden Movie Retriever 1996*. Visible Ink, 1996.

Web Pages

The Internet Movie Database: http://us.imdb.com/
The Episode Guides Page: http://www.xnet.com/~djk/main__page.shtml
The Magrathea SFTV Homepage: http://www.indirect.com/www/leew/index.html

Periodicals

Cinefantastique
Cinescape
Cult Times
Dark Side
Dreamwatch
Entertainment Weekly
EpiLog
Fangoria
Not of This Earth
The Official X-Files Magazine #1–2
Scarlet Street
Sci-Fi Entertainment
Sci-Fi Universe
SFX
Shivers
Spectrum
Starburst
Starlog
Television Chronicles
TV Guide
TV Zone
Wrapped in Plastic
The X-Files Magazine #1–2
The X-Files British magazine #1–21
XPosé

Introduction

Entertainment Weekly, March 18, 1994, "X Appeal," by Tim Appelo.
Entertainment Weekly, November 29, 1996, "Unseen Forces," by Mike Flaherty.
Starburst #216. August 1996, "Howard Gordon's Scary Things," Joe Nazarro.
Starlog Yearbook #15. August 1997, "X-Factors," Ian Spelling.

Mitch Pileggi Bibliography

Austin Chronicle. "Skinnerview," Chris Gray.
Cinefantastique. Vol. 26 No. 6/vol. 27 No. 1. October 1995, "F.B.I. Boss Skinner," Paula Vitaris.
Cinescape X-Files Special. "A Friend Indeed," Frieda Noone, 1996.
Entertainment Weekly. March 6, 1995.
FREETIME. July 31–August 31, 1996, "X Communications," Caroline Vincent.
Office of the Assistant Director Web page, June 21, 1995, "An Interview With Mitch Pileggi," Robin M. Mayhall. (http://www.hieran.com/office/)
People. May 6, 1996, "Senior G-Man," Calvin Baker and Craig Tomashoff.

People Online chat. May 16, 1996, moderated by Dylan Jones.

Reno Convention Report, September 22–24, 1995 on the Mitch Pileggi Estrogen Brigade Homepage by Paula Mackey. http://members.aol.com/TheMPEB/index.html

Sci Fi Fall Preview. October 1995, "Caught in the Middle," Steve Bonario.

Scarlet Street No. 20. Fall 1995, "Mitch Pileggi," Jessie Lilley.

Shivers No. 34. October 1996, "Aliens and Avatars," Nigel Adams and David Miller.

TV Guide. October 12, 1996, "X-Man," Mark Nollinger.

X-Files, The British magazine No. 8. January 1996, "Principle Skinner," Dave Hughes.

XPosé No. 3. October 1996, "Skinner Deep," Philip Zonkel.

Texas Monthly, "Ask Mitch Pileggi" http://www.texasmonthly.com/texas-talk/tmpileggi/index.html

Jerry Hardin Bibliography

Age, The (Green Guide). October 19, 1995, "X Marks the Big Revival Spot," Greg Burchall.

Starlog. February 1995, "Keeper of Secrets," Bill Florence.

TV Week. November 4, 1995, "Deep Throat Talks!" Shane Sutton.

Steven Williams Bibliography

Cinefantastique Vol. 26 No. 6/Vol. 27 No. 1. October 1995, "X, The Unknown," Paula Vitaris.

Cult Times No. 14. November 1996, "Need to Know," Steven Eramo.

Dreamwatch No. 18. February 1996, Kathleen Toth.

Dreamwatch No. 25. September 1996 "X-Celerating Action," Kathleen Toth.

Dreamwatch No. 27. December 1996, "Ex X," Kathleen Toth.

Fangoria No. 143. "Keepers of X-Secrets," Anne Moore.

SFX No. 19. December 1996, "The X-Man," Paula Vitaris.

Unofficial Channels (German). December 1995 "Steven Williams Interview," Mike French.

X-Files, The British magazine No. 20. January 1997, "X The Unknown," Dave Hughes.

Official Steven Williams Web page: http://www.celebrity-network.com/actors/stevenwilliams/

Nicholas Lea Bibliography

Cinefantastique Vol. 26 No. 6/Vol. 27 No. 1. October 1995, "F.B.I. Judas," Paula Vitaris.

Dreamwatch No. 16. December 1995, "The Howard Gordon File," Brian J. Robb.

Freetime. July 31–August 31, 1996, "X Communications," Caroline Vincent.

Fox World IRC. December 16, 1996, Nick Lea Chat.

Official X-Files Magazine, The No. 1. Spring 1997, "Alien Nation" and "The Rat's Back," Mo Ryan.

People Online conference with Nick Lea. May 9, 1996, moderated by Dylan Jones.

Satellite Time. September 1996, "Two Types of Spy for the FBI," Alex J. Geairns.

Scarlet Street No. 24. Spring 1997, "Nicholas Lea," Danny Savello.

Shivers No. 34. October 1996, "Nick Lea: Bad Boy Makes Good," Nigel Adams.

Starburst No. 209. January 1996, "The X-Men," Joe Nazzaro.

Toronto Sun. September 28, 1996, "It's Work That Woos Nick Lea," Claire Bickley.

Toronto Sun. October 17, 1995, "Opening the X-File on Krycek," Claire Bickley.

TV Guide. May 17, 1997, "From A to X," by Rick Schindler and Stephanie Williams.

TV Guide Online. "Nicholas Lea," Jeanne Wolf.

X-Files, The British magazine No. 9. February 1996, "Ice Cold Alex," Dave Hughes.

X-Files, The British magazine No. 17. October 1996, "Enemy Mine," Dave Hughes.

XPosé No. 2. September 1996, "Middle Man," Jane Killick.

The Nicholas Lea Homepage: http://members.aol.com/nicci73813/nicklea.htm

Nick Lea bio Web page: http://members.aol.com/Leanan7/nlbio.htm

William B. Davis Bibliography

Benson, Eugene and L.W. Conolly, eds. *The Oxford Companion to Canadian Theatre*. Oxford University Press, 1989.

Who Was Who in Theatre: 1912–1976, Volume II. Omnigraphics & Gale Research Company, 1978.

Wagner, Anton. *Contemporary Canadian Theatre: New World Visions*. Simon & Pierre, 1985.

CBC Times, February 10–16, 1952, "Here Come The Robinsons."

Starlog Yearbook, No. 15, August 1997, "Deadly Enigma," Ian Spelling.

Dreamwatch No. 31. March 1997, "Cancerous Growth," Dave Hughes.

The Lone Gunmen Bibliography

Cinefantastique Vol. 26 No. 6/Vol. 27 No. 1, October 1995, "The Lone Gunmen" Paula Vitaris.

Entertainment Weekly No. 313, February 9, 1996, "X-Tra Credits," BW.

Official X-Files Magazine, The No. 1. Spring 1997, "Three's Company," Mo Ryan.

Vancouver Sun, The, May 27, 1997, "Comic Conspirator," Alex Strachan.

X-Files Magazine, The, No. 2, Summer 1996, "Three of a Kind," Devon Jackson.

Episodic Bibliography

X2 *Cult Times Christmas Special* No. 1. 1996, "CX Files No. 2," Jaspre Bark.

X3 *X-Files, The* British magazine No. 11. April 1996, "Stretching as an Actor," Paula J. Vitaris.
Trekker, The No. 58. July–August 1996, "K & A Interview With Doug Hutchison," Kathy Krantz.
Starlog Yearbook No. 15. August 1997, "Mutants, Psychics, and Freaks," by Julianne Lee.

X5 *TV Zone Special* No. 21. May 1996, "Beauty and the Beast," Steven Eramo.

X7 *TV Zone Special* No. 23. December 1996, "Computer Whiz-Kid," Steven Eramo.

X8 *TV Zone Special* No. 21. May 1996, "Cinematic Chameleon," Steven Eramo.

X9 *TV Zone Special* No. 23. December 1996, "Deep Space Memories," Steven Eramo.

X10 *Cinefantastique* vol. 26 No. 6/vol. 27 No. 1. October 1995, "Casting Call," Paula Vitaris.
X-Files, The British magazine No. 10. March 1996, "Connecting the Dots," Dave Hughes.

X13 *Cinefantastique* vol. 26 No. 6/vol. 27 No. 1. October 1995, "Episode Guide," Paula Vitaris.

X18 *Cinefantastique* vol. 26 No. 6/vol. 27 No. 1. October 1995, "Episode Guide," Paula Vitaris.

X19 *Wrapped in Plastic* No. 25. October 1996, "1996 Twin Peaks Fan Festival," Craig Miller.

X20 *TV Zone Special* No. 21. May 1996, "Fun-Loving Forest Ranger," Steven Eramo.

X20 *TV Zone* No. 88. March 1997, "Et Tu, Brian," Steven Eramo.

X26 *Sci Fi Universe* Vol. 3 No. 1. September 1996, "Weird Science," Kevin Stevens.
X-Files, The British magazine No. 17, October 1996, "Brother From Another Planet," Paula J. Vitaris.

X27 *Femme Fatales* Vol. 5 No. 3. "Space Siren Kimberly Patton," Paula Vitaris.

X28 *TV Zone Special* No. 21. May 1996, "Sleepless in Vancouver," Stevan Eramo.
Starburst No. 226. June 1997, "On His Todd," Nick Joy.

X30 *Cinescape Presents* Vol. 3 No. 1. Fall 1996, "Barry Good," Kristin Kloberdanz.

X33 *Shivers* No. 30. June 1996, "Monster Maker," Joe Nazzaro.

X34 *Entertainment Weekly*. December 9, 1994, "Fences X'd Out," Richard Natale.
X-Files, The British magazine No. 10. March 1996, "Red Museum," author unknown.
TV Zone Special No. 21. May 1996, "Beauty and the Beast," Steven Eramo.

X36 *XPosé* No. 2. September 1996, "Strange Days," Steven Eramo.

X38 *Starlog* No. 227. June 1996, "Fantasies in Dark and Light," Joe Nazzaro.
Graham, Jefferson. *Frasier*. Pocket Books, 1996.

X44 *Entertainment Weekly,* February 9, 1996, "A Gillian to One," Bret Watson.
Shivers No. 30. June 1996, "Monster Maker," Joe Nazzaro.
Starlog No. 227. June 1996, "Fantasies in Dark and Light," Joe Nazzaro.

X47 *TV Zone Special* No. 21. May 1996, "Me and My Shadow," Steven Eramo.

X48 *Shivers* No. 29. May 1996, "Frank Spotnitz: Of Colonies and Cannibals," Joe Nazzaro.

X53 *Sci Fi Universe* vol. 3 No. 1. September 1996, "Weird Science," Kevin Stevens.

  Cult Times No. 13. October 1996, "The X-Files on 1," Steven Eramo.
  Dreamwatch No. 31. March 1997, "Boyle's Law," Kathleen Toth.
  Starlog Yearbook No. 15. August 1997, "X-Factors," Ian Spelling.
X54 *Cult Times* No. 13. October 1996, "The X-Files on 1," Steven Eramo.
X55 *TV Zone Special* No. 21. May 1996, "Weight Watcher," Steven Eramo.
  Cinescape, X-Files Special. 1996, "Dating Sucks," Kristin Kloberdanz.
X56 *TV Zone* No. 87. February 1997, "Galactic Gypsy," Steven Eramo.
X57 *Cinefantastique*, Vol. 28 No. 3. October 1996, "Oubliette," Paula Vitaris.
X59 *Shivers* No. 40. April 1997, "Making up the X-Files," Joe Nazzaro.
X61 *Entertainment Weekly,* September 27, 1996, "Fox's Den," Bret Watson.
X63 *XPosé* No. 11. June 1997, "Looking Into the Abyss," James E. Brooks.
X68 *Starburst Special* No. 29. October 1996, "Fearsome Physician," Pat Jankiewicz.
X69 *Sci Fi Universe* Vol. 3 No. 1. September 1996, "Weird Science," Kevin Stevens.
  Shivers No. 40. April 1997, "Making up the X-Files," Joe Nazzaro.
  Starlog Yearbook No. 15. August 1997, "X-Factors," Ian Spelling.
  Dreamwatch No. 31. March 1997, "Life of Reilly," Kathleen Toth.
X70 *TV Zone Special* No. 16. February 1995, "Vash Opportunities," Pat Jankiewicz.
X72 *Cinefantastique* vol. 26 No. 6/vol. 27 No. 1. October 1995, "Family Ties," Paula Vitaris.
X74 *TV Zone* No. 84. November 1996, "Roy Thinnes: Miracle Man," Steven Eramo.
X75 *US.* May 1977, "Duchovny Anderson," Chris Mundy.
X77 *Fangoria* No. 163. June 1997, "The Scripting Secrets of *The X-Files*," Abbie Bernstein.
  Entertainment Weekly. June 13, 1997, "In Characters," Bruce Fretts.
  Starlog Yearbook No. 15. August 1997, "X-Factors," Ian Spelling.
X78 *Starlog,* No. 220. November 1995 "Space: Above & Beyond," Ian Spelling.
  XPosé No. 10. May 1997, "Field Days," James E. Brooks.
  XPosé No. 10. May 1997, "Somewhere in Time," Steven Eramo.
X80 *Starlog,* No. 220. November 1995, "Space: Above & Beyond," Ian Spelling.
X81 *TV Guide.* May 17, 1997, "The X-Files A to X," Rick Schindler and Stephanie Williams.
X82 *The Official X-Files Magazine* No. 1. Spring 1997, "Alien Nation," Mo Ryan.
X84 *Sci Fi Universe* No. 12. "3's the Charm?" Kevin Stevens.
X86 *Starlog,* No. 220. November 1995, "Space: Above & Beyond," Ian Spelling.
X92 *Cult Times* No. 21. June 1997, "In Sync," Steven Eramo.
X94 *TV Guide.* May 17, 1997, "The X-Files A to X," Rick Schindler and Stephanie Williams.

            •

PHOTO CREDITS

Page 1:   Mitch Pileggi. Photo courtesy and © 1997 Paula Mackey
Page 23:   Wayne Duvall. Photo courtesy and © Wayne Duvall
Page 26:   Ed Lauter. Photo courtesy and © Ed Lauter
Page 30:   Amanda Pays. Photo courtesy and © Amanda Pays
Page 34:   Christopher Allport. Photo courtesy and © Christopher Allport
Page 40:   Jason Beghe. Photo courtesy and © Jason Beghe
Page 42:   Henry Beckman. Photo courtesy and © Henry Beckman
Page 44:   Mimi Lieber. Photo courtesy and © Mimi Lieber
Page 46:   Zeljko Ivanek. Photo courtesy and © Zeljko Ivanek
Page 47:   Lindsey Lee Ginter. Photo courtesy and © Lindsey Lee Ginter
Page 49:   Jerry Hardin. Photo courtesy and © Jerry Hardin
Page 66:   Raymond J. Barry. Photo courtesy and © Raymond J. Barry
Page 70:   William Sanderson. Photo courtesy and © William Sanderson
Page 72:   Tony Todd. Photo courtesy and © Jeff Hyman/Shooting Star
Page 75:   Steve Railsback. Photo courtesy and © Steve Railsback
Page 82:   Teryl Rothery. Photo courtesy and © Teryl Rothery
Page 86:   Bruce Weitz/"Highlander" Photo © 1997 Gaumont TV
Page 88:   Dan Butler. Photo courtesy and © Dan Butler
Page 90:   Daniel Benzali. Photo courtesy and © Daniel Benzali
Page 91:   Megan Leitch. Photo courtesy and © Megan Leitch
Page 96:   John Savage. Photo courtesy and © John Savage
Page 97:   Vincent Schiavelli. Photo courtesy and © Vincent Schiavelli
Page 102:   Kevin McNulty. Photo courtesy and © Kevin McNulty
Page 105:   Peter Donat. Photo courtesy and © Peter Donat
Page 106:   Publicity photo of Steven Williams and © 1996 Steven Williams
Page 123:   John Neville. Photo courtesy and © John Neville
Page 126:   Jack Black. Photo courtesy and © Jack Black
Page 138:   Bobbie Phillips. Photo courtesy and © Bobbie Phillips
Page 140:   Kurtwood Smith. Photo courtesy and © Kurtwood Smith
Page 143:   Ari Solomon. Photo courtesy and © Ari Solomon
Page 148:   B. D. Wong. Photo courtesy and © B. D. Wong
Page 150:   Charles Nelson Reilly. Photo courtesy and © Charles Nelson Reilly
Page 153:   Nicole Parker. Photo courtesy and © Nicole Parker

ABOUT THE AUTHOR

Living in Portland, Oregon, for the last decade, **Andy Mangels** has carved out a diverse writing career since his first published work in the book *Focus on George Pérez* in August 1985.

Since that time, his main body of work has been in the comic book business. Past comic series he's written include the best-selling *Bloodwulf, Elfquest: Blood of Ten Chiefs, Nightmares on Elm Street, Child's Play: The Series, Annie Sprinkle Is Miss Timed,* and *Friday the 13th: Jason Goes to Hell,* as well as stories in *Quantum Leap, Justice League Quarterly, Badrock & Company, Ultraverse Premiere, Troll Halloween Special,* and MicroSoft Kids' Network's online interactive comic series, *RE-Man.* He edits the award-winning *Gay Comics,* and is currently the cowriter of the *Star Trek: Deep Space Nine* comic series, and various special *Star Trek* projects for Marvel.

Another focus of his work is genre films and TV projects in Hollywood. His regular columns have appeared in *Amazing Heroes, Marvel Age, Fantazia* (England), *Edizione Star* (Italy), *Wizard, Hero Illustrated, FAN* magazine, *Cinescape,* and now in *Marvel Vision* and *MANIA Magazine Online.* He has also written for *Hollywood Reporter, Comics Interview, Comics Scene, Starlog,* and *Wild Cartoon Kingdom.*

He is the author of the book *Star Wars: The Essential Guide to Characters,* now in its third printing, and other *Star Wars* projects, including the script for a full-cast audio drama, two successful trading card sets, a best-selling Boba Fett comic, and more. He is a regular writer for *Star Wars Galaxy* and the British *Star Wars* magazine, and writes text for *Star Wars* licensees.

His more politically-charged work has appeared in *Gauntlet,* and in such gay-themed magazines as *In Uniform, Advocate, Outweek, Frontiers, Just Out, Bear, Drummer, Leather Journal,* and *Oregon Gay News.*

In his free time, he collects uniforms and action figures, and participates in gay activism.